Dear Reader . . .

There's no place like England when it comes to ro~~mance~~
From the glorious cliffs of Dover and the lush green hills of
country estates . . . to the grand courts of royal intrigue
and foggy streets of London . . . England is a beautiful
and timeless place that fires the imagination.

Tea Rose Romance is a wonderful new line of novels that
captures all the passion and glory of this splendid nation.
We asked some of our favorite writers to share their most
romantic dreams of England—and we were delighted with
their enthusiastic responses! Whatever the period and style—
adventurous, playful, intriguing, lusty, witty, or dramatically
heartfelt—every *Tea Rose Romance* is a unique love story
with an English flavor and timeless spirit.

We hope you enjoy these special new novels.

**Sincerely,
The Publishers**

Stolen Kisses

KAREN LOCKWOOD

JOVE BOOKS, NEW YORK

STOLEN KISSES

A Jove Book / published by arrangement with
the author

PRINTING HISTORY
Jove edition / November 1994

ISBN: 0-515-11490-1

A JOVE BOOK®
Jove Books are published by The Berkley Publishing Group,
200 Madison Avenue, New York, New York 10016.
JOVE and the "J" design are trademarks
belonging to Jove Publications, Inc.

PRINTED IN THE UNITED STATES OF AMERICA

10 9 8 7 6 5 4 3 2 1

*Dedicated to my aunt
Patricia Kirkland,
who was "across the border"
for me when I turned six.
Thanks for the birthday cake
and the lessons in courage—
always with a smile.*

Stolen Kisses

"Lord, what fool it was that first invented kissing!"
—Swift

❧Prologue

The Legend . . .

"Tell me, please, Aunt Clare, tell me about the statue. The one at the border."

Clare Charlton stopped walking, shielded her eyes from the wind, and peered upriver through low-hanging mist. Had they walked that far already?

Yes, there it stood, barely visible, frozen in time. Carved from granite, the figure of a woman in a flowing gown stood poised on the banks of the River Tyne. She perched at the boundary of their world, one arm outstretched, pointing toward Scotland, while looking back over her shoulder to England. The expression on the statue's face was unreadable.

"What does she mean?" her young charge asked beside her. "Why is she there? Did the reivers fear her?"

Clare glanced at Vicky, noted her pale face against the windblown red curls. The child needed a bonnet, so there'd be no lingering in this cold. "Now you know perfectly well no reivers have come thieving for three centuries now."

"Then who is she?" Vicky stared up, awestruck, mystified.

The sculptor was as long buried as the roots of heather and broom entrenched at the stone lady's base. If there was a history to her, it was lost back in the days of the reivers, when the border was a place of passions roused.

"The tale," Clare began, "is very old, and most of it you already know."

"She is pointing toward Dundroma," Vicky prompted.

"Where it is forbidden to travel. Never forget."

"Then why did she go there?"

"She crossed the border, stole away in the night from England with one of the reivers who had swept down out of the north. He gave his solemn oath that he'd kiss her once and send her back. But she never returned."

"Did her father not try to ransom her?"

"With the ashes from a burned cottage? An empty purse? The reivers took everything."

"He offered himself in her place then, surely."

"Yes, so the legend goes, but by then she had kissed the laird from the north, the laird from dark Dundroma, and he had bewitched her. And she did not return. Her family erected the statue at the border as a warning to young lasses: Danger befell young ladies who dared to venture beyond this point. Ignore men from the north. They deceive."

"With one kiss?"

"It was a stolen kiss. A forbidden, bewitching kiss." She removed a woolen scarf from about her shoulders and tied it over Vicky's hair. The mist was turning into a light drizzle.

"How can a kiss bewitch?" Vicky asked, twisting to stare up at the statue.

"That you would have to ask the lass who did the kissing."

"But she's made of stone . . ."

"Then you'll have to ask a lad, but not until you are older."

"How old?"

After a pause, she said quietly, "You'll know." And then without another word, she led the way back to the great house. They made it inside just ahead of the summer downpour.

Well, Clare thought as she stood in the recessed shelter of a doorway, shaking out her scarf . . . she had not exactly lied, but Vicky was so young . . . It would be years yet before she was ready for kisses of her own. And real kisses were not at all the same. Bewitching kisses, like long-vanished reivers, were the stuff of exaggeration.

And a governess ought not to be telling such tales . . .

⊶Chapter One

Reiver's Noose, Northern England, 1868

The news spread faster than a winter wind across the moorlands, and servants at Thornhill Manor, when they heard, fell on their knees to pray for mercy.

Alec Douglas, Lord Strahan, major in the 45th Borderland Regiment, and great-grandson of the Black Douglas, was returning home, and everyone from butlers to scullery maids knew what that meant.

The old feud between Dundroma Castle and Thornhill Manor would begin again. North versus south. Scotland versus England. Douglas versus Charlton.

"May God have mercy on our souls," the grooms muttered as they pulled themselves up out of haystacks. So fearsome was the news that pleasures like kissing wenches paled beside the task of warning the good ladies of Reiver's Noose. The men of the borderland pulled together and before Lord Strahan returned the word was passed.

The devil of Dundroma was on his way. It was said of course that one of his ancestors had sold his soul to the devil and been boiled alive. Yet another ancestor had pillaged and looted the English side of the border by night and by day returned to share Scots whisky with the English warden—to ensure the good fellow would look the other way at Black Alec's exploits. Wild blood ran through the veins of Alec Douglas, that much was certain.

Alec Douglas knew of course what his English neighbors called him, and even after twelve years he didn't expect they'd have altered their opinions of him.

Twelve years had not made him forget much either. On the contrary, the time away had taught him a great deal. He had learned that he was an excellent soldier, an even more excellent lover, and an eligible catch. He had also learned that women had been put on earth to hurt men. But in the end a fall off a horse had done him in.

Alec touched his hand to his pant leg, grazed the kneecap where beneath his trousers behind his scarred skin, the bones lay in painful pieces. Ugly. Painful. Humiliating. At least if he could say a tiger had attacked him, there'd be some marks for adventure. But a fall off a horse. As humiliating as if a woman had taken a stick to him.

He grabbed the strap to steady himself from the pitching of the coach. The damnable roads up in northern England rivaled the ocean. He sank back against the cushions of the coach and grimaced with pain. All during the ocean voyage home from India he'd debated his predicament. Over and over William Graham had argued his options. If William were seated across from him now, he'd still try to dissuade him from his course and persuade him to a more foolish course of action.

"You've decided what you'll do when you reach the borderland, haven't you?" he asked endlessly.

And Alec's reply had been firm. His resolve unbendable.

"A military man with a shattered knee has few options."

"I think you should consult with the Royal College of—"

"I'm not allowing a pack of grave-robbing butchers to cut up my knee. I'm lucky enough I didn't end up with the leg amputated." William had been there in sick bay. If it hadn't been for his intervention, it would be amputated now. You'd think a friend like that could leave well enough alone. But William was a peacemaker, a healer.

"You'd rather have a limp forever than risk healing? Healed you could return, have a chance at general——"

"You've taken too much sun, forgot to wear a hat over in India. What good would I be to the Queen's regiment with one leg?" Military ambition beckoned like a jealous mistress, true. But Alec had come home a wounded soldier.

"I'll learn to live with a limp," Alec said. "It suits the borderer in me."

"Coward . . . If you were as good as ever, if the blood of a reiver still coursed through your veins, you'd not be afraid. Surgery has advanced beyond amputations. It's gaining respectability. Only cowards fear the surgeon's knife."

"There is a difference, man, between being a coward and being an outright fool."

"Not in this matter."

But William, stubborn to the end, promised to send a physician to invade Dundroma. As borderers were renowned for hospitality, there'd be no turning away a friend of William's, but perhaps William would forget his threat. They'd parted amicably enough in London, and now Alec was alone on the road north.

Shadows clung to his soul, followed him from dawn on into dusk, and at night enveloped him. Only the discipline of the military kept the shadows lined up in their place. He was, he admitted, bored, angry, and hurting. No regiment of the Queen's army, no woman, no physician, no servant, could ease those feelings, so, in irritable border fashion, Alec decided to indulge them.

The coach slowed, and Alec peered out the window through the mist. A flicker of anticipation swelled in him at first sight of the River Tyne. Home. A place of windswept moorland, winding riverbanks, fortified towers, bold men, and bolder women. The borderland.

Thornhill Manor had not been his home, but he remembered it well. It perched down in the valley, unchanged: red brick, Georgian, and pretentious. His gaze swept from the windows, where servants pulled back draperies to openly gawk.

As a Dundroma man, he'd always despised this side of the border, but if he was going to carry out his plan, he'd have to call at Thornhill. No one save two people would know him. He held the element of surprise.

A clever reiver, if he wanted to succeed at plundering, never arrived at the front door and announced his intentions. A good reiver gave the enemy no chance to think up reprisals when shadows fell. Which is why he'd given the Charltons no forewarning.

He was about to claim the child he'd left behind. *His daughter.* The shadows of the past pressed closer, almost as painful as his knee. He pushed them back. Pushed all of it away.

He leaned back, sweat breaking out on his brow. With his cane, he poked at the coach roof. "Take the shortcut to Thornhill," he hollered up at the driver. "The servant's road. It'll be well marked."

"Sir?" The driver was peering down at him. He was a good man, a Dundroma man, who could be counted on like death himself to be loyal. He repeated himself. "You know the crossing."

Generations of Douglas reivers had hidden at the crossroads in the dark, waiting for their chance to loot the Charltons. One of his ancestors—a Douglas whose horse came up lame—was hanged from a tree on the very next bend . . .

With a doff of his cap the driver retreated from view and moments later the coach passed a grove of yew trees. They were almost there. Alec settled back, satisfied. Yes, this was more like it.

Soon now, the coach would arrive at the juncture in the

roads, the place where men chose their allegiance to
England or Scotland. Where lovers betrayed allegiances and
where reivers rode in shadow to plunder as he did
not . . . A place where a man's word was worth his life.

His hand tightened around the ivory-handled walking
stick he carried and as the coach jolted over a nasty rut in
the road, he winced in pain and touched his hat to his knee.

Oh, aye, his course was set. He'd divert himself from
pain, amuse himself with fatherhood. The child would be
about twelve now, too young to know the wiles of women,
and old enough to appreciate all the Dundroma ways he
could teach her. And the child—he'd never learned her
name—deserved to be raised a Dundroma lass. His daughter would be spoiled of course by life at Thornhill, in need
of a father's strong hand. Best of all, he'd have her all to
himself, with no interference from any traitorous Charlton
women.

For above all, Alec had learned never again to trust
females above the age of sixteen. Never. In that matter, even
more than his shattered dreams of military glory, he was a
confirmed pessimist.

The coach slowed for a flock of geese, and the coachman
climbed down to inquire if Lord Strahan was quite sure of
the turnoff in the road.

"Reiver's Noose," he snapped. "Look for the wooden
sign," and he settled back in keen anticipation.

The ax was too heavy, Clare realized, and nowhere in her
manners book was there any instruction on how a lady
carried one. She hoped dragging the tool behind her was not
too unseemly. Adele, if she could see what the governess
was up to, would be horrified, yet an uncustomary spark of
mischief propelled Clare on. Clutching the new wooden
signs to her breast, she dragged the ax through the rose
gardens and across the manicured lawns of Thornhill and at

last came to the place where wild daisies bloomed—the main road. She dropped her burden and rubbed her calloused hands.

It was a gray day in June, with the wind blowing down the bleak English moorland, whipping the heads of the daisies back and forth. Rain clouds hung on the horizon, and so the deed, if it got done today, would have to be done quickly.

It had been Vicky's idea to replace the crossing signs, and a fine idea it was. Only now Vicky had run off to say farewell to a visitor, and the carpenter had hit his thumb with a hammer. They'd left Clare with the ax and new road signs—sawed by Thornhill carpenters, hand-lettered, and painted by her charge. They'd also given promises to meet her by the crossing, and Clare was adamant about replacing the signs today before the rain fell. On Clare trudged up the moorland road. Splinters from the wood dug into her palms, but she didn't mind. Too much of the child's time was taken in rigid indoor lessons. This was a welcome outdoor respite.

She looked back. Vicky should have fetched her friend and said good-bye here, yet Clare arrived at the site of the decrepit old signs all alone. The signs pointing the way to Reiver's Noose and Black Cloak Crossing were rough-hewn and pushed to a crooked slant by some long-ago reiver, the names washed away by the rains and wind. Since no one could read them save for the initial letters, they scarcely served their function for strangers. Worse, they were sordid reminders of Thornhill's checkered past, telling all this was the road trod by unsavory thieves and murderers on their way back to Dundroma. The road deserved a more genteel marker.

Alone, she dropped the ax at her feet. She'd never swung an ax. Still, the old crossing marker looked so rickety that she gave it a swift kick. It stood. Something in Clare rose to the challenge. Something in her that tired of days on end shut up in a schoolroom with a twelve-year-old made her kick it again. It wobbled, and she knew a sense of power. She lifted the ax and swung back, then whacked the marker midway with the butt of the ax.

A crack rent the air and the withered old sign creaked and fell. It split like a tree struck by lightning. She was still staring at it, lying dead in the dirt, when horse's hooves pounded the lane, out of sight, but coming closer. Tack groaned and jangled, and suddenly a coach rounded the bend.

Unfamiliar in markings, she expected it to keep going. Instead, when it came alongside of her, it slowed to a stop, and to her horror the door opened and a man appeared.

He was dressed all in black, from his black top hat to his shiny boots. In his hands he held an ivory-headed cane. He swept off his hat to reveal tousled chestnut hair and leaned out, staring at the place where the ancient signs lay toppled, and then at her.

"Is there any good and legal reason why you're chopping down the road signs?" he asked at last. "What was wrong with Reiver's Noose and Black Cloak Crossing? Those names had history to them."

"My ward and I decided to paint new signs with more modern names," Clare said, adding, "No one asks for Reiver's Noose. Strangers always want to know the way to Thornhill."

He stared at her as if she'd said she was going to restore the Stuarts to the throne of England. "Well," he said, measuring his words carefully, "my coachman was depending on the old road signs."

Clare chewed on her lip. Eligible men did not come to Thornhill—certainly not the sort who would look twice at a widowed governess of twenty-eight. Clare's earlier bravado faltered.

"Actually," she admitted, "the man they call the devil of

Dundroma is returning, and they say he's worse than any plundering reivers. Without the old signs, he might get lost."

After a pause, the stranger smiled slightly. It was a pleasant expression. "Indeed. And Thornhill Manor sends out a gentlewoman to knock down the signs. To make him lose his bearings? Don't you think the devil of Dundroma knows his way?"

Under other circumstances, he could have charmed her.

"*I* don't believe all that nonsense about any man being a devil . . . the border's been calm for three centuries, and no Dundroma laird can destroy the peace. But . . . it amuses my charge."

He stood in the doorway of his coach, smiling even more.

Her heart picked up a beat. He was unnerving really. In seconds Clare took in crucial impressions. Compelling blue eyes and that arresting chestnut-brown hair. Unconfined from his hat, it blew about his face, a full face of strong lines and uncompromising expression. He stared up at the place where the old sign used to dangle from a worn bridle strap.

"Where is the hanging tree?" he asked, looking about.

"The hanging tree's been long cut down . . . you have been a long time between visits, haven't you?"

He glared, and she studied him a bit closer. If he stood straight he'd be tall. Moreover he was a big man. The harsh planes and craggy look to his face hinted at a dissolute life. He was not exactly handsome, but compelling to gaze upon, especially the eyes and the firm, well-formed mouth.

Her hands went back to her nape to touch her bun. "If—if I've inconvenienced you, I shall be happy to give directions. What is your destination?"

"Thornhill."

"How lovely. Thornhill is where I live."

He pushed the door open wider and used the walking stick to limp down out of the coach. She saw then he was crippled and felt pity, which he'd never want. Light rain began to fall. Too late today to nail up the new signs, but not too late for hospitality.

She wanted, for the sake of the Charltons, to make him feel welcome.

The same idea apparently occurred to him. He gazed directly into her eyes. "May I offer you a ride there then? In case the Black Douglas comes along while you're alone out on the road."

She paused, wondering if accepting his offer would be a breach of ladylike manners. But it was beginning to rain harder, and besides, he seemed to know everything about the borderland. Remarkably well informed.

"I think that would be lovely . . ." He held out a hand to assist her in, and she brushed rain off her skirt.

"Well, lass, and who might you be? I don't recall a bonnie lass living in that museum full of geegaws."

His trace of brogue rang an alarm bell in her, but she didn't know why. She passed it off to her imagination.

"I'm the governess and the daughter-in-law of the house. Thornhill needs a bit of company," she added. "Are you an old friend of the Charltons then?"

His smile was fleeting. "Unfortunately yes. An old family acquaintance . . . if not friends. It's been a long while since they've seen me."

"Does Vicky know you?" she asked while settling against the plush seat.

He seated himself opposite her and slammed the door.

"Vicky?" His face creased in bewilderment as he traced a finger around the ivory head of his walking stick.

"She's the Charltons' granddaughter. My charge."

The bewilderment faded, replaced by the smile.

"Vicky. So that's her name . . . I had the pleasure of meeting her long ago when she was but an infant. Not christened yet."

"Did you know her parents then?"

He was silent a moment. "Yes."

"Mother or father?"

He turned to look at her.

"I'm sorry. I'm being impertinent, but I've been so hoping someone who knew her poor parents might come and visit the poor little orphan."

"Orphan?"

"You did know about her father?"

He was silent, and the coach rocked along.

"Tell me then," he said at last. Deep blue eyes pinioned her. "What you know of her father."

She eyed the tiger's head on his walking stick. Ivory. Meticulously carved. "Tell me," he urged.

It all came out in a rush. "He was a missionary, and he's been missing ever so long. Presumed dead after the ship he was sailing on crashed."

There was a long pause while he stared at her.

"I'm sorry," she began. "I'm sure that I broke the news in a dreadfully blunt manner . . ."

"You did . . . but may I for once be optimistic and suggest he, like Robinson Crusoe, survived all these years."

"Oh, doubtful. He'd at least have written."

"Then I am sorely out of date on developments. Tell me more about the poor fellow . . . it would be a favor, so I don't put my foot in my mouth so to speak when I meet the child's grandparents."

At once Clare understood and sympathized. "I know very little . . . except she reveres the idea of an upstanding missionary father who is renowned for hundreds of conversions of heathens and for his Bible translations into tropical languages. Though I never met him, I've done my best to make his image worthy in her eyes. You won't tarnish that image, will you?"

"I doubt my memories could do that." Alec could barely conceal his displeasure. They'd lied about him. Alec was a disbeliever. Nothing spiritual had touched him in twelve years. Faith was a yawning void. Once in a while he peered over into what looked to be a black hole. Black emptiness.

Worse, a coddling English governess was raising his child. All the more reason to remove her from here and take her up to the less rigorous atmosphere of Dundroma.

"Do you know her father's name?" he asked.

Now she turned a suspicious look on him.

"Who are you? Did you truly know Vicky's father?"

"Aye . . . why don't you believe me?"

"You can't."

"Pray tell why not."

She never hesitated. "Because—as I explained—her father's been gone for twelve years."

"That doesn't mean I couldn't have known him twelve years ago—or even longer. We go back to boyhood, Alec Douglas and I."

She was silent, dubious . . . For Alec Douglas was *not* the name of Vicky's father. It was *William* Douglas, so Adele said.

"What's wrong? Do you fear the truth might be far different from this fiction you've preached to the child?"

"Fiction? You play at games with me. It's not fiction."

He made a scoffing sound and tapped his walking stick against his knee.

Again, she stared at him, thoughtfully studying his profile, the reddish glints in his dark hair.

Clare gulped. *His hair held reddish lights. A rare color.* A darker red than Vicky's but still . . . an awful suspicion filled her. But no, she would not give it a name.

"Who are you?" she asked in a small voice. "You're no missionary. And you're no friend of William's, are you?"

"The only William with which I am acquainted goes by the surname . . ."

She reached for the door handle, but his hand covered hers.

"Wait, lassie—"

Lassie. The pieces came together like a newfangled daguerreotype thrust in her face. Lord help her, he was a Scotsman. Alec Douglas. Alexander. The Black Douglas. The accents up here were similar to the untrained ear, but she could after a few minutes of conversation tell the difference. At once, she half stood and with a fist pounded on the roof of the coach. Thornhill Manor—its reassuring red brick facade—was in sight, but she wanted out. "Stop, I say. Stop!" The coachman obliged, and reined in.

She shoved at the door and stumbled from the coach, running across the lawns for Thornhill to warn the Charltons while servants peeked between drapes through the windows. Oh, she'd been duped, ruined! It was the devil of Dundroma himself beside whom she rode. A friend of Vicky's father! The deceitful cad.

She slammed the heavy front door and leaned against it catching her breath, pushing her hair back into its knot, praying servants would not gossip. She'd been seen consorting with the devil. Oh, there was no escaping her duty. She had to seek out her employers and confess. They must be warned.

She found them in the parlor, most unceremoniously posed, their noses pressed against the glass. They acted like children, staring out at the circular driveway as if for St. Nicholas. Only this was summer, not Christmas, and outside sat a coach, not a sleigh.

"A stranger's come—"

And their words came crystal-clear, like a knife to her heart. "It's just like him to come without warning. Out of the past. I suppose he wants to see his child." Percival's voice held no expression.

"Pish, what would that Scots devil want with the child?"

Adele asked. "He gave up his fatherly rights. But he'll think of some way to make trouble. Mark my words."

Clare sank back against the wall, the breath sucked out of her. Vicky's father . . . Unbelievable. Worse than she'd feared. Worst of all, she'd committed the borderer's ultimate sin, a crime worse than killing—she'd led the enemy right into the home of his prey.

"Do you think he'll finally be more civilized than when he left?" Adele was asking.

"I wager after all that time in a tropical climate," her husband said, "he'll be more of a barbarian than ever . . . Look there, he's limping. Perhaps the heat took some of the fight in him."

"I worry more, dearest, about what the father will do when he finds out we 'killed' him off prematurely?" Adele sighed. "This won't sit well with the servants, I suppose, to find out we've lied."

Distraught, Clare backed away, intending to find Vicky, but Adele Charlton's voice stopped her. "This is your fault, Clare. Haven't I told you to beware of strangers' motives up here in the borderland?" Adele Charlton did not turn. "He deceived you. Let this be a lesson."

Clare, numb, could only stare. Yes, he'd deceived her, but so, it seemed, had the Charltons. "You lied to Vicky and me."

Adele turned and her voice was deadly calm. "We've kept a dreadful secret in this house these twelve years past, but it's over. Now find her and bring her to us. But say nothing about her father."

Clare moved in a daze, whirling just in time to see him—the devil of Dundroma—invade Thornhill Manor. Limping into the grand hallway, leaning as crookedly against the stick as the old sign to Dundroma had, his face was set with purpose.

The Charltons followed her out. "You can't have her!"

Adele's voice rose a notch above its usual well-modulated tone.

"The law says I can have my daughter, madam, so you'd best break the news of my resurrection. Bibles have not been my career."

"You devil."

"That would be closer to the truth."

Adele's face paled with the shock of it.

"At least have the decency to wait in the library, for I won't spend one minute longer with such a duplicitous man."

She swept back into the parlor and slammed the door, leaving Clare alone and staring into Lord Strahan's amused eyes.

"The library door is behind you. Since you've no qualms about walking invited into the house, you will find a decanter of whisky and plenty of books. Dispose of them as you will, but kindly leave the Charltons and Vicky alone until . . . until—"

"What?"

"Until they break the news about you—you liar."

He opened the door to the library and looked around with disdain. "Me? A liar?" he said over his shoulder. "I recall *you* telling me the lies and making wrong assumptions. What is it I'm supposed to be? A missionary?" He gave a short laugh, then reached out with his walking stick to snag a stool and pull it toward him. Carefully, he eased himself down onto a chair, as if he were in much pain.

Clare pushed away all thoughts of sympathy or pity. "You should have told me straight off."

"But I was amused by your storytelling," he said while adjusting the stool beneath his aching leg. "An unexpected end to a tedious journey." Suddenly he looked up at her, blue eyes cold with resolve. "She's mine, and no one in this house has any choice in the matter . . . not even bold lasses."

"Vicky's feelings come first and foremost. I'll stop you from taking her."

He laughed outright. "Pray tell me what you intend to do . . . Stand in my way with a board and ax?"

"You selfish man." Clare's only prayer was simple: to find Vicky before this news spread outside the walls of Thornhill. She picked up her skirts and swirled out. "Whatever it takes to prevail. I shall never let anything but Vicky come first. She's an innocent."

⮤Chapter Two

"He kissed you?"

In a tree in the walled orchard of Thornhill Manor, Victoria Douglas, granddaughter of Percival and Adele Charlton, drew a blanket over the head of both her companion and herself as a makeshift shelter from the drizzle. Pesky geography lessons and comportment lectures could wait.

Right now, Charlotte Warnick's lessons held far more value, for Charlotte was bragging about something more important than the length of the River Thames or the proper order in which to use forks.

"Was it a real kiss?" Vicky Charlton perched in an apple tree in the gardens of Thornhill Manor, legs dangling from the lowest branch, cheek pressed against the trunk. "You know—one where lips touch?"

On the branch opposite her sat Charlotte Warnick, a distant cousin from her grandmother's side of the family. Once a year, Charlotte came for a fortnight to visit at Thornhill. This was Charlotte's last day, and true to her word, Charlotte had done what she'd vowed and won a kiss from the gypsy groom.

"Of course it was a real kiss," Charlotte said dreamily. "A kiss on the cheek counts."

Vicky was envious. Everything thirteen-year-old Charlotte did was wonderfully grown-up, and this late spring visit had been better than any other—ever. Charlotte was one year older, and dressed with the town polish of Newcastle. To Vicky, who'd been raised in this remote old house with Spartan strictness, everything about her city cousin sounded adventuresome—especially daring to let a boy kiss her.

Which is why a kiss was a milestone—way better than hiding rabbits in the gardener's watering cans or locking the privy doors.

"It was right here." Charlotte, leaning around from the other side of the tree, pointed to her cheekbone.

Vicky, who'd spent twelve years of increasing boredom shuttered up here with the same quiet governess as her companion, desperately wanted to measure up to Charlotte's coup.

But what could outdo a kiss from the stable boy?

"Have you ever had a boy kiss you on the lips?"

There was a quick intake of breath.

"Course not."

"Haven't you ever thought about it?"

"Yes. I saw the maid kiss the groom once, and she made moaning sounds."

Moaning? "Do you think it hurts or what?"

"Of course not, you goose."

"How do you know?"

"I just do. The maid looked like she'd had her cheeks pinched, that's all." With a bored sigh, Charlotte plucked a leaf from the tree and waved it idly. The rain stopped.

"Do you think Billy would kiss a girl on the lips?"

"Find out yourself."

"You're a coward, Charlotte Warnick. I wager I can get kissed on the lips before you."

"Who'd kiss you? Billy won't, because then your grandfather would sack him. And besides, I'm leaving today."

"There are other lads about besides Billy."

"Where? None who would kiss you."

Vicky bridled at Charlotte's conceit and her challenge. This was the border country. It was her, not Charlotte, who lived within sight of the kissing statue at the banks of the River Tyne. That meant maids got kissed up in this bleak moorland country. But by whom? She wanted something memorable, something worthy of the lady in the statue. On the other hand, she didn't want to turn to stone.

"I'll find someone. Let's go look at the statue and we'll decide on the wager." She shot a peek at Charlotte's velvet cloak. Pretty enough for a wager. Everything about Charlotte was pretty. Long blond ringlets. Long-lashed brown eyes. Not the red curly mane and blue eyes with lashes so light they were all but invisible Vicky had inherited.

"Papa says nice girls don't wager."

"Nice girls don't let grooms kiss them either," Vicky said.

"You won't find anyone to kiss you."

"Will too." Heedless of her dress, Vicky shimmied down the trunk of the apple tree and bent to brush the scuff marks off her high-top shoes. A short run ahead bubbled the River Tyne, the boundary between England and Scotland. Hair flying, she ran right up to the statue of the kissing lady and slapped a hand against it.

"Beat you."

"Who cares about the statue?" Charlotte said.

Vicky stared up at it. Oh, she cared. Always. It was where she and her governess came to sit for their history lessons in September when the heather bloomed across the heath.

"We wouldn't be bewitched, would we, if we kissed a boy, I mean?" Vicky, glancing nervously over the river into Dundroma territory, frowned. She never could figure it out. The heath looked exactly the same on both sides of the river. So it couldn't be Scotland that was bewitching. It must be the way Scots lads kissed.

"Of course not." Charlotte's voice held a superior air. "I dare you to let a lad kiss you this summer."

"Double dare if it's a Scots lad."

Vicky stared over the border into Dundroma territory. It was a scary thing to wager, but she was bored. "Yes, then, what shall we wager?"

"If I get a boy to kiss me first, then you have to give me your rabbit."

"Wellington? I can't give him away."

"You goose . . . You're not old enough to kiss."

When will I be ready? You'll know . . .

"I'm past twelve . . . and if I kiss a lad, you give me your blue velvet cloak."

Charlotte was so pretty and daring, but that wasn't all Vicky envied. Charlotte had something else Vicky lacked—a father, a father who indulged her every whim. Mr. Warnick gave her gifts instead of backboards for her posture. Sent her on holiday instead of locking her up in her room for dribbling ink on her good dress.

But since Vicky could never have a father, a kiss seemed a more realistic goal to hope for. A kiss and a blue velvet cloak.

Not any boy was worth kissing for a velvet cloak, but someone would turn up.

And someone did.

Her governess.

Too soon, she could hear her aunt Clare, calling from the distance, her name drawn out in the wind. "Victoria . . ."

Then Aunt Clare was there, right beside the statue, and giving orders, telling her to hurry up and climb up from the river's edge.

"You said I had the afternoon to spend with Charlotte."

"That was before."

"Before what? Did the road sign break?"

"Just come. Your grandmother wants you."

Vicky moaned. Whenever her grandmother wanted to see her, the meeting usually involved dress fittings, backboards, recitals, and sundry punishments for random misdeeds.

"Has the carpenter nailed up my new road sign?"

"Not quite, but we've more urgent business to attend to than renaming the roads." Aunt Clare told Charlotte to run along and pack for her journey home. "Say good-bye now. You might not have time later."

And so Vicky hugged Charlotte farewell. "We shall write each other on Michaelmas and tell all about our success with the wager . . ."

Aunt Clare tugged her away. "There'll be no wagering between young ladies. Come along now and change to meet your . . . your grandmother."

There was a wobble in Aunt Clare's voice. Serious indeed. If her grandmother was going to insist she start up harp lessons again, Vicky was having none of it. Nor dancing. She detested pirouettes almost as much as arpeggios. Embroidery was only tolerable because she could use the needle to prick the scullery maid when she bent over to lay the fire. Another bread and water offense. A small price to pay, especially since she had a stash of biscuits and jam under her bed, pilfered from Cook's pantry.

"What's wrong?" she asked automatically. "Did my rabbit break out of his cage? What's wrong?"

"Nothing's wrong . . . there's news. Important news about . . . well, it's for your grandmother to tell . . . Now, above all, stay out of the library. She's waiting in the parlor."

Hinges creaked and Alec watched as the door opened. When the governess appeared in the doorway, the even tenor of his breathing broke, but just for a split second. Without moving a muscle, he said, "Did you bring the child?"

The distance between the doorway and the wing chair in which he was seated spanned at least forty paces, and he watched her take every single step. He wouldn't call her beautiful in the manner of women he'd known, certainly not as beautiful as Cecilia. She held her cloak together at her throat as if she'd grabbed it in a hurry. With her other hand, she was holding up her hoop skirt, soaked with rain. Dark blond hair streamed out around her hood. There was an allure to the lass, something that intrigued him.

Perhaps it was the demure dress, with its wide crinoline skirt hiding her figure. Perhaps it was the anger sparkling in her eyes, turning them a deeper shade of green. Aye, he'd forgotten the attractiveness of the border lasses—even though this one was English . . . His loins stirred with longing, and he shifted restlessly, gathered his own control.

No, by God. He was done with women. For twelve years he'd avoided the wiles of women, no mean feat with the fishing fleet full of spinsters docking in India once a year. He was battleworn. Disillusioned. And obviously vain to think a pretty lass like that would look at him, title or no. And how, by the devil, had he made that mental leap from admiring a lass's figure and face to affairs of the heart? She stood there, hood slipping down from her hair, gown sodden, and crossed her arms as if she were a one-woman sentry. Too bad she'd not been here thirteen years past, else he might have, in his youthful indiscretion, chased after her instead of Cecilia.

He reached for his knobbed cane and carefully eased himself up out of the chair. She reached out as if to assist him, but he shook her away.

Her glance slid once to his leg, then up again to his face, and never once did she take her eyes off of him. Her voice, filled with the northern accent, rippled gently over her. He could not seem to pull his gaze away from hers. "Where is my child?" he repeated.

They stared at each other, silent.

"She doesn't even know you. This is madness."

"The child, if she's a Douglas, will want to come away with me. Now, where is she?"

She gulped.

Rain poured down the windows, streamed off the eaves outside.

Leaning on his cane, he circled her, suspicious, male instincts aroused. He liked a bold woman, and one who masqueraded as a prim governess was a distinct challenge.

"Lass," he said quietly, "I've been halfway around the world in India these twelve years past, but now I'm back in Britain and come to claim my child."

"You speak as if she were a piece of property."

"Legally I have that right—as her father. I own my child, and I shall take her."

"Stop calling her a child. She's Vicky. Victoria Augusta. We call her Vicky."

"By the ghost of Mary, Queen of Scots, they went and named her after the English Queen," he muttered, disgusted. He'd fought for that same Queen in India. Still, that didn't mean he wanted his daughter named for her. The Charlton sense of humor had been at work. Giving the child a name they had to know he'd abhor.

"It was Thornhill's right and obligation to name her. Do you not approve because it's not—biblical enough?"

"It's missish . . . and what surname does she go by?"

"Douglas, of course," Clare said, hastening to add, "but she doesn't know the laird of Dundroma by any surname or face even. To her, like the villagers, you're simply the absent Lord Strahan. There are so many Douglases about that—"

"Enough!" He didn't want a lecture, only the reassurance that she at least bore his surname. "I detest the Christian name."

"Then you should have stayed long enough to christen her."

Aye, he should have. Cecilia should have stayed faithful too. But life didn't work in shouldn'ts and what ifs.

Clare walked over and stood in front of the fire. The light traced a delicate frame about her, brightening her soft hair, darkening her eyes. "You're not really going to take her, are you? You'd not be that cruel?" she asked.

"What's cruel about giving her her birthright? Some adventure beyond the confines of this mausoleum?"

"This is the only home she's ever known. For a dozen years she's barely set foot off of Thornhill."

"Pity. She'll like Dundroma."

If only it were that simple. "But you can't just come back to life."

"Ah, pray tell why not? Is there a law against it?"

"Lord Strahan, there are human considerations at stake here, not just the law." She gazed up at him, pleading.

"Very well. It is for her grandparents to explain away the stories—missionary stories. Hah! And if they can't, I will."

She blocked the door, clearly nervous. "Give them a bit more time to talk with Vicky. Oh, but I'm being terribly disloyal talking to you."

"Be disloyal then," he demanded, eyes gleaming slyly. "Any good border lass worth her salt doesn't let a thing like loyalty stop her."

"I could lose my position."

"You will anyway when I take her home . . . Now, tell me what you know about *me*."

"I've told you all I know."

"I'm a missionary."

"Who died."

Dead. It still galled him beyond belief. Lord Charlton had the temerity to tell his child her own father was dead. He clenched and unclenched his hands about the head of his cane. His hands whitened with the pain, far greater than anything his leg had given him. He looked up to find pity in her eyes.

"They merely misstated the facts for Vicky's sake."

"They're from Thornhill, and I'm from Dundroma. That's all the reason they'd need. For three centuries the families have feuded and lied and plotted. No reason to change that now. I wasn't good enough for Adele Charlton's daughter, and so when she thought I was conveniently out of the way—forever—she invented someone more to her liking."

As the governess shrank back, he added, "At Dundroma we prefer to be bold and forthright. Now be so good as to reciprocate and tell me when I will meet my daughter."

"She's with her grandparents who are telling Vicky you've arrived."

"You mean, breaking the news that I'm alive."

"Yes."

His mouth thinned. "And no missionary."

"I think restoring you to life would be sufficient."

"Miss Clare—is that how my daughter terms you?—Miss Charlton . . ."

"Mrs. Charlton, but Vicky calls me Aunt Clare."

"Well, Aunt Clare, I've traveled halfway around the world—limped rather—and I'd rather not spend any more time dallying at Thornhill. If they can't rectify your lie then I'll do so myself—"

"I never knew about the lie." She looked up at him, eyes fearful, lips trembling.

He studied her, from her delicate English face to her tiny waist where she wrung her hands. Vulnerable? Totally at odds with the spirited lass he'd met at the crossing.

"Is it important that I believe you?"

She nodded, eyes welling with tears. "I'd never have agreed to such a lie over the years. Never. But though I abhor the lie, I abhor even more the idea of uprooting the child and sending her off with a complete stranger." She turned her back and dabbed at her eyes.

He had a momentary stab of conscience. "Miss Charlton, in India it was customary for children to be shipped home to England or Scotland for schooling. *That* was uprooting, sailing halfway around the world with only a nanny or governess or companion." He tried to sound reassuring, if only to forestall her tears. "Traveling across the border into the Cheviot Hills, is merely a holiday in the child's own backyard. Why, you can see them from here. I wager she's snuck over there already to inspect Dundroma."

She turned back, dry-eyed, in control again, as she tucked the lacy handkerchief up her sleeve. "It's forbidden territory."

"How insufferably smug of the Charltons."

"You left her, as I understand it. They raised her as they saw fit. And so did I. You could leave now, you know. She'll never know you were here. That would be best I think. Think of the child, her fear going off somewhere new . . ."

Her spirit amused him again. "You're negotiating for no reason, wee march warden."

"Don't call me that. I'm her governess, and no one knows her better. I'm not playing some game from days of old. I'm trying to do what's best for a child." She paused, looking at him. "Why did you leave her?"

"That's my affair. Why I returned is my affair also. And the fact remains that I am her father, legal and indisputable, and a father's right is paramount. I shall claim the child, Miss Charlton, and if she's half Douglas, then Douglas blood runs through her heart, and she'll get used to Dundroma in record time." He tapped her lightly on the arm with his cane. "Make no mistake, the child will want to come with me. You'll see."

Adele Charlton was, at sixty years of age, still a beautiful

woman. Despite salt in her brown hair and fine lines about
her eyes and mouth, her smile still revealed dimples,
laughter lurked in her eyes when she wasn't careful, and her
thin figure rivalled a girl's. She was more beautiful, in fact,
than any woman within a day's riding distance of Thornhill.
It had been said that her beauty was the subject of much
speculation and mystery—and most of all, self-satisfaction
among rival ladies.

For if a woman of Adele's beauty had ended up wed to an
untitled suitor like Percival Charlton and living her life up in
the wild border country, then she must have had to settle for
second best.

Though if anyone knew the tale—the tale of Adele's
"spurned" suitors, the reason she'd settled on stodgy
Percival—no one was daring enough to tell that tale aloud.

Oh, but there was a story to why Adele had had to settle
for a Charlton, and ladies old enough to recall Adele's
coming out vowed to live long enough to hear it. For her
part, Adele vowed only to outlive them all.

At the moment she was reconsidering that vow. Adele
Charlton had been trapped by many lies in her life, had
married because of a tarnished reputation. She was adept at
landing on her feet after impulsive lies and half truths got
her into trouble. But never in her wildest dreams had she
imagined this lie could come back to haunt her.

She watched as Vicky, summoned by the housekeeper,
came forward. In another room, alone, meek Clare held the
devil at bay, a decidedly lopsided match. There was nothing
for it but to get it out.

"Your father's returned for you, child."

Vicky's face went white, but she spoke right up. "My
father is a proper English missionary who was swept away
at sea."

Adele cleared her throat and stared at her hands.

"I know it's a shock, but in the end you'll feel glad. Perhaps." That was the easy part. That a father was alive.

"Y-you said he was drowned."

"Yes, well, these big ships have many people on them and mistakes can be made. We were mistaken."

Vicky gave a half smile, then reached up to twine a curl around one finger. "I'm glad."

"Well, I'm not. For now he's come to see you. And you're all I have left in the world. I don't want to lose you."

A long silence stretched out as Vicky stood there putting all the pieces together in her head. Having raised two children of her own, Adele expected anything from sullenness to excitability. Vicky expressed no emotion whatsoever. Her face was drained of color, and she stared straight at her grandmother, then glanced at her grandfather's face, as if looking for reassurance that this was a tasteless jest.

"You lied to me."

True, it had been a straightforward announcement, typical of Adele Charlton, who when faced with potential emotional situations reverted to bluntness. At once, she began to apologize, not for the news itself, but for her inability to break it to Vicky in a more genteel manner.

"Vicky, dearest, I've made a shambles of telling you. There was just no graceful way and, you must admit, not much protocol for this awkward situation. I dislike blurting out information in such a manner. Do say you'll forgive my shoddy manners. In most other circumstances, you'd want to remember Clare's fine teaching, and lead up to the subject delicately."

Vicky had nothing delicate to respond.

"But it was still a lie."

In the back of her mind, a tiny voice whispered that she was glad she had a father . . . a most handsome, tall, brave father . . . Alive and come for her. A chance to leave her grandparents' musty, rigid house. A chance to have a father like Charlotte's, an indulgent spoiling father. A real one. The wager was immediately filed away in the back of her mind.

A father. Hers.

"I don't mind that you weren't tactful."

Her grandmother sat back in her chair as if she'd been struck. "My dear child—"

"I'm not a child. I'm past twelve."

"Vicky, remember your manners."

"I don't care about manners. You care more about manners than my father."

Lady Charlton adjusted her pearls as if they were choking her lined neck. "I wouldn't put it quite so harshly, child. Your father was far from home. Misinformation can come from so great a distance. Obviously . . ." She glanced at her husband as if for confirmation. "We obviously were misled."

Vicky pinned a condemning glance at her grandmother, whose dimples and sweet smile had faded. Despite her grandmother's habit of trying to force her fussy ways on Vicky, the girl had always been proud of her genteel grandmother. Now shame and disgust filled her.

"Why did you lie to me?"

"Dear child, we didn't—"

"You lied about my father. He's not dead at all, and he's here. Where is he?"

"I wouldn't be in a rush . . . I believe he's got designs on taking you off with him, but that's out of the question. This is your home, and he can't walk in after twelve years and take you."

After her outburst, silence again.

"Well," Adele prompted. "What have you got to say for yourself? You look white. You're not feeling feverish, are you?"

Vicky looked up into her grandmother's innocent eyes. "Why did it take him so long to come for me?"

"He's not exactly who I told you. Be strong now, child."

"But you said you liked him." Vicky tugged at her dress and looked around, as if expecting to find him behind an urn.

"I don't like him."

"You were mistaken?"

Adele sighed. She hated admitting her mistakes.

"How?" Vicky asked.

Adele swallowed hard. Why did this child have to be so inquisitive? Why not dull-minded like her son, Clare's husband? Or dreamy like her dear departed Cecilia, the child's own mother.

"Where did he do his missionary work?"

The thought occurred to have Vicky ask the man herself, but she didn't want the child stolen. She'd have to answer the questions herself.

"All right, child, if you're brave enough for the truth, here it is. Your father was never a missionary. We only told you that to spare you the truth. He's a military man."

"You mean you lied twice."

Adele, who hated confrontations, reverted to bluntness. "Your father is a Scotsman from Dundroma."

Silence.

"There. It's out. I was ashamed that my own daughter, your darling mother, could be seduced by one of those barbarous heathens from over the border, but it's done."

She looked expectantly at her granddaughter, expecting the child to say, I forgive you.

"But you said my name is Douglas."

"The laird of Dundroma has a surname like the rest of us."

Vicky's eyes widened.

"Alec Douglas, Lord Strahan. One and the same. More's the pity. The devil of Dundroma. I'd hoped he'd stay away forever for your sake."

Vicky's eyes grew wider still. "I don't care who he is. I'm glad he's come for me."

"Now you're being melodramatic. Don't tell me you're happy to have a father who's descended from generations of reivers and plunderers?"

"It's better than having a grandmother who lies."

Adele stood, face flushed. "He's here and asking why or how doesn't matter now. It's done, and it was my doing, and now you'll have to get used to the idea. If you don't want to see the man, we'll send him off. Get the grooms to deposit him near the old drowning pool. Give him a taste of reiver treatment, as your grandfather likes to say."

"Where is he?"

"You want to chance meeting him? Risk being snatched across the border, and forcing your grandfather to come up to rescue you? He should have stayed dead, you know, deserting you when your mother died. Cursed at you like a madman. Blamed you. Helpless infant in your cradle. Well, he can't come back now, all done grieving, and have you. You belong to me."

"No!" Vicky stamped her foot. "I've always wished for a father, and now that I've got one, I'll meet him."

❧Chapter Three

Alec sat in the Charltons' bric-a-brac strewn library, knee throbbing in pain, pulse beating in pleasant awareness. It was a surprising reaction to the young woman who'd led him here, and a reaction he detested. He'd rather live with bone-numbing pain than allow himself to respond to another Thornhill woman. But try as he would, he could not push away the picture of clear hazel eyes and the sight of honey-streaked hair pulled back into a demure knot. Aunt Clare . . .

Then he heard a girlish voice saying those same words. "Aunt Clare, why? Why did they lie? . . . You taught me it was a sin to lie. My grandparents lied."

A voice of spirit. And then "Aunt Clare" pushed open the door yet again. This time she was accompanied by a gangly but pretty girl, a lass on the verge of adolescence. The woman in her was but a faint promise like heather in late spring.

A unexpected warmth gripped his heart. This was his daughter. Alec leaned forward in his chair, drinking in the sight of the child. A delicate face like Cecilia's, yes, but framed by bright red hair. Not chestnut like his own, but the color of the heath in summer . . . burnt red. And curly. Those curls came from Cecilia. He saw little of himself in her looks, but her spirit he had yet to size up.

The child walked across the room bravely enough,

defiance in her gaze. He liked that. Oh, she'd want to go
with him. There'd be no need to reassure this child about
strange and new places. If she was half Douglas, there'd be
a roaming in her blood. And if not . . . well, as a military
man, Alec knew how to calm such fears, and as a ladies'
man, he knew how to charm any female, even a daughter. It
was simply a matter of finding out what a female wanted out
of life and offering it.

Still, he had to marvel at the idea of a daughter. The lass
belonged to Alec. After twelve long years in self-imposed
exile, he was ready to claim her, and all the governesses in
the world would not stop him.

As for the old Charlton couple, well, they didn't worry
him. Retaliation from their side used to be a worry, but not
anymore. The English Charltons had absolutely no reputation with a sword or knife. Neither did they possess the most
basic characteristics of the borderman: endurance.

Their blood was tainted, nay thinned, now with intermar-
riage from Londoners—milksop sorts who held faith with
diplomacy instead of fighting. His ancestors had swept
down on them by the dark of the moon to raid their cattle
and houses. And his ancestors had, by the dark of the moon,
bedded Charlton women. Only Alec had been fool enough
to marry one.

And now the child of that marriage stood before him. He
dropped his cane and when he stood to retrieve it, his knee
buckled. He dropped back into the chair.

Vicky ran and picked it up and, after looking at the
ivory-knobbed handle, handed it to him. "Is it true you've
fought tigers?"

"Aye, child. But it wasn't a tiger who mangled my
kneecap."

"What did, then?"

"A fall off a horse. While playing polo."

"Was the horse hurt?"

"Fortunately, no. But the pottery vase we fell on was crushed to smithereens. The cobra hiding in it was so alarmed he slithered off without even bothering to bite me."

Vicky giggled. The lass knew a tall tale when she heard one.

"You don't have to go, you know," Clare whispered.

He glanced at "Aunt Clare." She was studying the hem of her hoop skirt and biting back a smile. Pert woman. He turned his concentration back to safer territory, like his daughter.

Vicky eyed his ivory-headed walking stick. "Does your leg hurt much?"

He exhaled. Hurt was relative. Since his accident Alec had learned how many degrees of hurt there were.

"All the time. But we Dundroma men, we're a tough lot. And so are the lasses."

They stood there eyeing each other, she gazing at his knee and the shiny black boot below it, he at her fresh little face with its expression of hope. The similarities, he guessed, outweighed the differences, and he felt relief about that.

What did not put him at ease was the scent of lavender. The governess was too close for comfort. It would have helped immensely if she'd been a horse-faced harridan. But she had the face of an angel.

And to avoid looking at her face, he fastened his gaze on the mother-of-pearl brooch at the neck of her dress. The brooch was in the shape of a rose, and despite his best efforts attraction stirred again.

He addressed Aunt Clare in a self-conscious voice, reminiscent of the way he sounded when he'd seen a woman naked for the first time. "I suppose you've taught her the English classics?"

"Of course."

"But no Burns, no Scott, no—"

"Nothing Scottish."

He shook his head and looked directly into clear hazel eyes.

"And she's had no training in Highland sports?"

"Of course not. She's about to receive training in ballet."

"You've coddled her."

The governess drew herself up straighter. "I have taught her how to answer her own questions."

Ah, a spark of mettle in the governess too. He only hoped she'd not planted radical ideas or English patriotism in his daughter with as much zeal as she argued manners. He turned a stern eye on his daughter.

The child beat him to the questioning. "Why did you go away and leave me?"

He drew back, startled at the child's directness. For the second time in an hour, she'd got the better of him. "It's a long journey to India," he said simply. "And," he added, "children don't belong in the military."

"But why did you stay twelve years? Why didn't you come for me sooner?" Vicky asked.

He searched for diplomatic words. "I didn't come because I didn't know what a bonnie lass I'd left."

Clare Charlton looked at him over Vicky's head and there was disapproval in her look. "The truth would be better."

He liked the governess's boldness. But not the way she probed into his emotions. If she could exercise supreme control, then so could he. Tit for tat. "I had to serve out my commission." Enough was enough. "Tell me, then . . . Vicky . . . how does your governess fill your days in the schoolroom?"

"I do needlepoint and watercolors and numbers and read history, and I hate it all. Do you have ponies?"

"Aye, child, is that what you want? To ride ponies?"

Eagerly, she nodded.

"Then you shall have ponies."

Clare Charlton stepped closer. "Vicky, don't listen. It's

common bribery and unworthy of his lordship. Here at
Thornhill Manor, don't forget, you have your grandparents,
a familiar staff, and Wellington, your rabbit."

Alec gave her a warning look. "Bribery? You accuse me
of bribery? I'll have no Thornhill animals at Dundroma."

"Children find comfort in familiar treasures . . . You
shouldn't bribe her into going with you anyway. She's
young and easily influenced."

"That, madam, is like the Highlander accusing the Low-
lander of hating the English."

Without warning, those clear hazel eyes looked up at him,
and the weakness in his knees had nothing to do with his old
injury, and everything to do with the length of Aunt Clare's
lashes.

"If you think I've taught her a lot of nonsense about
hating the Scottish, you're wrong. Actually, I've taught her
to be tolerant of her northern neighbors, and beyond that
concentrated on England."

"Tolerant! Then it's high time we moved on to my castle.
She'll learn to be more than tolerant. She'll learn enthusiasm."

"She's never seen Dundroma. It would be a dreadful
adjustment for an innocent child. To do it suddenly, I mean."

"Children adjust quickly, and so will the Charltons."

He'd no sooner spoken than from out in the hallway came
a dreadful ruckus. Metal clanged against metal, and a war
cry echoed off the rafters of Thornhill.

Alec's mouth thinned in annoyance.

While Vicky stood by her governess, he limped to the
door and opened it. There, down in the grand hallway,
sword aimed at the library, stood Percival Charlton. The old
man cradled a steel bonnet and in his hand grasped the
handle of an antique sword, which he was trying unsuccess-
fully to remove from its scabbard. His face was flushed with
the effort.

Adele stood nearby urging him on. "Pull harder, Percival, for heaven's sake."

"My dear, this sword hasn't been used in nearly three hundred years. Have a little patience."

"Well, you should have kept it oiled. You know Dundroma men can't be trusted, but you just wiled away the years staring at the thing as if it were a museum piece."

"Adele, this is the nineteenth century. One hardly expects reivers to come plundering down from Dundroma anymore."

"Well, what do you call that dreadful man holding our granddaughter captive?"

"He's our own daughter's husband, and if we hadn't lied, you'd not be so upset. That's what this is about—you're angry at being caught in another lie, not about the rusted sword."

"What do you mean, caught in *another* lie?" Adele crossed her arms and confronted her husband.

Alec cleared his throat.

Percival whirled and held out the sword. "You're a thieving devil, all you men of Dundroma, but you'll not get out of here alive. You're trapped and my prisoner."

Suddenly Vicky was beside her father and giggling. "He's drunk," Alec said tonelessly. Good God, the old man was getting senile. Reason enough to take the child out of here. And Adele—the grandmother. She stood ranting at Percival as if she were a fishwife.

"If you were a real man, Percival, you'd know how to handle this. For forty years now, I've wondered if you could have held your own against an invasion from Dundroma, and now I've got my answer. You're inept. And when I think of the titled gentlemen I passed by to accept your offer . . . real men who would know how to defend their household—"

"You had no other offers, Adele," her husband said

coldly. "I was your only choice. Why, pray tell, do you want me to remind you while the entire house is listening in?"

"You're no gentleman."

"You didn't need a gentleman, Adele." Percival's words were slurred. "You needed any man you could find to salvage your reputation."

"Say another word, and I shall never speak to you again."

"That would be a mercy and easier to bear than an invasion by Dundroma." The steel bonnet fell to the floor, and just then the sword gave way with such force he fell backward. He teetered, then tottered, and clattered to the floor, his rear end crashing into the great clock. His spectacles landed by a mouse hole.

"Adele, get my manservant."

"You are a disgrace, Percival," she said as she sailed up the stairs. "You couldn't defeat Vicky's rabbit if he were coming at you with a sword."

"Where are you going, Adele?" He was on his hands and knees feeling about the floor for his spectacles. "Where are you going?"

"To see to Vicky's packing. You don't think Lord Strahan is going to be stopped now, do you? And do get up, before too many of the servants see. Perhaps it's just as well our children did not live to see their father disgrace me so thoroughly, in front of our enemy no less."

Beside him, Vicky put her hand to her mouth to stifle another giggle and rushed out to hand him his spectacles. "I'd make your escape now, Lord Strahan, if you want out of here in one piece," the old man said.

Alec stood watching. Percival sat in the middle of the hall and adjusted his spectacles. He hiccuped.

"Do they behave like this often?" Alec asked Vicky.

"Only when the subject of Grandmother's coming out is referred to, and Grandpapa refers to it whenever she catches him at a disadvantage." She sighed. "Then they don't speak to each other for days on end."

"Impossible," Alec said.

"Vicky," warned Clare, who stood with hands folded, her emotions as controlled as if she were at a tea party. "Please remember your manners—this is a private family matter."

Vicky tossed her hair. "But Lord Strahan is family. Anyway, it's me who has to run back and forth with messages. Me or else Aunt Clare. One time at least forty days passed before they spoke again, so, you see, if they're going to stop speaking, I'm really glad you're taking me on holiday because I'm tired of conveying messages. It's actually worse than doing my numbers with Aunt Clare."

"I expect so." Alec gave the child a pat on the shoulder and himself a mental lash for staying away so long. "They say," he said with resignation, "that at some point old people turn back into children."

"I don't know why. I can't wait to grow up and I never want to be this age again. I want to be in charge of myself."

"You are, you know. At Dundroma, children are raised to make their own decisions—within the boundaries of safety."

Alec moved forward to help Percival Charlton to his feet, but the old man shook him off. "I can do it myself."

"Grandfather says Dundroma is a dangerous place."

"Now, Vicky," Alec said, driving home his advantage, "you are halfway grown-up. And I promise you this— Dundroma may be a bit musty and have some cobwebs to sweep away from my absentee years, but it's a fine place to visit . . . and I promise you there are no grandmothers there waiting to stuff a wooden board down your back for posture . . . and no grandfathers lurking around the corners with steel bonnets and rusted swords."

"Truly? Are there no backboards there?"

"They're forbidden on Dundroma property."

"And what about penmanship lessons?"

"Dispensed with while the heather blooms."

"And lectures on how ladies write condolence letters?"

"Letters have no rule other than stating a message."

"And young ladies spend time outdoors?"

"All the time they want."

"Lord Strahan?"

It was the governess. Alec tried to ignore her, but the scent of lavender was disturbingly haunting. Her reprimand, on the other hand, was futile.

"We here at Thornhill have devoted our lives to raising her to be a proper lady."

Alec considered the scene between Adele and Percival and could not resist a half smile.

"Pity you've wasted all those years, because when she comes to Dundroma, I'll spend the rest of her growing-up years allowing her some freedom and teaching her to be a proper Scots lass."

"What if she doesn't want to be a Scots lass?"

"She already is, and there's no changing that." He looked down at his daughter. "What do you think, Vicky? Shall we go on up and look at Dundroma? You can choose your own pony."

From out in the hall came Lord Charlton's voice, bellowing for a manservant.

"Why does Grandfather hate you?"

A twelve-year-old girl was too young to hear all the sordid details of his ill-fated marriage to the Charltons' daughter. So Alec surprised himself and took the high road.

"Your grandparents don't want to lose you. I expect that's what precipitated this . . . uh, disagreement."

"Fie, all they do is ply me with rules and schoolwork and comportment. While they argue about whether Grandmother was the most beautiful, more Incomparable whatever at her coming out. Or else they're arguing over whether Grandpapa married her out of love or duty."

"Vicky," warned Aunt Clare, "you're betraying family secrets. They cared for you when your father was halfway around the world."

Clare Charlton knew how to cut where it hurt and didn't let up.

"I'm sorry you've witnessed all this, but being privy to some secrets at Thornhill Manor does not give you leave to take advantage."

He didn't have leave, but he did have the strongest urge to take liberties with Aunt Clare's prim knot of honey-colored hair. And he'd noticed more than once now that whenever she talked one dimple came and went in her cheek. He rather enjoyed watching her talk . . . but it was time to leave.

He turned to Vicky. "Now, lass, the longer we put it off, the harder it will go for your grandparents."

"Yes . . . yes . . . then I want to go and see Dundroma. Aunt Clare's always made it sound so dreadfully frightful. She'll be surprised to see it, won't she?"

Alec Douglas, Lord Strahan, blinked. The child had chosen him. Chosen to join his camp. But she was making wild assumptions about this Aunt Clare.

"If you come, lass, you come alone," and his glance at Clare was a warning. "I have no time to coddle an English governess. I'll have my work cut out undoing all your Thornhill etiquette. So your aunt Clare can be the message carrier in your absence."

Vicky gulped, but stood there unflinching. The governess turned pale, and her bodice moved in and out. She wore a gray dress with a row of pearl buttons marching down the bodice. The color washed her out, and she went even paler. One strand of honey hair was enticingly loose, grazing her collar at the back of her neck.

"Go and fetch her grandmother for a farewell. I'll hold the grandfather at bay." His orders to Clare were quiet and precise, spoken in the tone of a military man. Control was essential. He had few defenses against dimples and enticing curls. Only military discipline.

"How long is she staying?" she asked, her voice tentative.

"As long as I stay. In other words, I've no idea. Don't pack much in any case because Vicky's going to be a Dundroma lass for at least the summer, and that will mean new clothing. Clothing from Scotland. I'll be waiting by the coach."

He limped off then, and Clare stood there watching him, torn between loathing and pity. Perhaps if he hadn't been injured, he'd have some likable quality. As it was she saw nothing to commend him. Most of all, she detested the way he burst into their lives and assumed he could have his way.

All because he was a father.

It was barbaric.

With Vicky at her heels chattering about how this would be her first adventure ever, ever allowed, Clare moved swiftly to pack. The fewer garments the better. As soon as Clare ran out of stockings he'd send her back here.

Vicky watched in silence. "Aunt Clare, why aren't we packing my winter clothes? My schoolbooks? My dolls."

Clare straightened and tried to think of a tactful way to explain the truth. "Vicky, this man will grow weary of playing at fatherhood, so don't expect much from him at Dundroma. He's rarely been around children . . . He'll send you back before two weeks are up, so don't expect a long adventure."

"A fortnight?" The girl sighed, and her expression drooped. "Well, that's how long Charlotte's father allows her to holiday here, and it's more than I've ever had before . . . but I'll give up Wellington for that."

"If Lord Strahan considers rabbits Scottish enough for his

castle, I'd suggest you ask him. If not, the rabbit will be here waiting when you come back. And so will your grandparents."

And on that note, they headed to the coach where Lord Strahan waited. The Charltons stood conspicuously apart, not speaking, neither looking at the other. Adele dabbed at her eyes. From windows all over the house, servants peeked out.

Vicky, who for the past hour had been full of spirit, now stopped in her tracks. And when Adele looked up, the child's face had softened. "Don't cry, Grandmother. You'd want a father too if you'd never known one, and don't worry that I'll be afraid to go to Scotland. I'll be brave, and he'll know you raised me well."

"Humph. A pretty speech when you rail out at everything we try to do to turn you into a lady. Come here then and kiss me farewell . . . but not good-bye. I shall see you soon. If I'm wrong, I was never the Incomparable during m-my season." Her voice caught. She dabbed at her eyes. "Be careful, dear, of the castle servants and ask for clean sheets on your bed and don't eat a morsel of food that is spiced . . . no uncooked vegetables . . . and none of that dreadful black pudding. Promise?"

Fingers crossed behind her back, Vicky nodded and then hugged her scented, powdered, prim grandmother. Oh, but what an exciting turn this summer had taken. And how jealous Charlotte would be when Vicky wrote her that she had a father, a father with a limp from riding horses in India. Oh, she could hardly wait to leave.

Aunt Clare had, strangely, nothing to say.

Clare stood, blinking back tears. The familiar pattern of her days was coming to an end. Worse, she was humiliating herself, losing control like this. She was fighting tears in front of this barbaric, handsome . . . male. The devil of

Dundroma himself. Through the haze of tears she saw him nod to Vicky, who ran over to her.

"Don't be sad," Vicky said, hugging her. "I'm the only girl I know who has no father, and he may be Scots but he's fought tigers, and that's ever so much braver than anything Charlotte's father has done." But for the first time, she realized Aunt Clare would have nothing to do without her.

"What shall you do?" she whispered.

"Me?" Clare patted her back, and stared with a mutinous look at the too attractive devil who was turning her life upside down. "I shall go to London . . . unless you change your mind and return tomorrow."

Vicky looked up at her father. "Do you have many bedchambers in your castle?"

"Not enough for governesses."

She gave a resigned sigh. "Then it's time to go."

"Very well," Clare said to Alec Douglas, "you've won the day, it appears, but not the war." Then she knelt down to Vicky. "If you feel lonely, remember Thornhill borders on Dundroma land, and after a few days your grandfather will send for you—"

"Oh, fie," called out Adele Charlton where she sulked by the parlor window. "Clare, tell Mr. Charlton that he'll have to be a brave man to do that."

At once, Percival glowered from his solitary vantage point—the holly bush by the library window. "Clare, tell Mrs. Charlton that she no longer has the beauty to command brave men to do her bidding and hasn't since our own Reginald departed."

"I think," Clare said, "that both of you are a disgrace to Thornhill."

There was a shocked moment of silence.

"Then, since you've led Vicky into our enemy's hands, you may go too."

Her shoulders slumped, ever so briefly before she looked

up with a forced smile for Vicky. "You see, London it is for me. Perhaps we all need a holiday." She planted a quick kiss on the crown of Vicky's head.

Vicky gave a brave wave. "Don't worry, everyone. I shall be busy exploring his castle and riding his ponies—" She turned to look up at Lord Strahan. "You'll give me ponies?"

"I promised, and a promise from a Douglas of Dundroma is not taken lightly."

Clare looked over the child's head and caught his gaze. For long seconds they stared at each other, taking each other's measure. Her words, though, were for Vicky. "But don't forget, you are a Charlton from Thornhill too." She took her hand and began to walk her to the coach. They were flanked on the other side by Lord Strahan, who limped along to the rhythm of his cane. He leaned heavily on the wooden stick; clearly the injury to his leg was still aggravating him.

His right leg was held stiffly, knee locked when he moved it. She felt a wave of pity for treating him so callously, given his handicap. He was going to be even more handicapped at fatherhood though. He had no idea of what Vicky needed in the way of nurturing.

Behind, Percival and Adele Charlton were watching in frosty silence from their separate vantage points. Too proud to see the child off together in case anyone should assume either of them had been first to forgive their angry words, it was left to the governess to officially hand her over to her father.

There were more hugs, and Clare fought back the mist in her eyes. "You have only to say so if you need me," were her parting words. She'd fight Lord Strahan, the devilish rogue, for Vicky's sake, if need be. But she restrained her less ladylike impulses, as she had for years. Clare had made it her task in life to remain in control as an example to

Vicky. Passion unleashed was embarrassing and highly discouraged in her ladies comportment book.

Alec stepped between them and pulled himself up into the coach. "Of course she doesn't need her English nanny. I am perfectly capable of caring for my daughter, and what I can't do, I have women at my castle who can do for her." With a casual gesture, he signaled to his driver.

"I hope you're right—about having women at your castle—because you won't know what she needs, milord."

He glowered. The wind blew mahogany curls across his forehead. She tried to ignore its appealing quality. His hand whitened over the ivory head of his cane.

"Food. Water. A warm bed. Of course I know what she needs."

And with that, they drove off.

As they jounced away from Thornhill Manor, Alec positioned his cane between his knees and balanced his hands on the knob. At last, he could study his child without that bossy little governess looking over his shoulder or feuding grandparents distracting everyone.

His child. He studied her as one would a purebred dog.

The cloud of reddish curls was good. Signs of Douglas in her breeding had come through. He liked her spirit and as far as he could tell she looked healthy enough, no thanks to that governess.

He smiled.

She gave him a wan smile in return. Her teeth were even.

If she were a Shetland pony or a sheepdog, he'd give her high marks.

"Aye, except for that prissy English dress, you'll make a fine Douglas, lassie."

The road ran alongside the River Tyne and they could see the statue alongside it. "We're at the border, lassie. You're home now, on Douglas ground."

She stared at that statue of the woman turned to stone and gulped. Her voice was the tiniest of whispers.

"I'm a Charlton too."

"Aye, but we won't tell anyone, and we'll soon have you eating and playing and dancing like a Scots lassie, and before you know it, there's not a soul in my glen who'll know you once came from Thornhill."

"But I'm a Charlton too." There was a wobble in her voice.

He backtracked. "Well, half. The good half is Douglas."

Her eyes filled with tears. Damn that governess. Damn Cecilia for playing him false.

"I don't want to turn to stone."

"What makes you think that?"

"Aunt Clare told me about the statue. That Charlton girls who go over the border turn to stone."

Double damn Miss Charlton. He had a mind to write the governess a letter and give her a piece of his mind. The trouble was that every time he thought of her he went rather weak in the legs.

Suddenly tears were sliding down the child's face. "I'm going to turn to stone."

"Here now, that's not so."

"Aunt Clare would never lie. I want Aunt Clare," she wailed.

"You said you wanted a father."

"I want both."

"Nonsense."

"It's the statue. I promised never to go past it without her . . . Never . . ."

Aunt Clare was quite a storyteller.

"Here now, you said you wanted to ride my pony, and you can't do that if you're made of stone."

She sobbed. Tears splashed off her face and onto her frock.

"Douglases don't cry." He'd never shed a tear in his life, not even when his parents had died of typhoid. Certainly not when Cecilia died in childbed, her English lover weeping like a woman in the next room. Especially not then. He had just stoically picked up the pieces of his life. Bordermen didn't cry, and he told the child so.

"Charltons do. Clare says it's not good to always keep a stiff upper lip."

Mollycoddling governess.

"That's why you don't need her while you're with me."

Now sobs wracked her shoulders. She put her fingers to her eyes as if to stop the tears. They leaked through.

"What do you want from me?" He felt more helpless than when the cobra had slithered past his face.

"I lied. I want Aunt Clare to come too."

"Why?" Homesick soldiers he knew how to handle, but not this. "Why? She's English. I'm going to teach you how to be a Scots lass."

Great heaving sobs shook her shoulders.

Perhaps, he considered, he had been abrupt in handling the situation . . . but it was the only way he knew or ever had known.

Soldiers didn't complain and certainly never shed tears. They were stoic to the end. But this was no soldier.

He had no idea what to say. A mistress, a woman . . . now, tears from them held messages that he could decipher: anger, jealousy, sorrow. Each message he knew the answer to.

But the tears of a twelve-year-old child? He couldn't decipher those.

And he suspected only one person in the world could.

Half a hour later the coach pulled up at the front of Thornhill Manor where the governess sat forlornly on a bench in the rose garden. At the sound of the horses' hooves, she straightened, then ran toward the coach. Actually picked up her skirts and ran. Alec watched her breasts move, her full skirts blow about and display tantalizing peeks of her ankles. Halfway there she remembered her station and, hastily dropping her skirts, slowed to a walk.

He leaned out. "We've changed our minds. We need a familiar governess, only for an interim period."

"I'll pack my valise," she said, calmly, with a controlled, measured voice. "If you'll wait, please."

"No . . . have someone send a bag after you. Get in. I've already wasted too much time."

He held out his hand. For a few seconds she stared at him, as if considering the consequences of such rash behavior.

"Clare," Adele Charlton called out of a window. "I need you to take a message to Mr. Charlton about his kidney pie supper."

Suddenly Clare reached out and allowed herself to be handed in. Her hand, he noticed, was warm in his, and very slim and soft. She pulled from his grip and took Vicky in her arms. He was, he realized, grateful and—touched. A momentary weakness.

He gave his attention to the coach as they headed back toward Dundroma, Vicky's sobs echoing to the clip-clop of the horse hooves.

Gradually, as they drove along again, the child's crying subsided. "What did you do to her?" Aunt Clare pinned a condemning look on him.

"Me? She was fine until we passed that damned border statue. Romantic nonsense about turning to stone as soon as she entered Dundroma land. Was that one of your English history lessons?" he asked.

Clare Charlton kept her pert profile to him, but her chin tilted out a fraction of an inch. "If you don't know, then you've no business asking a twelve-year-old to leave the only home she's ever known."

Alec and the governess looked at each other from across the coach. The look of natural enemies sizing each other up.

"A fortnight, Miss Charlton. As soon as she's used to being alone at Dundroma, you leave. The Charltons will have tired of their feud by then."

"You'll tire of fatherhood well before then."

"Just so you don't think you've won."

"Oh, but I have."

"Only for the moment. The battle perhaps, but not the war. And since we're now on Dundroma territory, henceforth I set the rules regarding how she learns."

"Indeed. When dealing with a child, you'll soon learn rules were made to be bent." Her bosom rose and fell with hypnotic regularity. Her honey hair was confined into too tight a knot. A woman of control. Her appearance, he noted, was completely at odds with the woman who'd come running to the coach moments earlier. *That* was the woman he wanted to know.

"The child is mine," he said stiffly. "You're to cease teaching her fairy tales and nonsense. Your only function is a companion to ease the change. Is that clear?"

The child looked up in chagrin. "I'm sorry I didn't welcome Scotland better," she said solemnly, "but it's better now that Aunt Clare's here."

He nodded. It might be better for Vicky, but it definitely made him uneasy. The dimples and honey hair were distractions he could do without.

The sooner he separated his daughter from the governess the better off he'd be. Two weeks, and he'd have Aunt Clare gone.

Gone or seduced. He snuck a sideways glance at that coil of delectable honey hair, and imagined it loose and pouring in thick coils over his face.

The choices might turn out to be more complicated.

⧼Chapter Four

As the coach clattered over a bridge, Clare caught her breath. For there was Dundroma rising up out of the mists, even more dark and imposing than legend had it. Nestled on an outcropping of rock, it looked down upon a village washed gray by time and rain.

Beyond, in the valley, stone walls crisscrossed the lowest land, where sheepdogs circled a flock of sheep. And higher up, the heath lay like tweed, nubs of purple flecking the hills and hinting of full bloom to come. Closer to Dundroma, the shrubberies grew willy-nilly. The wildness was all in a stark contrast to Thornhill.

Inside a central courtyard, the coach stopped. Dundroma Castle had a scarred, battle-weary air about it, as if the dust of past centuries had not settled.

Servants in common dress—no livery anywhere—bustled over to assist Lord Strahan out, but with impatience, he waved them away and, leaning heavily on his walking stick, limped toward the oaken door.

His progress wasn't helped by a sheepdog bounding about his walking stick and barking. Lord Strahan wobbled in place, while the dog continued to circle him, sniffing and yipping.

"Quiet now," commanded an otherwise soft-looking woman. "Sit," she ordered. "'Tis your master now. Sit."

After a shake of black and white fur, the dog lowered its haunches right beside the returning laird.

The woman, in flour-dusted apron, curtsied. "I beg your pardon, milord, but you've been gone so long she doesn't know you. She warms up to people quickly, though."

"No matter, Mrs. Drummond," he said easily, leaning heavily on his cane while he bent to ruffle the dog's ears. He was instantly rewarded with a thud of tail-wagging, and the austere planes of his face softened briefly.

"You see, an animal friend already," he said as his daughter bent to pat the dog. "Mrs. Drummond, I should like you to take care of my daughter the same as you would me."

The housekeeper, eyes wide, stared at Vicky and bobbed her head. "Aye, milord."

Clare followed the housekeeper with a sleepy Vicky by the hand. There was a brief glimpse of a great hall and then without a word to her, Lord Strahan vanished into a cavernous parlor.

Mrs. Drummond touched Clare's arm, and she started.

"You'll be wanting to see the young lass to bed."

"Of course," she answered and followed the woman, who led the way by lamplight up a staircase. Earlier emotions had taken their toll: Vicky was yawning. Quickly Clare helped her change into her nightdress and waited while she climbed into bed—a large canopied affair not unlike the one she'd left at Thornhill. But the room was smaller, the walls completely filled with either windows or gilt-framed portraits. The entire Douglas ancestry of sheep-dogs was enshrined here.

Mrs. Drummond, instead of being dour as Clare had expected, was remarkably cheerful and efficient. "There," she said, "the wee lass'll sleep till morning, and then after a hearty breakfast she'll have much to explore. And Mrs. Fraser will be over to welcome her. Himself will see you now."

"Himself?" She had no chance to ask about the mysterious Mrs. Fraser. Himself was the greater worry.

"The laird."

The barbarian. Lord Strahan was wasting no time at all in getting down to business, and she steeled herself for a barrage of rules. Better, Clare supposed, to get a meeting over with.

Retracing her steps, Clare found the great parlor. No bric-a-brac or vases of flowers as at Thornhill. Just enormous portraits of kilt-clad ancestors wearing wicked expressions and holding guns and daggers. Stag heads stared down over the dark green tartan furniture that was arranged haphazardly upon tartan rugs. A fire roared in a massive rock fireplace. It would be quite oppressive for a young girl. But it wasn't Vicky of whom she thought. It was Lord Strahan, who stood staring out a window at the dusk.

Mahogany flecked his dark hair, and lines of weariness wore grooves into his face. He'd removed his coat and had loosened the cravat at the neck of a white shirt. The boots, which came up to the knees of his trousers, were as shiny as black onyx. Though she made no sound, at her entrance he turned and limped over to sit in a chair by the fire, then balanced his walking stick across his legs.

The sheepdog rose, shook its black and white fur, and came, tail wagging, to greet her.

"Reiver!" The dog returned to his side. Then he reached for a glass of whisky on the table nearby, took a long swallow, and with his other hand reached out a hand to nuzzle the fur of the dog. "Whisky, Miss Charlton?"

"I don't partake of spirits."

"Most Scots enjoy their dram."

Desperate, she decided on a change of subjects. "How can you know the dog if you've been gone twelve years?"

He remained in profile, but his mouth turned up in a near smile. "He's descended from a long line of dogs, each in turn named Reiver. It's a tradition. Just as it's a tradition for Dundroma to raid and plunder Thornhill Manor."

Clare thought a change of subject was needed. "Vicky may be your daughter, but she's young and in need of a familiar companion."

"You wouldn't be here now if I didn't believe that, but her fears are temporary and come from her soft, coddling Thornhill upbringing. I intend to instill some Dundroma boldness in her. Be assured, she won't need you for long."

"If that's true, then we should be able to dispense with this interview in short order."

"Aye, we could, but I choose to prolong it." With a wave of his hand, he gestured for her to sit in the chair opposite his, and now he turned his gaze upon her.

She sat and self-consciously reached up to make sure her hair was tucked into its net.

"Your hair is a bonnie shade of gold," he said.

She lowered her hands to her lap.

"Have you never learned," he went on, "that gold is meant to be enjoyed, no' hoarded?"

"You talk in riddles."

He shrugged. "I was giving you a compliment. About how you hide your hair away like a miser."

"I don't want any compliments."

"Of course not. I suppose you've learned to be wary of compliments from Dundroma. Beware an enemy who bears gifts or compliments, is that it?"

She glared up at him. His return gaze burned through her consciousness.

He drank, but watched her over the edge of his glass. Silence stretched out between them, and desperate to escape his scrutiny, she stared at the walls.

"What do you find so fascinating about this place?"

"The paintings of your barbarian ancestors."

"Looking for resemblances?"

A bitterness edged his words and then he raised his glass

of whisky and toasted her before taking another long swallow.

Clare bristled. "I care little about the feud between Thornhill and Dundroma. I only care for Vicky's welfare."

"Ah, idealism," he said with scorn in his voice and mockery in his eyes. "Tell me, is that quality bred into you? Or did you learn it from your late husband—Reginald?"

She blushed under his relentless scrutiny. "We were only married a month before he died."

"Damn unthoughtful of him." He eyed her up and down. "I've never known a woman widowed so close to her wedding . . . neither virginal nor a woman of vast experience. 'Twixt one and the other. Tell me, does that leave you hungering for a man's arms?"

Shocked, her embarrassment deepened.

"That was the least of my considerations when Reginald died."

"Were you a passionate woman with him, Miss Charlton, or did he die too soon?"

Aghast at his perceptiveness, she jumped to her feet. He knew women better than she'd given him credit for. "*That* is none of your business."

"Perhaps I'm testing you. I'm merely curious at your control. You do not slap me for such ungentlemanly talk?"

"Ladies do not lose control."

He was silent, staring at the way the firelight glowed off her golden hair. "Now I know your husband did indeed die too soon. You obviously missed out on the passionate side of marriage. A bitter draught, but then you couldn't know that . . ."

She blushed to the roots of her hair. "A gentleman would not talk so before a lady, for any reason. I cannot imagine how you lured a Charlton lady into marriage."

"You scold me for prying, but pry yourself . . . Actually,

Aunt Clare, I married her because she was with my child and
needed her reputation saved."

Silence. She was appalled at this man's candor. She was
equally appalled at the bitterness in his voice. She turned to
leave.

"Stay," he said and to her back he added, "you think me
a barbarian, I know. Perhaps you would prefer that I had just
stepped out of one of those portraits. My ancestors, you see,
did   not   pretend   with   a   veneer   of   gentlemanly
behavior . . . and as for the Charltons, they've never
welcomed me, especially not when I married their
daughter—"

She turned. "I don't want to know."

"But know you shall . . . Adele never considered me
good enough. She'd have preferred Cecilia bear the child in
disgrace than tarnish her reputation with the Douglas
name . . . But I was young, and fancied the lass . . . and
she fancied me. Such attractions transcend the boundaries of
feuds. But little did I guess she'd fancy more than one man
while carrying my child. An English cad, and he had the
nerve to compound my grief with humiliation by weeping in
the hallway even while Cecilia lay dying in childbed."

"I see," Clare whispered. Poor Vicky. Such a tragic start
to her life. "I see," she repeated, other words failing her.

"I doubt that . . . but we have one thing in common. We
both married into the Charlton family . . . We each buried
our spouses."

She drew a deep breath to gather her composure. "We
have more—an abiding interest in Vicky. And you can
threaten to remove me with whatever weapons you hide
about this dank castle, but I shan't budge as long as Vicky
needs me."

"Not even curious what my weapons are?"

She shook her head.

"But well you should be, Aunt Clare, for the weapons I

intend to wield are more potent than the pieces of steel and iron in those portraits."

Wary, she stood and backed up toward the fireplace.

"Are you cold?"

Mute, she could only turn her head from side to side. No.

"Then you must shake out of fear."

It wasn't fear. It was something new. Longings his every word stirred within her. She half turned. "I am going to disappoint you and tell you I'm not curious—or afraid of you."

"Oh, that I have no doubt of, but are you not curious how you might respond to my lips, Miss Charlton? Or to the touch of my hands on you or—"

"Stop!" She pressed her hands to her ears. Ruthless and perceptive, Lord Strahan needed no more ammunition to use against her. Her pulse was racing, her heartbeat quickened by his nearness.

His laughter was soft. "No need to play at dramatics. I can hardly chase you about with this bum leg. I prefer a battle of wits."

"I'm weary and should like to sleep, and this conversation has no point other than to intimidate me."

At that he turned and looked her up and down. "Oh, but you're wrong. There is a point."

She waited.

"We are about to draw a line in the sand, so to speak, and make some rules here."

She'd known it. "There are no rules in war."

"Or lovemaking. But since we're engaged in neither, that's irrelevant. We shall for the next few days—or until you leave—have a bit of military order. Ergo, rules. Not for Vicky. Vicky is going to receive lessons in how to be a Scottish lass. I don't need or want any lessons on the subject from an English governess. I want her to learn unrestrained freedom. This is my castle, my estate, and I rule supreme."

He held up a hand to stay her protests. "Be warned—we Scots are a bold lot—bolder than our more restrained Charlton neighbors across the border . . . and I might open the wrong bedchamber door."

"Lord Strahan, that is a veiled threat."

"Veils have never suited me. The naked truth appeals more. It's a simple rule of life at Dundroma. The laird enjoys whichever female suits his fancy. And no female ever finds that rule contrary to her own fancy."

"I wouldn't find you appealing if you were the last man in Dundroma."

"Harsh words to lay on a cripple."

"You do not strike me as a man who bargains with pity. I can fend for myself. As for Vicky, heed my advice: A father earns and loves his way." Talking longer would serve no purpose at all. "Now where do I stay?"

His chuckle rumbled deep in his throat, and against her will her gaze fastened on the open neck of his shirt. "Choose any chamber you like. They're all alike to me. Whatever suits you for your . . . short stay."

Goose bumps went up and down her back. "W-which is yours?"

"That, Widow Charlton, is for you to worry about."

Vicky was up and gone the next morning when at her customary time Clare came for her. She'd taken the room next door, reasoning that Lord Strahan, as laird of the castle, would have far more expansive quarters than these smallish rooms. Besides, it would never occur to him to spend the night close to a child. He would know nothing of nightmares, illness, or homesickness.

Clare stared around at the dim room as rain ran down the windows. Everything Vicky had brought from Thornhill was here—everything English—her Thornhill frock, her cape, her doll, her nightdress. Even the ear cap that Clare had tossed into the valise. Adele Charlton insisted Vicky wear it to flatten her ears, though last night out of deference to her strange surroundings, Clare had not made Vicky sleep in it. Now, all of this lay in a heap on the floor. Discarded.

On the bed were bolts of tweed, a book of poems by Burns, and a plate of crumbs. Clare dipped her fingers into the mess and licked.

Shortbread. The devil was wasting no time.

Seething, Clare scooped up the pile on the floor and took it to her room. If the devil of Dundroma thought he was going to strip his daughter of everything in her past, he was sorely mistaken.

She sought out Mrs. Drummond in the servants' hall. "Where is Vicky?"

"Riding ponies, miss. The laird rose at dawn, and he took the child with him, of course. She was most anxious."

A man of his word. Twelve years in India had not changed that. A borderer's word was honorable, even if he was thieving while he gave it. Suddenly Clare had her weapon.

His word. His sacred word. If Lord Strahan wanted to teach Vicky how to be a Scots lass, he'd also want to teach her about the meaning of one's word.

The housekeeper stood watching her.

"May I walk to where they ride?" Clare asked.

"Oh, but he took the wee lass way up on the heath, miss. "'Twould be a long tramp and here it is drizzling. I'd wait near the stables. They'll return for breakfast soon."

Clare did not trust Lord Strahan's definition of "soon." After all, the man had been gone twelve years.

Already she was wrapping herself in her cloak, wishing she'd slept better so she'd have her wits about her. Instead she'd tossed and turned. She strode out to the stables to meet them, and Vicky, clad in a new cloak of black and white checks, ran to meet her.

"Aunt Clare, my father gave me a pony, just like he said."

"He's a man of his word then, isn't he?" She was looking at Lord Strahan. "I should like to be informed when Vicky goes out."

His smile was brilliant, his eyes dark blue, deeply set. "Why? She's safer with me about Dundroma grounds."

"Because she might need me. That's the reason for my being here at Dundroma."

"Did you need a governess this morning, Vicky?" Lord Strahan looked at Vicky.

Vicky, shaking her head, grinned from ear to ear. "He was as good as his word, Aunt Clare. A nice groom gave me my first riding lesson. And I've got a cloak just like the shepherds wear." She whirled for Clare's inspection. "Did you know it's supposed to be only men who dance, but I'm going to learn the Highland fling. He's promised I can ride the pony anytime . . . and go on picnics and own my very own fishing tackle."

"Don't ask him for too much at once, Vicky, or he'll think you only take. That would be greedy and not polite of you as a guest."

Lord Strahan handed his pony over to a groom who'd caught up—a handsome lad, barely past boyhood himself. Then he walked over to her, close to her. "I've given Andrew instructions to go slow with the lessons."

Clare stared at him. "A mere boy."

"Who by the way is knowledgeable and careful. Vicky, being half Douglas, clearly will thrive on the freedom."

"Well, I see no difference in Vicky from yesterday."

"If you want to know what the difference is, I invite you to join us this afternoon. A lady friend is coming to meet Vicky. I believe you'll be pleased to make her acquaintance."

"Vicky and I won't be here long enough to need friends."

He stared at her, as if startled to hear his own threat come back in his face. "It's true you won't, Aunt Clare . . . but you have enough spirit to enjoy Mrs. Fraser. In time she might be a good replacement companion for Vicky, then you can leave with peace of mind."

She could hardly wait to see what old crone he dragged out of some village croft and tried to pass off as a womanly influence for Vicky. "Very well, but now while we're alone with Vicky, I should like to ask you something."

"While we eat breakfast then," he agreed. "You do like oats?"

At last, something upon which they agreed, and they headed to the dining room. "Vicky has eaten porridge every day of her life."

To her consternation, he proceeded to explain to Vicky about Scots porridge and how it was vastly superior to English.

"One would think the oats actually know which side of the border on which they grow," she said dryly.

He laughed at that. "It's in the preparation. Part of the reason Vicky hasn't liked it is the bland way they serve it there at Thornhill, especially in the nursery."

"What would you know about Thornhill's oats?"

"My late wife." The three words hung in the air while Vicky looked from one to the other. He pulled out Clare's chair for her and as she sat began explaining. "Now, here at Dundroma the cook does more interesting things with oats." As if on cue, a servant entered.

A plate of oatmeal-coated fish was set in front of her. She stared at it, and her stomach roiled.

Lord Strahan whipped his napkin onto his lap and tucked into the fish. Vicky, eyes shining with happiness, picked up her fork and imitated the man's every move.

He took a bite and chewed.

Vicky took a bite and gagged. She spit out the unchewed bite of fish onto her plate.

Clare could talk Vicky into leaving by half past breakfast.

"It takes a few bites to acquire a taste for it . . . unless you've eaten it from early on. Try again. Any lass who can ride ponies at dawn and dance the Highland fling like the laddies can learn to like herrings in oatmeal."

Clare waited until the fish course was gone, and she'd sipped a cup of strong tea to wash away the taste.

"Tomorrow we shall have Scotch woodcock," Lord Strahan boasted.

"Dare I ask the ingredients or do you plan to surprise us?"

"Whatever you wish."

"We wish plain porridge."

"Too bland. Vicky has to learn to eat bold food."

He reached for the marmalade to slather on a scone, and she set down her spoon. Enough was enough.

"I want your word about something, and I want it given in Vicky's presence."

He looked at her over the scone. As soon as he'd taken a large bite of it, she began.

"I want your word that if Vicky decides she's tired of Dundroma when two weeks are up, that you'll give her up."

He gave up chewing and washed down his scone with tea. Clare pressed her verbal advantage and kept talking.

"No fight. No retaliations. No further raids on Thornhill. If Vicky wants to return to Thornhill with me, you won't stop her."

His teacup clattered in its saucer, and he looked up, his eyes bright with challenge. "Ah, you're wagering heavily, Aunt Clare. What has Thornhill got that can compete with a pony?"

"It's got grandparents. Loving family. Since the pony and other material possessions are gifts, they'd surely go with her."

He inclined his head in assent. "But she won't want to leave."

"How can you be sure?"

"She'll like it here. She's half Scots, whether she knows it or not. Vicky, lass, those red curls give away the Douglas in you, don't they?"

"Yes."

"Aye," he corrected her.

"Aye."

Heaven help them, he already was teaching her brogue. His own soft brogue warmed her, made her turn over inside. But from Vicky it sounded unnatural.

"That's sounding more like a lass born and bred to Dundroma already." His soft burr felt pleasant to Clare's ears. "You're a bonnie lass, Victoria Douglas. Would that you'd been christened with a more Scottish name. But I can live with Vicky as long as you sound Scottish. Do you like it here?"

"I'm having a grand time, Lord Strahan."

"Aye, so am I, considering . . . and you shall from now on call me Papa."

"And what of Aunt Clare? What shall she call you?"

Without missing a beat, his gaze slid to Clare and his reply was silky smooth. "Your aunt Clare has her choice of many names to call me. I shall leave it to her."

Clare was not to be distracted. "I'm waiting for your word. The word of a borderer."

"Ah, the one thing I can never take back."

"That's right. If, after a fortnight, Vicky is homesick, you'll let her return to Thornhill."

"My rights as a father mean too much. The child is mine."

He spoke as if Vicky were another sheepdog. She negotiated. "Then when Vicky says she does not need my companionship, I'll leave."

He tilted his head, studying her, as if looking for motives. "You have my word," he said, nodding. "My word as a Scotsman."

"Your word as a borderer is what I want, Lord Strahan."

"You play to win, lass."

She was silent. It was that or nothing. His solemn word. And a borderer's word was worth even more than a Scotsman's or an Englishman's. A borderer would never, ever go back on his word, no matter what, and it had nothing to do with family or national loyalties. A word given was kept.

"You have it then." He spoke with easy confidence. "By then she'll be a dyed-in-the-wool Dundroma lass, complaining you're in her way. Perhaps you ought to begin packing now."

"Lord Strahan, my valise has not yet arrived from Thornhill." She gave him an innocent look and lifted her teacup. "Actually, I'm considering sending for more items—an entire trunk of clothing."

"You'll never need it, Aunt Clare." There was a wicked gleam in his eye.

"I do wish you'd cease calling me Aunt Clare."

"Why?"

Why? "Why, because I'm not your aunt, and furthermore, it makes me sound like some doddering gray-haired maiden crone." For some reason it was very important that he not see her that way. She might be a straight-laced governess, but she was not past her prime.

He examined her face, then looked down to her bodice and suddenly back up to her face. "You're certainly not an old crone. My apologies if I've failed to tell you how enthralled I am by English governesses."

With a scrape, she pushed back her chair and stood.

"Leaving us? But you've barely touched your herring in oatmeal. A poor example to your charge, Aunt Clare."

"I'm not hungry. Thank you, Lord Strahan."

He suddenly set down his napkin and stood, a tall figure in black, towering above her at his place. "Very well, if

Vicky can call me Papa, I can call you something other than the doddering Aunt Clare. Will plain Clare satisfy you?"

"More than the herring, yes, thank you," she said and marched out, his laughter soft behind her.

While Vicky bent over her paper and quill, Clare stood by the window of Dundroma Castle. It was a recessed affair, the better to keep out the wind—and presumably musket fire. Doubtless for the same reason it commanded a sweeping view of the rutted road up to the castle. And at the moment a modest coach rumbled toward the castle. The lady friend. Clare admitted to too much curiosity for her own good.

After all, two weeks was all she had. Two weeks to convince a twelve-year-old that this man could not buy her affection with gifts. And hope that the novelty of having the entire castle doting on her would wear off. Part of it was selfish on Clare's side. For if Lord Strahan kept Vicky here, then Clare's services as a governess would not be needed. And she could not imagine life without Vicky.

No, it was inconceivable that Vicky should remain here.

Vicky set down her pen and sighed. "The groom is only fifteen and he knows ever so much about ponies. Too much to tell my grandparents."

"Merely tell them you've arrived safely." Perhaps a letter would thaw the frostiness back at Thornhill.

"The groom taught me how to sit, how to use the stirrups, and the reins. And do you know that Andrew—that's his name—is also an expert on Shetland ponies? He says—"

"First finish the letter . . . Tell your grandparents the name of your pony, if it pleases you, but finish the letter, Vicky, before your father comes for you. His guest has arrived." She glanced at the clock in the room. Time mocked her.

Two weeks. A fortnight.

It was, she reminded herself, Vicky's interests that came first. The problem would be convincing the father of that. And the law favored the father. By law, he could keep Vicky forever, no matter how homesick for Thornhill the child became. Oh, yes, Clare would stay with her and do all in her power to convince Lord Strahan to put his child's interest first. A tall order.

"I should mention to them why my father limps, so they'll soften toward him."

That would never happen—not in a hundred fortnights, but she said nothing. Instead, she leaned closer to the window. Two people were getting out of the coach, not one. A woman was accompanied by someone in trousers. An indefinable tension in Clare relaxed. Inexplicable relief.

"Perhaps if I tell Grandmother how Papa almost died, she'll like him better."

Curious now, Clare turned, her expression quizzical.

"He nearly died, you know," Vicky said. "I heard the grooms talking."

"Then I'm sure it's true." At Dundroma, she'd noticed, the servants tended to be family, related, and so likely knew everyone's business. Even the business of Thornhill. In that respect, servants were borderers first.

"Do you enjoy the time with your father?" Clare asked.

Vicky didn't hesitate but nodded vigorously. "I never thought to have a father, so I like him for that, even if he is stern and sometimes grouchy."

Clare sighed. "Fathers tend to be that away, especially after they've grown accustomed to you. It's their role to be stern patriarchs. I recall how my father's eyebrows knitted together when he preached."

"Well, then I'm lucky mine came back from the dead. And I'm lucky he's given me a pony. He might give me a velvet cape too. He asked what I wanted more than anything in the world, and that's what I told him."

Clare stared. "Since when did you want a velvet cape?"

A pause. "Oh . . . Charlotte and I made a wager. If I win, I get hers . . . but if Papa gives me one, Charlotte can keep hers."

"I see." The devil was still bribing the girl.

"Finish the letter, then sign your name. Put 'Affectionately' before your name, as I taught you."

"Oh, fie. Why should I be affectionate to them when Grandmother and Grandfather are not affectionate to each other?"

"You will sign the letter in a cordial manner. As it is, that note you wrote barely suffices."

A brisk rap rattled the door, and then it burst open. Lord Strahan, the devil of Dundroma, stood there, leaning on his walking stick, looking like the very devil of handsomeness in a black coat and a dark green kilt.

For seconds only the ticking clock dared make a sound. Then Clare became aware of her heart, pounding rather more loudly than usual. Lord Strahan, knuckles whitening over his walking stick, stared at Clare for too long.

"What is the child doing shut up in her room? I made it clear she's done with such confinement."

They stood staring at each other, and it was Vicky who answered, her expression panicked. "I'm writing my grandparents, Papa. It would be rude not to. Aunt Clare says so."

"Aye, so it would." He turned to Clare. "But you don't have my word to shut her away this long. She can write anywhere in the castle."

"As it is, her letter is too short, hastily scribbled."

With painful slowness, he limped toward the table.

Clare felt something tug at her heartstrings and quickly handed the letter to Vicky. "Vicky, take it to your father. Don't make him come for it."

He stopped and stared at her, even when Vicky handed him the letter. "I'm not an invalid, Clare."

Clare. Not Aunt Clare. Just Clare. No one at Thornhill said her name in those dark rich tones.

He scanned the letter's contents. "They are informed that she has safely arrived. I find it quite efficient and her penmanship needs no further work. Adele Charlton will accept it."

He looked up at her over the letter. Seconds ticked by, then suddenly he turned, dropping the letter on the table. "Come along, Vicky, and bring your aunt if you must. You're going to learn lessons out-of-doors. Flora and fauna of Scotland. History lessons about Dundroma. Tales of warriors past. There are other ways to learn than in a stuffy room . . . and Mrs. Fraser is here to meet you. She's more adept at outdoor lessons."

So. He was trying to supplant her in Vicky's affections by bringing in another teacher.

Clare had to deal with the letter first, but then she followed, smoothing down her gray dress and tucking back a loose strand of hair. For some reason she needed to prove that no other female could possibly replace Clare in Vicky's affections. No one, and it was very important that Clare be there. If only so Lord Strahan could see with his own eyes how Clare's refinement far exceeded that of some crude Scots woman.

❧Chapter Five

At the entrance to the parlor, Clare, dismayed, hung back in the shadows. Mrs. Fraser was not the gray-haired crone she'd imagined. And her male escort had vanished.

Young and beautiful, the woman wore a crown of thick black hair. She was a study in winter—her black hair framed a perfect oval face. Her snowy complexion was accented by wide dark eyes and a full red mouth. Her gown of black velvet was trimmed in tartan, a slight bending of the rules of mourning.

Her laughter was throaty, and Clare silently dubbed Mrs. Fraser the Merry Widow, a judgment verified by her manner.

"My, Alec," Mrs. Fraser said gaily, "the child is charming, and how she favors you with this incredible hair. Shall I help you outfit her in some fine gowns? I know a marvelous dressmaker in Edinburgh. Blue, without a doubt, is the color to favor that marvelous red hair. I see now that all your children will be redheads." And she cast a coy look at Lord Strahan.

He chose to ignore the remark. Instead he glanced over at the doorway where Clare stood.

He took a step toward her and extended a hand to beckon her inside the room.

"Isobel, may I present my daughter's . . . companion, shall we say."

Isobel turned, the gay expression on her face fading. "You mean her governess?"

"Former governess. She's come to lend a familiar presence until Vicky gets used to the idea of Dundroma as her home."

Clare took exception to that and stared up at him. "She's on holiday. Thornhill is her home."

He smiled back, his blue eyes bemused. "Our wager is not yet resolved, Aunt Clare. I am her father, and that makes Dundroma her home."

Her heart plummeted.

And then Isobel Fraser, the merry widow, stepped between them, smile tight. "I'm pleased to make your acquaintance . . . was it *Miss* Charlton?"

"She's Reginald's widow," Lord Strahan explained. "And she prefers to be called Clare. Not Aunt Clare. Just Clare."

"Well, Clare," said the merry widow Fraser, "I've never met an English governess, but I'm certain you've taken good care of Alec's daughter."

Lord Strahan moved away to listen to his daughter recount again the wonders of her pony. Clare was alone with the widow.

"I've been her sole nanny and governess both since she was six months old."

Isobel's smile was patronizing. "I'm afraid I'm out of touch with what's been going on in the border country. You see, like Alec, I've spent most of the past decade in India enduring the heat."

Clare couldn't resist a glance down at her black gown.

"I'd still be over in India if Malcolm hadn't taken ill. But as fortune would have it, Alec returned too, and it's a great comfort to have an old friend nearby to help me through my mourning."

She turned toward Vicky and her father, as if Clare were

dismissed. "Alec, you must be sorry now you stayed away
so long . . ."

Lord Strahan looked up. "I'm sorry I didn't discover my
daughter sooner. She's been raised English on me. She
should have had me home sooner."

"Fie, Alec. Children thrive just fine without a parent. I
sent my son back here to school as soon as possible, and you
must admit he's turned out admirably—even in English
schools."

"Where is the boy?" Alec asked.

"Oh, at the ponies, I'm sure. You don't mind, do you?"

"I envy the lad his mobility. Don't let convention and
stodgy conversation stop him."

Mrs. Fraser turned to Vicky. "Your papa is looking out for
my poor fatherless son. So you see, perhaps his accident
was a blessing. Otherwise, we'd not have him home to help
us."

"I'm sure he'd rather have his knee like it was," Vicky
said with childish candor. "It hurts, you know." Trust Vicky
to forget all Clare had taught her about talking to one's
elders and speaking her mind.

Isobel smiled tolerantly and batted her big black eyes at
Lord Strahan. "Does it hurt, Alec? Are you suffering
dreadfully from the pain still? I thought you merely used the
walking stick as an affectation . . . to prove you were still
sulking over this setback to your military dreams."

Alec glowered and rose to his feet. "Shattered kneecaps
are painful, and the walking stick is no affectation. As for
my military dreams, they matter little now." Pride made him
lie.

He took a few steps toward the sideboard. Halfway there,
his bad knee buckled beneath him, and with a curse, he
grabbed for the sideboard, missed, sent a decanter crashing
to the ground. Two seconds later, he landed on his knees in
a pool of whisky.

Clare rushed over and held out a hand. "Milord, you shouldn't be walking without some support." Vicky came and, joining her, offered another hand.

He waved them both away. "I can get up."

And by grabbing onto the sideboard he struggled up. To spare his dignity, Clare set about picking up broken pieces of glass and dumping them into the cuspidor that Vicky brought over.

Isobel Fraser stood watching and tapping her foot. "Well, Alec, I didn't mean to send you to your knees so soon. And in your kilt yet. "

Lord Strahan's face was dark with anger. "Go and see the new pony, Isobel, and persuade your son to come inside. Dinner is postponed while we clean up the room."

"But, Alec, don't be angry. It was your own fault."

"Spare me my dignity, Isobel. Go and get the boy."

Clare stood close by until he steadied himself and then handed him his walking stick, waiting while he grasped the ivory-headed top. "Be careful, milord. The whisky might be slippery."

A maid had appeared within seconds of the crash and was picking up smaller slices of glass as she mopped up. Just to be safe, Clare took Lord Strahan by the arm. Without being told, Vicky rushed over and took the other arm. "No arguing now, Papa. We'll help you sit."

Isobel Fraser watched with bemusement. "My, that knee does have ways of garnering you female attention. I believe my son can fend for himself. It's you who needs the chaperoning." And she sat down, skirts billowing about her, expression amused.

Clare said nothing, just waited until Lord Strahan was seated. "Your knees—does the whisky burn?"

"No," he said tersely. "The advantage of a kilt is clear, you see, over trousers. No need to change."

Clare took a clean towel from the maid and hovered with

Vicky until he mopped the whisky off his knees. He winced once or twice.

"Does it burn?"

"Whisky, Vicky, is what the surgeons used to dull the pain in India when they almost amputated my leg. I'm lucky I had a sober friend who could talk them out of it."

Alec cast a bleak eye on Clare. "What were we talking about?"

It was Isobel who answered. "About your crushed knee, of course. You don't mind that much, do you? I mean, I know you wanted to stay in the military. But look what you've gained . . . a daughter . . . *and*, we can resume our friendship. That's what we were talking about."

Ignoring Clare, who stood quietly nearby, the merry Mrs. Fraser reached out a hand and pulled Vicky close against her crinolined skirt. "Oh, don't worry that my son can take your place . . . He's back to school soon."

Alec glowered. "A lad with his mother's taste for flirtations."

"But his father's discretion, thankfully. He's rather sweet on the baker's daughter, you know, but too shy to tell her so."

Vicky moved away from the widow, and Alec stared off out the window. "Malcolm and I would be grouse hunting soon. Even that's out of the question for me now. Pity. By odds it ought to have been me that died."

"Don't feel guilty, Alec. Malcolm's gone, and the past can't be changed. He wouldn't want us to brood overly long."

"I'll brood till I've had my fill," he growled.

Isobel smoothed back her skirts and sat down close to Lord Strahan while Clare, feeling out of place, looked on from the sideboard. The entire room reeked of the spilled whisky, and there was a scratch—red and angry-looking—on Lord Strahan's leg beneath the tartan.

But the widow was oblivious. "Oh, Alec, dear," she said, batting her eyes up at him. "We'll go for walks on the heath and that will strengthen you up. In no time, you'll be fine."

"Isobel, shattered bones don't become fine again."

Isobel stroked his arm briefly. "You must learn to look at the whisky glass as half full instead of half empty, Alec. You're angry at losing a chance to be promoted to general, when you should be glad to be home in Scotland surrounded by a daughter and old friends who are ever so glad to see you. That's worth more than being a general, isn't it?"

"No."

"Alec, if I were an apothecary I'd toss out that laudanum and whisky they're giving you and suggest a picnic. A short hike will strengthen your knee, and in time—"

"No."

"But Vicky could go with you and learn about flora and fauna and fishing and . . . well, you know. You see that I'm right."

Alec shut his eyes, praying for strength to endure the pain. Yes, for Vicky's sake. So he could win the wager with the prim Aunt Clara from Thornhill.

Prim and compassionate. He'd been surprised at how she'd rushed to his side, as if he were an invalid, and he'd been far too humiliated to properly thank her. All she'd received was a snarl.

Now he looked at her. She was standing still by the sideboard, a cloth in her hands, looking very pale and wide-eyed, that honey hair slipping out of its net. Her gown was stained with whisky splashes.

"Well?" Isobel urged.

He was looking at Clare as he answered. "Yes, then, a picnic for Vicky's sake. You won't mind if her companion joins us?"

"The governess, Alec? We were going to catch up on old

times, old friends from Simla. Vicky's governess won't
want to hear us talk about people she doesn't know . . ."

"Forgive me, Isobel, but gaining my daughter for this
holiday involved a truce of sorts with Thornhill. I'm turning
my daughter into a Scots woman, and the English governess
has wagered I can't do it."

Clare blushed prettily, and he saw a glimmer of the
dimples that had intrigued him whenever she spoke. He'd
tried to ignore them, pretend they weren't there, but it was
no use.

Isobel gave Clare a dismissive look. "Well, if you insist,"
she said quickly. "We'll tramp the heather at a child's pace,
and that will be good exercise for you."

There was little enthusiasm in her voice, but then as Alec
knew full well Isobel was never one to be threatened by a
meek companion nor be overshadowed. Isobel might have
watched while Alec wed Cecilia out from under her nose,
but he doubted she'd be so careless with Dundroma women
again—not even with gray sparrow governesses. The pain
of limping about might be worth enduring just to watch
Isobel work her wiles.

"Agreed then. The first clear day we picnic in the moors."

Two hours later Isobel was sitting in the musty dining
room of Dundroma—at the right hand of Lord Strahan, and
she was holding court with Vicky's father on subjects of
which Clare had no knowledge. They worked their way
through the courses of salmon, mutton, and vegetables. The
stag heads stared down on them in here too.

Nothing seemed to dim Isobel, not even the tardiness of
her son. Even if she hadn't been sitting down table with no
one to speak with, Clare would have felt like a sparrow, gray
and fading into the woodwork. Which was just as well, for
while everyone forgot she was there, she could observe
Isobel Fraser, the merry widow in black velvet. Secretly, she

wagered that the lovely widow was not a bit sorry to be widowed. Though she tried to make it sound otherwise.

"What was India like?" Vicky asked, fork poised between bites of salmon.

"Hot," replied her father.

"Exotic and lovely," Isobel Fraser added. "Oh, but, Alec, we did have some lovely times there." Then she added for Vicky's sake, "You see, Victoria, I knew your father for many, many years. Why, I was friends with your mother. In fact, I was the one who introduced them, isn't that so?"

Alec reached for his wine. "Is that how it happened?"

"Well, you know it did." Isobel leaned across the snowy tablecloth to speak to Vicky. "I knew her before your father did even. You take after him, you know."

"Did my mother go to India?"

Clare jumped in with a plain practical explanation. "Your father went to India after she died."

Lord Strahan did not look at her, but stared off at the far end of the dining table.

"Where he fought tigers," Vicky said, a bit confused.

"Pathans," Alec corrected and at last tucked into his fish and pudding.

"He and my Malcolm were best friends, you see," Isobel explained. "Best friends here in Scotland . . . we were wed just months apart, and we welcomed your father to India. We were inseparable for ten years . . . until Malcolm caught a fever, and the doctors sent him home. I returned here to Thistle Lodge with him—and it was supposed to be a temporary stay, but then my husband died. It's very lonely here in this border country when you don't know anyone. I was ready to herd sheep or take over managing the Fraser family's woolen business . . . oh, it was tedious, Alec," she said, turning to Lord Strahan with a smile.

She toyed with her wineglass, then held it out for a refill

and sipped ever so delicately. "I admit I've never been more glad to have an old friend back. Why, it was almost fortuitous. Here I sat, widowed and distraught because in my hour of sorrow my dearest friend was halfway around the world. And then a fall from a horse injures him, and he's sent home too. Oh, but it's so good to have neighbors here again—even a crotchety old major like your father. So you see I'm not in the least sorry."

Vicky had sat wide-eyed through this. "But he could have died."

"Your father? Alec lives a charmed life."

"Is that why I must live with a walking stick?" he asked.

"Oh, Alec, you're ruining dinner with your glum comments. Now we won't allow such a mood to intrude on our picnics. I know you're used to the outdoor, active life. In time you'll perhaps heal—"

"In time counts for nothing with the army. I'm finished."

Clare stared at her plate, hurt for Vicky's sake. He was taking up fatherhood as second choice because the army was done with him.

"Miss Charlton, you haven't touched your wine."

Clare looked up to find Lord Strahan watching her.

Her cheeks flushed. "I—I don't care for wine."

"Nor for good Scots cooking."

"I fear I'm not becoming acclimated very quickly. I'd have a terrible time in India."

Isobel gave her a condescending smile. "But how do you know until you try something? When Lord Strahan arrived, he was determined to hate it, but Malcolm and I soon made him see the good aspects. And as for Dundroma, well, I dreaded living here alone in this glen, but now that you're home, Alec, I know I shall like it very well indeed. You shall take my mind off my grief for Malcolm. And I shall keep you so occupied you'll forget your ill humor over your leg. You'll see. There's so much to catch up on . . ."

"Are you going back to India?" Vicky asked her father in all innocence.

"God willing, child."

"And take me?"

He paused, as if he'd not thought of how a child fit into his plans beyond possessing her here at Dundroma. Clare looked directly at him, and just briefly he met her taunting stare.

"Why not?"

"And Aunt Clare?"

"Aunt Clare would detest India."

At this Isobel turned to Clare. "He's right of course. We who've been there gloss over it, form a sort of club of former residents. But I wouldn't recommend it, especially to such meek, sweet, naive sorts as yourself. The women who go out on the fishing fleet arrive mostly seasick, you know, and few catch a husband."

"I was thinking of London, of another situation."

Isobel traced the pattern in her crystal goblet.

"How perfect . . . For now, though, Lord Strahan must be glad to have you along to comfort the child." She turned to Vicky and smiled overly much. "Is it nice to have one's aunt be governess? I only had grouchy stern creatures as my governesses."

"I've never known another governess."

"Your mother and I shared one once. She was most strict, and we put frogs in her valise. That was my idea, of course. Your mother was very pretty, child, but I always had all the adventuresome ideas."

Vicky's hand shook, and she put down her fork. She turned emotional easily when any references to her mother came up. Adele had told her so many overly sentimental stories—true or not—that Vicky automatically grieved.

Alec scraped back his chair and reached for his walking stick. He stood abruptly, hands on the table for support.

"Join me in the drawing room and we'll reminisce, Isobel. You never were shy about making conversation with the men, were you?"

Isobel tilted her head. "Did I tell more than you wanted? So sorry, Alec. It's been so long. I had no idea you remembered all these details . . . Good evening, Miss— Mrs. Charlton, I do hope your trunk arrives soon from Thornhill. I can imagine how tedious it is wearing the same gown day in and day out. If it doesn't, let me know. I've gowns from before my widowhood that I can lend you."

Clare stood out of politeness and felt Vicky reaching for her hand. "A kind gesture, but I'm sure I shall manage one more day."

Isobel nodded. "Gray serge is so serviceable that way."

And on that, she sailed out, petticoats swishing beneath her voluminous velvet skirt.

Clare scraped in her chair, relieved the dinner was over. She felt strangely bothered by the entire tone of the meal. She wasn't certain what bothered her more—Isobel's acerbic observations or Lord Strahan's barbaric mood.

Yet, she had the distinct feeling Isobel Fraser, the merry widow, had been baiting her. As if she were any threat to the lady's designs on Lord Strahan. And designs she had, for Clare hadn't missed the roguish, sparkling glances, the affected blush, the too gay laughter. She felt empty, hollow.

"Clare . . ."

She looked up. Lord Strahan stood there in the doorway, leaning heavily on his walking stick. "I don't want Vicky to spend her evening shut in her room. She's to take a brisk walk outdoors while I entertain Mrs. Fraser. Is that clear? Take her into the gardens. They're walled."

"You mean that mass of unpruned shrubbery?"

"Here in Dundroma, the heather and the trees have a wildness about them. That's the way of Dundroma."

And so did the master. A depth of wildness she could only guess at.

Clare turned to Vicky, who sat there, glum. "Are you tiring of life in Dundroma, Vicky? We could return to Thornhill, you know." It was worth asking.

Her father answered for her. "She's yet to see the best of Dundroma. We'll send Andrew out to join you."

"Andrew?" The name vaguely rang a bell.

"Mrs. Fraser's son . . . the lad who helped Vicky ride her pony."

Vicky looked toward the gate, gaze fixed on a handsome lad in coat and tie who had just come in. The pony groom.

"Andrew?" Clare asked. "Andrew Fraser is your groom?"

Vicky nodded and then sat there mesmerized. This was the same lad who was giving Vicky pony riding lessons?

"Vicky!" Her whisper was hasty. "*This* is your groom? Why didn't you tell me it was Mrs. Fraser's son?"

"I—I didn't know. He never said his surname. Just Andrew. He's ever so smart with ponies, you know."

And a flirt with the lasses. His own mother had bragged about it.

Andrew joined them then, and Vicky begged permission from Clare to go see the ponies.

Clare looked Andrew up and down.

"Would you like to come?" Andrew asked politely.

"I'll follow along behind just to have a look."

"Andrew will show you how to ride too."

"Never, I should fall off and break my neck."

"Oh, Aunt Clare, you're so proper."

"And so have you been raised. Remember your manners around Andrew. Go on, I'll be along."

At last, at long last, Vicky had Andrew to herself.

He walked with his hands in his pockets, and his hair was fair and tousled. Vicky went warm from head to toe.

"I've never had a governess," Andrew observed.

"Mine's nice, only my father doesn't want her to stay."

"Oh."

"Did your mother make you come see me?"

He glanced at her. "Well, she said it would be good manners."

Vicky giggled. "What else would you do?"

"Stroll the village. Steal whisky and drink with the fairies and ghosties."

"Doesn't your mother care?"

"Of course not. She only cares about talking with your father."

"Did you live in India with them?"

Andrew shrugged, and the wind chose just that moment to blow his fair curls about his forehead.

"I don't hardly remember it, but aye, for a while. I hardly remember it—except for wearing a funny domed hat when I played in the sun . . . and I slept under a gauze tent . . . oh, and I rode an elephant once, led on a rope by my ayah."

"What's that?" They were at the stables and Vicky wanted to keep Andrew talking forever.

"A kind of governess in India."

"Wizened and crabby?"

He smiled at her, then chuckled. His laughter made her tingle all over. Colors took on brighter hues, sounds were muted. She forgot they'd come to see the pony.

"Well, there's the pony . . . and your governess."

Vicky looked back. Aunt Clare stood in the stable doorway, maintaining a safe distance.

"He's small," she said. "Not as big as Thornhill animals."

"He's a pony."

Andrew headed out. "I have to leave."

Vicky ran after him. "Will we have a lesson tomorrow?"

He shrugged, as if she were a gnat on his heels. "Of

course," then he leaned down and whispered in her ear.
"Hear now, Vicky, if Mother asks, tell her you met me, will
you? Tell her I was a gentleman, and we played at
revolutionaries and soldiers."

"No one plays that anymore."

"Mother doesn't know."

"Why do you want me to tell her that?"

"I have to go back to the village."

The baker's daughter. Jealousy coursed through Vicky.
For the first time in her life. Jealousy. Andrew's breath was
still warm against her ear.

"Farewell . . . don't forget, I did my duty, and watch
out for the ghost of Dundroma. He's a green ghost."

"Why?"

"All ghosts in Scotland are green, didn't you know that
yet? Goose."

She was not a goose.

Andrew was gone then, leaving Vicky and Aunt Clare to
stroll back to Dundroma to those ugly shrubberies. They
didn't speak. Vicky was in a daydreaming mood. Clouds
hung about everywhere above, yet an eclipse had occurred.
Somewhere inside her. She pondered the feeling, the yearning she felt.

Suddenly she knew what she wanted from Andrew.

But she'd best not tell her aunt or she'd haul her posthaste
back to Thornhill, and then her father would chase after her
and that would be the end of pony riding with Andrew, and
there wasn't a boy around Thornhill who could compare to
Andrew Fraser, certainly not Charlotte's Billy.

"You'd rather stay here longer and ride ponies than stroll
the grounds with me, is that why you are so quiet?" Aunt
Clare asked.

"Oh, Aunt Clare, I love riding ponies. Andrew can teach
most everything in the world—about ponies."

Thornhill had nothing to compare, and Aunt Clare was

going to have a hard time winning the child back from her father. It was all so silly anyway, the way these grown-ups argued over where she should live. Dundroma. Thornhill. The heath grew the same on both sides of the dividing line. And as for that mysterious statue, well, maybe, if she could win a kiss from Andrew, she'd know what it meant. Oh, aye, Vicky had a wager of her own to win before she could pacify the feuding grown-ups.

It was evening when the traveler begged directions at Thornhill. Percival and Adele, still not speaking, had taken to spending their time in separate quarters of the estate. Servants kept them informed as to each other's whereabouts. Percival would take his after-dinner brandy in the rose garden; Adele would take her after-dinner sherry in the rose salon. A hapless servant, hopelessly confused by the barrage of written communications, delivered the sherry to the rose garden by mistake. And the stranger as well.

Adele, when she learned of the error, was at her wit's end, and rather than risk more miscommunication, she ventured out to the rose garden herself, but stopped at the end farthest from Percival—the section where white roses were cultivated in abundance. An embarrassed maid curtsied.

"Please inform my husband that he has my sherry by mistake."

Moments later, the maid returned with a message from the other end of the rose garden. "Mr. Charlton says to please inform his wife that he has offered her glass of sherry to the unexpected guest."

Unexpected guest? Curiosity was ever so much stronger than this tedious feud, and swallowing her pride, she plucked a white rosebud and marched through the carefully tended garden—past her own favorite roses, the whites, which bloomed like gentle nesting doves. Across a cobbled walkway, until at last she joined her husband at an alfresco table set up right beside the bloodred roses. Red climbing roses grew up the wall here, and an army of crimson, blood, and vermillion blooms surrounded him, all extravagantly perfuming the air.

"Good evening, Percival." Those three words were the first exchanged since Vicky left for Dundroma.

Percival stood as did the guest and replied, "Good evening to you, Adele. We have a guest." And he promptly ordered more brandy all around for the three of them.

The maid scurried off and Adele could well guess what was going on in the servants' quarters: In the housekeeper's room at Thornhill, a hoarded bottle of vintage wine would be popped open so the servants could celebrate the return to normalcy.

That, Adele decided, might be a premature celebration. It would depend on how this conversation went and on the nature of their visitor's business.

Adele, who had never lost her eye for a man's attributes, looked him over from head to toe. Fate had neglected him when passing out looks. He was stout and bespectacled. On the other hand, he was young and well spoken. A shame Clare was not here. He'd do for her.

"Your name, sir?" she said with her best London polish. Percival needed reminding that she could have done better than this isolated drafty mansion.

The guest cleared his throat in a prelude to pomposity. "Wilmot. Dr. Wigston Wilmot, and I apologize for the intrusion, but I am searching for a castle called Dundroma."

Percival and Adele exchanged a knowing glance. A physician would do for Clare. Yes. For of course someday Vicky would be grown-up, the feuding with her father would be a moot point, and then there'd be the problem of what to do with Aunt Clare.

"This is Thornhill Manor, sir."

"Am I close?" the Londoner asked. "Are you familiar with the castle? Much legend surrounds it, you know."

Adele's voice was frosty. "We know."

"If you're going there to search after the legend of the kissing statue—"

"No, not that. Other business."

"Well," Adele said, "we don't give out directions."

The fellow sighed and explained his other mission besides a fascination with travel—a medical pioneer, it turned out. "And so," he finished, "being a loyal Londoner, who's never socialized with Scottish nobility, I at first agreed to come and examine this Lord Strahan's injury as a favor owed to my brother-in-law who served in the military with the man."

"Occasionally, I suppose, one must perform acts of mercy," Adele said. Oh, she'd known his type in her youth. It was this same sort who had caused her social failure and left her wed to Percival. Dr. Wigston Wilmot was, in short, a man who considered his every word and thought superior. Irksome and yet, she knew this: Such a man generally wanted to prove his superiority so much that he'd do favors to prove his worth. All he needed was to be asked.

"Oh, indeed . . . but then it occurred to me this case might prove the ideal one to meld two disciplines in medicine. You see, very few parts of the anatomy can be improved with surgery. But a kneecap—yes. I was on my way to Edinburgh . . . my colleagues—medical colleagues—have a great debate going as to the value of surgical advances at the Royal College there." He plucked a faded red rose and put it with the white that Adele held. "Imagine a melding of white and red roses."

Adele could not.

"What would you have?" Dr. Wilmot asked.

"It's never been done."

"Not with medicine. But in war, it has. In politics, it has. Witness the peace between England and Scotland today."

"There is no peace up in this borderland." Adele tossed the roses onto the table.

Dr. Wilmot plucked a petal from each. "Not yet. But if these two were melded, made into a hybrid, you'd see something new. Progress."

"There will never be progress between Thornhill and Dundroma. Their histories are far more complicated than roses."

"Sad indeed. That's how the physicians and surgeons are—separate, like your two beds of roses here. Have you ever seen a pink rose?"

Adele sighed. This Dr. Wilmot was tenacious, she'd give him that, and fascinated by his logic, she listened now with interest.

"It's no secret we physicians have never muddied our hands associating with the baser work of surgeons, but perhaps the time has come. At any rate, since I'm on my way to Edinburgh, I needed to pass this way. Dundroma can serve a double purpose." He drained his glass in one gulp. "Is it true they call the laird there the devil of Dundroma?"

Again, Percival and Adele exchanged a look. Mutual agreement passed between them without words. A plan.

"He's a man who'll have his own way," Adele said, bending the truth. "But while he's not a devil, he is, after all, not quite one of us. Our own granddaughter was taken up there because he demanded his father's patriarchal rights. She's written us the briefest of letters, and we do worry about the influences up there. So much of Dundroma is mysterious."

"Then you know the way."

"Yes, you're almost there, but the route winds through burn and valley and across heath. One wrong turn and a Londoner can find himself in the hands of reivers."

"Surely not in this day and age. The nineteenth century?"

"The borderland is sadly backward and barbaric. But an educated man like yourself does not sit in fear of murdering, plundering Scotsmen? Would you trust our guidance to Dundroma?"

Dr. Wigston Wilmot stood and looked with longing out across the windswept moorland that stretched beyond this rose garden. "But of course. Why do you fear giving me the directions?"

Percival Charlton stood and for the first time in Adele's memory spoke without any dithering hesitation. "I fear nothing from any Londoner. Not even my wife's past suitors. In exchange for directions we need a favor. Do you agree?"

❧ Chapter Six

"A surprise visit," Lord Strahan noted. He leaned rather more heavily than usual against his walking stick, as if yesterday's fall pained him still more than he wanted anyone to know.

As Clare watched from the staircase, Isobel held out her hand for Lord Strahan's kiss and simpered prettily all the while. Then Isobel swirled down the great hall, looking for all the world as if she were rehearsing for the role of mistress of the castle already. Widow's black did not slow down her ambitions. Oh, yes, Clare thought as she moved downstairs, she could picture Isobel as Lady Strahan.

The widow made it no secret how much superior she found Dundroma Castle to her own more modest estate, Thistle Lodge. And someday, of course, even that would belong to the fair son, Andrew. Then Isobel would be out of a home entirely. Unless, of course, the merry widow captured Dundroma for a new home.

"I'm out paying calls to the poor villagers today," Isobel said too sweetly. "Gifts of jam and fruit from the Fraser orchard."

"Ah, a package of pears," Alec guessed and gave Isobel a wry smile. He and Clare gazed in curiosity at the wrapped bundle under her arms. The widow Fraser tossed her head and her dark ringlets shook.

"For you, I've brought nothing at all."

"Am I out of favor then?"

"You forget, Alec, I'm in mourning. How very forward of you to flirt."

His smile froze. "Is that what I was doing?"

"This offering is for Clare Charlton."

Clare had just selected a book of poems to read during Vicky's riding lesson and stood, speechless still, in the library doorway.

Lord Strahan called out to her. "Come here, Clare, and see what Mrs. Fraser has brought."

She stepped forward. "But you shouldn't have. There's nothing I need."

The widow wrinkled her nose at Clare's humble gray serge. "But of course you do. You can't wear that gown day in and day out."

True, the gown was hopelessly wrinkled, and spotted here and there with the remnants of whisky from Lord Strahan's fall. But taking castoffs from Mrs. Fraser would be demeaning. Adele Charlton would be horrified. What would the neighbors around Thornhill think? The servants?

Isobel Fraser did away with such objections. "Oh, I know your belongings are not here yet. Servant talk, you know, and anyway, Adele will take her sweet time about ordering any of Thornhill's servants to pack for a governess. So I've brought you one of my gowns. Obviously since I'm in mourning I can't wear it, and it never was my best color. The waist may need to be let out, but otherwise the fit should do. Then you won't have to wear that same old gray thing . . . I see you tried to blot out the whisky, but really, do wear this, with my compliments."

Clare was too stunned to manage anything more than obligatory phrases. "You're too kind," she murmured, taking the package.

"Not at all. It's the least I can do after all Alec's done for my Andrew. Now please try it on." And she'd barely spoken the words before she looked at Alec. "I shall take you up on refreshment. Sherry, please . . ."

And with that she turned her back on Clare and the package, the gift forgotten. Clare backed out into the hallway. Clearly, Isobel had brought the gift merely as an excuse to see Lord Strahan, and as Clare retreated up the stairs to her bedchamber, the widow Fraser's merry laughter followed her up.

"She's such a goose. Aren't you glad you took control of your daughter when you did?"

Privately, Alec agreed with Isobel, but he wasn't about to give her the satisfaction. So he lied. "There's no harm in having her here. Oh, I didn't want a starchy governess around either, but for the child's sake, if it makes her feel better for a while . . ."

"For the child's sake? Alec, where do you get these ideas? As her father, she's yours, and you need no governess to tell you how she's been raised. You may raise her in whatever manner you please. Father was a barrister, and I know these things. The child is yours."

"As Andrew belonged to your husband more than to you." He let that thought sink in then added, "Yet you urged Malcolm to send him away from India at age eight to attend the best school in England?"

Isobel flushed slightly, and Alec decided to make her squirm—just a bit. Malcolm had been his closest friend, and had confided his uneasiness over sending Andrew at so young an age away on a journey halfway around the world. But Isobel wanted the lad gone.

"That was different. That was India, and it was only proper and safe for the boy to send him away to school. Malcolm didn't see it, but I did. Besides, it's the way all the gentry and officers handled their children."

Alec leaned back in his favorite chair and stared up at a stag head. Oh, Isobel had a way of twisting the truth. Alec knew better. Isobel was relieved to be done with the duties of motherhood. Malcolm sorely regretted giving Isobel her way with the boy, but had never been one to rule the roost with a heavy hand like most fathers.

"I wrote to him. So did Malcolm. He thrived. You can see that," Isobel said while posing prettily by the fireplace. Her dark ringlets framed her face, and she busied herself rearranging the dried heather on his mantel.

Watching her, Alec knew he'd done right to take matters into his own hand for his godchild. In his boyhood, he'd attended the same school as Andrew, knew the headmaster—and the headmaster's wife—and privately wrote to ensure that Andrew was assured a bit of mothering, and a bit more food than the gruel and potato and bread fare that he'd known. Too Spartan a regimen, he'd always felt.

Alec never told Malcolm, let alone Isobel, of his behind-the-scenes maneuvering, merely advised the boy of paths to steer clear of and traditions to follow at his school, and Andrew, who luckily had been blessed with a resourceful nature, wrote that he preferred England to India. Later, Alec learned that in the headmaster's wife, Andrew had found a nurturing tenfold than ever afforded by his mother.

And now the lad was without a father and Alec was anxious to talk with him as together they helped Vicky master pony riding. A servant brought a tray of sherry and for a few minutes that occupied them.

"Do you want to come and see how adept your son is at pony riding? He'll be an excellent teacher to Vicky."

Except for sipping at her sherry, Isobel didn't make a move. "Alec, for a man who wanted no part of fatherhood, you've certainly become besotted with the role. Much more so than Malcolm ever was. He left so many decisions on Andrew to me. If he were to walk in that door today—alive and well—he'd ask after the army's position on the Khyber Pass before he'd inquire if his son were alive."

"He was fond of Andrew. Perhaps he should have told you how much."

"Well, but that's past now, isn't it?" And she gazed at Alec while absently twirling the stem of her glass. "Let's stay here and catch up on old times in India. Remember the dinner party during the last monsoon season? The one that lasted all night?"

"We were, as I recall, housebound due to weather."

All India reminded him of was the pain of his knee and his lost opportunities. Other men with better horse sense than he were commanding troops at the Khyber Pass, at Calcutta, and Bombay, all of them sprinting ahead to the glory of general while he sat here with a fanciful widow who behaved as if her gown were any color but black.

Outside a coach rolled up the lane in a clatter of horses' hooves and tack. He expected no one, but anyone was welcome to break up this forced tête-à-tête with Isobel. So it was with gratitude that he looked at the servant who suddenly appeared on the scene.

"Milord, a gentleman caller."

"Send him in by all means."

Sighing, Isobel walked to a chair and settled into it, as if the prospect of two gentlemen with whom to flirt suited her to perfection.

Then, before his eyes her face dissolved into distaste, and hastily she set down her sherry glass.

Turning, Alec looked upon a homely little runt of a man, knock-kneed and plump of belly. Balding and round-faced. Not at all Isobel's sort.

Alec stood, and quickly it became clear who this was.

"Dr. Wigston Wilmot of London."

Alec nodded. "So Graham made good on his word and sent you here."

"He spoke ever so highly of Dundroma's hospitality—

and its mystery is legendary. Naturally, he told me of your injury and suggested I can help."

"Humph. Graham is an old woman. You're welcome to stay, of course. Dundroma never turns away a wayfarer, and if you admire the tales of Scott, you're welcome to poke about the scenery. As to my knee, it'll be a cold day in hell before you examine me. Whisky, Doctor?"

Dr. Wilmot accepted.

"Isobel?" he offered. "You'll stay and visit with us?"

She was standing now, eyeing Dr. Wilmot with ill-concealed distaste. "Actually," she said, backing toward the door, "I'm expected elsewhere—at the wife of the farrier."

She looked, to judge by the way she moved about the edges of the room, as if she'd seen a reptile. The good physician, on the other hand, could not seem to take his eyes off of Isobel.

"But you said you had time to visit," Alec said with the devil in his voice.

"That was before your visitor arrived. I'll not linger. So many mercy calls await now that I think on it. After the farrier, there's the butcher's wife, the minister's wife expects me for tea later . . ." She was backing out of the room.

Dr. Wilmot was now staring openmouthed at her, rapt admiration clear on his pudgy face. "I trust we shall meet again."

With an uncharacteristically lame smile, Isobel tossed her ringlets. "Doubtful, Doctor, and I have to tell you that I quite agree with Alec. Who in their right mind would sacrifice a leg to surgeons? Your mission here is a waste of time."

Her words only served to encourage his attention. Now he followed her, eyes glowing in unmistakable admiration. "But, madam, these are Edinburgh surgeons with whom I will discuss Lord Strahan's case. The world's finest."

"Edinburgh makes fine gowns. I've heard little to recommend its surgeons. Good day to you, sir."

"Isobel," Alec called after her, unable to hide the trace of amusement in his voice, "Dundroma thanks you for your charity. Was that an Edinburgh gown you dropped off?"

"Does it matter, Alec? It's one of mine, and that's all you need worry about. Gowns are something only women understand." She fled.

The gown stunned Clare. Oh, the style was conservative enough, but the color . . . not at all in fashion, certainly not for a governess, someone who was a model of sedateness to a child.

"Well, now," said the maid who assisted Clare. "I can't recall ever seeing a gown of this color worn. It's likely a color from India. A native color."

"I can't wear it."

"But the master expects to see you in it. It's a gift, and at Dundroma it's rude not to use a gift."

Where, oh, where, was her trunk from Thornhill? It would be filled with tasteful colors like gray and black and brown and one or two gowns in the more fashionable vivid shades of purple and crimson.

"You know, ma'am, it reminds me of those wild berries on hedgerows, it does. Not the fashion, but pretty in its way." The maid held the gown up against Clare's wrinkled and stained gray serge. "Oh, aye, it'll go nicely with your hair and eyes. Brings out the green in them, it does. Go on then. Put it on. One wearing, and everyone will be satisfied. I promise to wash and iron the gray one as quickly as I can."

She gave in. But she was under no illusions about this gift. This was Isobel's way of making her look like a laughingstock in front of Lord Strahan. Nothing else. Isobel Fraser was worrying over nothing. Only when Clare took too heavy a hand with Vicky did Lord Strahan notice her.

But when she ventured downstairs, Isobel was gone already, off on more calls to the needy. Lord Strahan was engaged in a friendly argument with a male visitor in the parlor doorway. Relieved, Clare escaped with a book of poetry to the garden. This was the best place to hide until her own gown was ironed.

She drew a paisley shawl about her shoulders—not because the day was cool, but to hide the garish gown. Then, satisfied she was well hidden, she opened up her book of poems.

Moments later, footsteps—uneven in tread—sounded in the garden, crunching on the gravel walkway, and then they stopped. She peered over the edge of her book. Black shiny boots stood facing her. And a wooden walking stick. Her gaze moved up into hooded blue eyes and a smile. And chestnut hair blowing across his forehead.

Lord Strahan had found her. Her own gaze dropped to her book. Maybe if she pretended to be occupied, he'd go away.

"Look up at me, Clare," he commanded.

Before she could obey, he reached over and, lifting one end of the shawl, pulled at it slowly till it trailed off her shoulders and finally dangled from his hand. "Look up."

Blushing deeply, she did so. He stared back at her, gaze intense, mouth a taut line, fingers clenched about his ivory-handled stick.

"You hate it, don't you?" Clare asked, voice trembling.

"Isobel may have hoped I would, but she's wrong. It flatters you."

"No one wears gowns of this color. I feel foolish, like some underripe raspberry. Utterly foolish."

The expression in his eyes softened. "Less foolish than me, slipping and landing in a pool of whisky."

"That was an accident."

"This is a gift. I don't recall ever seeing it on Isobel, but it suits you—aye, most admirably."

"I don't want to talk about it."

"Very well, what do you want to do?"

"Read. Don't let me keep you from your visitor."

"He's a physician sent here by a friend to bribe me into putting my life and limbs into the hands of butcher surgeons."

"Then you've sent him packing?"

He shook his head. "You underestimate Dundroma hospitality. He's welcome to stay because he's Graham's friend, and I've given him leave to poke about. He belongs to a literary group—Londoners who admire Scott's border country. I warned him to stay clear of the stables. That will give me a safe haven should he wish to pursue his radical medical ideas."

"Aren't you going to watch Vicky on her pony?"

"In time. I should like to visit with you."

"Why? What do you want to know?"

"Well, Clare, tell me what you and Vicky observed last night in the garden, so we can discuss future lessons."

She was silent.

"Tell me what you learned," he urged.

They were quiet, except for the crunch of footsteps on the cobblestones of the stableyard. Clare's heart was hammering. "Vicky learned not to climb out onto narrow tree limbs because they can break."

He smiled, briefly. "It's called backing yourself into a corner, Clare. Out on a limb. Meaning, nowhere to retreat. A Douglas will go out on a limb, but a Douglas is prepared to land on his feet if the branch gives way. Vicky will handle herself when out on limbs. The questions remains—can you?"

"I've never been out on a limb."

"You are now, Clare. Coming here to Dundroma has put you out on a limb. What I'm waiting to see is what you do next."

Clare chose to ignore his comment. "I also observed a bird's nest Vicky discovered."

"Empty?"

"Of birds, yes."

"Then what was left to see?"

"One tiny shell. Cracked open. Brown speckled."

"And the birds had all flown away."

"Every one."

"No doubt Miss Charlton wishes she'd flown with them. The gown you wear—that shade of underripe raspberry—reminds me that you want only to fly away from here, back to your brown and gray world."

"Your wish also."

"My hasty first reaction, aye, but now I find you a challenge, Clare. I should like to make you like Dundroma as much as Vicky."

"I can be stoic and endure what I dislike—including this dress."

"Such a waste of time and life, though, Clare."

She bristled. "I shall try for Vicky's sake to enjoy her progress with rigorous Dundroma sports. Let me know when I am required to watch."

And she settled down on a bench and opened a small book she'd brought. But still Lord Strahan did not leave her alone.

"The poetry of Burns?" he asked.

"Of course not. Keats."

"Heresy here at Dundroma." He yanked the book away and sat down on the bench, so close his thigh grazed her crinoline. All her senses were suddenly keenly on edge. Pleasantly so.

"You cannot censor what I read—only Vicky's reading."

"True, but I *can* recite my favorite poetry in your presence, Clare."

"Out loud?"

"Is that not the meaning of a recital?"

"Yes, but—"

"But you've only heard poetry from bairns. Never from a man. Reginald, as I recall, was one to recite the results of grain futures and the prices of horseflesh at Tattersalls. Not poetry."

"No," she admitted.

"Aren't you a wee bit curious, as a governess, to hear how well I recite? I should like your comments. To know if I earn high marks from you."

She was silent. Anything she said would only bait him all the more, and so he took that silence as assent.

He was sitting across from her, staring out at the hills. His voice was husky as he explained how the poem was inspired, and then still looking out at the hills, he began.

> *"But pleasures are like poppies spread,*
> *You seize the flower, its bloom is shed;*
> *Or like the snow falls in the river,*
> *A moment white, then melts forever . . ."*

As he rose and towered over her, Clare turned weak. A poem by Robert Burns was breaking down her defenses. Scottish verse, recited by heart by a mercenary man.

Potent. Sweet. Shattering.

His voice was deep and sent shivers down her back, and inside, deep inside some secret recess of her, she ached, yearned for fulfillment. On he recited, words spoken in alternately dark and soft tones. Oh, he was a man who would break hearts. No wonder Dundroma maids blushed in his presence. Not to mention his effect on the widow Fraser.

She was blushing like a schoolgirl herself. While he smiled down at her. Her in her raspberry gown. Yes, she realized he'd temporarily made her forget her self-consciousness over the gown.

He finished "Tam o' Shanter," and the last words drifted off into the wind. Her heart pounded in her throat. It took all her willpower to control her impulses. She looked up into his eyes, intense and oh, so blue.

"It was lovely."

"Burns is powerful."

"Your recitation was very good."

He bent down to look close into her eyes, a smile lurking in his own. "Was it, Clare? Don't be charitable now, because I'm the master . . ."

"I'd never be kind to you or grant you charity."

"Then give me a mark for my recital."

They stared into each other's eyes. So close. A breath away. She could see the stubble on his jaw, smell the tangy scent of him, and the wool of his checked cloak. His recital echoed off her heart.

> *But pleasures are like poppies spread,*
> *You seize the flower, its bloom is shed;*

"You earn top marks."

He handed her back her shawl, his voice now matter-of-fact. "Has any man ever recited poetry to you?"

"Reginald was of a more practical bent."

He moved then and his walking stick slipped. His leg half buckled, and she reached out to catch him. Instead, he caught his own balance. Her hand covered his, felt the hard strength of his where he gripped the walking stick, and before she could remove it, he covered it with his free hand. Warm and strong.

Yes, this man could break hearts.

"Please, Lord Strahan, let me go."

"Tell me one thing more, and then I will.

"Did the poetry stir some passion in you?"

"I admire Burns's flair for dramatic imagery."

"You hide your reaction," he mocked.

"How do you know?"

"Because I know lasses—I know the lasses better than you realize."

Clare also knew him a little better. His enjoyment of women was not a wicked thing; he truly believed in and enjoyed the attraction between man and woman. And for his tough military exterior, his frustration over his career and his stubbornness over having surgeons fuss over his knee, he was at heart a romantic.

Vicky chose then to call from afar. "Clare, Papa—come and see me."

This time Clare gladly grabbed at the chance to escape. Ponies were far, far safer than the seductive voice of a border lord reciting Robert Burns in a secluded garden.

And as if the intimate moment in the garden had never happened, a few minutes later Lord Strahan ignored Clare totally and stood out on the moorland watching his daughter in approval.

The next day they did the same—ignored each other in favor of watching Vicky ride a pony. After two days in a row, Clare couldn't deny the bloom on Vicky's face. As for herself, she had stuffed the unwanted dress in her armoire and donned again her freshly pressed gray serge. That, she decided, was what had caused her reaction to Lord Strahan in the garden. That raspberry gown was too passionate a color. Combined with the soulful poetry recital, her equilibrium had been skewed, her control disturbed. Garbed again in plain gray with white collar and cuffs, she felt in control. Totally.

Until Lord Strahan joined Vicky and her and Andrew at the stables. He watched awhile, then said without warning, "Now it is time to ride out on the moors, lass."

The moors. Heaven help them, the man was serious. "You're giving her too much freedom. Twelve-year-old girls—"

"Lasses."

"—don't gallivant about astride ponies."

"Here at Dundroma, the lasses learn young."

Clare was not used to chasing after Vicky in hoydenish activity, and she wasn't going to do it without letting the devil of Dundroma feel the sting of her tongue. Perhaps if she gave him enough bite, he'd grow weary of this forced arrangement; fatherhood could lose its novelty when it entailed an ill-humored governess.

As if he read her mind, he said, "If you think to wear me out by the sternness of your tongue, you judge me wrong, Miss Charlton. I am a major, a laird, a Scotsman, and a borderer. As a major, I've wielded a sharp tongue; as a laird, a commanding tongue; as a Scotsman, a stubborn tongue; and as a borderer, an uncompromising one. I want my daughter to ride out on the moors."

"You are, milord, a thistle when it comes to good cheer toward your guests. And you still don't know anything about fatherhood if you put having your own way above the welfare of your daughter. You take the law and use it to prove you are a patriarch. What Vicky needs no law or judge or court can provide."

"You would dispute the entire British court system?"

"Indeed. If I could make you see how selfish your stubborn following of a law is. She's a person, not a horse."

"What accounts for this passion lurking beneath your calm?"

"I understand Vicky . . . I too was raised by a father, who used the law as his weapon. He kept my own mother at bay, just as you would keep Vicky from her family."

"But did you suffer?"

"Did you never have a mother? Did you never pine for her? Or were you truly, as they say, the devil's spawn? If your memory cannot call up longing for an absent mother, then you are truly not human, and I say they who call you devil are correct in their judgment. Would that I could be a judge to decide Vicky's fate and make the laws work for her, not you."

He stared at her so long she knew at once she'd gone too far. True, she'd lived in the far north in a house of drafts and eccentric in-laws, but she read the newspapers—when the coach brought them up. She read with keen interest of the so-called bluestockings, the women who debated to change the laws. If she had not been fated to the ordinary life of a governess, if she had had her choice in life, had money to choose her fate, then she would have chosen law . . . and not let gender stop her. Percival Charlton had a small shelf of legal books in his library and she had read them all in her time alone in her room. Read and stared out her window at the endless moors. Trapped. Reading to try to find out why, how her mother had been ripped from her. Did her mother voluntarily leave, or had her father, in the ultimate act of cruelty, banished her? She had to know she had not been abandoned, and she read on until she found the laws . . . and she of course saved the newspaper accounts of the Norton case, of the woman whose husband had retaliated for imagined sins by hiding her very children from her. Oh, the injustice of it, especially to the children. It was scant comfort after *her* mother was gone, but it eased old hurts to know her mother had had no choice—and that Clare was not alone.

And now history was repeating itself. That was her ultimate lesson. Men owned and ruled and made the laws, and women were at their mercy.

"I release you from our wager," she said with suddenness.

"You're leaving."

"I'm staying. Even if Vicky, in a rash moment, were to say she no longer needed me, I fear it might be her concern for my homesickness. I hate it here, but Thornhill holds no love either. So even if she releases me, I shall not leave, but endure as long as she does. It is best for Vicky, and if you're a man of reason and emotion, you'll know I'm right and extend your famous Dundroma hospitality to me. Not as a wicked wager, but out of fatherly compassion. Your daughter deserves a trusted companion."

He watched the ponies in the enclosure and for a while she thought he was going to ignore her. At last he turned to her. "You may stay then—a hostage from Thornhill—and your fear not the consequences?"

"You do not frighten me. Only your worship of laws holding father's rights more sacred than a young girl's feelings."

"There is passion beneath that prim gray exterior, Clare."

"Intellectual passion, yes."

He smiled. Other kinds as well. Enough of this intellectual talk. Bluestockings had never before attracted him, but a challenging woman did.

"Aye, and as to that, since you're my guest, I prefer a little less formality around here. Since I call you Clare, you shall call me—"

"Don't I get a choice?"

"The devil? My daughter has tender listening ears," he mocked, though Vicky was out of hearing distance, climbing over a stile.

"I prefer formality."

"At Thornhill, too much formality prevails. That's the point. I want Vicky to become accustomed to a looser atmosphere."

"You're turning her into a hoyden. She'll get lost."

"Miss Charlton, you're welcome to come along."

She pulled back. "Me?"

"You ride ponies."

Not for years. Still, she'd vowed to look out for Vicky.

"I—I haven't received my trunk with my riding habit, my gloves, my hat . . ."

"Nonsense. A Dundroma lass doesn't need all that confining clothing. You're only backing out onto a limb . . . which I'm about to saw off."

"How?"

"I'll have a groom lead you. Andrew is expert at leading novices. You shall have our gentlest pony."

Then Vicky came running. "Aunt Clare, you're coming, you're coming. Aren't you?" As Clare shook her head, Vicky hopped around her. "You must come, Aunt Clare. You promised to follow me all places, remember? If I needed you, you said you'd come. I need you."

"You are learning naughty tricks here at Dundroma."

"Nonsense. She is just her father's daughter," put in Lord Strahan.

"And I suppose you're going to lead me up into those cliffs."

"Oh, no, not this first time. We'll stay low down, on the road below the heath. That way I can follow in the pony cart and if you get weary you can ride back with me. It's perfectly safe."

Vicky was looking up hopefully.

"You're risking your daughter's safety." She tried to sound as dignified as possible.

Lord Strahan smiled crookedly. "The martyr, trying to make me feel you care for her more?"

"Aunt Clare, do come."

It was useless, and she knew it. "Very well, but on one condition."

"Which is?"

"That if I get on that pony, Lord Strahan shall submit to having his knee examined by the good physician from London. You'd not be risking a thing. Merely an examination. I, on the other hand, risk losing life and limb getting on one of those ponies. It seems to me a small thing for you to do."

Now it was his turn to concede.

"Please, Papa. I want Clare to come with me on the ponies. I once was examined in my throat, and it didn't hurt a bit."

He nodded slowly. "Very well. A deal it is."

❧Chapter Seven

The groom led a swaybacked pony named Ghost out of the paddock and headed straight for her. Clare backed away. Lord Strahan laughed, and she stopped. Self-control, she reminded herself.

The closer the animal came, the harder she gulped. It was snorting and pawing the ground and shaking a mane of creamy hair while simultaneously swishing its tail. Her single thought was daunting: It might be shorter than a horse, but it was in motion. And they actually expected her to mount it. Not even the sidesaddle eased her qualms.

But she was here on behalf of Thornhill, and she was here to keep a stiff upper lip, to remind Vicky that good manners were paramount. Duty to Thornhill involved smiling even when performing distasteful chores.

In short, she'd ride Ghost, and no one would know she was going to lose minutes off her life and turn from gold to gray before her time. On the contrary, dignity and side-saddles had something in common. She wasn't sure what, but she'd do her best to maintain her prim image.

"Do you know how to mount him?" Lord Strahan asked.

"Of course," she snapped. "Don't you think we've got horses at Thornhill?"

"This is a pony, whereas Percival only indulges in English horseflesh."

"Well, what difference does it make? He's got four feet,

just like a horse, doesn't he?" Smiling gamely, she walked toward the beast.

"Aye," Lord Strahan admitted, "but those feet are closer to the ground. You want to take that into account."

She gave him a sour look. "I noticed that." And gave silent thanks. For the closer his feet were to the ground, the less distance she'd fall.

An hour later she was feeling quite smug about the entire outing. She'd not fallen once, not even slipped from the saddle. She merely got jolted around inside, and her thighs were chafed through her gray serge. But the ride itself was pleasant enough. They made an odd little procession— Andrew and Vicky out front riding side by side when the road allowed, Clare following on her slower mount, and Lord Strahan behind her, wearing a black and white checked cloak, in a pony cart.

It was disconcerting at first knowing he could see her from behind, and she sat back ramrod-straight, the model of the prim English governess. But gradually, lulled by the sway of the pony, she relaxed. After all, except for Lord Strahan, the surroundings were not so different from those at Thornhill Manor. This border country was the same on either side of the kissing statue. Up here at Dundroma the hills also rose steeply and were heather-clad. The River Tyne threaded its way through the valley. Sheep grazed on either side of stone walls and hedgerows. And overhead the sky was the same north country blue as at Thornhill. Outside a humble croft an old woman sat carding wool, and except for larks singing, they saw no one else. Only occasional nettles and brambles, tossing in the breeze, dotted the road.

If Clare concentrated on all of the scenery, she could nearly forget the image of the darkly handsome man who followed behind her. Almost.

Ahead, Vicky and Andrew stopped at a bramble patch for

a rest. It was a perfect place to take a stretch before heading back to the Dundroma paddock.

Vicky plucked a few plump berries from the edge of the road and popped them in her mouth. She shared one with Andrew, then stuck out her tongue—dyed blue—and laughed. The child obviously adored Andrew, that was clear, and Clare had to admit that Dundroma was agreeing with her.

Not that she'd ever confess such feelings to Lord Strahan. She had to keep up her stern, forbidding image. That poetry reading had taught her a valuable lesson. Forbidding and domineering as he might be, Lord Strahan knew his way around a lady, and that made him more dangerous than all the pikestaffs and broadswords in the castle.

Clare, thirsty from the ride, anxious to rid her thoughts of Lord Strahan, slid off the pony and walked toward the roadside brambles. She was feeling rather proud of herself for handling the pony. Smug, even. She turned around to see Lord Strahan's reaction, and too late felt the reins sliding through her hands.

Andrew called out from the edge of the road, but through his mouthful of berries, his message was not clear.

The pony turned, rump first. Clare grabbed for his reins but couldn't reach him. As she leaned toward the pony, fabric tore. Her skirt was caught up in the bramble thorns. Furiously she tugged at her gray serge, but all the time, second by second, the pony's rump moved closer.

The pony's rump grew larger and larger, took up more and more of the view. She screamed. The sound of fabric tearing punctuated another scream. Clare and that rump collided, and Clare was the loser. Immediately, she went flying down—down—down through a prism of prickles. Down and down she crashed, bramble thorns slowing her as they tore through her dress to her skin. That's all she heard—tearing sounds and the humiliating snap of blackberry stems, and her own angry sobs. Her hands and face had taken on a new life—that of a giant pincushion.

There was a moment of stunned silence, then came Vicky's voice. "Aunt Clare!" she hollered over and over. "Don't move, don't move."

As if she could.

Clare wasn't about to move an eyelash. Vicky's voice was so close she guessed she was peering through the brambles. She peeked through one eye to see her charge, mouth blue from berries staring down in horror.

"Get your papa!" she said through gritted teeth. And she hoped he got good and scratched pulling her out of here. "Tell him to bring a knife." The devil carried poetry around in his head. Surely he could come up with a knife.

"Will he need gloves?"

"I don't—care—if—he wears a—crinoline. Get him, Vicky. Now . . . please . . ."

The brambles were like the bars of a cage. Tears of humiliation welled up and ran down her face. To top it off, one plump blackberry hung just an inch above her face, daring her to move so it could fall and land with a splat.

Oh, but she'd changed her mind. The scenery had deceived her. There was a difference on this side of the border. It was cursed. Ruled by a devil who made bad things happen. She had no control over the order of her life, and events swept her along on this side, made her feel she was losing control.

Losing control.

She'd lost it when the pony's rump batted her.

Oh, but she hated this place! And that devil who'd talked her into this pony ride.

And then, as if she'd conjured him up, there he was. Vicky was gone and there was Lord Strahan, chestnut hair tousled, face ever so serious, peering down at her.

"Are you all right, lass?" His voice was the model of innocence.

"You knew the pony would do that," she said. A bramble leaf got caught in her mouth, and she spit it out. "You knew!" she choked.

"Aye, but it doesn't matter what I know. I'm not the one who let go of Ghost at a sloping bramble patch."

"Get me out . . ."

"That'll take a wee bit of time on my part, lass, and some of that Thornhill stiff upper lip on yours."

"Don't jest . . . do something."

He rattled the brambles, and the big plump blackberry wobbled on its stem a second before it landed right between her eyes.

"Sorry, lass, now hang on tight."

She couldn't answer. Just the slightest movement drove brambles right through her thin gray gown. Lord Strahan broke them off and gently lifted them away from the parts of her that were bare. As he worked she held herself rigid, every movement driving thorns through the thin fabric of her gown.

"Owww," she moaned. Tears ran unchecked down her cheeks. She was humiliated.

He paused and looked at her, all traces of teasing gone. He grew serious all of a sudden, and brandished a knife that Andrew handed over to him. "Hold very still now," he said gently. "This may take a few minutes. Hold very still, Aunt Clare."

On top of all else, he lied. It took forever. She began to think if all Scotsmen were this methodical, then it was no wonder tartan was so valued. It must take years to weave in all those tiny stripes.

And to make matters worse, he spoke to her in endearments.

"A wee bit of bruising and a few scratches. But your

fleece is none the worse for wear. Only your gown. You'll fetch the same price when we shear you of that gray thing."

"Stop talking as if I'm a sheep," she snapped.

"Now, lassie, it appears you're in no position this time to be giving me orders, are you?" Deftly he pulled aside one more bramble, snipped it, and tossed it away. "It seems to me it's the pony you should have given orders to."

"I told you I didn't want to come on this ride."

"You'd prefer to return to Thornhill."

She was silent, teeth gritted as much from holding back her angry retort as from the prick of the barbs.

"Just cut me out of here."

"Steady, lass."

One by one he cut away brambles, stopping after each cut to toss them aside. Closer and closer he came. Nearer and nearer his hands came to rescuing her. Another bramble was slashed and another. He worked swiftly and without any sign of pain to himself. A trickle of blood dripped from his thumb onto her bodice and then he peeled away one last bramble and reached down to lift her up. The devil of Dundroma was going to get his hands on her proper and stiffly corseted figure.

She didn't care. He reached down, ripped her skirt away from a last few bramble thorns, and then he reached into the brambles and lifted her into his arms and out. After setting her down, he held her in his arms while crooning soft things in her ear. Things that sounded comforting. While he whispered soothing words, his hands were busy plucking bits and pieces of brambles from her hair, then he turned her around and pulled one from her back.

She realized his own arms bore traces of blood, were more scratched then her own.

"One more." His soft burr enveloped her.

"Does it hurt, Aunt Clare?"

Lord Strahan answered for his daughter. "Of course it

hurts. Get the pony cart. Bring him here by the reins, so your aunt can ride back."

"No, I'll walk."

"I don't think so," he said.

"No—" His thumb touched her mouth then, and she went numb. Numb except for the touch of his skin, its tender touch as he dabbed at her lower lip. "No—"

"Hold still, you're bleeding. A tiny scratch just to the side here. Don't flinch. I could have my way with an English governess if I wanted. But I don't. I don't want blood dripping on my pony."

"I don't care about your pony."

"Aye, he was wicked to bump you into the brambles. No oats for him tonight."

Alec was at pains to retain his patience and composure both. As he dabbed at her lips, he studied her face— porcelain skin and rosebud mouth, and enormous eyes of a blue-green. Not so different from Cecilia in coloring. But smaller, more fragile. A scared little bird. A wren. The gray gown was torn and ruined. He ought to be glad and hope she'd decide no child was worth this trouble. Then she'd go back to Thornhill, and he'd be rid of her.

But she stirred a tenderness in him. An emotion long dormant flickered, tried to touch the darkness in him. Abruptly he handed her a handkerchief. "Here, you blot it."

"Where?"

God help him, but she was too naive to know a man couldn't stand like this blotting lips without a natural response. And she was English, like Cecilia. That meant forbidden. He'd never let another English lass, especially one from Thornhill, under his skin. For the Charltons were like those brambles that he'd just pulled out of her. Worse. They might be pretty to look at, but they got under your skin, and when they did that, a man ended up hurt. And healing took forever.

Briskly he guided her hand to her own lips. "There." He tugged the hem of her skirt away from the last brambles. He wasn't gentle. The dress was too far gone for that, and good riddance.

He turned away. "Come along, or we'll have the entire castle thinking my daughter is lost."

Clare had too many sensations running through her to know what to think—pain, numbness, longing, the memory of this man's touch. Awareness. It happened more suddenly than the fall.

But she'd never let him know. The world had plenty of men. Just because her husband had never made her melt with desire did not mean this man was anything special. He was the devil of Dundroma and melting women was sport to him like shooting so many grouse.

He looked back over his shoulder to where she stood, immobile. "Come along."

She stood there, too hurt to move, too stubborn.

"You took liberties when I was in a vulnerable position."

He turned and faced her. "Aye, true enough. I warned you that you'd be dealing with a borderer. You don't think you can extract promises from a borderer and not expect me to behave like a borderer in return."

"If I did, I was optimistic in my thinking. I misjudged you."

"You wanted a borderer's promise and you got it, but you have to take what else goes with it."

Over his shoulder he gave his daughter swift instructions about bringing the pony cart closer. Clare didn't care if she paddled back to the castle in a boat. She only wanted to get away, and for that she was totally at Lord Strahan's mercy.

"Papa, give Aunt Clare your cloak. Her gown is ripped," Vicky called.

He did as his daughter bid, and wrapped Clare in the black and white checked cloak that was distinctive of the

Dundroma shepherds. Without warning, he took her hands in his. Gently, he pulled out another thorn from between her thumb and index finger, then helped her into the pony cart.

It was at least a mile back to the castle, but he limped the entire way, leading the pony cart on the smoothest part of the dirt road. Vicky and Andrew rode on ahead, at Lord Strahan's behest, to find where "that bothersome physician from London is prowling about and bid him be waiting in the parlor."

"I'll be fine." Even in pain, a governess did not complain. She'd steeled herself through twelve long years to ignore bodily ailments and put appearances first. For Vicky's sake.

"The physician will decide that, lass."

"Th-thank you."

"You'd have done the same for me, would you not?"

"I—I'm not sure."

She wasn't sure of anything. She was sore and blackberry-stained and torn and anything but prim and in control. And most of all, through all the pain, she kept hearing like an echo somewhere deep inside her the sound of Lord Strahan's voice soft in her ear.

> *"Or like the Borealis race,*
> *That flit ere you can point their place;*
> *Or like the rainbow's lovely form,*
> *Vanishing amid the storm . . ."*

He was reciting Burns again. Soothing her with love poems while she reacted with utter loss of control.

She knew "Tam o' Shanter," though she'd never give him the satisfaction of telling him so. And she knew its last line too.

The de'il had business on his hand.

Oh, yes, he was a devil.

And after this humiliation, he'd not get the upper hand. Not ever again.

She forgot, when she made that oath, about her tattered, blackberry-stained gown. The gray serge would be rejected by the ragman. She had no choice upon arrival at the castle but to discard it. Once again, she had to don the garish raspberry gown. Either that or lock herself in her room until her trunk arrived from Thornhill, and Adele could be taking till the Restoration of the Stuarts to pack the thing.

She chose to stay in her bedchamber. She sat on the edge of the bed in just her corset and pantaloons, and with a cloth dipped into the icy water of her pitcher, she dabbed at the scratches on her hands and arms.

Lord Strahan pounded on the door. "Come out and show yourself to Dr. Wilmot."

"I'm not showing myself to any man, physician or not," she called back.

"No one will laugh at a few scratches."

"I have no dress."

"You have the gown from Isobel."

"If you think I'm wearing some paramour's gown—"

"You flatter me. It's not easy coercing mistresses up to Dundroma, and Isobel is my best friend's widow."

"Go away, before the servants hear such disgraceful talk from Vicky's father."

He pounded louder. "And you think the servants at Thornhill see nothing ill-advised about the Charltons' behavior?"

"At least they're quiet when they argue. Go away."

"Come out, Clare, or I'll take an ax to the door. The Dundroma servants are not easily shocked. They'll take it in their stride and guess I've merely taken a fancy to your bed—"

The door swung open and she stuffed her gray serge

gown in his face, then slammed it shut and leaned against it. Fancy *that*.

An hour later, she was shivering and able to think. It was Vicky's best interests that counted here. And so she dressed in the dreadful raspberry gown. She smoothed down the skirt, trying not to feel like a tropical bird that should have flown the nest by now, and after patting her hair, she glided down the dark staircase to find Dr. Wilmot. The examination was brief, and before she could run back upstairs to hide, Mrs. Drummond blocked her way. "Lord Strahan would see you, Miss Charlton."

At once, her heart pattered a bit faster.

"He didn't say what he wanted. Doubtless to ask what the physician said about your scratches."

Clare doubted that. She couldn't say what he wanted, but one line of Burns echoed over and over in her head.

The de'il had business on his hand.

And so did the dark laird of the north. Steeling herself for more banter, she lifted her chin and headed for the parlor.

He'd be sitting in the dim room, walking stick on his lap, staring back at all those glassy-eyed stag heads, and feeling sorry for himself.

She paused in the doorway, gaze automatically going to the fireplace. He sat there, back to her, hair tousled and glinting reddish by the firelight.

"I'm glad you decided to don the gown," he said without turning.

"It's annoying how you ask me questions before I'm even in the room. How did you know it was me and not a servant—or Vicky?"

"Come in, Clare." As she strode over to him, he explained. "You see, everyone has a distinctive footstep. Mine is accented by the walking stick. Yours is hesitant, as if you were finding your way about. A few steps, and pause. A few steps and pause. A maid would have come right in and bobbed, and Vicky would have ran and skidded to a stop."

She stopped in front of him. His gaze was on the walking stick, playing with the tiger's ivory head. But suddenly he looked up, straight at the gown of raspberry.

"It suits you. I said it before and I don't give compliments lightly, nor do I give much stock to the rules of fashion. Nothing in your trunk will suit you like that. Now then, did Dr. Wilmot give you some salve for your bramble scratches?"

Clare had seen him in the kitchen. "Yes, thank you, he did, and they shall heal." At once she turned the tables on him. "And you? You promised to let him examine your— you." Best not to mention his knee by name, because then she'd drop her defenses and look at it, and from there it was but a short look up to the rest of him.

"You're afraid to look at me, now?"

The devil could read her mind. "No," she lied. She turned her gaze fully on his. "You promised."

"Aye, as I promised, I allowed an examination, but alas, the good doctor cannot heal me."

"Of course he can't. But he can tell the surgeons—"

"There is a vast difference between what physicians do and what surgeons do, Clare. You know that as well as I. Physicians don't have the means to fix me. And while these surgeons up in Edinburgh might know how to dispense chloroform and slice open a man or take out a bone or hack it off, they're grave-robbing charlatans."

"If you gave them the chance, perhaps they would prove you wrong. It takes time for new ideas to gain respectability," she argued.

"Ah, the wee bluestocking is at it again. Wanting to mend everything in society. From father's custody of children to the social standing of surgeons. You are truly wasted at Thornhill."

"Not if I've taught Vicky the same open-minded thinking."

He thought that over while silently staring at her, his blue eyes boring into her, melting her.

"Well, you can't have a double standard, milord. If you want the child to learn freedom, that should extend to her mind, and who's to say that because I kept her in a schoolroom these years, I did not open her mind? You, on the other hand, are limited to physical activity in your curriculum."

"I am a physical man, which makes my present predicament doubly hard. In any case, Dr. Wilmot could do nothing but poke around a bit and stir up the pain. As you remind me, he must tell the surgeons of his findings before they'll even take me as a practice case." He gave a short laugh. "I hoped to go down in history as a great general. Now my chance at immortality comes down to no better than a grave robber's corpse."

"I would expect you to defend anything Scottish, milord."

"Except surgeons. No, it would take more convincing than nationality to lead me to the knife."

"You surprise me then, milord. I took you for a man of courage."

Slowly his gaze moved up the gown. He paused and studied the scratch by her mouth. "And you surprise me, Clare—when I least expect it."

Before she knew it, he'd stood, limped over to her, and touched the skin just below the tiny scar. "I would say your activities today were almost hoydenish. You're setting a bad example, something I would never expect from you."

She moved back out of reach. "I'm not. I only went because I was afraid for Vicky."

Again, he advanced on her. "It's yourself you're afraid for, not Vicky. It's yourself and your attraction to me."

"Pity your injury did not break your conceit."

"And you should never have made up stories about that silly statue at the border. You were teaching my daughter to be prissish, Clare, and I don't approve."

"Wh-what do you mean?"

"You know very well what I mean . . . teaching her that if a young lady kisses a man, she'll turn to stone."

"What would you like her taught at age twelve?"

"That kissing is natural and pleasurable."

"She's too young."

"Agreed, but that doesn't mean she has to believe it's something to be feared or endured. Otherwise, she'll grow up to be a cold wife in her wedding chamber."

"Your teaching methods are too radical, unorthodox."

"They're natural. Scots lasses don't walk around looking at men as creatures who will turn them to stone. And I don't want my daughter to have such fears about the laddies, hence there is to be a new story about the border statue."

"And you're going to share it with me."

"That would be best—so we can keep our stories straight and be in accord about what my daughter learns."

"What do you want her to know?"

"About kissing?"

"About the statue. I have no intention of telling Vicky anything about kissing."

"Better nothing at all than this myth about English women turning to stone when kissed and bewitched by Dundroma men."

She backed into the stone walls of the parlor, right beneath a stag's head, and he loomed over her, his walking stick touching her leg through her dress.

He gave her a mocking look. "I suspect your wedding night was a shock to you, Clare."

"You've no business asking private questions. Have you no shame?"

"Borderers may give their word and hold high their honor, but shame is unknown to us."

She tried to dart away, but his walking stick came up to block her way. And then he caught her chin between his thumb and forefinger. Her heart was like a wild bird in her chest.

"Milord, tell me about the statue."

His words came out as a whisper. "I'll show you and then you tell me what you're going to teach her about that statue."

Ever so slowly, his head dipped down toward her, and his lips touched hers. Just a gentle kiss, and then he backed off an inch. "Are you turning to stone, Aunt Clare?" he said in a husky voice.

On the contrary, Clare was melting. Though he stood as motionless as a statue, inside she was filled with sensations that could only be described as warm and liquid. Warm enough that just his male scent, the husky timbre of his voice close to her, would dissolve her from the inside out, and she wasn't sure what her body would do.

He leaned down to kiss her again. And again, gently. The merest brush of his lips on hers. Her legs went weak. She pushed against his chest and ducked away. His walking stick went rattling across the cobblestones.

She was tempted to leave him helpless, but picked it up and handed it to him from a safe distance, ivory tiger head aimed at him.

His hand closed about the tiger head.

"Tell me, Clare, please," he pressed, "just to satisfy my curiosity—are you stone at this moment?"

She didn't answer. All she could do was shake her head, for she was afraid to tell him how warm he'd made her, how mellow, how much longing he'd conjured up.

He came close and touched her lower lip with the pad of

his thumb. "I'll tell you what you are then—soft and pliant, like a spring flower ready to bloom, overdue to bloom."

She ducked away from him, and left him propped there on his walking stick. "You win. I was wrong to teach Vicky fanciful lessons. We shall confine ourselves to more scholarly matters." She gathered up the skirt of her gown and turned, prepared to flee.

"Clare," he called back, "it was a Dundroma laird who built that statue and it was to warn English women off because too many were coming up here, throwing themselves at us."

"You are revising history."

He smiled. "Are we done with the subject of kissing then?"

"Forever." But as she stalked from the room in her raspberry dress, she knew she'd never, ever forget the touch of his lips on hers. Oh, but this kissing was a dangerously sweet business. And once again, she cursed the gown for making her lose control.

Through her haze of pleasant numbness, a servant's words drifted in to her. "The lady's trunk has arrived on Dundroma territory."

Her trunk. Saved from wearing this garish dress another minute. She could hardly wait to get back to gray or black.

She came out into the great hall and looked around: no trunk. "Where is it?" she demanded. "Where?"

"Right on the border. The Thornhill servants set it just this side of the border statue."

Of course. Because of the legend no servant—male or female—from Thornhill would venture any farther.

She ran upstairs for her cloak. She couldn't wait to get her hands on a fresh piece of gray serge. Some nondescript color that would allow her to blend back in with the shadows. A gown that would allow her to regain her control.

❧ Chapter Eight

"Can you hear me, Percival?"

After three hours of silent waiting in the coach, Adele Charlton decided it might help to pass the time if she gave in first and spoke to her husband. Besides, she rarely ventured up here to the mysterious kissing statue, and it made her nervous. Percival might have his faults, but he possessed a gentleman's protectiveness. She clutched the rope of pearls at her neck for courage.

"Can you?"

"I seem to have no choice, Adele, for you are determined to give me something to hear. What brings on this change of heart?"

Adele Charlton peered anxiously out the window and then across the coach at her husband. Percival refused to meet her gaze. "This is an affront to our dignity sitting hiding behind the bend in the road like common reivers."

Percival thought that statement over for about a half hour and then replied, "Don't you think, Adele, it's rather late in life to worry about dignity? Besides, for my granddaughter, I can lower my standards of company, considerably."

"Do you think Dr. Wilmot's idea will work?"

He put down his field glasses and turned back to where she sat like a new-sprung crocus stem, ramrod-stiff in a cloak of green. "In the old days," he began stiffly, "a march warden would call the disputing parties to a mutually agreed on site to forge a compromise. That's all we're doing—a bit of playacting to flush out our granddaughter. What have we to lose?"

"Vicky, if this goes awry. And our reputations."

Percival lifted the field glasses again and aimed them at the kissing statue at whose feet sat a battered trunk. "Reputation is a cold bedfellow, Adele. It does not skip about, or beg stories read, or laugh at an old man's tales."

"What do you mean?" Adele's voice grew alarmed.

"Lately I've been reconsidering the importance of our appearances."

"Whatever do you mean? The Charlton family is an institution, a model of appearances."

"What is an institution," he muttered, "compared with our granddaughter's happiness?"

"Happiness?" It was not a subject on which he'd ever spoken. "Percival, are you turning sentimental? I'm not certain I want that."

Silence. She couldn't stand to bare her feelings. It wasn't done. Percival couldn't change on her now. She'd rather he stayed angry and never spoke to her again. The best way to deal with this was to change the subject . . . and quickly.

"We've sat here so long. Perhaps Clare never received the message." There, feelings were swept under the coach again, and the air was clear and comfortable, the subject impersonal.

"She'll be along. The worry is whether she'll bring Victoria . . . I believe we can trust Dr. Wilmot, and if he's wrong and we don't gather Victoria back into our bosom, then we've lost nothing but a bit of dignity."

"A great deal of dignity if any of our neighbors should come riding up this way."

His voice grew uncharacteristically irritated. "For heaven's sake, I want for once in our lives to put Victoria first and dignity second. You certainly put dignity second when you deigned to accept my hand in marriage."

"Well, are you suggesting I had no choices? Percival, after nearly forty years, surely you've gotten over this notion I married you to save my dignity?"

He laughed abruptly. "I may have been last choice among your suitors, but I was never naive. I married you, Adele, to spare your reputation. You had no alternatives and I wanted a comely wife. It was as simple as that. An arrangement of convenience. So are our dealings with Dr. Wilmot. For mutual benefit." He glared out the window.

Adele was weary of having the cold, raw facts thrown in her face—ever since—since Alec Douglas returned. Yes, that barbarian's behavior was affecting Percival—deeply.

Adele Charlton was effectively silenced. Percival was upset over his granddaughter—more so than she'd realized. He had insisted they plant that trunk at the border as a decoy to lure Victoria back to them. He was trying to prove to her that he could perform as adequately as his reiver ancestors. That's all. And she felt remorse for her worry and for her words.

Always, her entire life, Adele had felt remorse for words spoken in haste.

Twining her rope of pearls about a finger, she spent another half hour considering her husband's longstanding accusation. She supposed she'd deserved it.

Yes, she conceded, she had married Percival solely to save her injured dignity. But now that she thought of it, she did care more for Victoria than she did her own dignity . . . not that a body went around announcing such things . . . it was rather "north of the border" to be so sentimental, and while it was one thing to share a border in common, she'd never go so far as to claim she shared sentimental leanings. Not out loud, for heaven's sake.

Not even to Percival with whom she'd not exchanged a

peck on the lips since their wedding day nearly forty years past.

It was enough to have started speaking to him again.

Vicky ran across the castle courtyard, hair flying in the breeze. She flew by an apple tree, for she didn't want to climb it. She had more important business on her mind.

Andrew. Talking to him alone, without her prim governess and watchful papa tagging along.

With Aunt Clare dragged into the castle by her papa to see Dr. Wilmot, all was in hand. Her papa had even gone so far as to give her instructions to play outside while he saw to her governess.

This was an unexpected boon. Vicky headed straight for the stables, where Andrew would be brushing down the ponies. This was her chance to get alone with him, without appearing, as her grandmother was always saying, unladylike. For of course Andrew would want to know how Aunt Clare was faring.

Good luck. He stood in the stable, brushing Ghost and Macduff. The ponies' coats gleamed handsomely, but not even they could outshine Andrew in Vicky's eyes.

Careful to remain silent, Vicky stood in the doorway, admiring Andrew. He was tall and fair of hair and had a profile like a Viking. Oh, but he was a braw lad, as the maids said. Then he slipped Ghost a forbidden handful of oats.

"Ghost isn't to have his ration of oats."

Andrew jerked around, the handful of oats pulled back. But when he saw who stood there—her, Vicky—his face relaxed. "Oh, it's just you." And he turned back to give the pony its treat.

"What are you doing?" It was obvious, but there wasn't much else to ask.

"Don't you have dolls to play with?"

"They're back at Thornhill, all packed away."

"Well, I'm going to play at dice in the stables with the grooms," he warned.

"Well, can't I play too?"

She picked up another brush and joined him in grooming Ghost.

Andrew stopped his own brushing and stared down at her as if she were a gnat, but inside Vicky melted at his stare. If he wanted her to be a gnat she'd not mind—not for a few minutes.

"Can't I?" she gently prodded, heart thumping. "If you're worried that it might vex my governess or your mother . . ."

Andrew knelt and threw a practice roll of the dice on the stable floor. "My mother," he said at last, "wants me to occupy you so you'll stay away from Lord Strahan while she's here visiting." He shook the dice and rolled a pair of threes. "Nothing will vex my mother—except me not keeping you occupied. But I'll not play at dolls into the bargain. So we play dice."

"What are you talking about?" Vicky was well and truly baffled.

"If you don't know, you're too young for an explanation."

"I'm not so young. She wants to kiss my father, doesn't she?"

Andrew looked up, dice captive in his hand.

He shrugged. "What kind of question is that?"

"Aunt Clare says there are only two kinds of questions— the kind that should be answered promptly and politely and the kind that are best ignored."

Andrew rolled the dice. A pair of sixes.

"Aunt Clare told me that at the kissing statue."

"Stuff and nonsense," Andrew muttered.

Vicky abandoned Ghost and came to kneel across from Andrew where she could stare at his fine Viking profile, his tousled fair hair. "Aunt Clare knows all about the statue. Don't you?"

"I don't much care."

"You mean about kissing."

"I never said that."

"Well, have you ever kissed a lass?"

He kept his head bent over his dice. "Aye," he said at length, "of course I have. You're a mite young to be asking so many questions. Are all Thornhill lasses inquisitive like you?"

"How should I know? Besides, half of me is really from Dundroma like my father."

His look was cautious. "My mother never tells me about kissing, except to say it's not polite for a gentleman to kiss and tell, nor for a lady either."

Charlotte had not mentioned that rule.

"Why not?"

"It's just not . . ." A dull flush stole up Andrew's face, adding to his appeal, and he got up to leave. Vicky tossed her hair and followed him out of the stable. She'd been hoping she'd find a chink in his armor, and the topic of kissing was it.

"Not what?"

"Not a public thing. It's private, I suppose."

"You suppose? You said you knew. Was it a kiss on the lips?"

He shrugged casually. "I told you, gentlemen don't tell, and if you're a lady, you won't ask."

And with that, he rode awhile in the paddock while Vicky stared at him in longing. She didn't want to be a lady. She wanted a kiss from Andrew.

Alec gritted his teeth against the pain, ignored the orders of at least ten physicians on two continents, and dug his knees into the flanks of a horse. He had to ride and ride fast.

He took the best mount in the stable and cut across the moors on a path only the old-time reivers had used.

He had to get to the kissing statue before Clare Charlton did.

Or else risk forfeiting his daughter again. Oh, but he'd been angry when young Andrew had told him that Clare had taken Vicky with her on the coach ride to claim her trunk.

"Whatever for?"

Young Andrew, unwise in the ways of Thornhill, had not a single suggestion. But Alec at once knew two possible answers to his own question: Either she was using the trunk as a chance to take his daughter and escape Dundroma, or else she was innocently taking his daughter along for the ride and the Charltons, hoping she'd do just that, had deliberately planted the trunk at the place of every young lass's fancy—that damnable kissing statue. If the latter were the case, they'd kidnap Vicky and . . . well, it wouldn't happen, for he'd beat Clare to the trunk.

And he'd not compromise on the matter of his daughter. He put his heels to the horse's flanks again, while the wind whipped his coat out and tossed his hair. Above him, the hills of heather were but a blur.

Faster and faster.

He had to keep Vicky.

And Clare . . . Clare . . .

Deceptive wench.

Plotting escape.

Clare.

Soft in his arms.

Lips petal soft.

Passion banked.

No.

He slowed his speed. Ahead, he could see in the distance the lichen-covered statue. Fanciful work of some love-besotted Charlton.

And his thoughts were running away from him faster than the horse.

Pain edged into his thoughts and with it brought sanity.

No English governess was going to cause him to whip a horse into a frenzy.

No English lass. No woman ever.

For that reason alone, his shattered knee served a purpose—a tangible reminder of what women brought to you. Pain. Pain that could not be healed.

No, he'd come only for Vicky, and he'd best keep his wits so he could be rational.

And he guided his horse through a cleft in the rocks of which only Dundroma men knew the dark secrets.

Alec waited behind an outcropping of rocks until coach wheels clattered on the road. His coach.

His daughter.

And her governess.

And then the expedition from Dundroma rounded the bend. At first sight of her grandparents' coach, Vicky burst out.

"Aunt Clare," Vicky called out. "Isn't this fine good fortune? My grandparents have come to see us pick up your trunk?"

She picked up her skirts to run, then stopped. Alec pulled out of the shadowy brush along the road.

"Papa!"

"I say it's a damn coincidence that's too good to be true."

"Lord Strahan," Clare cautioned. "Put your borderland suspicions aside. Good manners call for her to greet her grandparents."

Greet. That would depend on whether she had in mind a formal exchange of words or something like an embrace.

He asked.

"The Charltons are a formal family. But I beg your leave to allow Vicky get close enough to shake their hands."

He considered Clare's request. A regular march warden she was or could have been, three hundred years past.

"Very well."

And if they did stuff Vicky into their coach, they'd not get far. He supposed it would be a kind gesture to allow a greeting. He nodded and Vicky walked over to the Charltons. All of her earlier spontaneity had vanished. The spontaneity he enjoyed so. The part of Vicky that reminded him of Douglases.

But it had nothing to do with him or his forbidding words. It was the Charltons who caused Vicky's spirit to close up, like a flower folding up in the shade. That's what she reminded him of. All the more evidence why she belonged with him. Besides the weight of the entire British court system.

Adele Charlton held out her hand and shook Vicky's. Typical of the frosty old girl. Percival held out his next, then suddenly knelt down and, holding out his arms, pulled Vicky into his embrace.

Alec watched, swallowing hard, as Vicky hugged her grandfather. A Charlton.

Clare turned to Alec. The glance she gave him was forbidding. Daring him to interfere. A short embrace, he guessed, would do no harm, and perhaps soften the Charltons to his position.

"What are you doing here, Lord Strahan?" she said to him with a trace of sarcasm. "Have you come to help me with my trunk?"

"This, Aunt Clare, looks like much more than a trunk waiting for you." His voice was withering. She deserved it, the traitorous little wench.

"I knew nothing," she whispered.

"Then how do you account for them?" he whispered back, indicating the Charltons. "You expect me to believe you did not know they'd be here?"

"Yes. Why would you not believe me?"

"I have three hundred years of reivers in my family to set the example. Also because you brought Vicky. What were you planning to do—hand her over and then return with your trunk to Dundroma to put me off the scent?"

She blinked as comprehension sank in. "You think I would deceive you like that? After all I've said about the emotions of children? I would never have Vicky yanked back and forth across this border. She's not a tug-of-war rope. Nor a croquet ball. And certainly no reiver's prize. She is a child, with feelings. . . .

"Who told you of our expedition?" Clare walked right up to Alec, and the horse would have skittered had he not tied the reins to a bush and limped to meet her halfway.

"Andrew," he said, unaccountably glad to see the way the way the wind ruffled wisps of dark blond away from her face. Against the colorful dress, her eyes glowed with anger and were a lovely shade of hazel. Almost green. The color had never been higher in her cheeks.

She was the bewitching one. He dragged his gaze away and sought out his daughter.

Vicky stood by the statue staring from her grandparents to her father. The Charltons and the laird of Dundroma stared each other down.

"The child stays on my side of the border, you deceitful old reiver. Your plan almost worked. Clare was desperate enough for prim dresses to come for the trunk. And brought my daughter. But you forgot about me. How good I am at scenting a trap. You had a greeting, but you shall not have her. She belongs to me. She is mine."

"Lord Strahan, there's no need to be angry," Clare cautioned. "You'll upset Vicky."

"Douglas," spoke up Percival, "we're meeting here on neutral territory to ask when to expect our granddaughter back. You can't take up fatherhood this late in life."

"You're a fine one to talk . . . She's not coming back."
Percival Charlton slumped slightly.

It was Adele who spoke up. "Of course she is. Why, look at her flushed cheeks. She's not coming down with a fever, is she?"

Actually, thought Clare, Vicky had never been healthier—far healthier than all the years she'd spent confined in stuffy rooms eating bland food like suet and bread.

If Clare was honest with herself, she'd admit that Alec Douglas's way with raising children was the healthier. The child had positively bloomed. And not just physically; there was an inner glow as well.

And to everyone's surprise, it was Vicky who prevented any arguing on the subject. "I want to stay."

Adele Charlton's jaw dropped. "Whatever for? You'd have to be bewitched to stay up there."

Vicky smiled, a grown-up smile. Secretive and more like a young lady than a girl, Alec thought, then dismissed the thought as fancy. She was only twelve. Well, twelve and a half.

"I'm not done getting to know Dundroma," she said in a tone of voice more reassuring than expected for her years.

"And you say you're well?"

"As healthy as a stag in summer," Alec replied.

"Has she had bad dreams?"

"Not that I've heard of."

"Has she missed her home?"

"She's enjoyed exploring Dundroma."

No matter what they asked, Lord Strahan and Vicky put the best light on it.

"Andrew is teaching me about ponies and India and fishing."

"Andrew? A playmate?" This from her grandfather.

She shook her head and explained his connection to the widow Fraser.

Her grandparents exchanged concerned looks and then turned as one to Clare, their gazes fastening on her scratched face. "You, on the other hand, appear to have been dragged through a loch by the kelpies."

"Mere scratches. I've been trying to keep up with Vicky, and she sets a fast pace."

Vicky continued to argue her case. "You mustn't worry. It's grand fun, and there's no green ghost lady, but I don't want to leave. I can't yet. Papa is good to me in his fashion, just as you are. Besides," she whispered to her grandfather, "if I stay, I shall convince him to let me come back. If you take me by force, it will only anger him and he'll behave like a reiver. Aunt Clare says he was born three centuries too late, and it will take time for him to get used to modern ways of treating children. I shall help him grow accustomed to those modern ways."

Adele blinked in astonishment. It was a new way of thinking—to put a person, especially a child, ahead of one's station in life.

"I was raised where children were seen and not heard and such talk would be blasphemy."

"Times are changing. Should not your granddaughter's feelings count for something?"

This from Clare. In her garish gown, she was a bold woman.

Adele thought this over. "I don't know," she said truthfully.

Percival decided it. "You have a right to know your father. And I can't deny you look well cared for. But don't forget your poor old grieving grandpa."

"Percival, don't be maudlin," Adele whispered.

He ignored her. "I've missed you, Victoria Douglas. But what must be must be."

"Will you stay and hear my father's version of the legend of the kissing statue?" Vicky asked.

This was beyond the pale. Percival sputtered and cleared his throat; Adele looked flustered beyond belief. In their decades of marriage, the pair had never once exchanged a public kiss, never mind any other displays of affection; to even talk of kissing in public was plebeian. What Percival had never grasped down there in staid Thornhill was that a man could both kiss a lass and juggle raising a child at the same time.

"Well?"

"Humph. Poppycock and nonsense. We shall leave then. Your aunt Clare has her trunk." Percival harrumphed and hemmed and hawed. He looked up. "I commend you, Douglas, on having put that bloom in her cheeks; I expect it will still be there when I next see her."

"The advantage of Dundroma ponies."

"That's all?"

"Of course. Good fresh air. And an excellent pony. What else do you want to know? If you can have your governess back?"

The grandfather and the father glared at each other. Unspoken was the thought that Vicky would never return to Thornhill.

"We have no need of her now," Adele said with a crashing lack of tact. "Our granddaughter surely needs her more."

For that, Alec felt surprisingly glad.

His gaze locked with Clare's. Her eyes were swimming with tears. "You'll stay?"

She nodded her head. "If you'll ride back with me. It would be an honor to have you help me carry my trunk back to Dundroma."

In five minutes his own horse was tied to the back of the coach, and Vicky, Clare, and Alec, the devil of Dundroma, headed back to the castle. Alec felt unaccountably pleased with himself. He'd averted a raid by the Charltons, and he had Vicky with him still.

And Clare.

Clare in her gown of raspberry pink.

"Thank you for helping to plead my case," he said.

"I did it for Vicky, not you. And now that my trunk is here, life will be so much easier."

He couldn't suppress an ironic smile. "Why do I have the feeling that mine will be quite the opposite?"

No answer was needed. It was enough to have her gaze up into his eyes. Bewitching green they were, and he almost wished he were a devil.

In the Thornhill coach, Percival stared at Adele, and she at him. "Do you believe the devil of Dundroma?" she asked.

"Too agreeable. All of them. Something's caught Vicky's fancy, else she'd have come home with us, straightaway."

"We could go up there for a reprisal raid and see for ourselves."

"Never." Percival's voice was gruff. "Do you think I'll stoop to the level of a Douglas?"

"Well," Adele sniffed, "if we're lucky, Isobel Fraser will snare Lord Strahan for a husband, and she'll not want a hand-me-down child, and then all this talk of British courts and a father's rights will mean nothing more than a feather in the wind. Rather timely of Malcolm to die when he did and leave Isobel free."

"Ever the practical one about matchmaking, aren't you, Adele? In this case, I hope you're right."

❧Chapter Nine

It was treachery! The worst betrayal!

The trunk contained nothing Clare needed. She'd been deceived, and by her own kin, her own mother-in-law.

Nothing . . . not one gown suitable for a governess. Why, Clare had several perfectly good gowns in the armoire in her bedchamber at Thornhill, and Adele had ignored them. She'd forgotten that Clare had left Thornhill with only the clothes on her back. Or else didn't care.

One by one Clare tossed the useless contents onto the floor—books on the history of England, another ear flattener, extra pantaloons for Vicky . . . All useless here at Dundroma because Lord Strahan would not allow his daughter to wile away good summer days in the schoolroom. Nor put her in any confining garments. Including English pantaloons.

Clare sat in the middle of the floor and despair washed over her. Books. Watercolors. Embroidery thread. Even dolls Vicky had long ago outgrown, including the once favorite oat-filled doll of cloth. Then there was the formal clothing for Vicky. Smocked frocks with fashionable satin ribbons. A spare nightdress. Hairbrushes. Stockings. Writing paper with the Thornhill monogram.

And not one article of clothing for Clare.

Only a letter.

On the very top of the contents had lain an envelope with her name written in Adele's spidery handwriting.

"Dear Clare . . . So many of Vicky's dearest treasures and clothes had to be left behind. We were fortunate to squeeze in this much. Naturally there was no room for anything of yours, but you probably don't require much more than a spare cloak. I'm sure one of the maids at Dundroma has something you can use . . ."

Wadding the unctuous letter, Clare stared in disbelief at the empty trunk as if she'd missed something.

Just one dark, prim gown would have been enough. Not even a crinoline. Just a gown.

Instead . . . this. Useless. All of it. So incredibly thoughtless of Adele. Writing her as if she, Clare, were no better than a servant. Less than that. Even servants were clothed.

For the first time in twelve years, Clare had left the safe haven of Thornhill, her only home, and found that no one worried over her. What was she to Adele? Clearly dispensable, judging by the contents of this mercy trunk. Quick tears stung her eyes, and she dashed them away. No, she couldn't turn soft. It's just that she felt so alone, so uncared for. Now that she thought on it, Adele had not had a word of sympathy for Clare's scratches—just a cluck of annoyance. That was Adele's way, and years of frustration at living in her mother-in-law's shadow shot up to the surface. A governess deserved better than a servant, especially a governess related to the family.

Yet, for Vicky's sake, she had to quell the pain. Had to maintain control.

It was this impossible audacious gown that was the cause of her turmoil. She needed something subdued, her usual dark governess colors. But they were back in Thornhill, lined up neatly in her armoire. Forgotten.

Adele was heartless.

Clare had allowed her to be.

If she were at Thornhill, she would give Adele a piece of her mind—even at the risk of her post.

No, she would never risk being sent away from Vicky. For the child's sake.

Logic led her to another solution. She was now at Dundroma, not Thornhill.

And since the master and mistress of Thornhill had given her nothing, she would have to swallow her pride and do the unthinkable: go to the devil of Dundroma and throw herself on his mercy.

But not garbed like a raspberry tart. First, she'd do something about this garish dress, for when confronting the devil of Dundroma, she had to maintain control.

"Miss Clare," came Mrs. Drummond's voice from outside her door. "You're summoned to see the master."

Clare would be summoned by no one at Dundroma. "Please," she called out. "Tell the master I'm indisposed." And that was that. She was in no condition to meet anyone, and the master was no exception.

After all, she was standing in her corset and pantaloons. She could play one of Macbeth's witches, she decided, as she stirred away, watching bracken roots and alder bark color the water. As far as the maids knew, Clare was taking a bath. Whoever collected the tub later was going to have plenty to gossip about in the servants' quarters. She could hear it now. *The water was black as tar as it was after the governess had her bath. Why, you'd think she'd been rolling in the dirt lanes. But those Thornhill gentry got no right to put on airs when their bathwater's muddier than our'n.*

If there was one wise servant in the lot, they'd recognize the color of the water for what it was: dye. Clare had taken Vicky for an outing to "inspect" the flora of Dundroma and collected every root and bark sample she could lay her hands on.

Natural dyes used for coloring Dundroma tartans would
do quite nicely to change the color of the horrid gown.

She set down the long stick with which she stirred. Time
to test the waters. She dipped the hem of the gown into the
tub, swished it around and pulled it out. The fabric was a
fine light wool, and the part she'd dipped had soaked up the
dye beautifully. The fistful of hem had in mere minutes
turned a dingy brown. Wonderful. Sedate. Prim.

And above all, a safe color. Without further hesitation,
she stuffed the entire gown into the tub.

Mrs. Drummond returned moments later and rapped
again.

"His lordship would know why," she called.

"I have no gown to wear . . . I've washed my solitary
garment." That would forestall any need to see him.

Again, Mrs. Drummond departed.

Moments later Clare lifted the gown out of the tub and
inspected its new color. The dress hung limply like a
bleached fish. Well . . . it wasn't exactly black nor brown,
but it was suitably dark—rather like the muck in the lane
after a good rain.

Again, Mrs. Drummond rapped. "Please, miss, his lordship says you're to come to the parlor."

Clare began to wring it in sections.

"I'll be there in the morning," she called. When her newly
dyed—and suitably subdued—gown was dry. She moved
to the fire, which she'd stoked up high. A chair was her
clothesline.

Mrs. Drummond would not leave. "His lordship says
that . . . that he doesn't care if you come in your wrapper.
He's summoned you to discuss Vicky."

"Is anything the matter?"

"Oh, aye, he's in a raw humor, and he's sent you a maid's
gown to wear. Please take it, miss."

Clare opened the door a crack and took the dress. Gray.

Just her color. True it was two sizes too large, but if he insisted . . . She put it on, tied her hair back in a severe knot, and, holding up the voluminous skirts of the maid's dress, walked out to meet the devil.

She bore the scabs of scratches on her arms and face, and her hands now were smeared brownish from the bracken and bark, but she had done away with the Isobel's gown. She had won that battle. She would remain in control. Two kisses were all she'd given. No more. Victorious, she smiled and walked down the stairs of Dundroma Castle and headed toward the parlor full of stag heads.

He did not keep her waiting. Five minutes after she entered the tartan parlor, he arrived, the dark green Douglas tartan of his kilt showing off muscular calves, a black and white plaid tossed over one shoulder. Russet lights glowed in his hair, and he looked the forbidding Scotsman. Clare felt a strange lightness in her chest.

Isobel, beautiful as ever in black, arrived right behind him, and glided over to the fireplace. A sharp pang coursed through her. Jealousy. She couldn't help wondering if he'd kissed the widow.

Which was unworthy of her. Isobel, after all, was still in mourning. Consoling his best friend's widow was a noble act. That the widow was beautiful and in need of much consoling was beside the point.

His deep voice rolled across the room as he told Isobel briefly about the way he'd outwitted the Charltons at the kissing statue earlier that day. Two or three sentences summed things up nicely enough for Isobel to laugh gaily.

"Oh, but, Alec, how melodramatic of you to ride to your daughter's rescue and put the Charltons in their place."

Clare stood, angry, her chair scraping the floor.

Isobel and Lord Strahan turned as one.

"You have a visitor," Isobel said with a half smile, though her eyes narrowed.

"I must have misunderstood the message. Pardon me."

"Stay, *Aunt* Clare. No misunderstanding, but you hide like a mouse back there in the shadows," Alec chided.

She took a step toward him, and could not contain her outrage. "How dare you laugh at me, at the Charltons, at—"

"I knew the Charltons were trying to trick you into bringing them Vicky, and now I see I was correct."

"How?"

His gaze fell to the outsize maid's dress. "Obviously there were no dresses in that trunk or you'd not have told me you had nothing to wear. And the Lord only knows how you disposed of Isobel's gift." His gaze roamed up and down the misfitting maid's dress before he continued. "So, was I right?"

"About my clothing—yes. But chasing Vicky like a common reiver? You were no better than her grandparents. Both of you should be ashamed."

"Ah, taken to task by the English governess . . . I gather Isobel's gown was taken to task as well."

"It merely changed colors." She held up her hands for him to see the brown dye stains. "The dress is still drying."

He digested this information. "Then I am fortunate to have escaped a caldron of dye and suffered no more than a tongue-lashing . . . tell me, why this determination not to wear such a lovely color?"

"It's not a governess's color."

"Ah, but it's a Clare color, and . . . the gown was Isobel's."

Isobel stepped forward with a soft laugh. "Oh, Alec, it's of no account. If she wants to wear mud-brown, I'm not going to object. I'll never wear the gown again in any case."

"I think we should discuss Vicky, not my gowns," Clare said.

Alec smiled. "But you are right. The Charltons played

you false—and Vicky too—and we must talk about how she fares." He glanced over at Isobel who stood tapping her foot. "Isobel, give us leave to discuss my daughter."

Isobel gave him an amused look and rustled up next to him. "See to your governess then. I shall see to the cook. Call if you need to be rescued from the caldron," she purred.

Isobel, observed Clare, was behaving as if she were already lady of the castle.

"Is Vicky suffering any ill effects from the border skirmish?"

"You could ask her yourself."

"I'm asking you." His hand closed around his walking stick, and he limped closer to her. Slow steps, as if he were in more pain than usual. Once, on the way to her, he had to stop, obviously wincing, and she moved to meet him.

"Have no fear, I'm not about to collapse again." He pushed his plaid up from his arm and clenched his hand over the ivory-headed stick. "Tell me about Vicky. It diverts me from my own pains."

"She's thriving here, no thanks to your melodramatic actions today. I'm surprised you left your steel bonnet at the castle."

His gaze narrowed on her. "Are you telling me if I'd not arrived you would not have vanished back to Thornhill with her?"

"Yes."

"Why?"

"Because . . ." He limped closer, so close she could see the deep blue of his eyes, the sparkle of auburn hair, the scent of damp wool from his plaid. Pressing a hand against her waist for control, she tried again. "Because, milord, I believe the child is thriving here at Dundroma, and it would not serve her best health to keep dragging her back and forth across the border. A child does best who stays in familiar surroundings."

"But the Charltons are more familiar than me."

"Are you going to give her back to them?"

"Of course not."

"Then would it be fair to let them take her, only to have you come and steal her back like a brass pot taken in plunder?"

He pulled back, as if struck. "I'd never thought of it like that."

"You should, milord. And as for the feud between Thornhill and Dundroma, I have no idea how it began, but Vicky will not be a pawn to further it, and it is for Vicky's good I serve, neither yours nor Adele's."

He gave her gray dress a withering look, then smiled. "Nor would I trust her either. Not one dress in the trunk?"

She shook her head.

Without warning, he reached out to touch her chin, and his hand was uncommonly gentle, gentler than any touch she'd felt from Reginald. Instinct made her take a step backward, but he was quicker and pulled her close.

"Tell me," he urged softly, "where did you learn these radical ideas on what makes children thrive? From your husband?"

Beneath his touch, color rushed to her face. "No, milord. He was rather sickly."

"Then you didn't thrive." Dropping his hand, he placed both on his walking stick for support.

"That depends how you would define it."

"Thriving involves the capacity to unfold and take pleasure in the company of a mate. A husband's duty is to make certain his wife thrives. Now, did you thrive?"

"I don't know. I can speak only of Vicky."

"Let me tell you then. You thrive when you wear the color of roses, and when you reach for ripe blackberries and when a man's hand grazes your chin——" He reached out to touch her face again.

Her desire to feel his lips on hers was far too potent, too intoxicating. This man was a potion, and she wanted never to drink from his lips again. Too much pleasure was unwise for a modest governess.

Footsteps clicked on the stones of the castle hall. "Alec, are you done yet?" It was Isobel, rustling in her black crinolined skirt and impatient to claim the laird of the castle.

He dropped his hand and sank into a chair. "No, but join us. She did not throw me into a caldron, merely took me to task, and now we have an unresolved question: However did the feud with Thornhill begin?"

Isobel clearly saw this as an invitation and sat down in the chair nearest Lord Strahan while Clare sank down into an overstuffed chair by the fire.

Isobel smiled like a woman who'd been invited to set the wedding date. "Well, who knows when it started, but it was Cecilia who made it all flare up again. Vicky's mother," she said as if Clare were too dense to comprehend. "I was her best friend, you see . . ." And Isobel began to relate the tale of how she'd introduced Alec to his future wife. Halfway through the telling, Vicky appeared in the doorway and with a waggle of her finger, Clare beckoned the child to come sit at the footstool by her feet. Isobel's tale would be fascinating to a child who'd never known her mother, and Clare did not interrupt. Yet . . .

On Isobel talked. "I met your mother, Vicky, at the same finishing school in France. Alec came to visit me, as a favor to my family, and as it turned out, I played matchmaker and introduced Alec and Cecilia.

"Love at first sight it was," Isobel told a wide-eyed Vicky. "At least that's what Cecilia told me." Her voice had gone flat.

"My, what an excellent memory you have, Isobel," commented Alec, frowning darkly at the ceiling, his fingertips steepled.

Isobel warmed to her subject and gave Clare a superior look. "But Cecilia and I were such close friends. I warrant I can tell Vicky all she'd ever need to know about her mother."

"Tell us more, then," Alec commanded. "As you can see, my daughter is all ears."

Isobel glanced absently at Vicky. "She reminds me, you know, of her dear departed mother—except for your hair, of course. But Cecilia had her spirit. I remember it well. I was always the one hanging back, being the lady, wondering about manners, and there'd be Cecilia racing off to play pranks. Why, once she tied the toes of two sleeping teachers together. A prank only the lads dared try, and she got away with it. But Cecilia got away with everything, didn't she, Alec?"

The room was quiet, waiting for Alec's comment. "And here I thought you and Cecilia were mere acquaintances."

"Dearest friends. Why else do you think I introduced you to Cecilia? Your spirits were a match." She turned to Clare, who'd remained silent. "It was my first try at matchmaking and then Alec returned the favor and introduced me to his best friend, Malcolm. Fancy that? We introduced each other to our mates and now we're both widowed and fate brings up both back to Scotland. Do you believe in fate, Clare?" she asked.

Clare stroked Vicky's long red curls, then with her hand resting on the girl's shoulder looked up into Isobel's eyes. There was challenge in them. A dare to say anything to contradict her story.

"Fate can cause us to take life for granted," she began. "Rather I believe in working hard and using one's God-given talents to attain our goals and achieve success in life."

Isobel scoffed. "But what you say is all good and well for men. Not for women."

"Times are changing. I've raised Vicky to use her talents, not her feminine wiles."

"Cecilia would be shocked."

"Cecilia would be pleased. For the Cecilia I knew—"

"You knew Mama?" Vicky turned, surprised.

"When Reginald was courting me, she came to London . . ."

"And?" It was Lord Strahan, a devilish grin on his face, who urged her to continue.

"And I'm afraid I have a totally different memory of Vicky's mother than yours, Mrs. Fraser."

"Oh?" Sheep left out in the snow did not wear more frost than Isobel's single syllable.

"Tell us what you remember, Aunt Clare," Lord Strahan said.

Clare paused, wondering how the widow would react to being directly contradicted. "The Cecilia I knew was quiet, soft-spoken, very much in awe of her mama, Adele Charlton. Adele took great pride in the behavior of both her children. Reginald used to tell me that Cecilia was too well behaved for her own good. Both of them were. Model children. Or else shy."

"Or else under the thumb of the dominant Adele," Lord Strahan put in.

"Well," Isobel said with a toss of her black ringlets, "that certainly differs from the Cecilia I knew. Perhaps she changed once away from Adele. In any case, I'm certain the spirited lady I knew is more to Vicky's liking, isn't it, child?"

They all stared at Vicky, who looked at Isobel awhile before replying, "I'm not a child."

"Well," a flustered Isobel said, "what are you then? May I call you Vicky?"

"Yes, ma'am."

"And wouldn't you rather have a mama like the one I

knew? Not a milksop mama as your aunt Clare describes?"

"Aunt Clare has given me Mama's letters from France."

"Oh . . ."

"And in them she writes about her hoydenish friend Isobel and how jealous Isobel is that Lord Strahan has taken a fancy to her. She feared the romance would harm their friendship."

Clare, horrified at Vicky's lack of discretion, stood. "No, Vicky, don't say that. Those letters were for you only."

Now it was Isobel, white-faced, who stood and stared in dislike at Vicky. "And how do you know your mama wrote those letters?"

"Aunt Clare said so."

"And Aunt Clare is always right." Her tone was full of sugar sweetness.

"Aye."

"Vicky, hush." It was one thing to prove a point. Quite another to show up the ambitious widow in front of Alec. If she said any more she'd be questioning the integrity of Mrs. Fraser, and Clare had more survival instincts than to do something that foolish.

"Forgive me for prattling on about Vicky's mother, milord," she said apologetically. "Vicky and I will leave you alone now."

Isobel's expression softened, and her mouth turned up in a smile. "So sorry you have to leave. But you do have your work cut out for you teaching Alec's child good manners, and that can occur none too soon."

"Isobel," Alec drawled from his chair, "I care less about Vicky's memories of her mother and more about her time here at Dundroma."

Isobel put on a smile for him. "Then we shall have a picnic, shan't we? A picnic it is." She lowered her voice. "And now that we've got rid of your governess, I have news from friends in India . . ."

Clare straightened her back and vowed to avoid the widow at all costs.

"Andrew, how long can it take you?" Isobel called up the stairs as she pinned on a silver thistle brooch at her neckline. If she was going to show up the Thornhill governess at pony riding today, she would do so with style.

"Andrew!"

She'd known better than to allow him to go fishing alone. And now they were going to be late for the picnic at Dundroma. Late to see Alec, when every moment Isobel was not with him was a moment in which that mousy governess could catch his eye.

He poked his head over the banister, his fair hair all wet and tousled. "A few minutes, Mother. Think how glad you are to have me back again."

"You weren't dawdling by the village school, were you? You've nothing in common with those lads."

"Aye, but the lasses, Mother, are pleasing to the eye."

"All the more reason to stay away. I can't imagine where you inherit such a common manner." Oh, but she did. Her son was picking up common tastes and manners from the grooms at Lord Strahan's stables. Isobel should have refused Alec's offer to allow the lad unlimited time at his pony stable. Alec knew nothing of how to raise a boy to be a gentleman. Why, he'd even tried to talk her out of sending Andrew home from India to school. Isobel had prevailed then, but now . . . well, now, she was a widow who very much wanted, as soon as convention would allow, to snare the key to Dundroma Castle for her very own.

For that reason, and none other, had she deigned to allow Andrew his heart's desire . . . work as a groom at Dundroma. It gave Isobel just one more pretext to drive over there. Asking Alec if Andrew was working hard enough was an excellent conversational opening. When she'd found out

Andrew was giving riding lessons to Alec's own daughter, Isobel had been elated. A chance to talk about both their children. Tedious as Isobel found the subject, it seemed to intrigue Alec.

Which is why she'd suggested today's picnic: a chance for Andrew to show off to Alec what he'd taught Vicky— hoydenish lass, if ever Isobel saw one, but she'd pretend to adore the child—anything for Alec. She could only hope he would not bring the governess . . . or that odious Dr. Wilmot.

But if the worst happened, she'd contrive a way to get them alone and out of her way. After all, a woman with only three more months of official mourning had no time to waste. She may have been cheated first time around, but not a second time. Lady Strahan. It was that or nothing. Oh, yes, a widow in need of a titled husband could do worse than use a strapping lad as a lure. Especially when that man had a daughter who needed distracting.

Dr. Wigston Wilmot was trying yet again to convince Alec to allow him to discuss his injury with the Edinburgh surgeons. Alec was barely listening to the rotund little doctor at all. From his vantage point at the fireplace, he had a perfect view out the parlor windows. Five minutes ago he'd spied a blur of black outside the windows. Aunt Clare strolling out in the Dundroma gardens. Unable to resist a closer look, he had pulled himself past the pain, past the shadows, and limped over to the fireplace. There he could both watch Clare and continue this conversation with Dr. Wilmot.

"I leave in the morning for Edinburgh," the physician said. "Weather permitting."

"So soon . . ." Clare was wearing the dress from Isobel. He half smiled. It was the color of mud, and she was quite pleased with herself for hiding behind dim colors again,

successfully pushing her passion back behind a prim gown.
They were a pair, each of them running from something—
she from passion, he from pain. A pale sun lit up the
gardens, and he noted with satisfaction that her dye job had
not affected the honey highlights of her hair, nor the play of
dimples that came and went as she spoke. Vicky ran across
the garden, which earned her a quiet reminder about
ladylike behavior from Clare.

Clare. How he longed to strip that ladylike Thornhill
facade from her. Tangle tendrils of her honeyed hair in his
fingers . . . breathe in the lavender scent of her . . .
gaze down into shy green eyes . . . tease her unschooled
lips . . .

"Is that agreeable with you?" someone asked.

"Aye, most agreeable," he said softly, still watching
Clare.

"I shall return as soon as possible to let you decide."

Return? Alec pivoted on his walking stick. He hadn't
been paying attention. "What did I promise you?"

"That I could return with the surgeons' recommendation,
and if they agreed to make you a test case, you'd be willing
to give yourself to the study of surgery by Edinburgh's
finest. A full report would go to London physicians and—"

"Spare me the details and yourself the breath, Doctor. My
reply will be negative." Dr. Wilmot could bring back
whatever recommendation he wished, but he couldn't force
Alec to willingly lie down on a table and risk losing a leg.
All so some Edinburgh surgeons could poke about his
kneecap in search of professional acclaim.

Alec was restless. His thoughts drifted to green eyes and
lavender fragrances. Clare. But Isobel had hinted broadly
that the governess need not come on their picnic.

The trouble was, Alec didn't want to leave her behind.
And not for Vicky's sake. He liked looking at her, would

rather look at her, banter with her, make conversation with her than spend the picnic fending off Isobel.

The good physician doctor could make up for all this nonsense over repairing his knee by rounding out the party.

"Will you accompany me on a picnic this afternoon?" he asked out of the blue.

"A picnic?" Dr. Wilmot frowned as if he'd never heard of the word. "I've never been on one," he admitted. "Not much opportunity in London, you know."

"Don't worry. The ladies will keep us entertained. You'll make up a fourth and round out the numbers."

Dr. Wilmot worried at his lower lip. "Is Mrs. Fraser coming on the picnic?" he asked suddenly.

"Aye," he said on a weary sigh. "It was her idea."

"She's a lovely lady, if you don't mind my saying so, milord. Most attractive."

Vaguely it registered that Dr. Wilmot was perhaps smitten with Isobel. The beautiful widow had smote many a man in her lifetime. Alec did not find it remarkable if yet another found her black-haired charms irresistible.

"Most attractive," Alec echoed, but it was not Isobel on whom he gazed. And with Dr. Wigston Wilmot's acceptance, the picnic took on new possibilities. Many.

❧ Chapter Ten

They said bad things happened in threes. When Dr.
Wigston Wilmot kicked over the jar of stewed apples on
their way up into the moors, Clare suspected the worst was
yet to come.

The widow Fraser—ambitious Isobel—rarely took her
eyes off Lord Strahan, except to cast cunning looks at Clare.
Isobel would retaliate for yesterday. It didn't take a gypsy's
skill to foretell that. Clare had contradicted her about Lord
Strahan's first wife, made Isobel look the fool, and for that
Clare was going to pay.

Clare didn't know how Isobel would get even, but she
suspected Dr. Wilmot would play a role. Next to her the
portly physician sat stuffing himself with a second mutton
pie, which he washed down with ale. Across from her,
Isobel reached into the picnic basket and brought out a
triangle of shortbread, broke off the tip, and popped it into
her mouth, then handed the tin across to Dr. Wilmot who
scooped out several pieces.

Clare peeked from under her lashes at Lord Strahan . . . at
his stone-carved profile, the dark chestnut hair blowing
across his forehead. Today, like Isobel, he wore all black
because, as he explained, he'd had no time to change from
a morning call at his solicitor's in the village. Now he was
leaning back on the plaid, frock coat open, one knee up, the
other outstretched, black top hat at his side. For a few

unguarded moments, he sat there smiling, watching his
daughter with evident enjoyment. At least he was no longer
treating Vicky as if she were a trophy he'd won from
Thornhill.

Nearby, Vicky, blithely oblivious to all the grown-up
intrigues, continued to show off on her pony, the brown and
white named Macduff. Andrew held the pony by a long rope
while Vicky wore out a circular track in the heath. Nearby
the calmer mount, Ghost, flicked his tail and shook his mane
in a sassy gesture. Innocent brown eyes stared at Clare. Not
a scratch on the beast. Even the Dundroma ponies were
devils . . .

"Papa!" Vicky called. "Come and see me . . . come see
what Andrew has taught me."

Isobel tilted her head flirtatiously. "She wants to show off
for you. A good sign. Your daughter has learned to ride her
pony like a native Dundroma lass. You'd never know she'd
been brought up by an English governess." This said with a
sly look at Clare in her hand-dyed gown. "You were right to
dye the gown, Clare," she'd said earlier. "This color suits
you so much better." Isobel was wearing black velvet again,
but with a purple petticoat. She sat on the blanket with an
inch of petticoat showing. Outrageous. Adele Charlton
would swoon.

"Perhaps," Alec said quietly, "my daughter's English
governess has been busy teaching my daughter other loftier
skills."

Isobel cast an impatient look at Clare. "I've heard that
your daughter's English governess has not learned to sit a
pony saddle yet . . . and from the looks of those nasty
scratches on her hands, I do believe it's true. I do hope Dr.
Wilmot has seen to them. Infection is always such a worry."

Dr. Wilmot was busy piling a plate with cold beef slices
over a mound of horseradish and mustard. Mustard and

pudding were colliding on his plate, and he licked his fingers.

"Isn't it, Doctor?" Isobel prompted. "A worry for Clare?"

Dr. Wilmot, plate balanced on his paunch, glanced over, clearly not certain on which body part he'd been asked to give advice. Clare hastily adjusted the folds of her skirt so it concealed her hands. The thought of Dr. Wigston Wilmot examining her a second time quite threatened her appetite, nearly as much as the mustard pudding.

Isobel stood and tugged at Alec. "In India," she said, "Alec and I were the best riders in our social set. Even Malcolm bragged about us—his wife and his best friend. Remember, Alec, remember our races across the plains in moonlight? Who won the most?"

"It was you, Isobel. You always liked to win."

"Are you saying you let me win?" she teased.

He shrugged.

"Never mind, you're too much the devil to tell the truth . . . but we were the best pair on horseback."

"Were we?"

"You doubt it. Must we prove it?" she said with obvious coyness.

Clare, disgusted at the flirtation, reached for a meat pie.

"No, I've a better idea." Alec's gaze rested on Clare, and on her guard, she paused with the pie halfway to her plate.

Isobel was smiling hopefully. "A contest to prove we can ride ponies as well as horses?"

"Aye," Alec said, "in a manner of speaking. The surest way to prove who's most adept is to see who can teach our Thornhill guests here—"

"I've already had a lesson," Clare protested.

"—in the shortest time," Alec finished.

Isobel blanched. Against her black gown, she turned pale as Ghost and her paisley shawl fell unchecked to the heath.

"What do you mean?"

"I mean, we take Ghost and Macduff—I'll take Ghost, you take Macduff—walk a mile in opposite directions and then return. Whichever of us returns the soonest—with our 'student' riding the pony still—shall be deemed the 'best.'"

Isobel laughed. "You can't mean it. That sounds like a duel."

"To the finish. The picnic blanket here."

He did mean it.

Clare jumped up. "I don't want to be used as sport."

"She doesn't want to, Alec," Isobel objected.

But Dr. Wigston Wilmot was interested enough to put down his plate. He eyed Isobel with more longing than he had the sliced tongue in aspic. "I'll be a sport then," he said.

"There, you see," Lord Strahan said, "it's three to one. Take Wigston and Macduff and go west, Isobel. Clare and I shall head east. One hour." By now, Andrew and Vicky stood listening.

Chin raised in a haughty gesture, Isobel snatched the halter of Macduff from Andrew, and tramped away across the heath, pony and Dr. Wilmot both close at her heels.

"What shall we do, Mother?" Andrew called out.

"Go off and teach Vicky some other Dundroma sports," his mother snapped. She never looked back.

With a shrug, Andrew looked at Vicky. "Come on then, we'll look for grouse." And they departed up a cleft in the hill and headed toward a small burn.

Only Clare and Lord Strahan remained, Ghost with them.

Lord Strahan looked over at her and raised his eyebrows, as if to question if she were game.

She wasn't.

"I don't need a lesson."

"No, but Wilmot does, and I am not up to teaching him. He will keep Isobel busy."

"Then why must we go anywhere?"

"I choose to."

"Is it me you choose to provoke or Isobel?"

"Clare," he said in a husky voice, "I am not making sport. You suffered a fright at the hands of Ghost, and it's an old truism that once you suffer a spill you must get right on again."

"All except for you."

"You have a sharp tongue, wee lassie . . . sharper than a bramble's thorn."

Suddenly she felt ashamed, taunting him for his limp. It was unworthy. But she had to maintain control here.

The wind suddenly came up and blew Clare's hair free of its knot. Worse, her crinoline was blowing about her ankles. Modest white or not, a lady did not show off her petticoats.

Clare stood her ground until Lord Strahan limped over, his deep blue eyes intense.

The only thing to do with a devil riled was to meet him head-on and speak before he could.

"You are a devil, well and truly, milord, but very well. I shall help you to win your contest." Without waiting for a reply, she began walking across the heath, eastward, leaving him to grab Ghost's halter and follow.

She finally slowed down, ashamed of herself for forgetting his limp, and waited for him to catch up. Then they walked awhile farther across the heath, both silent. She had to walk slowly to hold herself to his halting pace.

"Stop here, Clare," he said finally, "and I will show you again how to move the reins."

She did as he bid, but only out of consideration for his limp. Even so, she kept her distance. To be unchaperoned with the devil of Dundroma up here on the heath, playing at ponies . . . well, whatever would Thornhill and its neighbors think? Appearances were all.

But Adele had not thought a whit about Clare, stranded up here with no gowns or spare nightgowns even. Who was up here to tattle on her? A lone lark? The pony? It was just her and Alec Douglas and the eternal wind. Not even Vicky was here.

Her prim facade slipped a bit. Let convention go . . . let it slip. What did it matter what the neighbors thought? For a prim widow nearing thirty, there was little gossip could do to harm her. For a few minutes, an hour perhaps, she could flout convention. Something she'd never ever done.

But what would it feel like to flout the rules of society with the devil of Dundroma? She raised her gaze to his face.

Silent, blue eyes smiling, he watched her. "Did your conscience win out?"

She shook her head. "Curiosity."

His smile held a touch of whimsy, and he held out a hand to her. Trembling, she moved toward him and took his hand, slipped her arm through his to offer him a second support beside his cane. Her full skirt brushed against his thighs, and the powerful grip of his arms came about her to guide her hand to the pony's halter.

Suddenly she stopped. The pony had no sidesaddle. She'd have to straddle the beast. Besides cope with swishing tails, unpredictable nostrils, and that swaying rump. Curiosity paled as more practical considerations loomed. The memory of Ghost knocking her flat. Humiliation. Pain. And herself in Lord Strahan's arms in full view of witnesses.

"I'm not dressed for pony riding," she stammered.

"When are you going to rid yourself of English modesty? Besides, you can't go back on your word now. You've anteed up. You're in the game. And as for your skirt, have you never seen the Scots lasses tramping the laundry?"

"What would a peer know of laundry?"

"When a maid pulls her skirts up between her legs and bares not just her ankles but her lovely legs as well to tramp on the bedsheets, class distinctions in Scotland have a way of melting away. I expect if linen were laundered the same way in your rigid England, you'd find class barriers

crashing. Lords and stable boys stand equal when there's a
lass's skirt pulled up on laundry day."

"Yes . . . aye. I've seen your Scottish washerwomen
down at the banks of the River Tyne. I find their way with
clothing to be most novel."

"But then, your modesty would get in the way—not to
mention your crinoline."

"Are you suggesting I sit astride this pony with my skirt
pulled up?"

"You're too frightened of what I might do to you if you
chose to be so bold, Miss Charlton."

Clare's anger broke. In the back of her head, she warned
herself that anger preceded passion. Beware of passion. Stay
in control . . . but the words tumbled out anyway.

"You forget. Although I'm Vicky's governess and companion, I am not a maiden lady, and Scots lasses do not have
a monopoly on boldness. I, however, have a monopoly on a
schoolteacher's curiosity. Whatever would a legendary
Scottish lord do if I shed my crinoline and tucked my skirt
up?"

"Dismiss you. And send Vicky back to Thornhill."

"Promises from Dundroma reivers, I've heard, are hard-
won at best."

And with that, she marched behind a rock. "Look away,
please. Your bluff has been called."

"Clare, no theatrics are necessary. We shall have a lesson
in how to work the pony's reins. You needn't ride astride."

"I know how to work his reins. It's his rump that
confounds me, milord, therefore, I want an advanced
lesson."

After some fumbling, she stepped out of her crinoline and
left it abandoned on the heath. She tucked her skirt up
washwoman style. She untied her boots and set them neatly
by the crinoline in the heather. And then, barefoot, ankles on

display, she took a deep breath, straightened her shoulders, and marched out toward the pony.

He said nothing.

Face expressionless, he stared.

"What is the saying, milord?" she said. "When in Dundroma, do as the Dundroma women do . . . Now, about the dismissal . . . or were you the one bluffing?"

His face was ashen. He took one halting step toward her. "Clare, you surprise me. You do hide passion behind those damnable drab dresses, don't you?"

Heart soaring at her daring, she was afraid to answer. "This is a contest, not a conversation, milord, so we'd best get on with it. What do I do first?"

Do? Alec tried to count the possibilities. He yearned to take her in his arms and kiss away the remnants of her primness, make her bloom . . .

"If you don't hurry up," Clare said, "Isobel will have Dr. Wigston Wilmot back to the picnic basket, and all the shortbread will be gone. Do get on with it."

Pony riding it would be. For now. "What do you remember?"

She put her foot in the low stirrup and slung herself over, then sat there looking at Alec, who stood staring as if he'd been shot and crushed under yet another horse. The shadows cleared away, and he forgot his pain, all his pains, past and present. All he wanted was to stand there, drinking in the sight of Clare Charlton, honey hair streaked by the sun, blown free by the wind, and hazel eyes flashing with passion. The lavender scent of her still clung to him.

As Andrew had done a while ago, he gathered up the halter and stood like a compass point while she practiced riding about him. Navigating both the halter and his walking stick was tricky. He was dizzy. He was hurting. He was unable to take his eyes off Clare, unbridled, uncorseted.

Prim Clare transformed to a woman of passion. He'd known this was in her.

Pity it could not be his.

Even more the pity, she would let herself go to waste, unappreciated at Thornhill.

"Now, you were going to teach me how to maneuver this animal . . . Do so before the wind comes up and gives me a chill."

Lord Strahan, in turn, face set, limped over, reached for her, and, letting his walking stick fall, put his arms about her waist and dragged her off the pony.

She resisted.

He tugged.

She let her weight fall against him. Against his bad knee.

He lost his balance.

And together they fell into the heather. The wool of his trousers scratched her bare legs. He shot up to a sitting position, pulled off his plaid, and quickly wrapped it about her.

Before she realized what he was about, he'd reached over and touched her cheek, right below one of her scratches. "Your English complexion is taking on a Scots battle look, but healing."

At his touch, Clare held her breath. She felt strangely light-headed; instinct said to pull away, but she could no more do that than the stone statue at the border could run. His touch, remarkably light, grazed her like a butterfly and yet had the ability to make her quake as if a steel bonnet had rammed her in the stomach.

"Please, forgive my behavior. I forgot the teachings of my manners book."

"Your manners book would be better served as fuel for a fire, lass. There's nothing to forgive. Forgetting is what you should be begging for."

Abruptly she pulled away.

"I must find Vicky. She's vanished in the moorland."

"Then hurry, Clare, for if she takes after her father, then any mischief is possible . . ." His low laughter made her heart lurch and speed through her veins, making the strangest parts of her warm with new kinds of aching. Hurry away from the Dundroma devil, before he bewitches you all the more.

He did not need to tell her twice. She stood, picked up her crinoline, and moved back behind the rock. With shaking hands, she stepped into her crinoline, reached back to fasten the hook and eye, failed, pulled it around and fastened it in the front. She smoothed her dress down over it and stepped out, his black and white checked plaid in hand. She held it out. "You dropped one of your garments."

He stood there, both hands clamped over his walking stick. She draped the cloak over his arm. At once, he flung it aside, and turning on his good leg, he grabbed her by the arm and pulled her back behind her rocky dressing room. Pressing her back gently against the rock, he said, breath warm against her hair, "This, Miss Charlton, is what happens to governesses, even Thornhill ones, who bare their legs and feet in front of the laird of Dundroma."

She ducked down, but so did he, capturing her chin in his grasp, fingers warm against her skin.

"You aren't going to kiss me?"

Her question made him blink. He shook his head. "Not on the lips."

And then he bent to kiss the crown of her head. His lips on her hair, a single kiss to the crown of her head. Like a moth to the candle. His mouth to her hair. Inside, she melted, and now it was *her* legs that threatened to buckle.

Devil's play. Any second now, he'd release her, step back, and smile at her in triumph at his outrageous behavior. Declare himself the more outrageous in their little game of outshocking each other.

The buttons on her bodice made a row of indentations down her middle, and her hair slipped undone against the rough rock wall. She stood stiffly. Any second now.

Any second changed irrevocably to any minute. Somehow, time took on new and different definitions. It was a shift somewhere inside of her. Invisible. Imperceptible. It happened halfway between the whisper of his lips on her hair and the glide of his hands up her waist, the whisper of breath, the tangy male scent of him mingling with the feel of skin on skin, the yearning of other places to be unconfined and touching skin on skin.

"Let go of me." Suddenly coming to her senses, she pushed her hands up between them to form a wedge and force him back. He stumbled, and guilt overwhelmed her. Followed just as quickly by righteous anger. "I suppose you think to intimidate me."

"I warned you what to expect of Dundroma."

"The play of boys. The legend in the statue is mere fancy, remember?"

He was looking at her, as if searching for chinks in her armor.

"You also forget again that I am no fainting maiden," she added.

"Nor am I a statue without feeling in my body, lassie, and you'd best remember it next time you take off your petticoats."

Alec stared at this pert little governess. Aye, he was devoid of heart. For twelve long years he'd allowed his heart to rust away. Thrown away the key. Buried it. Never again would he give his heart, and he'd best be careful.

She reached up to tuck her hair back into its knot. His gaze slid down to where her blouse moved up and down with each breath. "Aye," he said at last when they were done staring each other down. "Heartless. And I will win whatever wager, whatever battle, whatever challenge you set for me. Especially any lessons regarding my daughter."

She tugged away. "Remember this, Lord Strahan, even Dundroma men must know that winning battles is all good and well . . . but it's the war that counts. That remains to be decided."

And she marched off in the direction of the picnic blanket.

She ought to pack up and leave.

But where to? Thornhill? Vicky came first, she reminded herself. For Vicky, she could endure anything. Even teasing by the devil of Dundroma.

Pony hooves sounded, and Isobel came limping back, the pony led by a halter. Dr. Wigston Wilmot sat astride, wearing an absurdly pleased expression. Macduff's back swayed closer to the ground than usual, and he clopped along at a slower pace.

Isobel was exhausted. The lesson had gone abominably. Twice, Dr. Wilmot had fallen off, once landing on Isobel's toes, and cursed at Macduff for bruising his tailbone. Isobel didn't care what happened to Dr. Wigston Wilmot's tailbone, but she did pray poor Macduff made it back to the picnic blanket without keeling over.

Shading her eyes, she peered ahead. Alec was nowhere in sight and neither was that sly little governess. She brushed mud off her skirt and pushed her hair back off her face. On top of all else, her hands were blistered and her toes bruised. Her best crinoline—the purple satin—was sadly torn from leading Wigston Wilmot out of thistle patches when the pony had bucked. A thistle burr under his saddle. Isobel had practically gnashed her teeth. The work of Vicky Douglas, no doubt. She couldn't wait to send that child off to finishing school. She'd had to unsaddle Macduff, brush him off, and saddle him up again, by herself, with no groom.

"I can ride Macduff to the finish," Wigston insisted when Isobel suggested they give up. "I want you to win."

With clockwork regularity, Macduff stalled again and again, and the fourth time, Wigston Wilmot, giving up, slid off. "Mrs. Fraser, I am slowing the pony, and you will lose the contest. We'll walk together."

"I don't care who wins," she said. And meant it. She didn't. As long as Alec was off with Clare Charlton, she was not winning the contest that counted. The contest for Alec Douglas.

Dr. Wilmot, for an educated man, was incredibly obtuse about affairs of the heart and insisted on trying to impress her. Reaching for the pony's halter, he tried to play the gallant. "Allow me to lead the animal, Mrs. Fraser. If the win is forfeited, I shall at least play the gallant."

"Dr. Wilmot, I do not wish to play at any games — races or chivalry," she told him, but he just wagged his head and spoke of false modesty.

Limping on, heartsick, Isobel forced her bruised toes back toward the picnic blanket, hurrying as much as she was able. God save her from this odious little man. Naturally, she attracted men; she always had, but usually she could beckon them or wave them away as she chose. She, Isobel, did the choosing.

But this one was different, either too arrogant to see he wasn't wanted, or else too stupid.

"It doesn't matter to me either if we win, you know," he said. "It is enough to have enjoyed your company."

Suddenly she stopped and turned.

"Please, sir, your words are too forward," she said. "Can't you see I'm in mourning still?" And she held out one black-clad arm practically under his nose. In case he was nearsighted.

"But, madam, there must be some misunderstanding . . . I have permission from the Charltons to court you."

Isobel's face burned with a slow-growing rage. "The Charltons are nothing to me. What do you mean?"

"In exchange for directing me to Dundroma, they told me I could have leave to court the fairest lady in the castle."

Isobel's mouth dropped open, and for a good minute she couldn't seem to make her jaw work.

The fool. The pompous fool. The Charltons had played him for a dupe. And he was too ignorant of the treachery among borderland families to know.

"What do you mean? The Charltons have no authority over my wedded state. If they gave you leave to court, it would be their daughter-in-law, the governess. Go and follow her. You have the wrong woman."

The man's stomach actually shook like a pudding that hadn't set. "I may have leave to court the governess, but, madam, it is you for whom my heart yearns."

Good Lord, the man was serious.

She picked up her skirts in case he actually touched the velvet and hurried on faster. She could see the picnic basket now, and the blanket. The square of tartan sat deserted on the heath. Alec was gone. Clare was gone. Oh, but how could fate conspire like this? And it was all the fault of Thornhill. The daughter. The governess. The Charltons.

And now, this fat and supercilious Londoner who had the nerve to admit he'd never been on a picnic. She ran through the heather the rest of the way to the picnic blanket, dropped down beside the basket, and, grabbing Wigston Wilmot's field glasses, scanned the horizon.

"Madam!" Wigston Wilmot, huffing and puffing, caught up with her. "Madam, pray do not be angry if I have spoken in too great a haste. I respect your widow's weeds. I shall only be a friend, a companion until your mourning ends."

"I plan to mourn forever."

"You are too grief-stricken still to know your heart, and I

assure you I would not want you to pledge your troth again until your heart is ready."

Imbecile. "Leave at once," she snapped, "else I shall have Lord Strahan remove you by your cravat and shoelaces."

Instead, overcome by the exercise, he dropped to the blanket, expression contrite.

"I have offended you," he said. "I offer my apologies for speaking too hastily and beg your forgiveness. Perhaps while I am in Edinburgh, you can see it in your heart to forget this episode."

Well. That was more like it. She'd already forgotten he was leaving for Edinburgh. Though men usually didn't rescind their attentions quite that rapidly, in this case, it was for the best.

"But," he added, "I shall return to give my report to the laird of Dundroma on his medical prospects, and I hope I may speak with you again. I am, you may be assured, a patient man."

Oh, fie. Patience, in Isobel's opinion, was no virtue, except in the arms of a willing lover. Damn Alec's limp. She prayed the surgeons would find no way to repair him, then Dr. Wigston Wilmot need not return. She'd marry Alec as a cripple. Dundroma would not care.

"You will not forget me," Wigston asked in all sincerity, his homely face wrinkling with worry. When she didn't answer, he reminded her, "You do believe me when I say I am patient?"

"Pity," she said, shading her eyes to seek out Alec. "For I am most impulsive and impatient. Do not expect me to wait for anyone, sir."

He shrank back, expression wounded. "Madam, I have dreamed of you, for more nights than you know, and I shall learn to hasten my business then."

Enough was enough. Isobel picked up her skirts and ran in the direction Alec had gone. She reached the crest of a

hill and pulled up short . . . for there came Alec, limping
through the heather, the simpering little governess at his
side. Oh, this was all wrong. Prissy Mrs. Clare Charlton was
supposed to give fat Dr. Wilmot someone to occupy him.
Everyone was mixed up.

"Hallo, Isobel," Alec called with maddening good cheer
and a wave. "You win."

She glowered. "No, I don't. Dr. Wilmot *walked* back."
Oh, bother. There was only one thing to do, and that was to
tell that little governess exactly where she stood here. In
speaking her mind, Isobel had never been shy. But Clare
Charlton, sly little mouse, broke away and headed up the
moorland, doubtless to finally search for Vicky, which was
what she should have been doing all along. As Isobel closed
in on Alec, she slowed down and caught her breath. It would
not do to appear too worried or desperate. Tomorrow would
be soon enough to handle the governess. Aye, tomorrow.

At Thornhill, Adele Charlton stared at her husband.
"Percival, when are we going to see Vicky again?"

Percival had hardly spoken to her since the abortive
rescue attempt at the statue.

"Percival, say something . . . Anything. I can't stand
the silence up here at Thornhill any longer."

Silence. Except for the relentless breezes across the
heath. And far off, the River Tyne flowing over
rocks . . . And a lark singing while it winged its way north
from the Traitor's Bride, the statue of stone. Day after day,
Percival sat and stared out the window, silent, immobile.
Not touching his food. Scarcely sleeping.

"When will you tell me what you're thinking?"

"Tomorrow."

Alec shook hands with Dr. Wigston Wilmot with more
enthusiasm then he'd intended. As a physician spouting

radical ideas about the worth of surgeons, the man was tetched. But, as a snare for ladies like Isobel, the man was worth all his trouble. As thanks, Alec gladly endured another painful probing of his knee.

Now, though, the fellow lingered, following Alec about.

"Lord Strahan, I must speak with you on an urgent matter."

"Not my limp. No more examinations." He'd nearly forgotten about it in the more compelling memory of luminous green eyes, sun-streaked hair set against the backdrop of heather abloom.

"Milord, 'tis a matter of the heart."

Had the good physician been eyeing Clare? Alec's knee buckled, and Wigston Wilmot caught at his arm.

Annoyed, Alec shook him away. "Later. I've no time for any more talk."

"But when?"

"When you return."

"I shall consult the Royal College of Surgeons post-haste."

"Take your time."

For Alec was resigned to life at Dundroma, limping about, living in the shadows of pain, and watching the English governess bloom along with his daughter.

It would suffice. And finally believing him, Dr. Wigston Wilmot departed Dundroma for even more northerly parts.

Alec watched him go. He was alone now with Vicky, with Mrs. Drummond, the servants, Andrew, and Clare. He had lied to himself. Watching Clare bloom would not suffice.

He wanted to grab her and kiss her lips then and there. But where was his vow to ignore all Thornhill women? Desire for women was, unlike the pain of shattered bones, something that vanished. It had to vanish.

Another dawn, and he would push away this yearning to pull Clare into his arms. Life would go on. The moon set.

The sun rise. He would limp along in tune to the rhythms of his own village, not to the annoying beat of his pulse.

Aye, tomorrow, he'd be his normal devilish self.

❦ Chapter Eleven

Isobel returned the very next day. Alec, not in the mood to limp across the parlor, waited for her in the garden, wondering what the widow had up her sleeve today.

A warm summer sun shone into the garden this morning. Apple trees grew here, along with broom and a few experimental bushes, like rhododendrons, imported in his absence. The box hedges had been trimmed since his return, and the place weeded. Aged pines, tall and wind-bent, stood outside a stone wall, flanking the outer gate. They helped to shield this secluded nook, the best place from which to view the heather on the hills, and the view was even better from a wobbly bench near the gate.

Isobel's skirts rustled, and her perfume, musky and reminiscent of India, preceded her. The scent, rather than stimulating him, reminded him of Malcolm, of how much he missed his good friend. Dundroma wasn't the same without Malcolm.

He was beginning to see that he'd made a mistake allowing himself to become so entwined in the Frasers' social life back in India. Summer parties in the hills of Simla. Horseback riding in the moonlight. Lazy afternoons wiling away the heat of the day under a waving fan . . . and doing what? Encouraging Isobel's flirtatiousness. Thinking because she was wed to Malcolm there could be no harm.

Now with Malcolm gone, there was danger. Not that Isobel wasn't an attractive woman, but she was far too obvious, and Alec liked his women less hungry. Besides, he wasn't at all certain it was him she was flirting with or the title of Lady Strahan. In any case, it was a title Alec had no intention of bestowing on anybody. He'd let Dundroma pass to his daughter; Vicky's sons would, in the Scottish fashion, inherit the estate.

"Another visit, Isobel?" he said in a languid voice. "You must like this drafty old castle," he added. "Most women abhor it." He reached down with his walking stick and poked at a stray weed amid the broom. Damn, but he couldn't even kneel to weed. Even as a gardener he was worthless.

Isobel glided toward him and leaned over, hand outstretched for him to kiss. "I did not come to see Dundroma. I came to walk with you. To strengthen your knee. And then to take tea."

"I did not come home to mend, Isobel. I'm unmendable and well you know it. I intend to hibernate and rusticate in the drafts of Dundroma."

Undeterred, she pressed the issue. "You've been alone too long." Pressing her hand in the crook of his arm, she tugged him forward. "And this place needs a woman's influence. You're surrounded by too many dead animal trophies."

Alec doubted the stag heads had anything to do with his mood. "Dundroma has too many women in it as it is lately."

Isobel paused in her tracks and looked up at him. Her smile was too forced, her laugh too brittle. "Too many women . . . but, Alec, that's your own doing. If this feud with Thornhill is making you unhappy, perhaps you should send the child back for a while——"

"No."

Isobel reached for his walking stick and caressed the

ivory head of it. "So decisive. What brought this on? Too
much pony riding yesterday?"

He snatched the cane away and jammed it back down into
the gravel walkway, the ivory tiger's head secure in his
palm.

"Are you going to start spouting this bluestocking nonsense about children's feelings—the same as Clare Charlton?"

"Do you think I'm the same as Clare Charlton?"

"Night and day, Isobel."

"And which am I? Night or day?"

"Which do you want?"

She looked up at him from under her lashes. "Alec," she
purred, "I'm in mourning still . . . why do you keep
forgetting?" And Isobel batted her eyes as only Isobel could.

Damn Isobel's habit of flirtatious questions. There was
only one way to end her game.

"Vicky is coming to join us," he announced.

With a shrug, Isobel left him and moved ahead to settle
down on the sole bench.

"Well, where is she?" Isobel asked, her voice impatient.
"You should raise her to show respect for your schedule."

Isobel had absolutely no mothering instincts. In fact, Alec
doubted if Isobel knew the date of Andrew's birth without
resorting to the family Bible. But it was amusing to watch
her pretend. Rather like watching an Englishman try on a
kilt.

Pain throbbed in his leg, the old pain, accompanied by the
shadows. The past closing in. His dreams. His hopes.

Damn, he'd give anything to sit, but Isobel would like
nothing better than to have a cozy tête-à-tête.

And so he stood, leaning with two hands against his
reliable tiger head, hoping his leg would not buckle beneath
him.

Tea was late, and so was Vicky. But Isobel used the time to her advantage.

"The villagers are all gossiping, Alec," she said. "Don't you pay any attention?"

"To gossip? No." And he didn't much care.

"Well, in this case, I think you should listen."

"What is it?" The pain was a growling thing, stalking him. The tendons in his forearms quivered, stretched, throbbed, almost more than his knee. Through a haze of pain, he tried to make sense. Gossip.

"The governess. Some groom says you were rolling in the heather with her, and you know how they talk. This isn't India, Alec, this is Britain."

"It's Dundroma, first and last before it's Britain, and I'm master here and shall do as I please."

"You must be lonelier than I thought. You're tempting history to repeat itself."

He knew enough of women's wiles to recognize jealousy when he saw it. There was satisfaction in watching Isobel, who'd had her way so often, squirm.

"The groom doubtless needs a pair of spectacles, and a reprimand for spying—"

"I never said he spied intentionally—"

"Papa!"

The door from the castle burst open at the same time Vicky called out to him. Vicky. His daughter. In the nick of time.

And Clare Charlton accompanied her.

The governess herself, looking uncommonly refreshing, even in that drab gown. Sunlight caught in her hair and made her hazel eyes sparkle.

"Good afternoon, Miss Charlton," he said merely to coax a reply. He liked to watch the dimples appear when she spoke. A stiff greeting, but the dimples were there. Beside her, Vicky, red hair brushed and beribboned, wore some white starched creation that had altogether too much Thornhill style to it. Vicky was tugging at its neck, and the bow in her tartan sash had fallen free.

The growling, stalking tiger of pain was too close for him to say anything about it.

And then everything blurred.

"Lord Strahan?" a soft voice asked. "Mrs. Fraser, please be so kind as to allow Lord Strahan to sit . . ."

The governess was directing a servant in his direction, a servant carrying a chair from the great hall.

"Hurry, please, and set it on the path. Lord Strahan must sit down at once."

Alec had sunk onto one knee when someone took his arm with a "Here you go, sir," and yanked him up. Gentle arms eased him down onto a chair and he sank onto it, too grateful to speak. At once, the blurring pain receded. Servants hovered all about. Male servants. Isobel was staring with resentment. Ladies swooned, not devilish Scottish majors from the British Raj.

"Is there anything else, milord?" the butler asked.

He stared at his hands, which were on his knees, shaking.

"Whisky," he managed.

"No, just tea please." Clare answered for him and handed him his walking stick.

"Your master asked for whisky," Isobel snapped. "Lord Strahan knows what he wants."

The servant looked back and forth between the two women, as if wondering which to obey.

"Tea for Lord Strahan," Miss Charlton said. "Mrs. Fraser may of course have what she desires."

"Tea." Alec regained his equilibrium enough to settle the matter. "Tea with sugar."

Isobel glared. "Since when did the governess become your Florence Nightingale, Alec?"

But Alec didn't bother to reply. Clare, with quiet strength,

was at his side, an arm on his sleeve. "Vicky, come and sit
by your papa," she said.

His daughter leaned on the arm of the chair. "Are you all
right, Papa? You aren't supposed to stand so long, you
know. Dr. Wilmot said so."

"It had nothing to do with my knee," he growled. "I'm
fine. And Dr. Wilmot is a doddering fool—visiting surgeons in Edinburgh."

"There'd be no ideas in this world if men like Dr. Wilmot
didn't explore the possibilities, milord," Clare said softly.

"I am not Christopher Columbus, nor is my knee the New
World, wanting to be explored."

But he was lying. For as soon as the weight was off his
leg, the growling tiger backed off into the jungle, and the
misty Scottish afternoon took its place. He saw not fangs,
but a twisted yew tree, and Isobel's bemused face.

"My, you think of everything," she was saying to
someone. "Quite the efficient English governess. Doubling
as Alec's nursemaid . . . and that doesn't count hostess."

The prim brown dress was in front of him then. "Your tea,
sir. It will refresh you. Vicky's right, you know. Walking in
the heath yesterday overtired your leg."

"So Isobel has already suggested."

Clare glanced over at Isobel who was looking at Clare
with something akin to hatred. She backed away. "I've
intruded. I'll leave."

Alec looked up into her naive little face. "On the
contrary . . . if you'd been a minute longer, I'd probably
have fallen over again and embarrassed myself."

Isobel stood and blocked Clare from his view. "Alec, you
should have said you wanted to sit. Your daughter's governess is far too busy to indulge you."

"I'm not being mollycoddled, if that's your implication,"
he said, irritated beyond measure.

"Well, I hope you'll tell Clare that. She obviously doesn't

know it's the Dundroma way to encourage stoicism—even in the face of pain. Think, Alec, how women endure the rigors of childbed. Your knee can't possibly compare to that—"

"You're right, Isobel," he said, unable to keep a trace of sarcasm out of his voice. "Kindly allow Clare to share the bench with you."

There was silence, then Clare obeyed.

Looking at her, he felt blissful. Isobel, meanwhile, chattered on, bragging again about how she'd introduced Alec to his late wife.

Never dreaming he'd marry Cecilia and rob Isobel of Alec. Isobel, he was sure, had wed poor Malcolm mere weeks later to save face. But she couldn't admit that of course. Instead, she concocted a tale about how she'd played matchmaker.

At last, she paused to take a breath, and Alec, aware that through all this, Vicky had been silently watching the woman who aspired to be her stepmother, turned to his daughter. "What do you think of Mrs. Fraser's story of my courtship with your mother?"

"I think Mrs. Fraser had a good imagination. My mother's letters don't say that at all."

"You still suggest I fabricate my facts?" Isobel's face turned dark.

"Yes . . . aye," Vicky said. "As you did the other night."

"Why, you brazen little girl."

"Bold is the word, Isobel," Alec warned. Privately, he was amused at his daughter's outspokenness. Ah, yes, she was thriving here indeed if she could stand up to Isobel. "My daughter is growing bold."

Isobel stood and angrily brushed at her black velvet skirt. The crinoline beneath bobbed in and out. "Well, you don't believe her, do you?"

"A Douglas always believes his own kin."

"But this . . . this child has been taught by a Thornhill governess."

"And taught well, in book learning. I've yet to teach her the history of the border feuds, so Vicky is still innocent when it comes to stealing, plundering, bending the truth . . ."

"You have your work cut out for you then, Alec, truly."

He set down his teacup and stood.

"You're not leaving me with the governess?" Isobel asked.

Astute Vicky handed him his walking stick.

"I'm taking my daughter to visit the ponies. Stay and straighten out your facts with Miss Charlton. Vicky might ask again."

Face flushed, Isobel leaned against the bench, and silently watched him limp off.

Alec and Victoria paused out on the path up the moors, the path that led to the view of that damnable statue. Yet, every time he thought of it, he thought of sun-streaked hair, hazel eyes, and the memory of a rose-colored gown . . . that and the way her primness melted away at his touch. She was temptation . . . But, he cautioned himself, it was one thing entirely to flirt with an English rose. A man could get stung by English thorns if he was not careful, and Alec had sworn never to form any more alliances that could sting.

Yet, he'd give anything to know if Clare could hold her own against Isobel.

Well, thought Clare, as she watched them go . . . Lord Strahan could stalk out and take Vicky but that didn't mean she had to feel so forlorn. What was the matter with her? One touch of her hand to his sleeve, one gaze from him, and her pulse had jumped.

Clare added more milk to her tea to cool it and swallowed
it quickly. She set her cup in the saucer and stood to leave
also.

Isobel's voice stopped her in her tracks.

"His first wife and he eloped, you know."

"I believe you, Mrs. Fraser. And I'm not trying to make
you look bad. Nor is Vicky. She simply has a child's lack of
guile."

Isobel motioned for her to sit, and Clare, out of politeness, sat back down on the bench.

"Well," Isobel conceded, "twelve years is a long time
ago, and perhaps my own memories are fading, but their
marriage was a mistake." Clare's head snapped up at this
piece of information, and Isobel continued. "From the start.
Alec acted impulsively and so did Cecilia. Both a bit
rebellious. I can't say I blame Cecilia; from what she told
me when we were at finishing school, Thornhill sounded
dreadfully repressive. I'd likely have rebelled too, though
not to the extent of marrying into my enemy's family . . ."

Clare sat ramrod-straight. "I thought it was a mutual
attachment. Lord Strahan never remarried, so it was assumed he was grieving all these years."

Isobel laughed. "And I suppose you assume he ran off to
India because his dear orphaned baby daughter reminded
him of his dead wife?"

Clare nodded. "What else would make the Charltons
invent a father for her?"

"The Charltons contort everything to put the best face on
the situation. Truth is often a victim. No, Miss Charlton,
Lord Strahan has not been grieving these twelve years, and
I'm the one who's been in India with him—until just a year
past. He was not grieving, but having a most gay time.
That's an even more compelling reason to invent a new
father for the child."

She sipped her tea. "And I imagine Alec has told you the sad tale of Cecilia's death in childbirth?"

Actually, not really. But Clare was fascinated by Isobel's gossip.

"Before the accident, that was the story he used to elicit sympathy. He knows better than to try such tales on me."

"Why should he want my sympathy?" Clare asked.

"Because once a man like him gets your sympathy, it's but a short step to more intimate behavior. Come, Clare, you were married to Cecilia's brother, so you're not that naive. I shouldn't have to spell this out, should I? Or perhaps I do . . ." She stood and gave a condescending smile.

Clare bristled. "You're suggesting I might be infatuated with Lord Strahan."

Isobel whirled in a rustle of black taffeta.

"I'm sure you already are. It takes little time for a man like him to make an impression on a sweet young thing like you."

"I don't expect a man like him to notice the governess."

"A man like Alec notices all women, and he takes what he wants."

Clare recalled his dark oath the day she'd arrived. Yes, she believed he might.

"It's the old code of the aristocracy," Isobel went on. "A double standard wherein the lord of the manor takes his pleasure by any maid or servant that catches his eye—but marries the ladies."

"Are you and he going to wed?" Clare asked boldly.

"My, what cheek. I'd hardly have expected it from a meek English governess."

Clare didn't see any point to this little discussion. She'd already guessed Isobel had more than a friendly interest in Lord Strahan.

There went her thoughts again . . . she got up. "Will

you excuse me, please? I have letters to write. To Vicky's grandparents."

"Not yet . . . Actually, Miss Charlton, it's Vicky I want to talk about."

"Yes?"

"I think you should leave."

"I *was* about to leave the garden . . . when *you* asked me to stay."

"Not the garden," Isobel said with a smug smile. "I mean Dundroma, of course. I know you hate it here, that you only came because of the girl."

The girl. How coldly Isobel reduced Vicky to a nameless thing. The girl. The child.

"I can't leave Vicky."

"But that's a convenient excuse to linger. A woman infatuated might find it harder to leave the father."

"That's not true."

"I don't expect you to admit it, of course, but let me remind you, you're only an English governess, and he'll never align himself with another Englishwoman from Thornhill, let alone a governess. You'd do yourself a favor if you left before your infatuation proved embarrassing."

Clare was too stunned at first to come up with words.

"You're very straightforward," she said at last.

"I'm a Scotswoman. Frugal with words, capable of reducing a situation to the most economical solution. And not always worried about what people will think. Leave, Miss Charlton, and I promise, if all goes as I hope with Lord Strahan—"

"You mean, if you become Lady Strahan—"

"You're learning quickly to become economical and blunt with your words as well."

"Survival up here demands it."

"Very well, I'm not afraid to admit my ambitions. It was me he came to see, you know, not Cecilia. It was an accident he wed her, and though I made the best of it once, the next time I wed, I'll have my due. You're distracting him, Miss Charlton, and so if you leave, I'll make you a bargain. I'll see that Vicky is sent home to Thornhill. There's no chance he can keep her."

"You'd tear her from her father?"

"Well, whose side are you on? Thornhill's or Dundroma's?"

"Vicky's. She is a borderer and a child. And she belongs to both places. She's not a sacrificial lamb to be torn apart. And whoever loves her best will know that and want what's best. It could be that here is best."

"My, spoken like Solomon, indeed. But that's all beside the point. I asked you to leave. You may even use my coach."

Clare was incensed. How dare this woman call herself a mother?

She strode toward the haughty widow in black. "I suggest you mind your own business. You have no authority to suggest I do anything. Convince Lord Strahan to wed you and then you may order me about, but until then, I take orders only from Vicky's father who is her legal guardian."

"Did you tell me to mind my own business?"

Clare stood straight.

"Lord Strahan is my business. And as widow of his best friend, Dundroma is my business. Servants talk, surely you know that, and they whisper already that he's stolen kisses from you."

She held Isobel's gaze. "That's my business."

"Has he?"

"Ask him yourself . . . and then look to yourself before you offer others moral advice. It's you Scots who have the reputation for lax behavior, and that's a well-known rumor at Thornhill. Charltons have always been the model of propriety. Perhaps too much so, but proper nonetheless. In

any case, I don't need lessons from a Scottish widow in how
to conduct myself!"

"You refuse my offer."

"You may take your offer and toss it in the loch with the
kelpies."

And brushing past the black widow's skirts, she turned
her back and straightened her shoulders and exited the
garden.

She never stopped until she was well out on the heath,
alone, walking beside a narrow stream.

And then she stopped at a clump of wind-tossed heather.
Telling off the self-righteous Isobel had felt good. More than
good. In fact, Clare had never told off anyone before in her
life. Certainly not dear Reginald, and never the
Charltons . . . and Vicky had never been in need of
serious reprimands . . . and well, no one. It was a heady
feeling, standing up for herself. Heady indeed.

She walked higher up into the hills, wild with purple
heather. The wind blew her skirt and loosened her hair, and
she lifted her face up to the sky. Her feelings were taking
over in this wild Dundroma, her inhibitions slipping. Else it
was a newfound confidence taking hold now that she was
out from under her mother-in-law's thumb . . . perhaps
something about the Dundroma life was making her bolder,
as Lord Strahan predicted.

But Isobel had hit the mark about her feelings. Her
feelings for the man were growing bolder too, and she'd
have to hold them in check. If need be, she'd sacrifice
something to keep herself from falling prey to her wild
emotions.

Even Vicky?

Could she go that far . . . as to steal her away from here
where she'd bloomed so happily?

And the answer came back like a whisper. Yes . . . if

need be. Otherwise, she'd be as undone as the poor woman
in that statue at the border . . . lost forever.

Vicky leaned on the paddock fence, heedless of her frock.
Her hair ribbon dangled from one hand. Poor Papa was too
tired to remain long at the paddock. After admiring
Macduff, he told Vicky her bold words to Mrs. Fraser had
pleased him and limped back to the castle. Vicky pondered
that.

Boldness pleased Papa.

Very well. That was the same as giving her permission for
even more bolder things. Like a first kiss. And perhaps to
win one, she would have to be bolder with Andrew as well.

Vicky found Andrew inside the stables. He stood in
profile, golden hair falling over his forehead, looking so
handsome Vicky's heart felt as if she'd been practicing a
Highland reel.

Vicky said the first thing that came to her mind. "Today
I interrupted your mother with my father, Andrew . . . will
she be angry at me?"

"Very . . . you'd better hide out for a while."

Andrew flashed her a bashful smile, one of the first he'd
given her. In that instant she ceased to care about the wager
with Charlotte. Only Andrew. Handsome Andrew.

"Where should I go?"

Andrew pointed up to the hills, and turning tail, the pair
of them ran, Andrew first, leading up the moorland into the
heather, Vicky following him, her feet carrying her as fast as
she could go.

At last Andrew fell into the heather and lay back laughing
and catching his breath.

Vicky flopped down too, but propped herself up on one
elbow, out of breath as much from watching Andrew Fraser
as from their escape. She decided now was the time for the
boldness her father had praised.

"You said you'd kissed someone, didn't you?"

He suddenly became interested in his fingernails. "Oh, that again."

"I still don't understand the kissing statue. Now that I'm here I know no Scotsman would turn a lass to stone, so it's got to have something else to do with kissing. What do you think?"

Andrew shrugged and finally turned to look at her. "I expect so. Kissing is nicer, and you don't feel like a stone statue when you do it."

"How do you feel?"

"I can't describe it."

"Then show me?"

"You're too young."

"I'm twelve, almost twelve and a half. And my friend Charlotte's already kissed the groom. I know enough."

She lay back down in the heather and smiled up at Andrew. "Coward. You've never kissed anyone."

"I have." He hesitated, then touched her cheek with his finger. "How does that feel?"

"Like dew. Like butterflies. Like—"

"That's how a kiss starts."

"How does it end?"

"The same."

"What happens in between?"

Oh, but Andrew was a stubborn Scotsman. She was almost sorry she adored him so, that he made her heart beat faster. But she'd get her first kiss from him, if she had to spend her life here.

"What?"

He shrugged. "It depends on the lass, ye ken."

"What about me?"

"You'd be like the stone statue."

Irate, she sat up. "I would not."

He shrugged. "You've never done it."

"You don't want to."

"I never said that. A lad doesn't just kiss any lass."

"Is it because I'm from Thornhill?"

"No, it's because you're too busy asking questions. A lad wants to think of it himself and take the lass by surprise."

Vicky was silent. He was right. "I'll shut my eyes and—"

"No—"

She sighed and opened her eyes again. Aunt Clare was tramping up behind them. Reluctantly Vicky got up and brushed bits of heather off her skirt. "I think you're afraid, Andrew, that's what."

Aunt Clare had ruined her chances today; Vicky was getting altogether too big to be followed about by a governess.

"Are you angry, Aunt Clare?" Vicky asked as they started back. "You look distressed."

"Not angry, but concerned. I heard you, Vicky. You're too young to be off alone in the heather with Andrew, talking about kisses."

No, she wasn't. Like the border at the River Tyne, crossing into the world of kissing would take her somewhere new and mysterious. Aunt Clare had told her at the statue that she'd know when she was ready. And her father had told she was free to explore here. She was going to kiss Andrew, and that was that.

"I'm not too young," she said and ran into the castle.

❦ Chapter Twelve

"Miss Charlton," Lord Strahan called from the midst of all the stag heads, "stop hiding out there in the shadows and show yourself."

Taking a deep breath, she slipped inside the doorway and, praying for control, walked across the tartan carpet. He was seated in front of the fire, Reiver at his side, his hand caressing the dog. Clare had mere seconds to steel herself for the devilish laird. Control. Self-control. No matter what he did, she would not let him affect her.

The room was lit only by scattered candles, the heavy draperies were pulled against the daylight, and so his face was cast in shadow. He wore only a white shirt over his black trousers; the checked plaid lay over a chair. Candlelight shone on him from behind and highlighted the rich reddish tones of his hair.

"What is it?" His voice was austere, his features drawn, and there was not a bit of welcoming warmth in his eyes. He looked at her as if she were a nuisance.

"Why have you come?"

"I need to talk with you about your daughter . . . naturally. What other reason could there be?"

He stared at her, his eyes going up and down her gown as if in disapproval.

Instead of asking her about Vicky as she expected, he said, "It has come to my attention that the servants gossip about your presence in my house."

"That is not my fault."

"Oh, but I take full blame."

"That is not fair."

"Fair? You are a lass concerned with justice, aren't you, Aunt Clare? When it comes to the lasses, I don't consider what is fair."

"But other people care."

"Isobel," he guessed.

She was silent.

"What did you tell her?"

"That what I did here was none of her affair."

He whistled low and gave her an appreciative look. "The Highlanders are not so brave in battle as you are . . . few Scotsmen take on Isobel Fraser. Well done, Aunt Clare."

She hated being called Aunt Clare. It made her feel he was seeing her as a wizened old widow.

"You're jesting. I apologize if I offended your late friend's widow."

"Isobel is a woman of boldness and so not easily offended. I admire that quality in her; it's the very quality I hope to instill in my daughter."

"Sir, if I may be so bold, there is a difference between boldness and rudeness, between spirit and breaking the rules of politeness."

"From your English perspective, aye, but here at Dundroma, we are not so concerned with rules as with survival."

"Then you're still a barbarian."

For the first time his face brightened.

This would never do. "Lord Strahan, I came on a serious mission and already you've turned the subject."

"Very well," he said. "How serious?"

"Vicky. We must talk."

"By all means." He stood and limped to where his

checked cloak lay on another chair. The sheepdog shadowed his every movement. Clare felt the breath slide out of her. She was rooted to the spot, unable to make her legs work. She watched as he slung the cloak over one shoulder, Scottish fashion.

Without warning, he turned to her, eyes dark as the loch at dawn. "Go on then, fetch your cloak, Clare Charlton."

"Can we not talk here?"

He shook his head. "To protect your reputation and mine, we shall not remain shut away in my library."

"Where are we going?" There could be greater hazards to her reputation. A hundred stag heads might be watching here, but at least they didn't talk.

"I'm going to the village, to see some of my people. I've been gone a long time, and they expect me. I believe it would be entirely proper for the governess of my child to accompany me."

"But we can discuss Vicky in a matter of minutes."

He strode to the door and held it for her. "Good, come along and tell me out in public, but bide a wee until we're clear of the castle."

Very well. If that's what he wanted. After all, he was the master here. And it would look as if he were driving her to market or to church. Propriety personified. Her talk could wait, and she admitted to curiosity about how such a barbaric man would relate to the common people. The villagers of Dundroma would doubtless shrink away from this cranky, devilish man . . . and that would help her retain control.

He limped toward the outer door, and quickly she went for her cloak.

Half an hour later they were nearing the village, and he'd been as silent as a loch at dawn. Only the clip-clop of the pony pulling the cart and a perfunctory query about whether she was warm enough broke their silence. But he faced her, and it was hard not to stare at his rock-hard body, at the soft wool of his cloak, the way he gripped the ivory head of his walking stick.

"About Vicky," she ventured.

"Not yet," he said bluntly. "We shall talk when we are farther away from Dundroma."

She waited. Trying hard to ignore his masculine attractiveness, trying to ignore the lock of hair that fell over his forehead, the blue-gray gaze that came back to her over and over. His harsh manner was the fascination. The man had no soft edges.

The pony cart slowed to a stop, and he leaned out. Clare peered out and saw a gypsy beggar, clothes ragged, pleading for coins. Years ago, gypsies used to come by the back door of Thornhill, but Adele left orders to have them beaten back at the road. Clare had rather enjoyed their colorful caravans winding through the borderland on their way up to Scotland, but in the past few years they'd been avoiding Thornhill property. So she assumed Dundroma would afford them even less hospitality. Beggars, begone. She could hear Adele even now. And of course it wasn't that Adele was thrifty. It was her inbred sense of appearances. The gentle folk of Thornhill did not want to be associated with such vagabond ragtag people. Appearances, always.

So now, Clare braced herself for the rattle of Alec's saber, or whatever weapon he'd use to chase the gypsy beggar away.

He did nothing of the kind.

Instead, he dug in his pocket for coins and handed them over. And then he gave the beggar a kind word.

Adele would have been prostrate with shock.

But it was doubtless done to impress her. No man called the devil of Dundroma would regularly befriend gypsy beggars.

"Adele says that giving to gypsies only encourages them."

"And what do you think, Clare?"

"To be honest, I miss visiting their wagons for scarves and the like. I used to listen to their violin music in the evenings—way back when Reginald had first died . . . I'd take my orphaned niece—back then of course I assumed Vicky was an orphan—"

"I'd forgotten. I was the missionary drowned at sea."

She smiled and for a split second their gazes met. Blue eyes. She looked away first.

"They don't come around anymore."

"Adele's chased them all away . . ."

She nodded.

"You still haven't told me what you think, Clare."

"At Thornhill, I'd never been asked what I think. I merely cared for Vicky."

"I can tell that, but I'm sure you have an opinion. I should like to hear it."

She thought a moment. She had expressed so many opinions already.

"Go on. I like it when you turn into a bluestocking. I'm assured then that Vicky's learned more about life than how to keep up appearances."

She cleared her throat, buying a few more moments to clear her thoughts. This was new. A request for her thoughts. A man wanting her opinion. Never ceasing in his quest to see beneath the surface. To taunt the passions she kept locked away.

"I think," she said carefully, "that there is a great deal of beauty in the Romany life." She was not used to speaking her opinion and so hedged her words.

"Roamers. I would be a roamer like the gypsies," he said, a trace of wistfulness in his voice. "Until my accident, I had roamed from the Crimea to India. I'd still like to roam some more. We Dundroma lads are not the sort to sit at home and warm a castle fire. For that reason, I would give all the gypsies a coin . . . because they can still roam to places I would only dream about now . . . Have you never dreamed of roaming, Clare?"

"When Vicky is grown."

"Aye, surely then. Where will you go?"

Beside him, she thought. Anywhere Lord Strahan went. There she would go too.

No. Her thoughts were turning fanciful.

"Lord Strahan, Vicky is not yet grown, and I must discuss her behavior . . ."

"Bide a wee." That was all he said, and they rode on past the thatched roofs of the village, the skies pleasantly blue above them, the summer day fragrant with strangely pleasant scents from the shops—the spices of black pudding, the yeast of bread cooling in the windows. The village of Black Cloak Crossing looked as English as her own familiar Reiver's Noose. Only the accents were more distinctively Scottish; the clothing too had a Highland look to it missing in and about Thornhill. But it was border country, bounded by heath the same as Thornhill's village, and it struck her then how much alike the border villages were. Distinctive in loyalties and yet bound by common geography. Thatch and sheep and heather. It knew no boundaries.

Nor did the heart. It was a fleeting thought, borne on her memory. Something she'd heard a while back. Men and women. Attractions of the heart. They could not be confined by a border that only existed on maps, which were scarce at best. Why, given that, half the people in this Black Cloak Crossing had intermarried with villagers from Reiver's Noose. Despite Adele's attempts to hold herself apart, the common people, the villagers, cared little for boundaries. Like gypsies they had roamed back and forth between the two villages for centuries, following their hearts' desires. Not caring how the politicians carved up the border. Simply flowing like the River Tyne between the heath and the hills.

Long ago, the people of the border had learned to live frugally, out of sheer necessity. Never knowing when a raid would take all a man owned forced a man to change his priorities. Here in the borderland, common men valued a crop that grew quickly, a loyal woman to warm a man's bed, wherever. That was all that could be counted on. That and the eternal feud between the high and mighty gentry in the big houses.

And neither, she suspected, if one could judge from his kindness to the gypsy beggar, did Lord Strahan confine himself to borders. His contempt toward the kissing statue was clear enough. And his marriage to a daughter of Thornhill spoke for itself.

But that begged the question: Would his unhappy marriage to Cecilia leave him forever cynical?

A village boy ran toward them, stuffing the last of an oat cake into his mouth. Face dirty, he scowled, and in one hand he brandished a long stick—still green with sap, its bark freshly peeled. He barely stopped to doff his bonnet at Lord Strahan and kept on going.

"Here then, but if he were older, I'd say he's hot trodding off to plunder—" Lord Strahan reined in the ponies and pulled the cart up short.

Clare turned. The gypsy beggar was walking barefoot some distance behind them. But now she cowered. The boy—younger than Vicky—raised the stick and struck at the beggar.

For a man in pain, Lord Strahan moved with unusual swiftness. Uncustomary speed. While Clare watched open-mouthed, Lord Strahan had eased out of the cart and hobbled back down the lane. He came up behind the urchin and taking the boy by the scruff of the neck, he removed the cane. As matter-of-factly as if he were pulling a bramble off the lane. Not harshly. But with a warning.

"Be off with you now, or I'll take the pony back. Leave the beggar alone, and count your blessings, lad."

The boy blinked. "Lord Strahan?" He stared from his crude stick to the polished one Lord Strahan balanced on.

"Aye, I don't walk as I used to, but it's me. And a stick is a necessity to me to move. To see a stick used to hinder someone is a grievous misuse, lad . . . Ian, is it?"

"How'd you know?"

"A guess, lad. Half the lads in Black Cloak Crossing were named Ian, just as half the sheepdogs are called Reiver . . . Now promise me you'll not cane any more beggars. Remember your golden rule, lad, and show compassion. Your mother's the widow, is she not?"

"Aye, sir."

"Tell her I'll send another sack of oats. Go on home with you now, and deliver her that news. Then report to my manager."

"For the oats?"

"For caning a beggar, you will help in the garden at Dundroma. The kitchen garden needs weeding. Take home potatoes for your mother, but you must do the harvesting and take a hoe home and start a garden for her. Busy lads, I've learned, do not have time to cane the unfortunate."

"You mean it?"

"As much as I want compassion but not pity for my bad leg. Think of the beggar as me, lad. He wants compassion, but no pity, and no cruelty. We are all alike that way."

"Aye, sir, aye." Wide-eyed at getting let off so easy for his naughtiness, the boy backed away, still staring at the laird.

Lord Strahan snapped the lad's stick in two and tossed it to the side of the road.

The old gypsy lurked behind a bush, half ready to run,

half taken by curiosity. Alec spotted her, but didn't move lest he frighten her.

"Be gone then before those coins burn a hole in your pocket. Both of you."

And a moment later, Ian was vanishing into the low-lying mist that hung about the edges of the village crofts. The old gypsy disappeared too, and Lord Strahan limped back to the cart where Clare waited.

She tried to think of the appropriate remark. "Milord, you surprise me every other moment."

"How is that?"

"Your kindness to a beggar, and then your discipline of a village boy. One of your people."

"We are all people, Clare."

His gentle reply encouraged her. "May we have our talk now?" she asked. "What I need to discuss has nothing to do with Thornhill and everything to do with Dundroma."

"Not yet," he said, waving to a passing carpenter. "I have one stop to make. Would you like to come in?"

"To a croft?"

"They're humble dwellings but the villagers take great pride in them, and I keep them maintained. Have even from a distance. I expected my estate manager to keep my people well. The Douglases have a tradition of kinship."

She was curious, and decided at once. "Yes, then." This devil of Dundroma was kind to beggars and merciful to small boys bent on mischief. What next?

He handed her down in front of a croft by the black-smith's and from the door she heard the grateful greetings of the smithy and his wife. The room was small: a black caldron bubbled over an open fire, and the beds were built into the walls. Somehow an entire family fit in here, and they parted to reveal a cradle. A newborn babe.

Lord Strahan turned to Clare. "Come along and have a look with me."

It was a girl, less than a week old and swaddled in white. Alec Douglas, the devil of Dundroma, touched a finger to the cradle and rocked it. Inside a lovely sleeping baby pursed its lips, stretched, and spread its fingers.

Clare hadn't seen such a young baby ever. "Vicky was as lovely as this." Her voice was a whisper. "Older, when I took over as nanny, but this lovely."

"Was she?" he said. "Pity I missed it. If I could change one thing it would be that."

"You'd have stayed?"

"I'd have taken her."

He laid a hand on the baby's brow and gave her the laird's blessing. "Her name?"

"Margaret."

"A bonnie name for a bonnie bairn. A proper Scots name and one suited for a Douglas."

"Ah, Lord Strahan, but your own daughter is named for the Queen, and for all the Queen's English and German, she's come to the Highlands and done all right by Scotland. 'Tis a fine name."

"Unusual."

"For Dundroma . . . but a fine name your Vicky."

Lord Strahan stood looking into the cradle, as if he were pondering what was past.

Clare studied him. Yes, he would have taken Vicky . . . and then she'd never have met him . . .

"Blessings on the babe. Don't let her languish in any sickness now. I'm to know at once."

"Mrs. Fraser—she came by and left a basket of jellies. She offered to help."

Lord Strahan paused. "If anyone is ill, send for me, or the governess here. Miss Charlton has cared for my daughter since she was an infant." He looked at her.

"Indeed."

They stared at the baby across opposite sides of the

cradle, and then she looked up to see him watching her. "We must go. I have next to discuss my daughter."

"Ta. Thank you, milord."

They touched their forelocks, and the mother curtsied, and they gathered in the doorway to watch him go, Clare in his wake.

So, thought Clare, as she settled back in the cart. The man had an unexpected side. Very much so. In fact, there was nothing barbaric to the man she'd spent the past hour with.

In England, what he'd done would have been considered too familiar, consorting with common people. Yet in England, she realized, beggars went hungry, gypsies were run away, mischievous boys were locked in workhouses, widows too.

And as for infants borne to the common villagers, why Adele had never visited a one. Oh, she'd dropped off food baskets from her coach. But never would she deign to alight and enter a humble cottage. Appearances. Appearances.

As for Clare, what had she gotten for her years of service? A roof over her head and an admonition to be grateful. Somehow, Dundroma's master seemed the more civilized. Thornhill, for all its outward facade of gentility, was at heart the more barbaric place. Simply for pretending the simple folk had no heartaches, for locking them away without a kind word. There was the boundary. Not geography at all. But a way of thinking.

"You're deep in thought, Miss Charlton, far away from me." The pony cart was heading toward the end of the village lane. And while she'd been lost in thought, the sky had turned dark.

"I was thinking of Thornhill."

"Homesick?"

"Not exactly." With Lord Strahan, she forgot what side of the border she was from. But he'd never know that, if she could help it. She sat up straighter, more primly.

"Then tell me what it is about Vicky that concerns you so?"

"It seems trivial now, perhaps my imagination."

"I'll be the judge of that."

"Very well." She cleared her throat, too aware of his intense gaze, his nearness. "I found her and Andrew together yesterday."

"Riding ponies?"

"Talking and . . . giggling. They were in the heather . . . like . . . like—"

"Like us?"

She managed a nod, her face flooding with embarrassed color.

To her consternation, he laughed.

"I scarcely think it's funny, milord."

"And that worries you?"

"She's terribly young to be alone with a young man."

He smiled. "Nonsense. Andrew is an upright lad. She idolizes him for his skills with ponies. It's natural for her to want to be with a lad she idolizes."

"But she's only twelve."

"Are you worried my daughter might turn into a bold young lady?"

"No . . . I mean, yes."

"I want her to be bold."

"You have succeeded in obtaining your wish—far sooner than you may have imagined."

"Ah—let me guess. You are suggesting she needs to learn about lads."

"Aren't you going to teach her?"

"About what?"

"You know."

How could he be so obtuse? They'd barely left the croft of a newborn baby. These things did not happen by immaculate conception.

"Ah . . . is that the father's duty now? To teach a lass about lads? I thought that was the duty of a close feminine acquaintance."

"But I'm the closest one to her." There was dismay in her voice.

He smiled again. "Aye, a dilemma indeed, since I'm not at all certain you know much more than my daughter. Did your late husband court you with kisses?"

"I fail to see what that has to do with your daughter."

"I want to know your qualifications for teaching a lass about the needs of lads and knowing the proper time to explain the ways of the marriage bed."

Shocked, she stared straight ahead. "You are too bold in your questions." And that is when the sky began to drizzle.

"You're blushing, Miss Charlton."

"It's the rain. The damp."

He reined in at the humble village school, deserted now of schoolchildren.

This was an unlikely place for a discussion about Vicky, and she asked him at once what he thought he was doing.

"An innocent place for the devil of Dundroma to hold a serious discussion about my daughter. What is your recommendation? That she cease riding ponies and give up her first friend? Dundroma can be lonely without a friend . . . come, come, let's go inside out of the drizzle. And let me remind you, this discussion was your idea, so we'll see it through to the end."

"Only till the rain stops."

"It rains often and long here at Dundroma. Surely you know that."

She did, and prayed for a miracle of sunshine.

He was already out, limping around to her side, coming toward her, reddish hair glistening with raindrops, his black and white checked cloak absorbing the rest.

"You don't need to—"

"Allow me to prove I've some gentlemanly traits, Clare—despite my knee." He reached for her and handed her down. She followed him up a muddy path toward a tiny whitewashed school. Wild grass came up past her black boots, and just then the mist gave way to outright rain. It fell on her hair, on her dress, too fine to be seen, but enough to make her run for the tiny covered roof of the village school.

Inside the village school smelled of sod and leather and chalk. Rows of benches lined the room, and Lord Strahan sat, patting the space next to him. "For propriety's sake, we shall leave the door open . . . now come and sit, Clare, and while we wait for the rain to let up, we shall continue this fascinating subject . . ."

She sorely regretted she'd ever stumbled upon Vicky and Andrew. But Vicky was twelve and a half and if Lord Strahan hadn't considered the delicate matters of helping a girl bridge the border between girlhood and womanhood, someday he'd have to. It might as well be now.

"About Vicky and Andrew—in England, it is not considered proper for young girls past a certain age to play unchaperoned with boys."

"What age would that be? She's not a young lady yet."

"I believe she's at that in-between time of life."

"A borderer in her own life, ready to cross from childhood into young ladyhood."

"Exactly."

"I see . . . then we do need to talk . . . about your qualifications to guide her through that time."

Clare nodded. "In my judgment it's not wise for her to go wandering off alone."

"Nonsense, Andrew is a sensible boy. And as for Vicky, look at how she's bloomed in the short time she's been here. The Dundroma freedom clearly agrees with her. She's healthier and happier than at Thornhill. If Vicky has

anything to overcome, it's smothering from too much
concern at Thornhill."

"There's still propriety to consider. In Thornhill women
are kept in innocence until marriage. The legend of the
statue is usually told and the girls ask no more."

"Ah, the wicked legend follows us still."

"Legend or not, it's a tale that Vicky has heard all her life.
She takes it very seriously . . . because she's in Dundroma, past the boundary of the kissing statue."

"Indeed . . . how did you think wee bairns came about
when you were a girl—from the kissing statue, I suppose?"

"When I was Vicky's age, I had not seen the kissing
statue, but I was certain kissing was the cause of bairns."

"Tell me quick. Vicky is not that naive, Aunt Clare."

"Of course not. The girls are more inquisitive nowadays."

He leaned back against the bench and sighed in relief.
"Then we can be at peace on the subject, Aunt Clare."

Clare bristled. "You're acting carelessly with your daughter."

"Have you no memory of your first kiss, Clare?"

"No."

"Ah, you were an innocent. Tell me," he said softly,
"what was lacking?"

"I—I don't know. I didn't know what to do."

"Did you shut your eyes?"

"I don't remember."

"Did you kiss the lad back?"

"Certainly not. Reginald didn't like it." She jumped up
and paced the little schoolhouse, stopping to peer out the
window at the rain.

"Reginald . . . Then he was lacking in kissing ability.
You see, if it's a good kiss, it's a pleasure, and a first kiss is
to be looked forward to. Have you filled Vicky's head with
these fearful ideas about kissing?"

She turned. "I've only told her about the statue."

"Fearful ideas. We shall have to do something about your education, Aunt Clare."

While he spoke, he got up, limped toward her. He stopped in front of her and reached out to touch her chin. Now the only sound was the rain and the pounding of her heart in her ears. His thumb moved up to caress her lower lip, and she began to melt deep inside. The rain was drumming ever louder against the windows, pounding on the thatched roof.

"You didn't learn a thing from me. We shall kiss again, and this time pay attention."

He bent down and touched his lips to hers, gently, just the featherlike brush of skin on skin.

She wanted to lean toward him, mold herself to him, but he pulled away.

His finger skimmed the outlines of her face, lingering on the softness just beside her mouth. "You have freethinking ideas on everything from fatherhood to children's feelings. I would expect you to think for yourself about the legendary Dundroma kisses. You disappoint me, doing no more than passing on fairy tales about a granite statue."

She couldn't think.

She answered on instinct.

"I'd do anything for Vicky. That's what I think."

"Even kiss me, the devil of Dundroma."

Silence. That was all she could manage. He was too close, too tempting; her pulse raced, the little stone schoolhouse was growing warmer.

"Lord Strahan—" She moved away.

He caught her wrist and gently pulled her back.

"You flit like a bird. Stand still. Were you like this with Reginald?"

"He never kissed me in—in daylight . . ."

With one finger, again he brushed her lower lip. Her heart trembled, caught in her chest "That, wee Clare, was Reginald's own fault, not yours." He leaned down and touched his lips to hers. Devastating in his gentleness. And far, far too swift.

He pulled back, tilted his head, and studied her, a half smile on his face. "Now imagine that as a first kiss? Do you find it so very dangerous?"

Her lips were parted in longing. Yes . . . yes, she wanted to say. Oh, so dangerous. Because they tempted her, made her yearn for more. One kiss from the devil of Dundroma was one too few . . . like steps along a beckoning path, it begged for one more, one more, until the mysteries he promised were revealed.

For the first time she understood the statue. The hand pointed ahead, not in warning, but to guide the maidens of Thornhill. The look was not sadness, but regret for innocence lost.

"Was it, Clare?" he asked again. "Was it dangerous?"

"No." Oh, yes it was. But never would she give him that satisfaction. "It was quite ordinary, as ordinary as our visit to the village."

"You concede that kisses are a natural progression in growing up?"

"This is Dundroma. I'm not sure."

Unexpectedly, his hand touched her hair. "Are you suggesting there is something different about Scottish and English kisses? Something to be feared?"

"Not a thing . . . now."

"Ah, Clare, you seek to deceive me now. For I know when a woman trembles in my arms."

"The subject was Vicky, not me."

"Ah, if you find my kiss ordinary, then why the worry over Vicky?"

Worry? Now that Alec had kissed her, she was terrified for Vicky. She could not reply. His breath brushed her lips again and then suddenly he pulled away. "Unlike you, I

won't lie. Your kiss shows promise, like heather, ready to
bloom. A bonnie taste, lass. And I've known my share."

"But it's Vicky—"

"Don't be alarmed, Aunt Clare. Be reassured. If I, her
father, have no fears over kissing, why should you? Besides
I've proven nothing dangerous will happen to you. And I
wager that green lad Andrew doesn't even know how to kiss
a lass. His head is in the fishing holes and the grouse fields
and the pony stables. Are we done with the discussion?" His
blue gaze bored into her. "All that worry over a trifle . . ."

She'd give the moon and stars to have him trifle with her
lips again and had to bend her head, press her lips together
not to say so.

"You're quiet."

"If so, it's because you've convinced me of the ordinari-
ness of kisses."

Suddenly he snatched up his top hat and limped away to
the pony cart.

"Come along," he called, his voice gruff, "before your
curious tongue gets you into more trouble than you bar-
gained for."

All the way back to the castle, they were silent. She knew
he was right.

Vicky was in no danger. But Clare, if she stayed under the
same roof with this devil, would be as bewitched as legend
warned.

✨Chapter Thirteen

The letter from Thornhill arrived with fortuitous timing.
Lord Strahan just happened to be away and so he never
knew of its delivery.

Clare, with a tripping heart, broke the seal and braced
herself for another plea from Adele to return Vicky.

Instead, she received a shock and had to scan the letter a
second time to be certain she'd read correctly. Yes, Percival
Charlton had taken to his bed, ill, wrote Adele Charlton.
And it all started with a fall to the floor in broad daylight.
He could have at least taken ill at night when no servants
were about to witness him swooning . . . There was no
telling how his health might turn, but he called for Vicky in
his delirium . . .

Clare sat down on her bed. A trick? Or genuine? In the
past, Percival had suffered bouts of gout. On the other hand,
it was typical of Adele Charlton to use health as an excuse
to get her way. There was a chance this letter was no more
than Adele crying wolf to try to lure Vicky home.

Clare got up and sent for Mrs. Drummond, whose
sensible advice might be helpful. She assumed of course
Lord Strahan was out for the day visiting his tenants again,
as he'd done daily since the rainy day in the village school.
He took no one, except his sheepdog, Reiver. He always
went alone in the pony cart and was gone for hours,
returning only to exchange his black frock coat and top hat

for the less formal kilt and shoulder plaid for afternoon hunting with Andrew or one of the villagers. The dinner table lately was laden with grouse, salmon, and venison. But Clare, who requested a tray of bland food in her room, managed to avoid him. And he likewise never requested her presence. Content with the company of his daughter, he ignored Clare.

And now, the letter.

Clare mulled over the message. The last line of the letter was the most ambivalent. "Think how it would appear if anything drastic happened and Vicky were not at her grandfather's bedside."

Even in sickness and death, appearances counted. But that was still not proof of Percival's illness.

What to do? Mrs. Drummond knocked on her door then and offered her condolences.

"On what?" Vicky? Lord Strahan?

"On Percival Charlton's illness. Forgive me if I'm speaking out of place, but the groom at Thornhill, Ned, is sweet on one of the maids here—Nessie—and he said that Percival's taken to his bed." She wrung her hands and apologized again. "Naturally, I'd not speak in hearing of the laird, but we're all human after all . . ."

"It's quite all right, Mrs. Drummond. Quite," Clare reassured her. "Thank you for your kind words."

She shut the door and stared down at the letter. It was true then. Nothing was more reliable than gossip back and forth between the servants of the two estates, and if Mrs. Drummond had heard it from another servant, then Percival was ill indeed.

She wavered. There were loyalties to Thornhill. To the Charltons. And to her English home. And rules had to bend for common decency. Vicky would have to visit her grandfather. But to avoid the wrong impression, she'd have to ask her father's permission. Surely, on a matter like this, Lord Strahan would show mercy.

"Lord Strahan is still away?" she asked in one room of the castle after another. "Shouldn't he be home by now from the village?"

"Aye," the housekeeper assured her, following in her wake. "But he's gone on to a house party at Mrs. Fraser's. An overnight hunting party."

Clare's heart sank.

She'd have to take Vicky to Thornhill without his permission. She wasn't betraying his rights as a father. Vicky was his, but in a time of illness a grandfather deserved compassion—especially one who'd filled in as father while Lord Strahan was roaming the world. It was all quite clear in her head. So clear she wrote it down in a letter. Alec Douglas might call it bluestocking thinking, but to her it was all quite logical.

Before she sealed it, she paused.

There was a slim chance he'd react with anger instead of reason. She could take a chance and wait for Lord Strahan's return. But if she left now, with Percival's illness as her excuse, she could retain her English virtue from this point on. In that way Percival's illness had a silver lining.

She could remove from her senses the constant reminders of Lord Strahan—a vase of dried heather, the mug of whisky he'd put to her lips, the scratches healing from the fall into his brambles, and books of Scott and Burns, which nightly he had delivered to her chamber for nighttime reading to Vicky. Oh, he was incorrigible.

She was falling prey to the same fate as the mysterious lady in the border statue—becoming bewitched and bedeviled into staying in this Dundroma of the mists and heather.

Yet . . . she recalled the way she'd melted beneath his kiss. His kiss was different from any others she'd known though she was loath to admit it to him. Perhaps his kiss would feel different if he were not from Dundroma, forbidden, mysterious Dundroma.

But she doubted it.

She finally slumped into a chair and allowed herself to admit what she'd feared in the back of her mind . . . she desired the laird of the castle, Lord Strahan, dour, stoic, grumbling, unpleasant barbaric man . . . She desired him.

She ought to feel ashamed, if she was a proper Charlton. Her loyalties were deserting her. Instead she felt exhilarated still, then panicky. If Isobel was to be believed, then the reputation of Dundroma's laird for going through women was legion.

He meant to seduce her.

There could be only one solution.

She had to leave. Now. She held the excuse in her hand. The letter from Thornhill pleading for Vicky to attend her grandfather's bedside.

Yet Lord Strahan's pride was formidable. She knew him well enough to guess he'd come after them. She'd have to be strong. Not just for Vicky, but to conceal her real motives, her personal reasons.

She could do it. It was time to go.

Looking out the window, she imagined him riding in, tall in the saddle, handsome in that black frock coat, hatless, his chestnut hair blowing about in the moorland wind. Something inside her ached; she wanted him, but that was like saying a mouse wanted the cheese in a trap.

He was gone.

The coast was clear.

Now was the time to leave.

There was no reason to wait.

Half an hour later she was in Vicky's room. Packing might alert the loyal Dundroma servants. "Vicky," she said gently, "we need to make a visit to Thornhill."

"With Papa?"

"Without."

"Am I being sent back then?"

Gently, Clare explained about her grandfather.

"Shall we tell Papa, so he won't worry?"

"Of course, why don't you write a note and leave it on his chair."

Vicky wrote the note and propped it on her father's favorite chair. As a goodwill gesture, Clare placed an English possession on the chair with the note—a cherished doll. The once favorite sack doll filled with oats and dressed in black. The one Adele had sent in the trunk from Thornhill. Alec Douglas had seen the doll, knew its meaning to his daughter. So if the note left him suspicious, the doll ought to reassure him that Clare would send Vicky back.

Only one other obstacle remained: how to steal a coach out of Dundroma's coach house. Luck was with her. Ned was there. Ned, the Thornhill groom who was sweet on Nessie. Nessie was there too.

"Are you going back to Thornhill, Ned? Vicky and I will travel as far as the kissing statue. To the border."

"It's no' a keen day for painting or reading. The wind is gusting up."

"We won't stay long," she promised. "And we'll dress in our warmest cloaks. Does the housekeeper know you're out here with Nessie?"

"I never stole a kiss."

Ah, but almost. Nessie ran back to the kitchen, and Ned gladly departed, Vicky and Clare his secret passengers.

The coach jolted over the border road, a place filled with the ghosts of robbers and murderers. A place the faint-hearted avoided. Clare boldly looked out at the passing heath. At the border, she told Ned to drive on.

Ned went pale. "Blimy, Miss Charlton, but the laird of Dundroma's going to have all our heads."

"Only mine, Ned. I'll never tell who drove us across the border."

"Promise?"

"Drive on, Ned."

Eyes big with fright, Ned put the crop to the horses, almost as if the devil were after him already. But Clare did not worry. She was too proud of her newfound courage.

Oh, yes, never let it be said Clare Charlton was a meek English governess with no bravery or courage to plot adventure . . . or escape. She'd done it.

And if he wasn't too angry, Lord Strahan might actually be proud of her boldness.

Still, she was nervous.

"Vicky, what did the note say?"

But Vicky, weary from all the excitement, had curled up on the seat and drifted off, lulled to sleep by the motion of the coach.

Isobel glared at the letter, then she read with dismay:
My dear Mrs. Fraser,

Neither time nor distance have dimmed my feelings of affection, and while I honor your virtue, I grow more impatient by the day to see your lovely face again.

To that end, I have concluded my business in Edinburgh in record time. Lord Strahan will be heartened indeed with the enthusiasm of the surgeons to experiment with his knee. He has the chance to make medical history and I predict be the man who brings physicians and surgeons together, the man who closes the great rift between their disciplines. I of course offered my services as intermediary to help bring this historical development about . . . but I shall send him a letter of reassurance on this matter. To you, dear madam, pray know that I shall soon be at your side again to plead my case and offer my heart at your feet . . .

Alec watched Isobel with interest. "An admirer in Edinburgh?"

Isobel decided it might better serve her purpose to keep Alec guessing. A bit of insecurity never hurt any man.

"For a man who's reluctant to travel to Edinburgh yourself, you're remarkably curious about the place. Are you actually considering going there?"

"What if I did?"

Good heavens, Alec might actually do something as rash as hand himself over to a bunch of surgeons. He could die in their hands. Die before she became Lady Strahan. For the first time, she realized the danger of Dr. Wigston Wilmot and his radical ideas.

Then again, perhaps there was another way to look at this. Instead of thinking of Dr. Wilmot as a toad and his attentions a bother, she could use him to make Alec jealous.

"It's only Dr. Wilmot," she sighed, as if she were weary of suitors pressing her hand. "He's promised to write you with the opinion of the surgeons. I'd listen, Alec, when he returns."

"You admire his opinion?" Alec looked at her with skepticism.

"I admire his mind, his forthright ideas. It takes more than a perfect physique to entice a woman, you know, Alec. That's why it's of no concern to me what you do about your knee. I admire imperfect men with keen intelligence—like Dr. Wilmot—and yourself . . . but don't ask me to choose. I'd be at wit's end."

"I'm sure you'd manage to make a choice, Isobel," he said with a smile.

She frowned. Alec knew her too well to have the wool pulled over his eyes.

"But could you make a decision?" she asked coyly. And she meant to keep his thoughts on her.

"About my knee?"

No. Bother take his knee. Why did he have to turn so deliberately obtuse whenever she turned the conversation to flirtation?

"Yes," she snapped, lying. "Deciding whether to let butchering surgeons mend your knee will make a difference to your military future, so do whatever pleases you." She stuffed the letter down a seat cushion. "Dr. Wilmot has written you a letter for your consideration. Now, since you can't play golf or ride with the others, shall we do something dreadfully decadent and play whist?"

"And where is my letter?" he asked.

"How should I know? At Dundroma, I would expect." Everything was at Dundroma. His daughter. Her son. The mousy governess. Everything she detested. And everything she wanted.

Dundroma. When it was hers, there'd be changes made. And the hands she'd slap would make Alec's bad knee feel like a mere rap to the knuckles in comparison.

What had made it short of a perfect outing, Alec realized with a jolt, was the absence of the governess to talk with and to tease. He wanted to watch the light glint off her hair, turning it from light brown to honey streaked. He was foolishly pleased with himself because he'd brought her a gift—the perfect item to entice her to the breakfast table—a jar of heather honey from a tenant. Now when she tasted *this*, she'd have to concede that something about Dundroma was superior to Thornhill.

He could have sworn his limp was less pronounced, his leg stronger as he entered Dundroma's courtyard. A maid, usually saucy, avoided his eye, and at once he felt the hushed atmosphere of the place, but just as quickly blamed it on his own cranky, dour mood of late.

He sought out his housekeeper and handing her the jar of heather honey instructed her to serve it up at the following morning's breakfast.

And as he leaned on his ivory-headed walking stick, he felt excited as a boy who'd caught his first trout.

"Miss Charlton's going to come around yet about Scotland and Dundroma. *And* she's going to return to the dining table."

"Oh, but, milord—" She never finished her sentence but bit it off, half said.

"What's wrong?"

With a quick curtsy, she took the honey. "Thank you, milord, I'll have it on the table. And a bonnie batch of honey it is, indeed."

"Is something worrying you?"

"Milord, I beg your pardon, but I only expected marmalade as long as your wee bairn was here."

"Well, put out marmalade for Vicky too, then. Whatever her appetite wants. And more haddock in oats. Scones. But none of that bland Thornhill porridge. Even their oats are anemic."

The woman's face was devoid of its usual ruddy cheerfulness, but he passed it off. She was, after all, juggling making shortbread in one room and overseeing the scrubbing of muddy paw prints left by Reiver from the tartan lounge chair. He tried hard to give his servants some slack—the Drummond family had served him well, even during all the years he'd been away.

In fact, that could be it—they'd grown used to running a castle without a master, and now as they became used to the master looking over their shoulder again, so to speak, it was natural for the servants to be slightly out of sorts.

He looked up on the shelf. The picnic basket was missing.

The governess and his daughter had spoken about a picnic. He'd surprise them and join them. Up in the moors.

He could walk it . . . no, he'd already walked about the village and he didn't want pain this afternoon. He wanted peace.

And so he told no one where he was going, nor did anyone ask the laird of the castle what he was about.

At the stable, he found Andrew brushing his pony and talking in hushed tones with a groom.

"What is this? It sounds like a ladies' gossip session. Is Vicky here?"

"Not yet."

"Well, when is she coming?"

Andrew stopped brushing in midstroke. Half turned. "I thought you'd know . . . We're going to ride today. I've only been here since the mist lifted. I came down over the heath, but it's deserted of people, so I assumed Vicky was in the house with her governess having lessons."

"Nonsense. Miss Charlton functions here as a companion; Vicky doesn't spend her days in stuffy schoolrooms. The outdoors is her classroom. Tomorrow I'm taking her grouse hunting and after that for a fishing lesson. These are where she learns her lessons in life. Fishing is the fine art of diplomacy, and grouse hunting is all she needs to know of tradition—"

"Besides the Highland games."

"This is the lowlands . . . but if she wants, we could sponsor a summer games—it would, I expect, make a perfect history lesson." Of course Clare Charlton would tag along to protect Vicky from all this barbaric outdoors activity, and . . . His thoughts drifted to Clare Charlton on a pony and the memory of her landing in the brambles and the feel of her clinging to him when he'd pulled her out.

All sorts of things could go wrong that would land the prim widow in his arms again . . . all sorts of lessons could be taught to her as well . . .

He pulled his thoughts up short. No, that was dangerous thinking. He was done with teasing kisses and flirtatious banter. For in such sport, a man did not bag a quarry, but got bagged. It was the one sport in which the man was most at risk, and he'd vowed history would not repeat itself with women from Thornhill. A groom passed by.

"Does this not sound like a fine way to show my daughter the advantages of Scotland?" he asked.

"Aye, milord, that it does," the groom answered. "But she's not here, ye ken."

"What do you mean not here?" Suspicion welled inside him. The hushed manner, the averted glances of the servants.

He grabbed the groom by the labels. "You—who are you?" It was not one of the Drummond family, but a new fellow. "As I live and breathe I command you to betray any other loyalties."

"I was in the stables when the coach rolled away with the lady, the governess."

"And the child?"

"They spoke of an illness in the family."

"What family?" Raw fear coursed through him.

The groom was white-haired and dim-witted, and now he scratched his head in bewilderment. "They headed south toward the border."

"Do you know where that border leads?" Alec's voice rose.

The man flinched, as if warding off the brunt of a storm that was about to break.

"It was a bloody escape. That traitorous governess stole my daughter back to Thornhill."

"Sir?"

"Saddle my horse."

"Your leg, sir?"

"I don't care if they cut it off. The child belongs to me, and no one else can steal her away. Only me! My horse!"

"Will you bring Vicky back, milord?" Andrew asked.

"Aye, she'll be back, with or without that governess."

Damn her, damn her to hell, betraying him. As he rode,

hell-bent for the border, he damned her for working her way under his skin and then leaving him. He'd befriended her, encouraged her to run off and have an adventure, spread her wings. Damn her, but she'd taken his own advice too literally! He dug his heels to his mount.

When he found her, if he was able to storm that prissy English stronghold, he'd wring her neck . . . no, kiss the breath out of her . . . no . . . aye . . .

He desired the woman. There was no denying that, and that was as much the cause of his fury as her treachery. How dare another English woman, a gray little wren, inflame him!

He pushed the horse ever faster.

He could not allow himself to be angry with her or anyone. Otherwise he'd follow through on his desire to kiss the breath out of her. A bad idea. All he wanted was his daughter, and the governess could go hang.

He knew the perfect spot—where his great-uncle had hung a Charlton for pilfering three cattle and a grouse, and for good measure, stealing a Scots lass to bed.

But he'd have Vicky back.

The prim governess would not elude him that easily.

No one outwitted him. Not pompous physicians from London. Not a roomful of surgeon butchers. Not his best friend's widow. Not even tigers.

So how the devil had a prim meek lass like her outsmarted him?

❧Chapter Fourteen

"Devil take her!"

No reiver ever rode the distance between Dundroma Castle and Thornhill Manor with greater speed. If the Queen's regiments could see him fly across the heath, they'd quick make an exception about promoting lame soldiers to general.

Deceptive females. They were all the same. Either dying on a man, or lying, or flirtatiously trying to marry his castle, or, worst, plotting treachery. Isobel was at least obvious in her goals. He could deal with Isobel. But Clare Charlton . . . she was enough to drive a man to distraction, acting all innocent about a lass's first kiss, getting him to demonstrate, reducing him to rice pudding for so many days that he had to resort to avoiding her . . .

Now this!

And they called *him* a devil.

Clare Charlton had just declared war, he decided as he banged the knocker on Thornhill's door. And the advantage was his. For he knew centuries of reivers' tricks. Reivers had been famed for the subtlety of their attacks. Sneaking up by the dark of the moon. Pretending neighborliness while plotting revenge. Smiling with knives and pistols hidden behind their backs. Oh, aye, Clare Charlton had best have her wits about her to take on a man in reiver country.

The door opened so suddenly he nearly fell in with it. Straightening, he put on his most forbidding expression.

No words were needed. The servant wore an all-suffering expression.

"Good afternoon, Lord Strahan. Mrs. Charlton is expecting you for tea."

"Of course." Adele would have Clare under her thumb again. He'd have to deal with Adele before he could get to Clare. Patience was becoming a second skin to him. He tightened his hand about the ivory tiger's head and limped in, pushing back the pain.

Vicky was his. The loss cut more deeply and unexpectedly than any broken bones.

For Vicky and for revenge, he could endure anything.

So ten minutes later he sat on the edge of a chintz chair. Nothing but four spindly Queen Anne legs held him up. Geegaws surrounded him. The room had always been overdone, but today it struck him as overbearing. On top of all else, he was held captive, like an Indian mutineer, by Adele Charlton, who had mastered the fine art of chitchatting about nothing.

"And was the weather quite nice for your ride down here?"

"Very nice." Colder than Hades with the furnace out. "A bit of a mist."

"We've had rather a lot of mist this summer. But the heather is blooming nicely."

"Indeed. I understand Percival is not up to snuff."

"Not quite."

"Pity."

Adele sighed. "He gave us all a fright, refusing to eat."

"I imagine so."

"His gout, you know. The strain and all . . ."

"How is Vicky?" he asked suddenly.

Adele drew back as if he'd lifted her skirt and exposed her crinoline.

"She seems quite well."

Damn Adele. "Where is she?"

"With her grandfather. He's most pleased to see her. She actually convinced him to eat some porridge."

"That is a commendable feat. She's not been able to convince me."

Adele's expression grew forbidding. "She suggested he try it with haddock and marmalade. But of course Percival had to decline—"

Alec set his teacup on her whatnot table. Gout. Nothing but a bloody case of gout, and for that the Charltons had lured Clare with lies and stolen his daughter away.

"I am here for Vicky."

Adele might never have heard him.

"Vicky's presence is good for Percival, I do believe. A godsend."

"How long will he be ailing?"

It was an excuse. Nothing more. Why wasn't Dr. Wigston Wilmot around when Alec needed him? If the pompous physician were here *now,* Alec would pay him to examine Percival. Pay to have him hauled up to the Edinburgh surgeons too. Anything to pry Vicky out of this cloying atmosphere.

"Naturally," Adele went on with a wan smile, "I would be remiss if I did not express my gratitude . . . that you granted permission for our dear Vicky to come back."

"I did not grant permission."

Now it was Adele who set down her teacup. She drew herself up straight. "Nevertheless, we're grateful for your understanding."

He ground his teeth. The ache throbbing in his knee increased a hundredfold. Perhaps another position . . . and he straightened it out, desperate to be out of pain, in control of life.

Clare glided into the room. Dressed in dark gray. Without even a white collar or cuffs to relieve the primness. Her

seductive honey-colored hair was pulled back in a severe
bun, bound in a snood. She edged around the far wall of the
parlor, stopped by a vase of roses, and looked at him, hazel
eyes oh, so innocent and free of guilt. There was challenge
in those eyes.

He returned the look. It took all his military training to
remain expressionless. And to ignore the quicker beating of
his heart. She was going to make it difficult to maintain his
anger.

"You see, Clare," Adele said to Vicky's governess as she
poured more tea, "I knew he'd be reasonable. And he is
reasonable, as befits a gentleman of the nineteenth century.
We're neighbors after all. I think you've managed to talk
some sense into him."

Clare paled a bit, then drew in a deep breath.

Oh, so she was not so sure of herself. With good reason.
Alec decided to continue this charade of a tea party awhile
longer. "The least I could do," he murmured. It was a lie, but
he enjoyed watching Clare, who came to sit beside her
mother-in-law. Demure, hands folded primly, innocent of
face, devoid of passion.

Frustration welled up inside him. As much for Clare as
for his daughter. Where was the Clare he'd sparred with in
the heather? The Clare he'd kissed beneath a rain-spattered
thatched roof? Held in his arms while her brambly tongue
matched the thorns he picked from her hands.

The realization came gradually over him, like clouds
parting in an uncertain sky. It was Clare he'd come after as
much as Vicky. And the Clare he'd glimpsed at Dundroma
had vanished as surely as Vicky had.

"It would be inhumane of me to pull her away without a
word to her relatives. Isn't that the modern approach, Clare?
To consider the child's feelings?"

She nodded stiffly. Her face betrayed no change of
expression, but the rest of her was not so controlled. The

buttons on her bodice moved in and out with each breath. He watched, fascinated.

Adele handed him more tea, and they drank in silence.

Clare got up without a word and pushed a footstool toward him. "Have you heard from Dr. Wilmot?"

"Yes." Subject closed.

The trace of a smile crossed her face. A fleeting dimple creased her face. "Would you like to rest your leg on—"

"My leg is fine," he said as sweat broke out on his brow. He was tired of being treated like an invalid. The only invalid in this house was Percival.

"Is Vicky ready to leave?"

Adele exchanged a private look with Clare. A conspiracy. He'd known it.

"Actually," Adele said stiffly, "Percival is more ill than we at first realized. We'd like Vicky to stay. Didn't you receive Clare's note?"

"What note?"

"I left you a note," she said. "So did Vicky."

"Where?"

"On your chair."

"Nothing was on my chair but Reiver's paw prints . . . and a scattering of oats."

"Then Reiver must have eaten the doll—and the note."

"Reiver does not eat my letters."

Adele stood. "That's past. Lord Strahan, as mercy dwells in your heart, I ask you to allow Vicky to stay until her grandfather is well. You are, of course, welcome to remain also."

Clare, clearly shocked, turned to her mother-in-law. "But he'd not want to stay at Thornhill."

Despite his bitter intentions, Alec smiled. She was worried. Wondering when he was going to end this facade of civilization and turn barbarian.

"On the contrary, Aunt Clare," he said easily. "You forget

about Cecilia. I know Thornhill. It's been many years, but I accept. Only to assure that I can watch over my daughter."

"I need to send Vicky off to bed." Clare stood, clearly anxious to put as much distance between them as possible.

He watched, tantalized as the dimple came and went with each word. His hands yearned to yank that bun out and watch her honey hair fall down her back. But not yet.

Let her watch over her shoulder. Let her wonder and worry when he was going to demand satisfaction for her treachery. By the candlelight her skin shone with a creamy glow. Oh, so touchable . . . Cursing himself for his weakness, for wanting the deceitful wee governess, he balled his hands into fists.

He watched her go, his gaze lingering on the sway of her wide skirt, the tiny waist his hands could span.

Adele was all formal propriety. "I shall have the blue bedchamber made up for you, Lord Strahan. Will that be satisfactory?"

Inwardly, he cringed. The most overdone of the bedrooms. And the coldest. Drafts blew down the fireplace from the moors, even when the thing was burning with coal.

"Delightful," he replied.

And with a smile and nod to Adele Charlton, he took his leave and limped up the staircase, a groom in tow, to rest in his room. Clare would make herself scarce, that he knew. But no matter. He could afford to bide his time and take a wee rest. Oh, yes, time enough to exact a borderer's revenge.

On he limped up the gloomy corridors of Thornhill to retreat to the drafty blue bedchamber.

To listen for the reassuring chatter of his daughter.

The silence of Aunt Clare . . .

And wait the coming of dusk.

Revenge always awaited the dark of the moon. And so could the stealing of kisses.

*   *   *

Clare slipped inside her bedchamber and with a sigh of relief leaned against the door. Refuge. Sanctuary.

Lord Strahan was behaving decidedly out of character. His English reserve was not fooling her a bit—no more than the mist about the moors fooled her. It was a facade, and just as beneath the mists lay the harsh moorlands, so beneath that facade lay a barbaric Scotsman—the devil of Dundroma. God only knew when he would toss his teacup over his shoulder and, like a wounded beast provoked once too often, turn into the Lord Strahan she really knew.

It was like guessing when the mists would lift, so for the rest of the day, she carefully made certain she was never alone. Her fears had been for naught. Not once had the devil emerged from the blue bedchamber. She had to pass it on the way to her chamber, and pausing she'd been tempted to knock, to ask if he needed food or whisky or if his knee pained him greatly.

No! The bewitching devil knew how to use her sympathetic thoughts to seduce her.

So after the briefest pause, she'd hurried on.

And now at last she could safely turn the key on her own chamber door. Her Thornhill bedchamber—with all its familiar belongings. Everything was still in its place, as it had been for twelve years now.

Her familiar washstand with basin and pitcher decorated with cabbage roses. Her armoire filled with identical and serviceable gray serge dresses. Her bed, high-canopied and covered with a coarse white spread, faintly scented with dried heather. And of course the daguerreotype of Reginald, dear innocent Reginald who knew little more of the marriage bed than she did. She could scarcely remember him. Poor Reginald. Dead from typhoid within a month of their wedding. If it hadn't been for "orphaned" Vicky she didn't know what she'd have done. Found a post somewhere, she supposed. But there was no use in speculating, for what was past was past.

Dundroma was past too, and she swallowed back a lump in her throat, blamed her sudden chill on the fireplace grate, in which the coals were unlit. Mullioned panes of glass looked down upon Thornhill's formal rose garden. The window was open, a stiff wind blowing in along with the first drops of rain.

A summer storm. Even nature conspired against her. She closed the window just before lightning struck, followed by the faraway rumble of thunder.

Decorum, Clare. Prim, correct behavior. Appearances above all, even in privacy.

Never once had anyone in the grand house seen her with her hair unplaited, her hems lifted above her ankles, her hands muddied. No matter how she'd felt, she had done her duty and behaved with perfect comportment.

Yet, her weeks at Dundroma had jarred those notions. True, the past could not be changed, but did the future have to follow the same monotonous path? If she'd forced Lord Strahan to rethink his notions about fatherhood as some sort of divine ownership, then he had forced her to rethink her notions about the need for prim behavior twenty-four hours a day.

Tonight for the first time, she allowed herself to drape her dress over a chair, and to splash water over her face and arms instead of scrubbing her face with a towel. She was simply too distracted, too drained.

Weary, she unfastened her corset and slipped on her nightdress, then unpinned the tight knot of hair at her neck. It fell in a single braided plait down her back. She had just reached up to unplait it when the knock came on her door, followed by another crash of lightning outside, the rumble of thunder, the memory of Alec Douglas's voice in her soul. It was a Tam o' Shanter night.

> *The wind blew as 'twould blawn its last,*
> *The rattling showers rose on the blast . . .*

Her door rattled. She started, then relaxed. It was only a servant at the door.

"Miss Charlton, I'm sorry to disturb you so late."

"What is it?" she asked through the door.

"The little girl, Vicky, miss, she's having a bad dream and asking for you. It's the storm, doubtless."

Clare drew in a breath. Oh, the familiarity of it all was comforting. She pulled on her wrapper and followed the servant next door. Vicky was sitting up in bed, white-faced, a single candle lit by her bedside. Outside thunder crashed again.

"A bad dream? It's not easy on you moving back and forth like this. Don't worry, dear, it will get easier."

"But will I go back to Dundroma? To the ponies. To Andrew . . . ?"

Ah, so that was it.

"Do you want to?"

"I was getting used to it."

That was for the best because she had no doubt Lord Strahan meant to keep his daughter. The best she could hope for was a concession to allow more visits between Dundroma and Thornhill.

"I'm sure you'll go back, but you see how glad your grandfather is to have you visit, and how concerned your father is that you do what is best."

"I had a dream."

"About what? Thornhill?"

"Dundroma."

Poor Vicky. This couldn't be easy, having her loyalties

torn at such a tender age. A draft rattled the shutters, and the candle flickered.

"Do you want to tell me about it?"

Vicky was silent a minute, then, "It was a good dream . . . I was riding the ponies . . . with Andrew . . . and then we were ambushed . . . musket fire, and Andrew vanished . . ."

"It was the storm, waking you," Clare said with as much reassurance as she could muster.

Vicky hugged her knees to her chest, her long red hair falling about the shoulders of her nightdress. "I have to go back," she pleaded. "Aunt Clare, I never got to say good-bye to Andrew. We had a wager." She turned stricken eyes to her governess.

"He'll be there still, taking care of Ghost and Macduff."

"He won't. Mrs. Fraser's sending him off to school again."

"A young man of his age must attend to his studies."

"But we have things to do before he goes."

"What did you want to do?"

She paused. "Go fishing with Andrew. Grouse hunting. You know."

Clare did not share the same passion for the Dundroma outdoors as her charge. "Then I'm sure there's plenty of time for those things before the summer ends. Young girls don't need to do everything the boys do, you know. You still have your lessons, your needlework, you music, your—"

To her surprise, Vicky slid down into bed and rolled over. "I'm not a little girl. I'm twelve. Nearly twelve and a half."

"Growing up."

"And not a child."

"Of course." No, Clare suspected Vicky did not want Andrew to see her as a child, but wisely kept her counsel.

"Don't you see—I want to be kind to Grandfather, but I want to go back to Dundroma."

"A dilemma indeed for a young girl to be torn between two places . . ." Clare pulled the blanket up. "The storm will pass . . . your grandfather will grow well . . . Dundroma will still be there."

"But not Andrew . . . and the ponies."

"Your papa would take you away tonight, but that would be unkind to your grandfather. I wager if you tell your papa of your dilemma he'll have a solution. Perhaps if your grandfather's illness lingers on, Andrew can come visit Thornhill." Isobel Fraser would bring Andrew for a chance to visit Alec Douglas.

"Truly?" Vicky asked, calmer now.

"Very likely . . . and even the storm is passing. Hear that? Silence outside."

"Mmm." Vicky rolled over and looked with sleepy gratitude at her governess. "Will you tell Papa to make sure the ponies wait for me till Grandfather is better?"

A tall order. "Of course. I'll talk to your grandmother tomorrow. I quite agree you're growing up. I've seen it coming on. Why, before long, you'll have no need for a governess."

Vicky half turned in bed. "Oh, but I didn't mean that. Even if you can't ride ponies that well, I don't mind if you tag along. You make Papa laugh."

"Do I? Well, it's you I'm companion to, not your papa, and someday you'll be grown up and won't need me."

No answer. Already, Vicky was drifting to sleep.

But Clare needed no reply, for it was entirely possible that her days with Vicky were numbered. She'd known so ever since the devil of Dundroma had first arrived at Thornhill and demanded his daughter. And should the ambitious Isobel snare him, certainly Clare would have to wean herself from Vicky.

"Good night, Vicky," she said and moments later shut Vicky's door and carried the candle to her own bedchamber.

Tomorrow she ought to ask Adele for a character so she'd be ready when it was time to place an advertisement for a new situation. The London papers would have the most opportunities.

Mentally, she roughed out the advertisement she'd need: Refined English lady of fine character desires post as governess in London. Character available. French, needlepoint, geography, writing, watercolors.

She shut the door to her room, candlestick in hand, her purpose sure.

Stopping, she stared at the grate. The coals were glowing, the fire warm.

A shadow fell across the floor, and even before she turned, she knew she was not alone. She turned, heart pounding, candle clutched tightly, and drew in her breath, heart racing.

Lord Strahan stood in her doorway. Inside her room. On this side of the latched door.

"How did you get in here? Get out."

He reached up and tested the latch to verify it was secure.

"You lied to me," he said, his voice soft as down. "Didn't you, Clare? You meant all along to steal Vicky back here to Thornhill."

"That's not true."

Her heart beat so loudly in her ears she could scarcely hear herself talk.

He smiled. And she recognized it for the devilish smile he'd hidden all day long.

"Now, lass," he said while advancing toward her. His limp made the shadows wobble, but her heartbeat, her breathing, were even more unsteady. "You didna think I'd cross the English border, muddy my walking stick and horse's hooves on Thornhill soil, just to take tea with Adele Charlton, do you?"

"You came out of concern."

"I came for many reasons. As a charitable Christian neighbor, concern crossed my mind, but was not chief among my reasons."

"Tell me one, then."

He stared deep into her eyes, as if he had never seen her before. "It is a Tam o' Shanter night, Clare."

"I know. I was reciting the lines to Vicky—the stormy part."

He took a step forward, an uneven step. "That night a child might understand . . . "

" 'The de'il had business on his hand,' " she finished for him. "State your business."

Her hands shook so, the candlelight brought his face in and out of shadows. Light. Shadow. Light.

His hands covered hers, steadied the candle, and then took it from her. The candlelight caught the strong planes of his face, showed the intense blue of his eyes gleaming. The devil was in him. Oh, yes, the facade of propriety had lifted, and he was here alone with her.

"Thornhill has many bedchambers, I know, so I'll assume you're lost. Go away."

He limped another step closer. "Now, lassie, where did all that Thornhill hospitality vanish? Even the devil of Dundroma is extended hospitality by fellow borderers. Among borderers, no matter which side of the border we claim, when shelter is needed, it is offered, and no host or guest betrays each other."

"You were assigned the blue bedchamber."

"I prefer your room."

"You are truly the devil."

"And you are no angel, little governess. You ran away today, and took my daughter, my own flesh and blood, my legal property. You betrayed me, after I offered you the hospitality of Dundroma."

"And so you think to punish me. How? String me up at the hanging tree? By the light of the moon?"

His laughter rumbled low in his throat. Trembling, she hugged her arms beneath her bodice, painfully aware that her wrapper of thin white lawn afforded little in the way of modesty.

His gaze raked her, while the candlelight played over the strong planes of his face, caught the chestnut facets of his hair.

"I don't think to punish you, lass. It is you, on the contrary, who have been punishing me by denying me your charms."

"They're not yours to have."

"Are they any man's?"

"You know they're not."

"Ever the proper governess, Clare."

"It is not proper for your daughter's governess to entertain you in her bedchamber."

"That rule must be in that book of comportment you quote to Vicky out of. Fie, and it's no' a Scottish rule. We dinna have comportment books at Dundroma," he said, deliberately thickening his brogue. "Our sole rule, wee lass, is to try to behave with honor at all times."

"You call this honorable behavior?"

"I said try. And a rule is sometimes stronger than the man."

She stood rooted to the spot, the cold floor numbing her feet. An invisible warmth stole up the rest of her.

"Go away." Her voice lacked conviction.

"You don't sound very stern about it," he noted. "Lassie, I claim one kiss freely given as your forfeit for your betrayal with Vicky. Then if you say to leave I will turn and limp out of here, a man spurned. You need never return to Dundroma."

He moved closer while she stood taking in his shocking

words. His barbaric offer. She was helpless as he reached up to touch her hair, which spilled wildly about her shoulders.

"Your hair shines like honey in the candlelight," he said. "I always knew it would look like this undone in the night."

And with his husky words, down went the last barriers of her resistance.

He pulled her to him and slid his hand inside her wrapper. "Come then, don't play the reluctant maiden, *Mrs.* Charlton. The custom may be to call the governess *Miss*, but we both know you're no novice with the laddies."

"That doesn't give you the right." Her voice lacked conviction. Inside, she yearned to cling to him. Curse her traitorous body. "Let me go. You have no rights with me."

"You gave me the right when you stole my daughter away. Here in the border country, right and wrong matter little, and English law is ours to use as we see fit. For every raid there's a retaliation. Fair enough?"

"One kiss then," she said, too limp to argue.

Gently, he took her hand and raised it to his lips. "One."

She could have bade him go but like a magnet was helpless against the pull of his touch.

One by one he kissed her fingertips, after each kiss looking into her eyes.

"You said one kiss. You're up to eight."

"I deceived you . . . Stop me, anytime. Tell me, Clare. Say it and I'll leave."

Words did not come.

They were lost in the fiery gaze. Consumed. Forgotten. She couldn't speak her name.

Then with his hands he pushed back her hair and he kissed her lips, once gently, the way a boy might give a first kiss. Hesitant. The kiss ended just as suddenly. He pulled back as if he were as startled at the contact as she was. He slid her wrapper down over her shoulders, and it caught midway down; he pulled it over her wrists and then it puddled at her feet. He tilted up her chin and kissed her again. She tried to stand as still as that statue at the border. Legend had it the devil could not pursue one over the river into Thornhill territory. She was a Thornhill lady. Her body, melting at his touch, said otherwise. She concentrated as never before. Counted sums backward. The alphabet. And she managed, barely, to resist.

He pulled back again, thumb tilting her chin, eyes vaguely amused.

"So your Reginald did not teach you how to kiss back," he observed.

"Perhaps I choose not to."

"A woman of reserve is always a challenge."

"You've taken your kiss, your forfeit."

He gave her a rueful smile. "Ah, as stiff as the river statue."

"It is my duty to behave with decorum."

"Did you ever wonder whether the devil or the Lord above sided with decorum?"

"No, but I have wondered about the necessity of kissing."

He touched her lips with his forefinger, gently kneaded them. With a little moan, she closed her eyes, and she bit her lip, hid from his probing touch. All that moved were the hands of a clock, the flicker of a candle, the moon outside the window. And the beat of her heart.

"A kiss was invented as a foretaste of pleasures to come. Didn't you know that, lass, or did Reginald never give you pleasure? Real pleasure."

"Leave now, please." She tried to pull away. "One forfeit. No more."

"Ah, but I've not had my pleasure. And the next time I kiss you, Clare, it will be because you want to know how I can pleasure you in ways that Reginald never showed you."

"Get out!"

He left her then in the darkened room, left her to lay

awake and stare at the night passing across the window. She had nowhere left to escape him—not even here in the safety of her own bedchamber could she escape her longings.

She hoped he returned to Dundroma on the morrow, for if he came to her one more time as he had tonight, she could not promise to restrain her desires. She was not, she admitted with rue, made of stone like that statue.

And she wanted him. She fell back onto the bed, and imagined them together, merging into one shadow, a shadow that moved as one. Intense. Clinging to each other. Savoring the nearness. Passion calling. She pushed it back, afraid.

He had found a chink in her armor, had well and truly bewitched her, stripped her of decorum and made her like every sensual moment. She slept, and when a tap sounded at the door—a maid to bring her morning tea—he was just a memory.

Only the dull heavy throbbing in the most secret places of her body were evidence of his nearness and her secret regret that he'd left too soon.

She lay abed way past her usual time of rising. Curiosity about Alec's embrace consumed her. She was by turns a girl yearning for her first kiss and a woman wishing to slake desire.

For both their sakes, she hoped Percival had overnight enjoyed a miraculous recovery, and her motivations were selfish. Only then would Alec Douglas, the devil of Dundroma, go back to his side of the border, to his castle, and stay there.

Vicky would have to return with her father, of course, but with a new companion, for nothing would drag Clare back to Dundroma. Alec Douglas, with his seductive words and touch, had nearly destroyed her prim facade, and she never wanted to set eyes on him again.

❦ Chapter Fifteen

Vicky spent the morning at the bedside of her grandfather, keeping vigil with her grandmother. Herbs and powders were dispensed. Prayers said for the imminent return of Dr. Wigston Wilmot from Edinburgh. Local apothecaries were not good enough for a man of Percival's standing. A good London physician was needed for appearances.

Aunt Clare sat alone in the parlor, reading her book of comportment. Vicky knew what that meant—an imminent lecture, probably on sick-room behavior. Rules. Rules. Rules. Always on the boring subjects. To her surprise, though, when Vicky wandered to the kitchen in search of a sweet bun, Aunt Clare complained of feeling indisposed and went to lie down. Aunt Clare? Lying down in the middle of the day. That was unheard of.

On her way back to her grandfather's room she noticed Aunt Clare had carelessly left the book unattended. She snatched it up as she passed by.

For the next hour, Vicky sat outside Grandfather's room, Aunt Clare's book of manners on her lap. Passing servants and family smiled and commented on what a model child she was.

She smiled and continued skimming the book—a treatise on good manners. So much of it she knew: family affection, church behavior, and delicacy of eating. Aunt Clare had drummed it all into her. She paused at ballroom etiquette, skimmed past baldness and wigs—useless. Christian principles—overdone. Old maids—perhaps, for Aunt Clare . . .

If her grandfather didn't get well soon, Andrew would leave before she could talk him into a kiss. And no one would care. Certainly not her father who limped the grounds of Thornhill with a glower. Her father wasn't even behaving like the same man. Pacing about with his limp, he behaved as if death were at his heels. He was unapproachable.

Nor was her grandfather someone in whom she could confide. He *never* ever kissed her grandmother, so he'd have no advice. Old fogies, that's what both her grandparents were. And she certainly couldn't tell Aunt Clare, who had said she disapproved of Vicky's giggling tête-à-têtes with Andrew.

Oh, but she was torn. She had a duty to keep vigil by her grandfather, but her heart was up at Dundroma. And no one in Thornhill, absolutely no one, understood. They were all too old and too caught up in what was proper.

She turned one more page. Ah-ha. The chapter title leapt out at her. *Love and Courtship*. Hastily she devoured the words, which were divided into topics. Wedding etiquette. Not yet. Duties of wives. And then the page she wanted. Promiscuous kissing! Vicky's heart leapt into her throat.

". . . the kiss seems to me too sacred an expression to be used lightly. We should take care of all personal intimacy . . . The custom of kissing lightly is bad, because it compels us to give tenderness to indifferent persons."

Bad? No wonder Aunt Clare had never allowed Vicky to read the book for herself. The comportment book didn't say kissing was bad; it said that kissing lightly was bad. Bad enough to bewitch the lady in stone at the border, she supposed. But her father had told her the legend of the kissing statue was false. And so if the lady in the kissing statue had done nothing bad, maybe this book was false. Besides, if kissing was bad, why did Charlotte say she'd seen her parents kiss? Grown-ups who lived their lives by the stuffy rules in etiquette books would not kiss if it were that bad. Oh, but it was a mystery, and Vicky needed Andrew to help her solve it.

She sighed three times. First her grandparents were not speaking . . . and now her papa and her aunt Clare weren't either.

"Vicky," her grandmother said, pausing in the doorway. "What are you so busily reading?"

Vicky slammed the book shut. "I was reviewing my French grammar."

Grandmother smiled wanly. "I knew returning to Thornhill would be good for you. Come along now to eat. I approve of your reading, but you need nourishment too."

The noon meal was no better—a subdued affair. No talk. Just the scrape of forks. The clink of wineglasses. The hushed footsteps of servants removing the tablecloth and bringing on dessert. And that was the signal for her grandmother to begin the conversation.

"I worry so," her grandmother began, "that we may have to resort to an apothecary for medical counsel." She looked at Vicky's father. "If Percival were to die, think of the indignity in having a mere apothecary at his bedside. Only workhouse paupers die with an apothecary in attendance. Why, even my second cousin, who was a blackguard and a rogue, had the honor of a real physician at his bedside. Wretched luck. Did you try the blackberry tart, Lord Strahan?"

And the forks scraped on. The glasses clinked.

Then the servant's footsteps suddenly held a quick hopeful sound. They heralded good news: Percival's fever had broken.

And more good news: a letter of good wishes from Isobel
Fraser.

Hopeful, Vicky looked up from stirring the bland tapioca
her grandmother insisted on giving her for dessert. She
hated the childish food here. "Is there news of
Andrew . . . and the ponies?" she asked, using the diver-
sion to scrape the tapioca into her napkin.

Her grandmother frowned at the letter, then back at
Vicky. Children allowed in the Thornhill dining room were
to be seen and not heard.

"Vicky, the letter is much too serious in nature to include
news from the stables. Isobel sends her best to Percival, dear
Cecilia's father. And to Alec, Lord Strahan." She smiled at
Alec. "Such a thoughtful lady, even in the grief of
widowhood . . . Oh, and she writes that Dr. Wilmot has
returned—just this past afternoon. Dear Isobel has gener-
ously offered to bring him down here to attend to
Percival . . . now when we don't need him—or apothecaries. Ah, well, Mrs. Fraser will be glad to keep Dr.
Wilmot nearby. He is courting her, isn't he?" she asked.

Her papa stared at his wineglass, twirled the stem in his
fingers. "If he is, he'll have his task cut out for him."

Vicky's grandmother gave him an astute look. "Ah, yes,
competition from you, I expect. Cecilia once confided that
she feared she'd stolen you from Isobel."

"Did she? Lucky for you Isobel missed out else you'd not
have Vicky as a grandchild."

Vicky tried her best to follow the back and forth of this
exchange. She twirled her fork, impatient to hear if her papa
would take her back to Dundroma today. But still her
grandmother chattered on. Her legendary beauty was
washed out today, and Grandmother's halfhearted smiles
showed to disadvantage her crow's-feet and a drooping
chin.

"You're so charming when you want to be, Alec. But I

never forget what a devil you are. If you ask me, Isobel should send coxcombs like you away. I have never recovered from your elopement with Cecilia, you know. It quite destroyed my social reputation for weeks."

Her grandmother droned on, reading tidbits of gossip from Isobel—gossip from old friends of Cecilia's. "Vicky, child, stop playing with the silverware and listen to this. Isobel Fraser writes about how your mama once declared I was the prettiest mama anyone ever had—"

Vicky clutched her fork. "Does she write of Andrew?"

Her grandmother laid down the letter. "What is the reason for this impertinence? I told you not to let her eat too much spicy food at Dundroma, Clare. Bland food. Anything else is upsetting to a child's delicate system."

Vicky allowed her fork to clatter onto her plate in a most unladylike manner. "I'm not a child. Grandfather's better. I want to go back. Andrew's promised to take me fishing."

Adele raised her brows and with a haughty voice inquired, "Is this Andrew the only friend she can find up there?"

"Ask Clare. She's sitting there unable to eat," her father replied.

"Vicky and Isobel's son. They get along famously. He's teaching her about Dundroma life," Aunt Clare said.

"Humph. Let the lad teach pony riding if you must. A trifle in the larger scheme of raising a young lady. You can take the child away from Thornhill but you can't take the training of Thornhill away from the child. Mark my words."

"I've not forgotten Aunt Clare's teachings," Vicky said. "But I like ponies."

"I hope you're not going to encourage any other hoydenish activities," her grandmother said to her papa. "Oh, you're the father with all a father's power, so I'll keep quiet, but I do wish you'd remained a drowned missionary, you know."

"I'm sure a lot of people do," he said, looking straight at Aunt Clare.

"I don't!" Vicky declared. "I'm glad I've got a real papa!"

Adele Charlton turned to her granddaughter. "A young lady does not speak in the company of her elders until spoken to. One more outburst, Victoria, and you'll be confined to your room."

Papa stood, knocking over his goblet. "One more threat to her, Adele, and I will take her back to Dundroma . . . so I suggest instead a truce."

Aunt Clare pulled out Vicky's chair. "Stand up, Vicky." And to the others: "Will you excuse us? Vicky needs some exercise."

"Exercise?" echoed her grandmother as if Aunt Clare had spoken of taking her to the moon. "Are you certain that's wise? She might take on a fever like her grandfather."

"She's grown accustomed to exercise at Dundroma. I think it would be best to allow her to continue her habits."

Vicky looked up, surprised. Aunt Clare talking back to her grandmother. This was new.

Her grandmother was looking at the three of them— Vicky, Clare, and Vicky's father as if they held the key to some conspiracy. "A young lady needs the company of other young ladies. Isobel perhaps does not know how much time her son spends alone with Lord Strahan's daughter. You may be the father with all the rights, Alec, but I have Isobel's confidence. She'll not want her son accused of leading a young lady astray—"

Vicky's heart plummeted. "No, please . . ." That isn't how it was. She and Andrew were friends. A kiss didn't lead a boy astray. Or a girl . . .

"She's only twelve," her father said. "When she's old enough to put up her hair, then I'll worry about the lads."

Her grandmother fingered the rope of pearls at her neck. "Very well. You're the father. But I do hope, Alec, you are not going to steal her out of here. I shall humble myself and beg leave of you to allow the child to remain a few days longer out of courtesy to her grandfather."

Vicky's father looked over at Aunt Clare before he answered. For a long heart-stopping minute.

Aunt Clare bent her head and blushed.

They said nothing to each other. Not a word. Oh, this wasn't good.

Finally he turned to her grandmother.

"I'll allow the child to stay another night."

"I don't want to stay. I want to go to Dundroma *now*." Vicky burst into tears and dashed out of the room and upstairs. She stopped at the top to listen.

"You see, this is all too upsetting to her. You could return to Isobel and your flirtation, you know, and leave Vicky here . . ." Vicky heard her grandmother say.

"You think I'm a bigger fool than I realized, Adele. I'm not that trusting of Thornhill yet."

"It's none of this." Aunt Clare actually sounded angry. "If Vicky's upset, there's another reason entirely. Adele, you're blind to it, just as much as her father."

"Surely, you don't take this obsession with Andrew seriously?"

"Yes. Were you never young, Adele, or have you forgotten?"

"Forgotten? Never! In my youth, I was the crème de la crème! No one knows what it is to be young more than me . . ."

"Lovely dinner, Adele," her papa said. The door shut firmly.

Words. Shut doors. And more words.

Vicky covered her ears. Why, why, couldn't the grown-ups stop arguing over her?

Why couldn't she live at both places, belong to both? Why couldn't the boundaries go away? First Grandmother

and Grandfather were not speaking, and now it was Aunt
Clare and her father. Why? Why couldn't they kiss and
make up, all of them?

Grandmother and Grandfather never would.

Aunt Clare and her father?

What a ridiculous notion. But they could at least talk.

She ran to her bedchamber and slammed the door. If no
one else could play peacemaker, then she would do it.

That evening Clare found a note in her room from Vicky.
It was propped against a pillow on her white muslin
counterpane. Fearing the worst, a runaway, she ripped it
open.

She read and relaxed.

"Dear Aunt Clare, please come to see me. I must know
about Andrew."

A fleeting smile crossed Clare's face. Andrew consumed
Vicky's thoughts. If only love were that simple. As simple
as the first tender blush of affection.

Love was far more complicated.

She bent over the note, stunned by her thoughts. Love.
She was falling in love with Alec Douglas, Lord Strahan.

No. Impossible fancy. She was behaving like her ward—
infatuated with an intriguing male. Nothing more. Vicky's
obsession was rubbing off on her. Certainly Reginald had
never made her feel this way, and he'd been her husband.
Yes, mere fancy on her part.

She rumpled the note and tossed it into the slops pail. It
had been a long day, trying to hide her feelings for Lord
Strahan. She'd been aware of him at every turn she took,
could practically feel his lips on hers from last night. Desire
filled her. But she didn't know what to do with this desire
burning inside her. Except to avoid Alec Douglas. And that
was easy, for he'd not so much as looked at her. Clearly, she

was now again nothing but the meek Thornhill governess to him, the governess he'd vowed to do away with.

Marching down the hall, she knocked and pushed the latch on Vicky's door. "What is the meaning of this note, Vicky?" she asked as she walked in. "What did you mean by . . ." Her voice trailed off, for the room was empty, but on the bed rested another folded note of ivory parchment.

"Vicky?"

"Gone." The masculine voice came from the doorway.

Clare whirled, heart racing at the familiar voice. There stood Lord Strahan by the door, leaning on his cane, a sheet of ivory paper crumpled in his hand.

"What are you doing here?" Already she guessed the answer.

"My daughter sent a note." He stated the obvious and held it out. "It appears she's conspired to get us in the same place. A ploy worthy of a border lass. Do you suppose she's hoping we'll talk to each other again?"

Clare gulped and then bent her head to read the newest note.

"Let me guess—it says Vicky wants to return to her pony."

"She misses Andrew."

"Ah, that again."

Clare moved to the bed and unpinned the note from the pillow.

"Read me the note so we'll know where to go next on this merry chase."

She drew herself up as tall as she could. She came to his chin—barely.

"This is a matter to be taken seriously, surely."

His mouth tilted in a smile. "Allowing a twelve-year-old to lead me on a merry chase? I think not. But watching you try to remain prim and serious, Clare, that I can take seriously."

"Lord Strahan—"

"Too serious. Try Alec."

She couldn't. She stared up trying to form the two-syllable name, but no sound came out.

"Read me the note then," he said gently.

She cleared her throat and forced her gaze down. Away from deep blue eyes, away from tousled mahogany hair. "Very well . . ." She would not let him disconcert her. The rogue.

She read. "Dear Aunt Clare and Papa, I'm in Mrs. Beedle's kitchen helping her make blackberry tarts. I'm sending some up for you to eat while you discuss how soon I can return to my ponies." The note ended with a girlish signature, smeared by a purplish thumbprint.

"Bribery," Lord Strahan said. "Aye, but the lass has Douglas blood in her veins."

"You are unconscionable." Clare wadded the note. "You're worrying more about her Douglas temper than her goodwill."

"And you, Aunt Clare," he said, limping closer, so close she could smell the warm wool of his coat, "you are too concerned with prim appearances."

"Better primness than making a mockery of a missing child."

"Missing? Are you suggesting her note is a deception? She's in the kitchens."

"I suggest we go look." Clare headed down the hallway, past generations of Charlton portraits.

He followed a step behind.

Then she stopped.

The kitchen maid stood in the middle of the hall, a tray of blackberry tarts in her hands. The sweet smell of berry juice and still warm pastry wafted over to her.

"Tarts, Miss Charlton. Sent up from Miss Vicky." She held them out.

"Sent up from Miss Vicky," she repeated, holding them out even farther.

Lord Strahan reached out with one hand and took the tray. "Is Vicky down there still?"

"Oh, yes, milord, she's eating as much as she's baking. Says something about blackberries meaning something to her aunt Clare and her papa."

Lord Strahan's expression did not change one iota at this information. "Aye, then, leave the whole tray with me."

The maid ducked a curtsy, then picked up her apron in two hands and scurried off, leaving Lord Strahan holding the tray.

"See," he said to Clare, "you've worried over nothing." And he was laughing. His blue eyes crinkled in laughter. His handsome profile softened in amusement.

She was furious. "No matter what the battle, you have to win."

"I'm a Dundroma man, lassie, and you're a Thornhill lass. It's the custom between our two estates."

"Well, I hate the custom, and so does Vicky."

"Do you?" he said gently as he set down the tray and poked at a tart. He tasted the blackberry center. "They're excellent. My daughter is as good a baker as she is a pony rider, it seems. Would you like one?"

"No."

"Blackberries do bring out the passion in you, Clare."

She stood, hands on hips, too mad to talk.

"What do blackberry tarts have to do with passion?"

He laughed and handed her one.

"And why must you twist everything back to passion?"

He rested both hands on his cane and leaned closer to her. "I like to see a lass resist passion. There's more challenge in cutting through all the prim and proper brambles you've hidden behind."

"You're incorrigible."

The tart broke in her hands and crumbled to the floor. She stalked to her room and slammed the door. Alone. Alone. Alone. She said it ten times. Trying, trying to restore her dignity. He played with women's defenses. Her naiveté was his sport.

And yet she couldn't stop her heart from pounding. One by one she licked the crumbs off her fingers, then stood stockstill, hands at her sides, listening to the distinctive uneven tread of Alec's cane as he approached her door. It was unlocked. She took a deep breath for control. She knew he'd come in. Deep down, she was curious more than afraid. Desire and propriety warred, like a pair of reiving bands. It was no contest. But that didn't mean he had to know it.

The door opened.

"Take those blasted tarts away and all your talk of passion."

He said nothing.

She did not move.

"One blackberry tart. Vicky meant them as a peace offering—for us. For her papa and her governess."

"I don't want to make peace with a borderer. I don't trust you."

"Aye, Clare, lass, I'd not trust me either, but take this blackberry sweet from me . . ."

He reached around and placed it in her hand. Tit for tat.

"Why?"

"So I can kiss the tendril of honey hair at the base of your neck." His lips grazed her skin, soft and tentative.

She turned.

The candlelight cast auburn lights on his hair. She stared into his dark, intense gaze. Control. Stiff upper lip. A stolen kiss from the likes of Lord Strahan meant nothing. It was as he said—a forfeit. A game. The same as the other kisses. It was all a game to him. She swallowed hard. It was hard to think. She was bathed in sensual feelings.

"We should talk about Vicky."

He didn't reply, just lifted her hand and kissed it, turned it over, kissed the pulse point at her wrist and let it go.

Clare backed around her room until the grate of her fireplace stopped her. The air between them was as charged as the sky before a storm. Pulsating. Almost tangible. She was powerless to turn the trembling off—unless he left, and he was limping closer. Ever closer. The wool of his black frock coat smelled good—damp and earthy from his walk through the Dundroma rose gardens. Her fingers ached to reach up and brush back auburn locks of hair that fell over his forehead, windblown, wild. But that would be like the devil's apprentice trying to put out a fire by touching the devil.

Alec's gaze went down her prim gray gown from the mother-of-pearl brooch to her full skirt. He was so close his trousered legs made an indentation in her crinolined skirt. A sinful throbbing began between her thighs. Warmth encircled her, magnetized her.

He gave her a wicked smile. "Do you know, Clare, that standing there you have a halo around your head from the light of the fire. Are you an angel come to save me from a deal with the devil?" He reached out to brush back a loose strand of hair from her cheek.

"You should leave . . . in case a servant saw you entering my chamber."

"Ah, appearances . . ."

"Someday, I'll need a character, a new position."

"When Vicky has no more need of you."

Or Lord Strahan. "I shall find a post in London. Which is why I need a character."

"Your voice shakes when you say that. Do you fear asking me for a character?"

"A character from you would be rather a contradiction in terms, don't you think?"

He laughed.

"You fear the unknown, like that statue pointing to God knows where. Everyone fears it because it's the unknown. You fear the unknown within yourself, don't you? Fear yielding to the passion burning even now in your eyes."

She backed up and bumped into her bedpost. "We all fear something, Lord Strahan. Even you."

"Oh. What do you suppose I fear? Blue-flowered bed-chambers? Or perhaps pert and prim governesses?"

"I think you fear being left alone in Thornhill." At his glower, she grabbed the bedpost. "Or perhaps you fear trusting your leg to the doctors in Edinburgh. If they fail to mend you, then there is no alternative, no hope. Is that it? Do you fear the end of hope? Are you brave enough to face the sepoys and the tigers and the Pathans of India, but not the knife of an Edinburgh surgeon?"

He drew back, as if surprised. Yet the change in his features told her she was not far off. "You're wrong, lassie. I am unmendable, and a man cannot fear what cannot be fixed. He can feel bitter and regretful, but not afraid."

"No, something about Thornhill scares the devil of Dundroma. Are you afraid you might become civilized here? Maybe it's the fear that in remaining here too long you'll actually begin to act civilized. The really crippled part of you, Alec, is not your knee, you know. It's your spirit."

Alec. His Christian name had rolled off her lips, just as easily as honey. "Your spirit, Lord Strahan, needs mending worse than your knee."

His face darkened, and he reached for her. "You've a vixen's tongue, lassie, and more passion than you know what to do with." He glared down, just a kiss away.

She stared back up, her lips tempting, her eyes wide with innocence.

A spark jumped between them.

"Clare, Clare. You are an innocent."

"Why?" Trembling, she sat down onto the bed.

"Desire is a complicated thing." He reached down and traced a tiny bramble scar that was healing on her chin . . . "Like the brambles, it can bear sweet fruit but lose your balance and you find yourself in a painful tangle. Some of us desire the fruit more than we fear the tangle."

"In the matter of your knee, you fear the tangle."

He flinched, inexplicable pain flickering in his eyes, then vanishing. "So you call me a coward." But if he'd lost his equilibrium he quickly regained it.

"Perhaps each of us is a coward in our own way. Do you fear desire's bramble, Clare?"

She closed her eyes. "I do not desire this conversation."

"Nor I—" He pressed his lips to her temple, smoothed back her hair, then trailed a line of tiny kisses down her cheek, his breath warm, tantalizing. "And like the brambles, lass, once caught in them, it's too late to back out . . ."

She turned and their lips met.

He was her devil, just like the legend warned, calling to her senses, awakening every pulse point, and God help her, she could not say no, but leaned back and allowed herself to be pulled beside him.

They were sworn enemies, honor bound not to trust each other, and yet her body seemed unable to listen to her head.

It was she who deepened the kiss, and he . . . he kissed her back even deeper. Desire, oh, it knew no boundaries, no borders.

And this border had nothing to do with geography, nothing at all.

⸃Chapter Sixteen

In one fleeting second she understood what in twelve years had been a mystery. The mystery of the statue at the border came clear. It was a wonderful thing, not a danger, to be so bewitched.

Alec Douglas pressed her back against the bed, then ran his hands up her arms, slowly, intoxicating her with longing. Her heart beat crazily, in a rhythm she'd never known. Never before had she yearned like this, felt this heat, this liquid yearning. It was intensely new, and she was unable to stop herself. Lost in his arms, his touch, his own ardor. Slowly he eased her down on the bed. Two halves, two worlds, that needed to be joined. Above her, his heart beat against hers.

For long moments neither of them talked. If Alec breathed deeply, held her still, he might yet back away from this. The only control left between them was his own conscience, and it was a tarnished thing. He levered himself up to gaze at her—long, dark lashes lying against creamy porcelain skin, wisps of honey-colored hair scattered across the counterpane. Her lavender scent drifted up to him, and he wanted only to undo the buttons of her prim blouse. He fumbled to unfasten the brooch at her neck, and his fingers trembled as they never had before. Giving up, he gathered her into his arms, close, and rained kisses on her hair.

Clare couldn't think. His kisses had turned her into a river of pleasure. She was aware of only sensations—a scent of bay rum and rain to him she could not ignore. And his heartbeat, the warmth of his breath continued to pound at her defenses.

He was kissing her throat, his hands caressing parts of her Reginald had never touched. Passion stalked her, closed in, begged for release until she held her breath to keep back a moan. If he didn't stop, the pent-up passion would betray her. She lay as still as possible. That's how Reginald had told her to behave in bed. Not move. He told her passion was wrong, disgraceful, common.

She tried to push back the memories of Reginald, but they flooded over her. With Reginald the marriage chamber had been a stiff, formal event. She had lain in bed, nightgown to her neck, and waited for him to come to her. Reginald had not looked her in the eye, but acted as embarrassed about being there, even more so about revealing himself naked to her.

He had made formal conversation, then blown out the lamp. She never saw Reginald naked, not in the month of their marriage. After the lamp was blown out, he slid into bed beside her, and lay stiffly beside her talking of mundane things until finally Clare, who had secretly yearned for her wedding night, felt slighted. Did Reginald not desire her? But as the minutes wore on, she felt his embarrassment in his voice and guessed Reginald, proper Reginald, son of Adele, was a virgin as much as her and that taking the initiative might be up to her.

She did not find the notion repellent. She wanted to know what the mating of a husband and wife was like. "Reginald," she said, "don't you want me?"

He was silent. She could almost see his blush. "Wives don't ask such questions," he said.

But she had.

"Will you kiss me?" she asked, prodding him along.

And so Reginald, in his nightshirt, had leaned over and chastely kissed her on the lips. One stiff kiss.

And then leaned back on his pillow.

Clare felt an instant flare up of sensual longing, not love necessarily, but a instinctive need to have a man join with her at the juncture of her thighs. It was the way of nature; she knew that much. And she knew at last she would have to initiate more.

"Reginald." She touched his arm, leaned up on one elbow and leaned toward him. "You *are* glad you married me?"

"Glad. What a question. Marriage is an institution."

"Reginald, do you want children?"

"When God blesses us with them."

"But, Reginald, God can't conceive them."

"Clare, don't talk blasphemy."

"Children are conceived between man and woman. I am not the Virgin mother." She dared to lay her hand on his chest, on his nightshirt.

He pushed it off. "Clare, don't be forward."

And so she lay back. Perfectly still.

A few minutes later she heard him take a deep breath and then he moved on top of her with no preliminaries, not even a kiss. His nightshirt tangled between them, and it was she who pulled it away. She who lifted her hips to pull her own nightgown out of the way. And then with mechanical precision, Reginald lowered himself onto her and consummated the marriage, barely touching her except in that most intimate place. She sensed his displeasure when her hips had moved in time to his, and so she schooled herself to lie still, to show no passion, as was proper here at Thornhill. Women did this as a duty; that's what Reginald expected.

A month later she was a widow. Not a virgin any longer, but always wondering what the marriage bed could have been.

"Clare," Alec's voice came soft and then feather-light kisses were on her face.

"What are you thinking? It is Reginald, isn't it?" he guessed. "Forget whatever he told you or taught you . . . Clare, forget. I don't want Reginald's widow. I want Clare. You. Only you . . ."

His mouth cut off her protests, and she was kissing him back. They clung, layers of clothing ignored as they pulled each other closer, craving touch, yielding to pent-up desire. Only closeness would satisfy. And yet more closeness. Alec Douglas, the devil of Dundroma, buried his head right where here heart beat, and there were no more thoughts of any other man. Tousled mahogany curls grazed her chin. His hands played her like a violin. She flung her head back, aching, melting, burning, turning liquid inch by inch wherever his hands roamed. He was on fire, as if he'd been contained for too long, like her, and now like spark to tinder, each of them was igniting.

Then her thoughts blurred, as Alec Douglas, the devil of Dundroma peeled away her gown, button by button, and watched breathlessly as she did the same with his shirt.

She clung to him while his hands and mouth caressed her hair, her skin. He flared to life against her, and instead of jumping away in maidenly embarrassment like Cecilia had done, she shut her eyes in ecstasy.

Prim Clare Charlton did indeed have a core of passion, and he intended to explore the limits of that passion.

With easy motions, he pushed up her dress, ran warm fingers up her thighs. She arched back against him, moaned, moved her hips. He moaned deep in his throat, a sound of impatience, then his fingers were gone, his trousered hardness pressed close to her, even while he fumbled for the openings.

She clasped him to her and slowly, ever so slowly he took her to release, unlocked a new door for her, then spent himself inside her, shuddered and fell against her. She lay spent herself, curled against him, and eventually remembered that she was breathing of her own accord.

This, this was what she'd been denied in marriage. It was a sweet ache, an endless void he filled. Endless. And she, lacking in shame. Taking, taking, taking . . .

She drifted asleep, and when she awoke he was gone.

Guilt washed over her and humiliation. Passion was her Achilles heel. Every time she opened the door to it, it took over, got her in trouble.

Tears blurring her eyes, she locked the door behind him, pressed her head to the door. She was so sinful, had betrayed everything at Thornhill, everything the Charltons had given her. Oh, if Alec Douglas had any doubts about her unsuitability as a governess, they must all be dashed by now. When they were together alone, she gave herself to him as easily as a Covent Garden strumpet. And he knew it, the devil.

She had to prove to him that she could face him and not give in. In fact, the more she thought about it, the more she realized she ought to apologize for losing control. Tell him she was deeply ashamed, and vow it would not happen again.

And her heart ached at how her weakness had betrayed her. All her life, from childhood on, passion had gotten her into trouble. Her parents were genteelly poor. Her rector father despaired of her lack of decorum, and girls' schools wrote endless letters to her father deploring her lack of discipline, until finally a new master came to her school, and with her father's permission, she was locked away in a school closet every time her spirits grew too high. Discipline was all. Rules were all. Running, laughing too loud, they locked her away over and over. Locked her away until her stomach rumbled with hunger. Until she cried herself to sleep. Until she woke up, aching with hunger and fear of the dark.

Finally the key would turn in the lock. She ate and retched and was locked up again. The key turned in the lock, a lamp held up to the dress she'd wet in her sleep. Her ears were boxed and back she went. She pounded on the door, but to no avail. The master and his evil wife would win. Eventually she learned to sit in stoic silence, reciting the rules of decorum. Her body ceased to betray her; her emotions were held in check. She buried her passions deep in the past. Survival depended on it, and only after she left the school and her father died did she accept the only escape life offered—a marriage proposal to the very proper Reginald, who like her father and the schoolmaster deplored any show of human frailty. Then she became a governess to Vicky and a valued companion. Dear, perfect Clare.

Alec Douglas paced Thornhill Manor, limping restlessly, scowling at servants who dared peer at him longer than five seconds. Room by room, he walked over the great house, deliberately inflaming the shattered bones in his knee. Pain was, he discovered, an excellent antidote to desire.

What had gotten into him in that charade over blackberry tarts? What? He was a man with a man's desires, but there were any number of suitable women at Dundroma who could slake his desires.

He ought to be ashamed taking advantage of a lonely widow. His behavior was unjustified, and a lonely woman like her might interpret it wrongly.

Clare was a good woman. Certainly too good a woman for the likes of him. And it was that goodness he was worrying about. Good women invariably wanted marriage. She'd be tapping at his door announcing in self-righteous tones that honor demanded a marriage of convenience.

And if there's one thing Alec did not want, it was marriage.

Aye, this cat-and-mouse game with Clare had to cease

and cease now. He'd have to apologize and assure her he'd never touch her again.

Clare could stand the tension no longer. She took a candle in hand and held it up high as she tapped on Alec's door.

He opened the door a crack and leaned against it, shutting his eyes briefly.

"I came to tell you I'm sorry. I behaved badly."

Wasn't she going to demand an honorable proposal? Part of him was relieved; another part, surprisingly, was disappointed. He tugged her inside the door and shut it.

"We must talk. I wanted to apologize to you as well. Clare—"

"It was unbecoming of my station as Vicky's governess."

He caught her by the arm. "Are we done apologizing then? Truce?"

She nodded.

He was silent a minute. "You are a bewitching little wren."

"Bewitching? Hah!" she scoffed. "If I were that, I would heal your leg. Instead, you shall have to take Dr. Wilmot's offer and trust your fate to the physicians."

"Why do you think I'm tarrying at Thornhill? I'm delaying my return to Dr. Wilmot, not Dundroma."

She was touched that he'd revealed a vulnerable chink in his armor. Yet his words were also a reminder. He *would* return. She, Clare, was a temporary fancy, an interlude for the devil of Dundroma.

She ached with longing, longing she'd never felt for Reginald. Tears slid down her face, and he wiped them away. She looked at his tousled hair, gleaming reddish, met his blue-eyed gaze head on.

"I'm afraid of you."

"It's passion you fear, not me, isn't that true, Clare?"

"No."

"Aye, lass."

"No . . . no."

"You live a lie, Clare. You lose."

And then from outside his room came a rapping. "Lord Strahan. I need you."

Adele Charlton herself. Serious business indeed if she acted as her own servant. Clare stood rooted to the spot, but Alec Douglas acted swiftly and pulled her behind the door.

Then and only then, he opened it a crack. "Mrs. Charlton, you're upset."

"Vicky is gone."

There was a long silence. "Do you mean by gone that she's nowhere in Thornhill? Just last night she left a note saying she was eating tarts with the cook. I assumed she was down there again."

Adele sobbed. "How do you know?"

"The samples were quite tasty. I complimented her today." It was true. Though he preferred her free spirited ways at Dundroma, he did not have the heart to squelch her pride over some simple little tarts. "She and I talked about the merits of blackberry tarts over apple."

"Yes, yes, she made tarts, and tonight she was going to make a pudding. Cook has been waiting for her. Oh, but I knew better than to give her freedom with the servants."

"Nonsense. She was enjoying herself. Wasn't she?"

"On the contrary. She's hid out in the kitchen as a ruse. She's run away, Alec Douglas. So there! What do you have to say now?"

He stared, dumbfounded, at Adele.

"Did you look for her?"

"Where? She's run away. Her note says so."

"She left me a similar note and she was in the kitchen eating tarts with Cook."

"But Clare's room is empty as well."

He reached behind the door and felt for Clare. His hand

made contact with her arm, slid down to grip her hand, and held her in place, out of sight.

"I'm sure Clare is somewhere about the place."

"No, she's not. We've searched high and low. She's gone too. Betrayed Thornhill and gone with Vicky."

"Then doubtless they've gone back to Dundroma. I'll go back and prove it."

Adele stood waiting.

"Come along then. I'll call for a coach."

He stalled for time. "As soon as I change into traveling clothes. I'm sure Vicky will be safe."

"Well," Adele Charlton sniffed as she twisted a handkerchief in her hands. "You certainly sound calm about the matter."

"Because I know Vicky as well as I know myself. There is no other place she'd go."

"You'll find her?" Her voice rose. "If you don't, Percival is certain to have a relapse. The child did him a world of good, and I admit it. But losing her will surely kill him."

Alec sighed, recognizing panic in the making. "I shall find her, I wager, in the pony stable at Dundroma. She's been anxious to get back there."

"Whatever could it be about that pony stable of yours she likes?" Adele's voice rose higher yet.

"Andrew is good with the ponies," Alec said calmly. "Vicky admires his skill."

"Humph. I feared Dundroma would ruin her, and now it has."

Alec squeezed Clare's hand in his. Meanwhile, he never missed a beat of his placating words to Adele. "Dundroma has exceptional qualities, Adele. You may come and search for Vicky yourself if you're so anxious."

"I've seen enough of it in you, milord. Lord Strahan, you try my patience."

"Do you care so little for Vicky that you would not set

foot on my property in order to find her yourself?" It was an offer freely made. "Not in three hundred years has anyone from Dundroma extended an invitation to Thornhill people to come visit."

"I have my reputation to consider."

Adele Charlton's selfishness amazed him. Appearances still mattered more than her granddaughter.

"Now please—please . . . hurry on up there. I want news of Vicky's safety posthaste."

"And of Clare?"

"She's dispensable. Surely you know that."

He felt Clare's hand go cold in his, her fingers slack.

He tightened his grip. "No, I hadn't realized that yet."

Adele of course had no idea who was listening. "She lost face the day she went off to Dundroma with you. Surely you knew that. The legend of the border statue, Lord Strahan. We take it seriously at Thornhill. Even if she returns, she'll never be truly a part of Thornhill again. She's tainted."

"I underestimated my reputation, I see." His voice was taut. "And Vicky?"

"Vicky's a mere child. The neighbors will make allowances for her . . . but Clare's reputation is already ruined."

He shut the door and looked into Clare's white face.

❧Chapter Seventeen

Adele Charlton made a concession to principle and loaned Alec one of her own coaches for the journey back to Dundroma. Haste was all. Waving from the bedchamber of her husband, she pondered what to do about Clare. She'd been perfect as governess to Cecilia's motherless baby, but now Vicky was clearly in need of a stronger hand. Perhaps the father's return was fortuitous. She'd think on it; she'd rather send the child away to school, to finishing school in France as she'd sent her daughter. Once Lord Strahan gained his strength back, he'd grow restless, and she'd be ready with advice on finishing schools for young ladies.

"I wonder who she takes after?" Adele mused to her husband, who sat up in bed, weak but speaking again. It was, she realized, good to have Percival talking again. Though she'd never told him so, Percival had come over forty years to be her best companion.

"I never ran away in my life," Percival muttered from his bed. "I think Vicky must get it from you."

"Me?" Adele turned a horrified stare on her husband. "Percival, there are times I don't think I really know you . . . or you me? Even after all these years. What do you know of me as a child?"

"I know what you were like as a young lady, and Vicky's not far away from young ladyhood."

Adele flushed. "Percival, do think straight. When . . .

when you met me, I was nearly nineteen. Vicky is only twelve."

"Eighteen, Adele, and caught kissing a rogue in the library of Lady Wattleston's town house during a soiree. That was hardly an innocent scene, Adele. It cost you your reputation in London."

"Must you keep reminding me that you helped me save face?"

"Save face? Such understatement is part of your fascination, Adele. And I married you, Adele. If it was nothing more than saving face to you, then so be it." He shut his eyes, face pained as if talking had brought on a relapse.

Adele bent over her husband and touched his cheek. "Percival? Are you alive?"

His eyes snapped open. "I've been more alive than you've given me credit for, Adele. I married you, dammit, and you've treated me for decades as if I were beneath your worth . . . Vicky, now, the child gives me reason to live."

"Percival, you're talking nonsense." But he wasn't, and she knew it. She simply wasn't used to such blunt talk. This was the first time Percival had made outright reference to the details of that fatal night when he'd rescued her from a cad and spared her reputation from potential damage.

Something would have to be done to nip such talk in the bud—even now—for Adele knew there were suspicions still lingering amid society's gossips.

Everyone in London had to go on assuming she'd married Percival and come to the bleak northland of Thornhill of her own volition. And it would never do, never, for people to learn otherwise. Oh, yes, the gossipy ladies would swoon to learn her secret. No, it would never do for the truth to out.

What did Percival want to bring up old history for? Oh, men had their pride—even Percival. She only hoped his pride didn't require anything drastic on her part. Marrying him had been drastic enough.

Well, whatever had been eating away at Percival's pride, she had her pride to consider too. Always. And she'd figure out some compromise. If she'd learned nothing else in all these years up here at Thornhill, it was the way of the borderer. Compromise.

At the border, Alec Douglas instructed the coachman to rein in.

"You can come out now," he said.

Clare worked her way out of a blanket, spitting woolen thread from her mouth. She shoved the dark tartan aside, sat up, and leaned back against the velvet-covered seat cushions.

She pushed her hair back with both hands and then made a great show of straightening her blouse.

What to do with Clare was Alec's dilemma, for he'd no intention of wedding, yet making her his mistress openly—assuming she'd even agree—would ruin her. He could take her to India, but there was the matter of his bum leg. He was not ready to go back, nor ready to have a woman in his life.

Pity she was from Thornhill, and that he was a cripple.

And a greater pity that he had vowed never, as long as he was less than what he was, to let a woman in his life again—except in the most casual way. Call it Dundroma pride.

Or the vow of a borderer.

Or the common sense of a wise man.

She pulled away toward the corner of the coach.

He stared straight ahead. He would, by God, ignore her. From this moment on. Ignore her. She despised him anyway.

Clare stared at the passing heath—purple and windswept. And lonely.

When they arrived at the castle, Vicky came running up,

with the sheepdog at her heels, apparently forgiven for eating her doll.

"You shouldn't have worried, Papa," she said brightly.

"I didn't worry," Alec said, his tone strained. "But for worrying everyone else on two estates you must be punished."

Vicky's face fell. "But you said you wanted me to run about free. That's the good thing about Dundroma—it's got none of those stuffy rules we had at Thornhill."

"Running about free is not the same as asking my permission to leave. I take pride in the freedom of Dundroma, but I'm also a military man, Victoria, and there are limits to freedom. What you did is no different than a soldier deserting his base. And in the military soldiers who run off are thrown in the brig and court-martialed."

"I'm not a soldier," she answered smartly.

"You're a Douglas, and here at Dundroma for running off without leave you shall spend three days locked in your room. Porridge and barley broth only."

Even Clare was shocked at the sudden military side to him. "Lord Strahan, she can't live on porridge."

"I'm not a child," Vicky pleaded.

"Your behavior is that of a bairn. To your room."

With a sob, Vicky ran off.

Stubborn Dundroma devil. If Clare could, she'd try to reason with the man for Vicky's sake. But after what had happened between them, she could hardly bear to look at him.

Dr. Wigston Wilmot was having a bad day. Dundroma's whisky was a soothing antidote to repeated rejection. Unfortunately it could not talk or give advice.

Which is why he was overjoyed to see the governess from Thornhill return. She seemed a sensible sort who might advise him.

His hunch proved correct. She allowed him to recount his findings in Edinburgh and chatted pleasantly with him over tea and scones.

"I'm certain Lord Strahan will come around when he learns of your news."

"I fear not. He refuses to allow lowly surgeons in the same category as physicians. Prejudice, pure and simple . . . but oh, the advances at the Royal College. You'd think one of his own—Scottish surgeons . . . well, we'll put it to him. It's quite a simple operation, really . . . when I tell the College of Physicians, they'll be impressed. We could join forces, the physicians and surgeons and pool our skills . . . but first we need the perfect case. Lord Strahan's injury would give us that perfect piece of surgery . . . he could alter the history of medicine."

"He's stubborn. I think perhaps he likes to make up his own mind, think it was his idea."

"Perhaps." Dr. Wilmot sighed heavily and laced his hands over his paunch.

His only hope for fame in this life—bringing together the physicians and surgeons, melding their disciplines, rested with stubborn Lord Strahan. And the laird of Dundroma had his mind in the dark ages, refused to give the luckless surgeons a chance to prove they were capable of medical advances more stunning than those of physicians. Worse, the widow Fraser would not give him the time of day. Not even when he'd asked if he could walk about the grounds of her more modest manor house. The widow had a military pension, a fine border house, and a winsome smile. Wigston had found his lady love.

"You sigh in discouragement, Dr. Wilmot," Clare asked gently.

"The widow Fraser does not invite my overtures. Perhaps you can advise me?"

Clare considered this. "Perhaps she is not wanting to be

claimed. You have a fascination with making medical history . . . but . . . well, sometimes we cannot change history, only ride the tide of it."

"I will change it, I know."

"Up here in the borderland, history is perhaps too complicated to change."

They were silent. Clare stared across the moorlands. She'd always held a secret fascination with this wild moorland. Unlike Adele who endured and complained and compared the place unfavorably with London, Clare took pride in loving this bleak windswept land—from its lowliest rock to its windy gray mist-shrouded skies. Not for her the soot-filled skies and crowded streets of Newcastle or Liverpool and the thought of London—teeming London . . . well, there weren't that many posts for governesses in this north country.

She'd sorely miss this place. But she couldn't stay. Not after what had happened. She'd see that Vicky was well cared for and then she would leave.

Dr. Wilmot cleared his throat. "You are very thoughtful," he observed.

Clare turned. "The widow Fraser is unaware of all this commotion, I hope."

"Oh, I think not, Mrs. Charlton. Lord Strahan was home less than a few hours when Mrs. Fraser arrived at Dundroma all concerned."

Isobel would know from the servants the second Lord Strahan crossed back into Dundroma land. "Then she must have a source of information—someone at Dundroma telling her what is going on . . . perhaps you should let it be known you have made a great medical discovery or that you are very rich . . . something to pique her interest."

Dr. Wilmot brushed off his hands and stared out across the garden of Dundroma at the purplish hills, pondering his

fascination with the widow Fraser. Clare's heart went out to
him.

Poor Dr. Wilmot. Bound to fail. For his was a grand
conceit. A knock-kneed man with a potbelly and supercilious manner who did not see his flaws was doomed to
failure and rejection. Especially by an ambitious woman
like Isobel.

Over and over in her mind she replayed Alec's kiss. Her
forfeit. And then their lovemaking. To a man like Alec
Douglas, it had all been mere sport. She'd leave Dundroma
soon, and like clouds scudding across the sky, her feelings
for Lord Strahan would pass. It was passing fancy. Certainly
for him.

And she'd best remember that.

"Isobel Fraser . . ." Dr. Wigston Wilmot sighed. "I have
no idea what would pique her interest."

"Make her jealous," Clare said automatically. "It's an old
secret weapon for making a woman take notice."

"Jealous?" Dr. Wilmot sat up, an expression of righteous
indignation on his face. "But Mrs. Fraser is above such
underhanded intrigue, not to mention far too refined to
possess such emotions."

Isobel Fraser seethed. She disliked the way Alec had
slipped away so easily into Thornhill territory. That's how
quickly he'd slipped out of her fingers and into Cecilia's
heart thirteen years ago. She was wiser now, on her guard,
but that governess and Alec's hoydenish daughter—they
were unknowns.

She'd have to encourage Andrew to take Vicky fishing or
perhaps off to some truly rustic activity like the Highland
games in a nearby village. All the villages were holding
games lately. It was becoming quite the rage, even in
Lowland villages, to dress up in tartan and sit over a picnic
lunch watching grown men throw logs and rocks about. Oh,

Andrew enjoyed it well enough, but eventually, Isobel
hoped with a shudder, such Highland nostalgia would pass.

Isobel much preferred French influences. Mary Stuart
was her heroine, and if—no, *when*—Isobel became chat-
elaine of Dundroma Castle there'd be some changes made.
Many. All the tartan would be thrown out and those odious
stag heads and Highlanders would be turned away at the
castle door. She'd redecorate with the more tasteful French
gilt. She'd add some elegance to the place. But first she
needed to snare Alec. She'd realized in the short time he'd
been away at Thornhill how close she was to losing him
again. It was time to do something drastic. The solution,
when she stopped to think about it, was so obvious as to be
laughable.

A simple letter to an uncle in distant London. Uncle
Henry never denied his favorite—his only niece—anything. And now that Alec was finally back from Thornhill,
she wasn't going to waste any more time or leave the title of
Lady Strahan to chance.

"Alec," she purred, pressing her hand to the crook of his
arm, "I missed you."

"I never left the borderland."

"You left Dundroma." She busied herself folding a tartan
rug.

"Two days, Isobel. You managed alone for six months
before I came."

"It was an eternity. And now that I've grown to count on
your friendship, I feel your absence all the more keenly."

"Malcolm was inconsiderate dying in so untimely a
manner."

"Indeed. But that's past, and we have our futures ahead of
us. Shall we go out for a ride? The heather is at its peak."
She set aside the rug and stood, all energy.

"I am not in the mood to tramp the heath," Alec said in
damping tones. "I saw endless hills of it traveling home

from Thornhill. It does grow on both sides of the border, you realize."

It took all her patience to retain her composure. "Alec, you're sounding tired. Shall I read to you? Scott. The Waverly stories. *Rob Roy*? You love those Highland adventures, don't you?"

"I can read for myself, Isobel."

Annoyed, she sighed and sat down amid all the stag heads and tartan. She whisked her skirt away from a potted palm and leaned back, staring up at a portrait of the heather on the hills. The butler handed Alec a whisky, and Reiver stood wagging his tail while Alec rubbed his ears.

"I'd like tea, Alec," she said.

He looked up from the dog, as if her request were distracting. "Pardon?"

She repeated herself. The sheepdog would have to go too.

And then the butler left and they sat there, each silent, the only sound Reiver's panting, and the wind blowing down the chimney.

She supposed she ought to ask Alec if he was tired, but it was a nuisance having to worry about his leg. His limp. His wound. He always commanded the attention. Now when she became Lady Strahan, the servants would learn in short order not to cater to his ill humor or to his bad leg. Stoicism was called for. That's how she'd been raised, and Alec needed a strong dose of it too now that he was back at Dundroma. Stoicism in the face of pain. A gentleman, no matter how poorly, always gave the lady the spotlight. Always. She was grateful for that part.

"Where's your daughter?" she asked with faint enthusiasm. "With the ponies?"

"Funny, Isobel, your interest in Vicky. I scarcely recall Andrew in India. You sent him home to school in Britain as soon as he was ready."

Isobel ignored that. "I told you—I could never find a

good ayah; he was better off here. It's different for an adult
in India. We had a social life, but for a child—no, Andrew
could have caught cholera or some other dreadful illness or,
worse, been caught up in the mutiny. I got him out of there
just in time." She paused. "I did not see much of him, but
he thrived. Now you, on the other hand, you are not thriving
being away from India, away from the military."

"How do you know?"

"I know your heart's desire—we always shared our
intimate thoughts in India. Remember the curry rice dinners
and croquet up in the hills, away from the heat? You'd
always confide in me."

That was before Malcolm died, before Alec's accident.

"What is my heart's desire?" he asked, brows raised.

If only he'd smile . . . like he used to. Isobel wished
they were away from prying servant eyes and that governess, who was always lurking in the shadows like a
mouse.

"Alec, I know very well you want the rank of general.
That was always your dream. Major was never enough for
you. Nor any ranks in between."

"How do you know?" He stared at her over his glass of
whisky.

"Malcolm told me about all you officers. The Crimean
War made everyone's career soar—especially yours, and
it's the cruelest fate that you should be treated with such
ingratitude by the military."

"I'm rather glad I met my daughter at last," he suggested.

"Well, of course. But that's family, and a man values his
career above all, doesn't he?"

Did he? He supposed so. His mind saw the porcelain skin
and honey-streaked hair of Clare. He forced himself to
remember endless military parades in the hot Indian sun.
His row of medals. His regiment.

"You're still dreaming of returning to India—of leading entire armies as general. Admit it."

Alec had to think about it. "When I returned I told myself it was only to gain strength and then I'd go back, but I'm still limping about Dundroma chasing my daughter back and forth from one estate to another like a border lord drawn back three centuries in time."

"Exactly. The men of Dundroma, the men on this side of the border, are the most valued as soldiers. A limp won't stop a borderer. Oh, Alec," she gushed, "I've taken a liberty. Do say you're pleased. I've written to Uncle Henry—"

"I don't want favors."

"He's been promoted too, you know. He holds influence with the army. Now, Alec, don't be stubborn with your pride. I know you want this."

"Aye, but the army, Isobel, does not want cripples in its ranks of generals."

"Fie. You could be general and command from a tent."

"I want no favors, Isobel. Besides, I'm getting used to fatherhood—rather more than I'd expected."

This was proving trickier than she'd expected. It was all the fault of that governess. "But, Alec," she said, grasping at straws, "Vicky will be grown someday. You've your entire life ahead of you."

She bent down and smiled. In case he wished to kiss her.

He didn't, and she drew back, smiling while he nuzzled that sheepdog again.

"Have you thought, Alec, how very much we have in common? A homeland, our memories of India, children, and now widowhood? We even share the loneliness of that sorry state."

"So does the Queen."

"Indeed, but none of the rest. Why, we even . . ." She thought of mentioning their mutual knowledge of Malcolm, then decided against it. When trying to interest a man in an affair of the heart, it probably wasn't wise to remind him of a prior husband. She led him out to the garden.

"We even have Malcolm in common," Alec said as if he read her mind.

"Malcolm would want us to console each other, don't you think?"

"Malcolm is barely cold in his grave, Isobel."

"You're not tempted by my offer."

"Oh, I'm tempted. Any man would be."

"Then you'll think on it." She laid her hand on his arm and looked up into his eyes. He had such remarkable blue eyes, such gorgeous chestnut hair. Their babies would be beautiful.

The wind blew through the garden, and the taffeta of her skirt rustled against her crinoline.

And there was another sound.

Footsteps in the hallway.

Isobel caught a glimpse of dove-gray and made a move to tug Alec back out of the place.

But it was too late.

He'd heard too.

And taken a step away from her.

"Miss Charlton," he called. "Are you lost?"

"Eavesdropping is what she's doing," Isobel whispered.

"She could learn much from you," Alec said with a sardonic smile. "Miss Charlton," he called.

The simpering, mousy governess turned, half hidden by a yew tree.

"What are you doing out here alone?"

"Waiting for Vicky, and reading."

"Reading what?"

"My book on manners."

"Don't good manners dictate that you come and greet us?"

"Not when you're entertaining a lady."

"You mean Isobel?"

"Mrs. Fraser, I mean."

He turned to Isobel, who nodded stiffly. The mood she'd carefully worked up to—intimacy borne of shared memories and her grand gesture—all of it was ruined.

Isobel extended her hand for Alec to kiss. "Don't bother seeing me out. Your leg, you know," she said with as much simpering concern as even the governess could muster.

Alec sat down and leaned on his walking stick. "Will you allow Miss Charlton to stand in for me?" he asked, smiling.

"It's not necessary. She's a mere governess, not the lady of the house."

He inclined his head in farewell. "Thank you, Isobel, for your generous offer. I shall spend the rest of the day contemplating it."

Isobel was mollified. The governess was scurrying off, manners book in hand. Yes, the mood might be broken, but he had a tempting offer to think over. Let him think of all he had to gain by courting her. Not just a career but all of Malcolm's property, and herself into the bargain. And she was twice as pretty as the governess.

Tomorrow she'd return and resume the discussion.

And if her offer was not enough to win him over, then she had another trump up her sleeve. A plan to rid herself of the enemy—that governess from Thornhill, who always managed to get in the way and capture his attention.

Oh, Isobel would have her way yet. She pretended to be all soft and helpless, but a Scots woman—a true one—was made of stern stoic stuff, and if she could deter a London dandy like that pompous Dr. Wilmot, she could take on a prissy Thornhill lass—and win.

No, not for nothing had Isobel been raised a borderer.

❧Chapter Eighteen

As soon as Isobel departed, Alec Douglas levered himself out of his chair and, leaning heavily on his walking stick, limped across the garden and returned inside.

Clare did not pause at the doorway this time, but marched right in and confronted him.

"You're too hard on Vicky."

He picked up his mug and limped back toward his chair.

"Moments ago, you were the meek governess. As soon as Isobel leaves, you turn inside out with passion."

"I was taught to be polite in front of guests."

"Isobel is not company."

Clare knew that. Isobel was going to be the lady of this castle. That made her far more intimate than mere company. Lord Strahan had probably forgotten all about Clare. Or if he had not forgotten, found their indiscretion not worth mentioning. He had stolen kisses and a few moments of passion with the governess. It was not the first time the laird of the manner had won the advantage with a servant.

Her spirits fell, but not her purpose. Heartache was of no account to a strong Thornhill governess. She'd been practicing the lessons in her manners book all her life for this moment—maintain a stiff upper lip, no matter how much despair you feel.

She repeated the words. "You're too hard on her." She let her gaze drop, then looked up to meet his gaze. "You must let Vicky out."

"That is not a judgment for you to make." He tipped the whisky and swallowed a generous portion.

"Less than an hour back in Dundroma and already you're reverting to barbarian behavior."

"Ah, your own passionate behavior is reserved for civilized men. Rather a contradiction, don't you think, Clare?"

"You want to know what I think? This, Alec Douglas— it's not your leg that got crippled in India as much as your spirit."

"So you've mentioned. I fail to understand."

"When that horse fell on you and crushed your leg, you weren't maimed as much as when your spirit was crushed."

"And how do you know where my spirit is?"

"I don't. But I am positive you don't have one. You have anger, you have rules—military rules—you have a grumpy facade, you have a body that moves, talks, drinks—you go through the motions of living, but you don't have a spirit."

He looked surprised. "And what do you think I did with it? Do you propose that I lost it somewhere? Shall we search about the castle?"

"You also have a sarcastic wit that masks any warmth you once had."

"Warmth?"

"The housekeeper, Mrs. Drummond, says she's known you since you were a boy, and you were a most spirited boy, similar to Vicky."

"Like yourself, Clare."

"I've learned to control my passions."

"Most of the time."

"I behaved in a manner unbecoming a companion to your daughter. I have apologized. I must concede you have proved me a less than exemplary influence. You have won."

He gave her a crooked smile. "I know the entire history

of Thornhill and Dundroma ancestors, Clare, and none of them conceded defeat as easily as you just have."

"Your ancestors dealt in thievery and plundering, not lovemaking."

"You are a heartless governess."

"Not so much as you are a harsh father."

"Because I would lock my daughter away."

"Yes."

"And what is wrong with that?"

"She's not in the military. She's twelve. And . . . and I know what it's like to be locked up. It will kill her spirit. Good discipline is measured, tempered with mercy."

"Who locked you up?"

The key turned in the lock, and she shut her eyes. Darkness stole over her spirit. "My schoolmaster at my father's request. I would spare Vicky from being locked up in any way. Lock up her person, and you risk locking up the very spirit you want to run free." Clare meant to stop there, but her words tripped over each other as she told him more and more.

He listened, and then rose and, without a word, leaned on his walking stick, the one with the ivory tiger's head, and limped toward her. She stood there, ashamed at having revealed the awful secret of her own childhood.

He stopped in front of her. "My leg pains me, Clare. I want to sit. Sit with me."

"That would not be wise."

"We are in the library. I promise to remain in control. My word as a borderer."

She wasn't certain she would, but sympathetic to his pain, she took his arm, and together they walked to the settee.

"There," he said when they were settled. "Is this not proper?"

Clare nodded, but didn't speak. She was so ashamed of her body, but the past could not be changed. Nor could people. No matter how hard she tried to be prim, always just beneath the surface, passionate, base needs hid, waiting to surface and besmirch her image.

"Look at me, Clare.

"Here now, little wren. Now I see why you've been trying so hard to hide a passionate nature. Clare, passion is not a thing to feel ashamed of, no matter what the comportment books say. They are written, I believe, by elderly spinsters. They are the ones who should be locked away in closets, not you."

Clare tried to smile at that.

She didn't ask him why he had left her bed if he felt that way. Instead she took a deep breath and said, "Now, I want you to reconsider Vicky's punishment."

He stared at her, expression stark. "Your story gives me pause as you knew it would, wee governess."

"Then I may set Vicky free?"

He nodded. "I would only have her thrive."

She was so glad she touched his hand. "You are a more compassionate man than your gruffness admits, milord." And she hurried out of the room to give Vicky the good news. Her father had a reasonable streak after all. *Kind* and reasonable.

The trouble was Clare didn't care. It was his *passionate* streak that lingered in her heart.

Foolish governess.

Clare's lot in life was a celibate, loveless existence, living on the fringes of someone else's family. Sensual pleasures were her forfeit for the privilege of caring for children.

She was here for Vicky, not Alec Douglas, and she could never have both.

An hour later Vicky sat with Andrew up in the heather, near a wooded area. Andrew was sitting cross-legged, scouting for grouse. Tomorrow was the twelfth of August—the opening of grouse season, and Andrew wanted to scout the area in advance.

He could have invited Vicky to scout for kelpies in the loch, for all Vicky cared. It was enough to be with Andrew.

Vicky, who lay on her stomach, hands propped beneath her chin, snuck casual looks at Andrew. He was in profile, squinting into field glasses. She admired him more than ever.

Andrew could do everything—ride ponies, fish, and shoot grouse. And he didn't mind talking to her. If he had any shortcoming it was the talking.

That's all he did with her. Talk.

She still hadn't succeeded in getting him to look at her as if she was a lass.

Time was running short. Her papa was angry at her for running away and who knew what her grandparents would do next? And even if she stayed at Dundroma Castle, Andrew would be going off to school. She could almost hear the clock ticking away. The sands running through the hourglass.

And still she was no closer to winning a kiss.

"Is your school all boys?" she asked.

He peered through his field glasses as a bird skittered across the heath and vanished. "Aye, all boys. Why?"

"Then there are no lasses there to kiss . . ."

He turned to her. "No . . . why?"

"How could you kiss one then, like you said?"

Turning back, he shrugged casually. "There are lasses in the village."

"Have you ever kissed a village lass?" She remembered now his visits to the blacksmith's daughter.

"Cheeky lass. Why are you so interested in kissing?"

"Aren't you?" She rolled over onto her back, the heather beneath her.

Andrew avoided looking at her. "Not with lasses as young as you."

She sat up, hugging her knees. "I didn't mean that. I'm only asking because you know everything." Especially kissing. Vicky suspected a kiss from Andrew would be very special.

"And you want to know what a kiss is like, don't you?"

"Well, the grown-ups won't talk about it, nor will you."

"Because I told you—people don't kiss and tell . . . anyway, it's nothing special."

"But how can I know what it's like if no one will talk about it?"

He shrugged and handed her the field glasses. "You ask too many questions, lass. Here, peer through the glasses at that fine specimen of a grouse over yonder." He pointed.

"I don't want to."

Andrew stood. "You've got your head full of that old legend. It's nothing. No one at Dundroma kisses anyone."

"That's not what Aunt Clare told me. I thought you were a wild border lad."

"I am."

"Well, then?" She lay on the heather, eyes shut, a strand of red hair twined around one finger so Andrew could admire it. This was his chance to kiss her. She pressed her lips together, waiting.

"If you want to try grouse hunting tomorrow, you can come, but you have to be still and not talk so much."

Eyes opened. She was on her feet in a second. "I hate you, Andrew." She turned her back on him.

"Aw, now, lassie, don't run off mad. I'm only teasing you."

"You're acting as if I'm a child. Well, I'm not, and I'm not going grouse hunting with you. What's more—I think you're plain scared."

"Me?" Andrew stood there, blond hair blowing in the

wind, looking truly baffled. "Of grouse? They're just birds with feathers."

"Not grouse. I'm sorry for the grouse."

"Then what?"

"Of kissing, that's what. You're afraid, Andrew Fraser."

She ran away across the heath, hair flying. Let Andrew mull that over while he was taking aim on his precious grouse.

She consoled herself by taking the entire shortbread tin to the parlor and devouring three pieces before Mrs. Drummond confiscated the tin. Vicky hid a fourth piece under the leaves of a potted palm and sat pouting in her papa's chair. Oh, Andrew was a stubborn lad. Why wasn't he more like his mother when it came to pursuing kisses?

Isobel was furious. Servant talk was rampant. More had gone on at Thornhill than Alec had let on. The rogue.

Now, she was learning the truth and could barely contain herself.

At Thornhill Alec had been seen entering the room of the mousy little governess after dark. Oh, but Isobel had grilled the servants.

"You're certain it was not his own room?" It had been years since Isobel had seen the inside of Thornhill; it was a maze of bedrooms. Someone might have been mistaken.

But no one was mistaken, for it was the upstairs maid, Polly, who passed the information to the groom Ned, who had told Nessie at Dundroma, who in turn told Ginger, who was Isobel's personal maid. Ginger had always been reliable with gossip. In fact, these servants knew less loyalty to their estates than to each other. In this case, Isobel was less annoyed at their gossip than grateful.

At first she'd refused to believe it—Alec and that—that mouse. He couldn't admire anything about her, unless it was her loose morals. But then she grew worried. If he had married Cecilia of Thornhill, if she had lost him once, she could lose him again. Only she wasn't going to. History was not going to repeat itself.

It sounded as if the little mouse of a governess was in want of pleasure. It was always the quiet ones who surprised you. But it wasn't fair. She, Isobel, was the perfect helpmate for Alec. It was she who'd taken all the trouble to encourage Alec that he had a future, she who'd put up with the attentions of the odious Dr. Wilmot, all because he was a London physician of repute who could provide a consultation over Alec's injury. She'd even written to her distant uncle. For no other reason did she curry the favor of these men.

And now here was Vicky, a bothersome girl, on her doorstep.

"Did you return for Andrew?" she asked.

Vicky nodded. "He promised to take me grouse hunting before he returns to school."

"Andrew's not leaving yet. And grouse hunting starts tomorrow you know. He'll be readying his gun and gathering up his boots. You'd be in his way, and that would annoy him."

"He gets annoyed at me anyway."

"Nonsense, lass." She had to encourage Andrew to be even friendlier. It was high time he learned to handle a girlhood crush. There'd be many more ladies setting their cap for him in the future. "Andrew, like so many men, hides his feelings behind gruffness. Hasn't your governess taught you the ways of men yet? There are times to approach them and times to leave them alone."

"Aunt Clare tells me I'm too young for lads."

"What about your aunt Clare? Is she too young?"

Vicky's confusion must have shown on her face.

"I'm asking you a bold question, Vicky. Have you seen her kiss your papa?"

"Aunt Clare would never kiss Papa."

"Then what does she do at Thornhill . . . how did your father spend all his empty time?"

"Walking on the heath. Playing cards. Reading. Paying a call on Grandfather's sickroom. I thought he'd be pleased if I came back here. But he locked me in my room."

"He is glad, but he's trying to prove to Clare that he knows how to father. He's had no experience at it, you see, and he has much to learn about raising a girl."

"That's why he's allowed Aunt Clare to return. They had an angry consultation about me, and they decided she should still be my companion."

"Do you want a companion?"

Vicky shrugged. "Aunt Clare has nowhere else to go."

"But someday, child, you'll be grown-up. Don't you think she wants to get on with her own life too?"

"You mean, leave me for good? She says I'm too young yet. Besides, she's a widow and says she'll never rewed."

The little liar. "I think your aunt Clare understands more than she's telling you. When you see Andrew, remember if he's gruff, it only means he's secretly glad, but doesn't want to say so. Men are that way—even at age fifteen. And above all, admire his catch of grouse, even if they're dripping blood and trailing feathers. Pretend they're as beautiful as that sheepdog."

Vicky's smile was so like her father's. "Thank you, Mrs. Fraser."

"You and I shall have lots of intimate tête-à-têtes before you go off to school."

And then Isobel headed inside. She sat down, closed her eyes, satisfied. She had the perfect plan to rid Dundroma of the governess and the child both. The first step was a letter, promptly written.

"Though our families have never been close, due to geography and patriotic differences, still we have in common a borderer's loyalty. Such immoral conditions exist at Dundroma between Lord Strahan and your governess that obligation forces me to cast aside all previous differences. It is my duty to inform you of the less than savory conditions in which your beloved granddaughter—dear Cecilia's daughter—languishes."

Her letter was a masterpiece. She sealed the envelope and sent it down to Thornhill by special messenger. If she were a wagering woman, she'd stake her sole possession— Thistle Lodge itself—that Percival Charlton would be mended and out of his sickbed within a day.

❧Chapter Nineteen

A coach clattered into the castle yard, disturbing Alec's solitary chess game. He sorely missed his old chess partner, Malcolm. The game was not the same when a man had to play for two.

He looked up at the noise outside. No visitors were expected at Dundroma, and though stiff from sitting, he half rose. His bad knee buckled, and he collapsed back into the chair, knocking chess pieces out of alignment as his full weight jarred the table.

"Damnation!"

A maid scurried in and bobbed a quick curtsy.

"It's the lady and gentleman from Thornhill, milord."

"My God, they're retaliating, invading us." And in one angry gesture, he swept all the chess pieces onto the opposite chair with a clatter. Clare rushed in and began to pick them up.

"No, milord, they've come for their daughter," the maid explained.

"Exactly. Retaliation. They've come thinking to steal her back. But they won't. A father's rights come first!" He fumbled for his walking stick and, gritting his teeth against the pain, pulled himself to his feet.

Adele Charlton was being shown in the door, followed by a palish Percival. At first scent, Reiver stood, barking.

"Reiver! Sit." With an impatient whine, the dog obeyed.

Clare turned and Adele pointed a blue-veined hand at her. "You traitor—living in sin with the devil of Dundroma."

"What are you talking about?" Alec demanded.

Adele whirled and, in a voice seething with righteousness, relayed the staff rumors.

"Who contacted you?" Alec demanded. His face was white.

"What are you going to do? Throw her in the dungeon?" *Her*. Isobel.

"Isobel," he said, answering his own question. Adele did not deny it, and he passed a weary hand over his forehead. "She has betrayed me."

"Isobel had the moral strength to write us about you and . . . and well, I'm ashamed to admit our own Clare is lacking in moral discretion."

Damn Isobel's soul to hell. Better yet, she deserved to be boiled in oil or hung from that tree back on the darkest curve in the road.

"Isobel Fraser is a traitor to Dundroma."

"She has done her moral duty. Did you think you commanded her utter loyalty because she lives near Dundroma, because she wed your friend? You forget that she was Cecilia's school friend, and feels a certain loyalty to us."

"Her only loyalty is to herself."

"You deny untoward behavior between yourself and Clare? You condone such behavior between the two people charged with influencing our granddaughter?"

He grabbed Clare before she slumped to the chair.

"Do not listen."

"Hell hath no fury like a woman scorned," she murmured.

"What did you say?"

She shook her head and stood tall. There was no use in telling them why Isobel wrote that letter, that the Charltons were merely pawns in a game of winner take all. The stakes were high. Dundroma Castle was the prize. The title of mistress more coveted than a silver cup in any Highland games.

"Take us to Vicky," Adele Charlton demanded, looking around at the stag heads and tartan with a proper measure of Thornhill indignation.

Too late to pull up the drawbridge, stock the moat with kelpies. The Charltons had pulled off a surprise raid on Dundroma.

This invasion was unheard of in three hundred years of border history, and even Dr. Wigston Wilmot crowded outside the library door with the servants, eavesdropping on this momentous event.

"We demand our granddaughter," the Charltons said. "She's living under unsavory influences up here. Tell that to the legal system that says Vicky is your property!"

"You have been sorely misled."

"I think not. I want my granddaughter!"

"Find her yourself," Alec said, then quickly added a sly condition. "If you dare explore Dundroma. The risk is yours, but I'll not lift a finger to have the child pulled back and forth like the knot in a tug-of-war rope."

"What?" Adele recoiled as if she'd peered into the Black Hole of Calcutta. "You expect us to go searching about this barbaric place?"

Alec smiled. "You'd better take a broadsword, Adele. You might need to defend yourself from a witch or a plundering ghost of some reiver past."

"And I'm certain it was a long line of reivers from whom your black heart descended."

"If that scares you off sooner, by all means, think what you want."

At last, the Charltons' gaze turned on Clare. "You have disgraced us."

"No more than you have shocked me," she shot back with

a new boldness. "I am ashamed of you, putting your reputation, your . . . your appearances with the neighbors ahead of a loving granddaughter! And who are the neighbors in any case but descendants of these plundering, thieving reivers whom you scorn?"

"You speak of good Thornhill neighbors."

"No matter what side of the border we live on, we are all human. We all have flaws. We all have checkered ancestors, so there's no use putting on airs. Our neighbors know us better than we know ourselves."

And she turned.

Adele's voice stopped her in her tracks.

"Well, I hope, dear Clare, that you can find a position without a character."

Twelve years of loyalty had been for naught, but she didn't care. "A character from a hypocritical woman is worthless," she said over her shoulder. "I shall make my way in the world on my own merits!"

As expressions ranging from disbelief to shock played across Adele's face, she sank into Alec's worn tartan chair. "Clare, you are obviously bewitched. I will overlook this outburst if—"

"I don't want to be forgiven. I intend to leave Thornhill and be free. Vicky will stay with her father. And if you truly love her, you and Percival will work out an understanding with Lord Strahan for visitation. I've spoken with Lord Strahan about the injustice of fathers owning children to the exclusion of the child's feelings for other relatives. If I've done nothing else right, at least credit me for loyalty to Vicky."

"What kind of traitorous idea is that? You suggest I applaud my granddaughter's loss to this wild castle? To our enemy's home? To this wretched Scottish heritage?"

"I suggest you applaud Vicky's tolerance, and I suggest you start learning some yourself. Look around you. Dundroma has many beauties if you look past your prejudices."

"Bewitched is what you are, Clare."

"No, free of prejudices that come dressed up as rules."

She stalked out to pack. Oh, but she was uncommonly pleased with herself. She'd done it. Told her vain mother-in-law off. The key turned, and she saw light and a freedom she'd not known in years. Freedom.

Freedom to leave Alec Douglas. The freedom to forget his arms about her, his tempestuous lovemaking.

Double-edged swords haunted her still. But that was her heartache, and clearly of no concern to Alec Douglas, Lord Strahan. But if one night of passion was all he wanted, at least he hadn't tried to make her feel ashamed for sharing it with him.

Alec watched from the fireplace and he relished this turnabout. Now the advantage was his. It always was when the enemy was on Dundroma territory.

Especially an enemy with no knowledge of his castle.

He grinned wickedly. "I would invite you to tea and reciprocate your Thornhill hospitality, but we seem to be fresh out. My fault. I was bundled off on a ship from India so fast, my pay taken from me by the physicians, that I neglected to pack some. So, won't you join me for some other refreshment?"

Adele Charlton eyed him with skepticism. "We did not come on a social call, and you know it. Don't patronize us."

"But as I see it, you're at Dundroma now, whatever the reason, and it would be rude to spurn my hospitality." A Dundroma servant hovered. "Whisky," he commanded.

Moments later, Adele Charlton sat on a tartan chair beneath the glassy eyes of a stag head and sipped at a glass of spirits.

"Now then," Alec said, "Victoria obviously ran off from Thornhill and returned to Dundroma because she finds

something here more to her liking than the stiff regimented
life of Thornhill."

"I can't imagine what that would be."

"A lad perhaps."

"She's only twelve." Adele Charlton half rose. "This is
absurd to suggest she's a coquette."

"Ah, but, Adele, you forget where you are—Dundroma . . . the mysterious castle to which the lass in the
statue ran off. Bewitched by the kiss of a dark northern
laird. Is that not how the story goes? Perhaps it is more than
legend. Perhaps it is true, and Vicky has been bewitched."

"Nonsense. This is 1868. No one is bewitched any more
than reivers still ride by the dark of the moon."

"Are you certain, Adele?" he asked with a smile. "How
can you be certain of what goes on up here in Dundroma
territory when you admit you've never set foot here before?"

Adele blanched and touched suddenly shaky fingers to
her cheek. A military man like Alec knew when to push his
advantage.

"What do you know of Dundroma? Except what Isobel
has told you."

"She told us enough to let us know Clare is bewitched by
you."

"Perhaps she enjoys bewitchment, the same as the woman
in the statue. Perhaps it is true. Every lass who ventures over
my border is captured here by passion . . . even you."

"You are talking fancy. I have never believed in that
legend."

"But Vicky does."

"Where is she?" Adele, with true alarm on her face, stood
and tugged at her baffled husband. "Percival, put down the
whisky. We must find Vicky. I fear something most dreadful
might happen to her."

Percival had a ruddier glow than usual on his cheeks. He

actually looked healthier than he had in days, Alec thought, and he tottered out behind Adele. "Something dreadful? Nothing could be as dreadful as your indiscreet youth, Adele."

"Hush, Percival, and hurry now. We must find her and spare her all the agonies of reckless kisses."

With a satisfied smile, Alec watched them go. Adele had walked right into his trap. He needed to add nothing more. He stood there, leaning on his walking stick, ignoring the pain riding roughshod over his knee, determined Adele would at last open her eyes and see past her limited horizons.

They might find Vicky. They might not.

But he hoped they'd find something else. At Dundroma, they might succeed.

Vicky spied her grandparents' coach from her hiding place up on the heath and, pulling a checked cloak about her, rushed to where Andrew was sitting admiring his catch of grouse. His gun lay beside him; he was done with sport and staring at the clouds.

Uncertain what fate awaited her between Thornhill and Dundroma, she decided to do what her father had suggested and ask for what she wanted.

She flopped down beside him and leaned back on her elbows, shaking her hair back, doing her best to look worldly, the way the beautiful Isobel did. And then she looked up at Andrew's handsome profile. Braw. That was the Scottish word for it. By English standards, he was perfect. Her father was just like Lord Byron—noticed by the ladies because of his limp. Andrew had no limp, but something else made her blood tingle strangely. Her heart fluttered, and her breath came fast.

If she was going to win the wager, it was now or never. "Have you ever kissed an English girl?" she asked.

Andrew dropped his pouch of gunpowder and swiveled to look at her. "I told you . . ."

"You told me you'd kissed a girl, but if it was a village girl, then she was from Dundroma."

"Kisses are all the same."

"Are you sure?"

"Aren't you?"

"How would I know, Andrew?"

He sighed, impatient. Yet as he stared at her, his face flushed deeply beneath his blond hair. "You're still too young to kiss." Yet he hadn't refused, only voiced an objection.

"I'm twelve and a half. I wager your mother was kissed by the time she was twelve. It's not so young."

"Maybe. Maybe not. Are you going back to Thornhill with your grandparents?"

She decided to leave Andrew in doubt. That would be best.

Shrugging her shoulders, she sighed. "I expect they're in there now with Aunt Clare, arguing over where I live. I'm getting tired of being fought over as if I were some prized cow or a pot of coins. But my father says I belong to him from now on. That doesn't mean I can't visit Thornhill, though. You can too," she added hastily.

"I might be off to school in a few days."

"And if the other boys ask you if you kissed any lasses this summer, what will you tell them?"

"Aw, Vicky, I told you, lads don't kiss and tell. Not lads who are gentlemen. All the lads talk about is who's going to be a barrister or a member of Parliament or a physician. Or else they talk about how many grouse they bagged and how many ales they stole from the cellar. That sort of thing."

"Then who'll ever know if you kiss me? I'll not tell."

He slanted a glance at her. "You won't?"

"Cross my heart." She leaned toward him, just as he leaned toward her.

"Close your eyes."

She clamped them shut. "Do you want my mouth closed too?"

"Aye, that's best."

She pressed her lips shut.

"Not like that. Just like a fish who's taken the hook. Like you're about to say something. Only not wide open."

She did as he instructed and lay there waiting, the sun warming her face. Beneath her, the heather made a rough bed, and she wished he'd hurry.

"What's next?" she asked.

"The kiss, I guess."

"Well, go ahead. I'm ready."

There was a pause. "Vicky Douglas, I'd get in trouble with your father. I don't want the devil of Dundroma after me."

"Papa won't know."

"He might."

She bolted upright, eyes open. "Then what were you teaching me?"

He shrugged. "Now you know how to lead up to it . . . in case some lad decides to kiss you."

"In case!" She leapt to her feet and picked up her cloak. "I hate you, Andrew Fraser. I hope your mother marries a mean stepfather, and you never get to ride ponies ever again."

Not only that, but for teasing her, she never intended to speak to Andrew. And she didn't care anymore if he kissed her. Ever. Not even if she had to lose the wager with Charlotte.

Panting, fretful, Adele finally lost her breath and was forced to slow down. While waiting for Percival to catch up with her, she actually looked around at the scenery about the loch.

There was no sign of Vicky, but now that she considered it, the view from this spot was rather soft on the eyes.

"What do you think, Percival?" she asked her husband when he had climbed over a last rocky ridge to reach her. Overhead the mist was giving way to a rainbow and a pair of larks flew up from a pine tree. Beside them on the road, a few brambles still held berries, overripe and wet with rain. Beyond, higher up, the hills were canopied in purple heather, fading now, its season almost done.

"My eyes can stand the view. I'd be tempted to admit it's even prettier here than Thornhill, except . . . well, that would be disloyal."

Adele stared off toward Thornhill, trying to fight back the regrets of forty years. At last, she understood that silly statue. It was perfectly clear. The kissing statue's message was a warning not to leave regrets behind—to venture into new territory without looking back.

"I suppose," Adele said on a sigh, "that if Vicky likes it here, the least we can do is try to like it as well. It's not as barbaric as I feared. And after all, it could have been worse. Her father could really have been a missionary."

"What's wrong with that?"

"Because, Percival, if he'd been a missionary returned from the dead, he might have dragged her off to some truly heathenish land. At least, Dundroma is just over the border. We can visit Vicky often, don't you think—or will Alec Douglas be unreasonable?"

"I believe he has a great deal more reason than we've given him credit for. I miss Vicky."

"So do I. But I see now, we were playing a lie."

"Yes. But I miss her nevertheless."

"Well, now, Percival, you have me to give your attention to."

"You?" Percival glanced at Adele, and his glance softened.

"What do you think of the men in kilts in this village?"

Adele had had just enough whisky to relax her; she'd wisely poured the rest in a handy cuspidor while Lord Strahan was not looking. Nevertheless, the glow of Dundroma's own brew still had her mellow. "I think you might look handsome in a kilt of your own, Percival."

"Brazen talk, Adele. Aren't you worried what the neighbors and servants will think?"

She stared off across the heather, off toward Thornhill. "I think not. Not anymore. Not as much as I used to."

"Do you know what I've wished for for nearly forty years, Adele?"

"That you'd never walked into Mrs. Wattleston's library and had to rescue my reputation."

Percival shook his head. "I've wished that I had that rogue's courage with a beautiful woman."

"What do you mean?"

She turned her head and to her amazement Percival took her in his arms and kissed her. He stole a kiss right up there in the heather of Dundroma.

Shocked, Adele pulled back. "Percival, are you sane? You've never kissed me flirtatiously, not in forty years."

"I apologize for taking so long."

She smiled as shyly as a debutante. "You've been jealous of that rogue all these years?" At his nod, she rushed on. "But I thought you considered me too fast a woman. You made me your wife, but not your sweetheart."

They stood side by side up in the Dundroma heather. "Then we both thought wrong . . . I wonder, if we'd ventured over into Dundroma years ago . . . what would have happened?"

"This," Adele said, and leaning over, she kissed Percival back.

Half an hour later they strolled back to the castle, arm in arm. Adele was satisfied. Vicky was riding her pony about the castle grounds, Lord Strahan's Dundroma was not as fearsome a place as she'd expected, and Percival . . . well, Percival had actually kissed her, had made her feel again like an Incomparable.

"Alec," she called out, "we compliment you on the scenery. A most rewarding view."

Though he still limped in pain, he managed a smile for them.

Truce. It was a start. For Vicky's sake.

Clare was happy for the reconciliation. Outwardly happy, that is. Inside, her heart ached. Vicky had given her leave to go. And after telling off her mother-in-law, she had little choice. Best, too, to leave before she let her feelings for Alec spill over.

Whatever passion, whatever kisses they'd shared at Thornhill was a thing of the past. Here at Dundroma he'd verbally sparred with her, even teased her, but nothing more. It was as she'd suspected—an interlude with a governess meant nothing to the laird of the manor. She was packed and could have lingered but tears blurred her enjoyment of the scene. Clare turned away from the happy chatter as the Charltons and Lord Strahan discussed Vicky.

Mentally she listed everything she'd packed. She wanted to leave nothing behind. Her manners book! She had found Vicky reading a chapter on courtship far too advanced for a lass so tender in years—and so had hidden the book under her mattress. Now she returned to her Dundroma bedchamber to retrieve it.

Without that book she had no compass. The kissing statue had led her down false paths, clearly. Stolen kisses brought happy endings only in legend.

❧ Chapter Twenty

Alec had made his peace and hated the terms. Clare Charlton was leaving. Isobel, who had betrayed him, had the gall to come calling. He had to bite his tongue to keep from yelling at her in public, a scene that would only make him look crass. No, Isobel deserved a more subtle, unexpected retaliation. All in due time. After Clare departed.

Even now Clare's trunk was being readied to load onto the Charltons' coach. Mere hours remained.

His hand twitched on the ivory-handled walking stick, and there was sweet, concerned Miss Clare Charlton approaching him, Isobel's borrowed gown in hand.

"Are you quite all right, milord?" she asked. "If Vicky needs anything, you may write."

Isobel sighed in exasperation. "Of course he's all right. He's a Douglas. And so is the child. At her age, Andrew had been weaned from a governess for years. I'll look out for her until she enrolls in finishing school."

"I'm tolerable, Clare," he said gently. "Give me that gown. Isobel would never want it back you know, not even if it were still its original color."

"You may use it for scrubbing floors," Isobel said. "Why don't I see about tea, Alec? You'll need a rest after all this company." Behaving like the mistress of the castle already, Alec noted, but he was too dispirited to care. She was right. When Clare departed, he'd want a cup of tea, laced with whisky. For the moment, he was glad to have Isobel busy—anywhere else—so he could speak privately with Clare.

He did not miss the sheen in her eyes, nor the dispirited slump to her shoulders. He wanted to console her, tell her how glad he was that she'd been the one to raise his daughter all these years. But words would not come. He'd gotten what he wanted. His daughter. All to himself. But still words would not come—because he was losing the woman he loved. In one brief flash, like unexpected lighting, he knew he loved Clare. But he had no idea what to do about his feelings.

"One stroll about this barbaric place to pacify our granddaughter, and we're heading back to Thornhill, Clare," warned Adele Charlton. "You'd best be ready to come with us. You're welcome to stay at Thornhill long enough to find another situation. But naturally, we won't tell the neighbors why you're leaving . . ." She met Percival's gaze, then seemed to think better of her hasty words.

"Well, it's of no account what they think, but you'll want to find a new situation as soon as possible."

Alec stared at her across the room, willing her to look at him, desperately needing to see what was written in her eyes. But she avoided his gaze, damn her. And he didn't know why that should anger him so. Or fill him with his hazy, vague unease.

He couldn't say farewell with Adele Charlton looking on. There were intimate things to say, things that were none of Adele's business.

"Miss Charlton," he said, "I would like a last word with you before you leave Dundroma."

"Is that necessary?" Clare asked, feeling her face grow warm. Her world was falling out from under her, everything she'd had in life was gone as surely as if a rug had been pulled out from under her. And Alec, the man who'd tempted her and caused her fall, wanted to meet. Still, she didn't want to argue over the matter.

"Very well," she said.

"The garden."

"The library," she countered.

He didn't blame her for not wanting to be caught alone with him, yet he had to have a few minutes alone with her.

"The tack room in the stable?" It lacked the genteel qualities but it was utterly private and there were pony blankets stacked in there on which a lady could sit . . . and on which a gentleman could ease himself with a servant lass. He despised himself. No, Alec, no need. You'll only talk, not touch . . .

Besides, she nodded her agreement with innocent pleasure. "Better to have ponies for a chaperon that no one. Yes, then, I would like to say farewell to Ghost. He and I need to make our peace also."

Relief flooded Lord Strahan's face. Relief at getting her alone again. But, oh, she was afraid, afraid of herself, of losing control at the last minute. His last memory of her *had* to be of her behaving prim and proper. Perhaps then he'd pretend they'd never made love, never so much as touched . . .

"Aye, lass, the castle tack room," he said and limped off without another word.

At once, she had a change of heart. Meeting Alec alone would be a mistake, could lead to nothing but bitter words or else reveal her heartbreak. Better she leave and never have him know of her love for him. Yes, she loved him. Desperately. Grouchy as a tiger. Dictatorial. Stubborn. Stoic. Rigid.

Dear, dear man.

Isobel appeared around the corner, like a godsend. Isobel was in love with Alec, that much was clear, and Isobel would be only too willing to help her out.

"Isobel, I need a favor from you."

Isobel speared her with a haughty look as if her time were too valuable to be wasted talking with governesses. Clare rushed on. "I've promised to meet Alec—Lord Strahan— but I don't think that would be wise."

"Indeed not." Isobel's chin was tilted up, her expression bored, but she listened intently. "What do you need me for?"

"Perhaps you would tell him why I cannot meet him. Perhaps you would rendezvous with him instead. It would be a favor to me."

Isobel smiled, obviously pleased. "For a Thornhill governess, you're finally thinking sensibly. Seeing him will only lead to more speculation. And we won't leave it to chance. I'll tell him myself that you're indisposed. Sometimes it takes another woman to explain things to him . . . and I know exactly how to talk to him."

She knew he'd be displeased with what she'd done, but it was for the best. In the end he'd see that.

It was settled then, and Isobel managed a smile for Clare, a smile Clare well understood. Clare had handed Isobel a golden opportunity to meet with Alec in intimate seclusion. Isobel thanked the lucky stars, and decided the tide was finally turning in her favor. Oh, but she'd love to announce her betrothal to Alec before those Thornhill stuffed shirts departed. What satisfaction. She wanted dearly to see the look on this mousy governess's face.

Clare returned to the castle to finish packing her few belongings. It was for the best, and when she walked in, she felt such a weight off her shoulders that she was able to smile for the benefit of Dr. Wigston Wilmot, who slouched in a chair, expression disconsolate.

"Have no fear, Dr. Wilmot," she managed to call in parting. "Perhaps Lord Strahan may yet come to his senses."

*   *   *

Alec decided he'd taken leave of his senses. Within moments, he regretted his impulsive request—oh, he wanted to see Clare. Too much. The black and white checked plaid swung from his shoulder in an unsteady motion, a reminder of his limp. It was selfish of him, to see her. He'd not be able to control himself around her, would end up compromising her again. She didn't deserve him.

He called for his manservant to deliver a note of regret and let her down easily. In the end she'd thank him. Yes, that would be best.

And within ten minutes he'd dispatched a groom with a note. It said rather more than he'd meant to put in writing, but better delivered in writing than said in person. This way she'd know how he felt before she crossed back over the border to her new life.

Dr. Wigston Wilmot, after a particularly hearty meal, usually could not see his feet for his belly. Consequently, within an hour of enjoying an excellent grouse pie with mounds of neeps and tatties, he tripped over the remnants of Vicky Douglas's rag doll that Reiver had discarded in the courtyard. A castle groom helped him to his feet and apologized.

"I'm so sorry, sir. Are you injured then?"

"Of course I am. I've twisted my ankle like a silly girl. Bother it all, but nothing's going right, right down to servants tripping me up . . . for no good reason either . . ." His voice trailed off. "I say there, you were reading on the job. I saw you. Reading a private note."

A serious breech of protocol, for which the groom instantly apologized, but Dr. Wilmot was not dumb. He seized the opportunity—and the note—and glanced at it. A note from Lord Strahan. To his dearest love. Dr. Wilmot read on. This was shocking. It was a love note. Lord Strahan writing love notes to a female? Though it bore no name, there was only one female whose name had been linked with the laird of Dundroma's—Isobel Fraser. If Dr. Wilmot didn't do something drastic, he'd lose his heart's desire forever.

"Where were you to deliver this?"

"The stable, sir."

The groom reached for it, but Dr. Wilmot held it out of reach. "I'll take it in person. Myself. And I'll make certain it gets to the lady in question without anyone else reading it."

Oh, my lady love . . . Mrs. Isobel Fraser would hear those heartfelt words, but she'd think that he, Wigston, had written them. True, Wigston was stealing another man's love poetry so to speak, but as Wigston had observed only too keenly, up here in the border country, stealing and deceit were the way business got done.

> *Pleasures are like poppies spread,*
> *You seize the flower, its bloom is shed;*

Very nice words. Lord Strahan had a feel for Burns he did. Of course, Wigston preferred Shakespeare himself, but whatever turned the head of Isobel Fraser would do quite nicely. Oh, yes, Dr. Wigston Wilmot was only a few moments away from claiming his heart's desire.

With Clare disgraced and leaving Dundroma, Isobel's moment was at hand. The stable was smelly and lacking in romantic appeal, but at least it was half dark back here on the haystack. She'd steal a kiss before Alec knew what was happening. Once he kissed her, he'd realize the wonder of her charms. Above all, Isobel was not going to miss out a second time on getting her heart's desire. She got there early, closed the shutters, and took a deep breath for luck and courage both. Alec was almost hers. One stolen kiss away from being hers.

Wigston's foot hurt like the very devil, but even that was a stroke of luck, for the lady would never suspect it was anyone other than Lord Strahan, and so he accentuated the limp. He regretted now the measure of garlic with which he'd doused his skin—a precaution against Scottish spirits and ailments. But in the surprise of his kiss, she'd never notice.

At the door, he straightened his coat and tie and smoothed back his hair. He turned the latch.

"Alec?" the woman whispered. She was all in black, he could see that much.

He wouldn't speak her name; words with him seemed to be wasted. Whether with squabbling physicians or historical society cronies, he made headway with action rather than talk. Which is why he'd come here to begin with—to forge ties between two factions. Now he was about to forge a tie between himself and a lovely lady. Only a man of decisive action could accomplish so much.

Isobel came toward him, her breath sweet against his cheek, and then he took her in his arms and pressed his lips to hers. Her lips responded, then froze, as all of her stiffened. She pulled back and sniffed the air, traced the contours of his face—and screamed.

"Who are you? Who?"

Wigston was touched. The lady was ready to swoon at his feet in ecstasy. "I'm the one who's yearned to kiss you and who will support and care for you always. Don't worry that you're still in mourning. We'll keep it secret."

The side door was yanked open and candlelight flooded the room. "Clare?"

It was Lord Strahan.

"Alec, what are you doing here?"

"What are you doing here, Isobel?"

"I came in place of Clare."

"What for?"

"To meet you. Who have you come for?"

"Clare. To talk with her. What is Dr. Wilmot doing here?"

"I came in your place, or rather in the place of your groom who was taking the liberty of reading your note."

By now, a small army of castle employees had heard Isobel's scream and had gathered outside the stable. Isobel and Dr. Wilmot kissing in the dark. Shocking.

"Shocking, indeed," proclaimed Adele Charlton. "And we trusted your moral integrity."

"Well, Adele," said Percival, who until now had been unaccountably quiet. "I think, given your own romantic history, you can afford to offer some charity and advice."

"Advice?" Isobel looked panicked and stared in horror at the beaming Dr. Wilmot.

"Dear Isobel, it's all right. You're not the first young woman—widowed or spinster—to be caught kissing in the dark. People will forget . . . of course you must marry."

"Who?"

"Why, Dr. Wilmot of course. You do want her, don't you, Doctor?"

Dr. Wilmot stared about dumbfounded.

"Don't they teach you at that Royal College about how to propose?" Alec prompted.

"Alec!" Isobel cried. "How can you do this to me?"

"Because I care about your honor, Isobel. As Malcolm's best friend and Andrew's godfather, I must ensure that nothing besmirches your name." While she stood there openmouthed, he turned to the physician. "We're waiting. A public proposal if you please. Nothing less will salvage the lady's honor."

Dr. Wilmot got down on bended knee. "You, dear Isobel,

would do me the greatest honor if you would consent to be my wife—as soon as your mourning is over."

Isobel, desperate, played her only card. "I told you—I shall mourn Malcolm forever." That line had worked before. It would work again.

"Nonsense," objected Adele. "You've been wearing black longer than most widows do. There's no time to linger in mourning up here in the border country. Time to put on gay colors again. When, Isobel, will you have the wedding? We'll of course make the journey back here just for your happy day . . . and to see Vicky of course. Plan the wedding for just before Vicky leaves for finishing school. Who'd have thought? Isobel and a London physician. A fine match—for the widow of a cavalry officer . . . Fine indeed. As good as you could hope to make."

"And Malcolm would want you to find happiness again." Alec held out his hand to Dr. Wilmot. "Felicitations."

And Isobel stood there, helpless, caught in a trap of her own making. For the second time caught with a man who was not of her choosing.

"Don't worry," Alec leaned down and whispered, "I won't tell a soul about your real intentions. Nor will the servants."

They all sprang back out of sight, and Isobel, face flushed, Dr. Wilmot waddling in her wake, walked with as much dignity as she could muster back to her coach.

Aye, one stolen kiss could be a gamble. Alec made a mental note to send Isobel a generous wedding gift—a consolation gift, if you would, for yet again losing out as Lady Strahan. Truth be told there would never be a Lady Strahan. Not until, the title went to Vicky.

As for Clare, well, he had memories of their lovemaking. For him that would be enough to take him through the decisions of the future. Through his life. Memories, that was all. She was not a part of his future.

Yet, he didn't want her to leave yet, not quite. If he couldn't steal a kiss, he would at least lay eyes on her, have one last look at her creamy skin, the green eyes, the way the sun streaked her hair. Aye, one last look, and that would be that.

Alec Douglas sat in his worn tartan chair in front of the fireplace, his dog at his side, leaning close as he stroked the fur.

He should have been a happy man. He'd won his way. And without resorting once to muskets, swords, ropes, or even a steel bonnet. Vicky was his to keep; her grandparents had accepted her happiness at Dundroma with her father. He in turn had made only one small concession—occasional visits to Thornhill. Despite his disdain for its fussy code of life, Clare had convinced him to think of the child. Vicky deserved the love of the Charltons, as misguided as their shallow lives were.

Compromise ruled. Clare Charlton had unwittingly served as mediator with as much effectiveness as a middlemarch warden of the olden days.

Vicky had to go on to finishing school. Alec's promise to send Vicky to an approved school in Edinburgh mollified Adele's sensibilities. A school in Scotland would sound better to the neighbors than leaving Vicky in the wicked environment of Dundroma Castle.

But there was the rub. For the first time Alec was forced to admit a bitter truth—in winning his case for father's rights, he had unwittingly set himself up to gain a daughter, but lose a governess.

Even now Clare was searching for her cloak. The minutes ticked away, and he had no law to keep her here. Nor could he very well kidnap her . . . He couldn't marry her. She didn't deserve an ill-humored cripple with no future for a husband. And all the time, Dr. Wigston Wilmot sat across from him, drinking whisky and lathering on about the Edinburgh surgeons.

"You're not listening, Lord Strahan. I've just laid out the boldest plan in a hundred years of medicine, and you've been woolgathering . . . where is your mind? Up in the heather with the sheep?"

Alec scowled. On the matter of his bum knee, there'd be no compromise. Just because Dr. Wilmot had outwitted Isobel didn't mean he could do the same with Alec.

"Impertinence and condescension will not win you your way. I refuse to be cut open like a cadaver."

"They're merely removing the shattered fragments of bone. I promise you'll survive. They're not butchers. They're quite skilled."

"Somehow the word 'quite' does not have the same ring as words like 'assuredly' and 'absolutely.'"

"If it's the pain, the surgeons report great advances with chloroform—"

"Pain is not an issue."

"Isobel . . . my dearest Isobel says she'll not give you her uncle's reply regarding military advancement if you don't gather your courage on this matter."

Alec gave a wry smile. Isobel's black eyes had flashed with anger the last time he'd seen her. But then, she'd been hoping for Alec's hand, not his best wishes on her upcoming nuptials.

And then suddenly there was Isobel, walking toward them, expression rather confident, considering. She spared not a glance at Wigston, but headed straight for Alec.

"Have I offered my felicitations?" Alec said mischievously. "You don't act like the blissful bride-to-be, Isobel," he noted. "Your groom-to-be is besotted with you."

Isobel had eyes only for Alec, and a sly smile. "Oh, but I'm delighted to have a future married life in London. As Mrs. Wilmot I'll meet so many interesting Londoners. I shall lead a charming life. Perhaps I shall meet you there at grand social functions."

"I doubt that." Alec felt a bit sorry for poor Wigston, condemned to a future with a woman intent on flirtation with other men. "I shall not be setting foot in London," Alec said.

"Won't you? But you haven't heard the offer from my uncle."

She suddenly had his attention more fully than before.

"You see, Alec, I still care about your happiness, and I want to share my uncle's offer. My letter caught up with him in London. Unlike the rest of the military, he values you. And whether you do anything about your limp is of consequence. It would further Wigston's career." She spared her fiancé a fleeting smile. "Naturally I would want him to be as successful as possible . . . but it would also help you in your new position. Help you to be incognito."

"So now both of you are ganging up on me." Her words sank in. "What new position? I'm through, I'm—"

She held up a hand to stay his objections. "Don't be proud now. Listen. My uncle's sent a message back posthaste only because he learned you had newly arrived in Britain. He's wanting a man of your abilities, Alec."

"What is that?" Alec, despite his wariness, could not contain his curiosity.

"He wants a borderer, a man skilled in duplicity, a man exactly like you—you specifically—for work in the diplomatic corps. Highly secret. Perhaps even espionage. A double life even. Think of the possibilities for your private life . . ."

"Isobel," he warned. For he knew her implications. A man with a double identity could more easily keep a mistress. Namely Isobel.

"Are you interested?" She paused, letting the offer sink in.

"Perhaps." He was interested in the lengths to which she'd go to have her way with him. And more, he was interested in the career offer. Any man would be a fool not to be. Diplomatic service. Men named their price. Claimed knighthood. Commanded respect. Earned glory and fame.

"It sounds too good." More tempting than he dared let on. He might do it. Now that Vicky was going to go to finishing school, he could. As long as he could hold Isobel at bay. And he would. "What else do I need to know?" There was more. He could tell by the sly look on her face she still held a trump.

"There's only one stipulation," she said, eyes flashing with delight. "The position is for a bachelor. A single man. A man with no wife to tie him down . . . you're ideal, and you deserve this, Alec."

Alec sucked in his breath in one great gulp. A deal with the devil it was. Oh, this was Isobel's ultimate revenge. If she couldn't have him, she'd make certain no one else did either. She didn't know that he'd already decided never to marry again. "Would you have told me of the offer had things turned out differently between us?"

Dr. Wilmot cleared his throat. "Now, see here . . ."

"Never mind." He knew the answer. Of course she wouldn't have. Only now that she'd lost him in a trick of fate would she ensure that no one else could have him either; only now would she tempt him away from all others with an offer no reasonable man could turn down.

Career or marriage? It was an easy choice, especially his avowal to avoid marriage.

"You are a true friend, Isobel," he said, leaving his answer ambiguous.

"And we shall continue to be friends, Alec. The best of friends. Do you accept?"

"I shall write your uncle at once."

An image of Clare, honey-haired and trembling in his

arms, intruded in his mind, but he pushed it away. He needed no woman. He wanted the glory Isobel offered.

Dr. Wilmot's voice cut through his reverie.

"Ah, woolgathering again. Either the sheep which you are woolgathering over is very large, or else your fear makes your mind ignore me——"

"Hah! I told you once. I do not fear pain."

"Then what is the obstacle to making medical history? You have a reason to try it now."

Or he could remain in painful pieces just as the borderland did. In time he would become accustomed to the pain, the walking stick with its ivory tiger's head was becoming his signature. His bum leg was like this wild borderland—a thing to be endured. Some things were not meant to be changed. And Isobel's uncle would take him as he was. "I'll let you know and Isobel's uncle as well. There is much at stake."

The physician frowned in bewilderment, but stood as if he understood he'd been dismissed. "You will do Isobel and me the honor of attending our wedding two weeks hence?"

"On that you may depend. With pleasure."

Dr. Wilmot stood fawning over Isobel, whose melancholy state he mistook for love. Alec knew better and relished every minute of her agony. It served Isobel right getting caught in her own trap, and Alec invited her and Dr. Wilmot to dinner so he could watch her, squirming like a fish on the line. Like a grouse captured in the sights of his gun. Irrevocably caught.

But first, the time for farewells had come. Piled high with valises, the coach from Thornhill awaited his English guests.

He limped out to the great hall, where everyone waited. Everyone including Clare.

❧Chapter Twenty-one

Farewells had never been his forte, and as a military man, he knew how to be brisk about it. For that reason, too, he made it clear his good-byes would be said in public. It was his one concession to appearances. Good-byes had to appear impersonal. In this case, with a feuding family departing from Dundroma, outside handshakes were appropriate.

They'd made a start. Mending. Healing. Everyone had much to do. His plaid kept blowing up muffling his words, and Clare kept her face averted, bade him farewell as if he'd been the stern master and nothing more. That was to be his memory. The cruelest hurt of all.

But then he hadn't counted on Vicky and the farewell she'd give to her longtime governess.

"Can't you just write her a letter?" he said, impatient.

"Papa—that's not nice. After all, Aunt Clare and I were together for all my life practically." Her voice caught.

Alec studied the ivory head of his walking stick. Anything save tears.

"You're certain you will be all right?" Clare asked.

Tell her no, Vicky.

But Vicky did no such thing.

"I'm going to be fine."

"No nightmares, no eating rich food—no kippers, no black pudding, and no more than one piece of shortbread at teatime. Oh, and no pony riding without a guide."

"Aunt *Clare*!" Vicky flounced away. "I'm old enough to stay here without a governess."

"Yes, all right then, I thought so. You'll wear frocks still, though." Clare looked up at Alec. "Just because you hope to make a hoyden of her does not mean she's to show up in the dress of a lad—trousers or such. She's to wear frocks."

"Aunt Clare, you are a conscientious governess, and I in turn shall be a conscientious father, in close touch with her grandmother, and with Mrs. Drummond's assistance, we'll survive admirably."

"Of course." Clare turned away.

"Wait," Vicky said. "I will miss you, Aunt Clare, more than I can say, but I'm ready to be on my own at Dundroma. Just me and my father and his castle . . . until I go to finishing school."

And Andrew.

"I understand," Clare said. "And I'll miss you too." Suddenly she reached down to hug her. "Write to me. I want to at least know you've not forgotten the fine penmanship I taught you."

They embraced and then Vicky pulled away and tugged at a long red curl. "Aunt Clare, where do I send letters?"

Clare paused, careful not to look at Alec Douglas. She had no idea if he was angry that she'd sent Isobel in her place. She was a coward, afraid of nothing more than an intimate meeting with this man.

"I . . . I'll write you and tell you of my new circumstances."

"Yes, then."

Vicky's voice wobbled at this leave-taking. Suddenly she thrust out a sheet of paper. "I have a letter for Charlotte Warnick—my friend. Can you give it to her please when she stops by Thornhill? We had a wager."

"A wager? Over what? Ladies don't wager." Her grandmother was looking on, half shocked.

"Nothing important."

Just then a gust of wind came up and blew the letter out of her hand. Vicky, horrified, stared after it, watching as the slip of paper went rolling, bouncing, flying, end over end. Coming alive, she tore after it. This was too personal for anyone to find and read.

She ran around the side of the castle and stopped in her tracks. Andrew stood picking her note up out of a mud puddle.

Andrew, whom she'd sworn never to talk to again. Worse, though, would be having him read this note. For the note contained a lie. She'd lied to Charlotte, told her friend that she'd won a kiss, and bragged on about how grand it was to kiss a lad.

"Don't you dare read it," she said.

"Come and get it then," he said. "Or else I'll take it to school with me and let all the lads read it."

She walked up to him and held out her hand. There was nothing to say. Andrew would only laugh at her. And then tell all the lads at school. This was his way of telling her he was leaving soon. She'd never see him again for months and months.

"Give it to me, Andrew," she said, her voice choked. She was embarrassed and heartbroken, both.

Then instead of handing her the note, he leaned over her, obliterating the sun. With one hand he grasped her by the shoulder, and then without warning his lips touched hers. It was ever so gentle a kiss, just a butterfly touch, the taste of dew.

She shut her eyes. Andrew was kissing her.

It was over as quickly as it had happened, and she hadn't even turned to stone. Except that she couldn't move; her legs felt like jelly.

"What's the matter? You look like that silly statue."

"I'm not. It was nice."

"Aye," he said, shuffling his feet. "Kisses are nice. Bye then. I'm leaving too."

He stuffed her letter in her hand and was gone then, running off through the mists, the opposite direction from all the rest of the people. She stood there watching until he was out of sight. And still she stared through the mists. She might be only twelve and a half, but she knew she'd always remember Andrew as surely as she knew the misty rain that was falling would yield rainbows.

Letter in hand, she walked back around the side of the castle to where the Charlton coach and her grandparents waited for their farewells. Andrew's kiss was still warm on her lips. Her first kiss. She couldn't imagine her grandparents had ever kissed. Not if Thornhill fell to Dundroma first. But she couldn't ask, because they'd never tell. That's how Andrew said it was.

People don't kiss and tell.

They were all staring at her. "Did you find it, Vicky?" Clare called. Her papa glowered. Her grandmother still looked aghast, but remained silent.

Aunt Clare held out her hand. "I'll give it to Charlotte. I hope you didn't wager anything important."

"I—I forget. Charlotte's blue cloak, I think."

"Nonsense. Ladies don't wager clothing."

And ladies don't kiss and tell. Now that Andrew had kissed her, the letter was no longer a fib or a lie. It was the truth.

Only the kiss was too special to tell Charlotte about.

While everyone looked on, she ripped the letter in half. "It's not important. Tell Charlotte I'll write her a new letter—later."

She held out her hand to Aunt Clare, the way ladies were supposed to. "Farewell. I'll write you often."

Aunt Clare's eyes glistened with tears, but she took her

hand. "You are a young lady now. I expect letters full of exciting news from finishing school."

"Yes, very." Her smile would not be contained. Andrew would return. In her heart she knew he would, as surely as she knew that statue stood at the border.

Clare lingered, wanting to postpone the farewell from Vicky yet needing to leave before she looked at Alec and lost her resolve.

The Charltons were waiting. It was time to board the coach.

"You won't miss us, we know, Alec. You've gotten your way," Adele said.

Alec stood ramrod-straight, unable to speak. Clare's trunk was strapped on top. She looked up once at Alec, her eyes luminescent, green as the dell in spring. The wind blew the hem of her prim dark gown, and one strand of honey-colored hair blew free of her bonnet. He could still feel her slim waist in his embrace, smell the lavender scent of her, feel her trembling, hear her impassioned plea for Vicky . . . her cry of pleasure at his touch and then her demure insistence on wearing anything but garish colors.

The coach door slammed, and the vehicle rolled away down the rutted lane from Dundroma.

Clare stared at her lap, oblivious to Adele's chatter. Her throat ached with an emotion she didn't want to explore. The rutted road jarred them about, but she scarcely cared. The driver finally reined in, and Clare didn't blame him. A coach could only take so much.

"We've stopped," Adele said. "Something's wrong."

Whatever was wrong, Clare was in no mood to care.

"What is it?" Adele asked.

"Calm down, Adele," her husband said. "The days of reivers are gone. It's nothing serious."

"If we're still on the Dundroma side of the border, I can't

be calm. Not unless you tell me we've passed that statue and are back in Thornhill land."

Percival peered out the window and hand on his heart slumped back into his seat. "Mercy . . . mercy."

Adele leaned over him. "What is it?" She grabbed the lapels of his frock coat and shook him, voice rising in panic. "Percival. What?"

"I don't believe my eyes. A highway raider, as I live and breathe. We're being raided. Don't argue. Unfasten your pearls, Adele. Reach in my pocket and pull out my gold watch."

When the coachman opened the door and peered in, he looked shaken. With hands cupped, Percival held out all the jewelry and money the three of them possessed. "Give them this, but we're not getting out. A fine nuisance having to put up with damnable highwaymen. In this day and age, you'd think the roads would be safe, but no, no one cares what happens up in our part of the world. I'd like to see a member of Parliament take an excursion on this wild road. Then we'd see some reforms in—"

"Please, sir," the coachman cut in, "it's not jewels and money the villain wants. It's the young lass, the governess."

"Clare?" Adele said. "What's she got to interest some thieving reiver?"

"Please, sir, it's not a thieving reiver. It's—"

"Clare!" came a agonized call from outside. "Clare, come out here."

She trembled. Alec? Could it be?

"Clare Charlton, bring your manners book and turn it over to me."

"What is the meaning of this?" Adele demanded, outraged. "This is highly irregular behavior for a gentleman, but then you never were a gentleman, were you, Alec?"

"Retaliation for all the tormented moments I have spent without Clare."

"Without Clare?" Adele sniffed. "I should have known he was beyond reform. Now what business do you have with her, you devil?"

"Pleasure," Clare whispered.

"What did you say, Clare?"

"Pleasure," she said in a firmer voice. Then looking at Alec, she said, "Pleasures are like poppies spread. You seize the flower its bloom is shed."

Lord Strahan wore the expression of a lovesick boy. "No man can tether time or tide." His voice was thick with emotion. "Come out of there, Clare. Come out and away with me. Or do you seek a life of glory in London?"

"I don't want to go to London. I love it here."

"And so do I. I want to be laird of the castle and laird to my lady love."

"The devil. He's propositioning Clare in broad daylight."

"Hush, Adele," Percival said. "Else I'll kiss you quiet."

"Well!" she said, then gave Percival a sideways glance. "Well . . . well, if you want . . ."

"Clare," Alec called. "Come. You feel the tide as I do."

Clare climbed out. They were stopped right at the border, right by the kissing statue. But it wasn't the statue she saw.

"Alec?" He stood there, alone, leaning on his walking stick, wind whipping his hair and cloak.

"Come to me, Clare."

Four words pulled her to him as if she'd been bewitched. The dark laird of the north was calling to her.

When she was a step from him, he let his walking stick drop to the dirt and he pulled her to him and into his embrace, and the next thing she knew he was kissing her. He took her in his arms in front of everyone—the Charltons and servants, and he kissed her as he'd never kissed a woman in his life. Oh, but he kissed her so thoroughly. His hands mussed her hair, and touched her face. She had to hang on to her bonnet to keep from losing it, and then while she wasn't expecting it, Alec kissed her again.

"Will you wed a man who cannot get down on bended knee to ask for your hand?"

"Alec . . . It isn't me you want out of life, Alec. It's something else, and I don't want to be second best to you or anyone."

"I never choose second best. Don't leave, Clare. Stay with me. You belong to Dundroma."

His leg buckled and he knelt. She knelt with him, heedless of the mud on the road. And they kept on kissing.

His kisses were drugging her objections. She wanted him so.

"I lacked the courage to meet you. Forgive me."

"It is for you to forgive me."

"Darling, Clare, you are my courage."

There, bent down on one knee in the mud of the rutted road, she knelt with Alec Douglas, Lord Strahan, descended from the Black Douglas, the man whom grooms and maids feared.

"Come with me," he pleaded. "I am an imperfect man, but with you whole. I need you, Clare."

She hesitated. It was one thing to need, another to love.

"I need you," he repeated. "It's the only decision I've made in my life of which I'm certain. You and only you have the power to make me whole. Your love, your courage. I told Wigston yes."

"You did?"

"For you. And I'm telling Isobel's uncle no."

"About what?"

"It doesn't matter now."

"No, you must do what you want—"

"I am, lass. I want you by my side."

"Then I will not leave you, no matter what you choose to do, for without you, my pain should be threefold your own."

"I love you. Can you love me back?"

Yes. She could give him that. She wanted nothing, only the chance to keep on giving, loving. Courage for the storms. She gave him her hand and helped him up, then handing him his walking stick walked at his side to his waiting coach, which was hidden amid the rough-hewn cliffs like the reivers of old. Some might say the dark devil of Dundroma had either captured or bewitched her, but it mattered little.

They headed north, the way the statue pointed, and as they crossed the border, Clare spared herself a fleeting glimpse of the statue. Only Clare knew now, it wasn't Dundroma to which the mysterious kissing lady pointed. Indeed, the legend had nothing to do with geography. Nothing at all.

"What, Clare Charlton," Alec asked, "did that manners book say about kissing?"

She smiled up at him and wrapped her arms about his neck. He gathered her close into his arms, so close she could hear the heavy beat of his heart. "The manners book?" she murmured, pulling back to look at his beloved face. "The chapter on kissing? Not one I ever read, so you, dearest Alec, must turn tutor. I expect to learn everything there is to tell."

"You have my word as a borderer," he said and then pulled her to him again, close enough to kiss her gently, and then closer yet.

Oh, the devil had delightful mischief on his mind.